EAST END JEWS AND
LEFT-WING THEATRE

To my husband Ivor Seddon for his overwhelming love, kindness and confidence and belief in my endeavours; my mother who helped to foster my passion for literature and research and to my daughters, Sophia and Anya

EAST END JEWS AND LEFT-WING THEATRE

Alfie Bass, David Kossoff,
Warren Mitchell and Lionel Bart

Isabelle Seddon

VALLENTINE MITCHELL
LONDON • CHICAGO, IL

First published in paper in 2021 by Vallentine Mitchell

Catalyst House, 720 Centennial Court,
Centennial Park
Elstree WD6 3SY, UK

814 N. Franklin Street
Chicago
IL 60610 , USA

www.vmbooks.com

Copyright © Isabelle Seddon 2020
First published in cloth 2020

British Library Cataloguing in Publication Data:
An entry can be found on request

ISBN 978 1 912676 35 4 (Cloth)
ISBN 978 1 912676 88 0 (Paper)
ISBN 978 1 912676 36 1 (Ebook)

Library of Congress Cataloging in Publication Data:
An entry can be found on request

All rights reserved. No part of this publication may be reproduced in any form or by any
means, electronic, mechanical, photocopying, reading or otherwise, without the prior
permission of Vallentine Mitchell & Co. Ltd.

Contents

List of Illustrations	vii
Acknowledgements	ix
Introduction	1
1. Alfie Bass	50
2. David Kossoff	75
3. Warren Mitchell	107
4. Lionel Bart	134
Conclusion	174
Bibliography and Sources	179
Index	191

List of Illustrations

1. *Winkles and Champagne*, Unity Theatre 1943: The history of the music hall © as stated at the copyright holder/Victoria and Albert Museum, London © permission (Clive Gellert, Unity Theatre Trust)

2. *Buster*, Unity Theatre 1950: Harry Landis stars in *Buster*, a play about working-class East End life, Unity Theatre 1950 © as stated at the copyright holder/Victoria and Albert Museum, London, © permission (Clive Gellert, Unity Theatre Trust)

3. Lionel Bart, 1959 (Pamela Chandler), courtesy of Lionel Bart Foundation Archive

4. *Babes in the Wood*, Unity Theatre 1938 ©as stated at the copyright holder/Victoria and Albert Museum, London © permission (Clive Gellert, Unity Theatre Trust)

5. Alfie Bass (left) and David Kossoff, *The Bespoke Overcoat* © Wolfgang Suschitzky

6. Kossoff family, 1924 © Simon Kossoff

7. Kossoff with his brother and sister in 1940 © Simon Kossoff

8. David Kossoff and Robert Taylor on film location in Holland for *The House of the Seven Hawks* (1959), © Simon Kossoff

9. David Kossoff in Italy whilst filming *Conspiracy of Hearts* (1960) © Simon Kossoff

10. Kossoff as Morry the tailor in *The Bespoke Overcoat* (1955) © Wolfgang Suschitzky

11. David Kossoff and Alfie Bass in *The Bespoke Overcoat* (1955) © Wolfgang Suschitzky

12. David Kossoff, 1970 © Simon Kossoff

13. *The Ragged Trousered Philanthropist*, Unity Theatre 1949 © as stated at the copyright holder/Victoria and Albert Museum, London © permission (Clive Gellert, Unity Theatre Trust)

14. Lionel Bart, 1959, taken for the launch of the LP record *Bart for Bart's Sake* (Pamela Chandler), courtesy of Lionel Bart Foundation Archive
15. Lionel Bart (Vivienne), courtesy of Lionel Bart Foundation Archive
16. Lionel Bart, courtesy of Lionel Bart Foundation Archive
17. Lionel Bart, 1994 (Michael Le Poer Trench), courtesy of Lionel Bart Foundation Archive

Acknowledgments

With utmost gratitude to Professor Tony Kushner for his great encouragement, support and tremendous patience. He is truly inspirational.

My appreciation goes to Dr James Jordan for his advice and suggestions, the staff at the British Library and British Sound Archives and to Brenda Evans of the Lionel Bart Foundation.

I am most grateful to Simon Kossoff for sharing photographs from his personal archive, to Peter Suschitzky for the photographs of *The Bespoke Overcoat* that were taken by his father Wolfgang Suschitzky and to Clive Gellert of the Unity Theatre Trust for his permission to use photographs from the Unity Theatre Archive.

Thank you to the following who gave their time for interviews, either in person or by telephone and email correspondence which gave me a great insight into Unity Theatre, the Jewish East End and the personalities featured: Ronald Davidson, Elliot Davis, Davina Gold, Geoffrey Goldstein, Margot Hilton, Gillian Jesson, Simon Kossoff, Martin Kraft, Harry Landis, Andrea Mattock, Gilda Moss Haber, Shirley Murgraff, Muriel Walker and Bonnie Yates.

Introduction

Contexts

The twentieth century and its two world wars led to enormous social change throughout Britain, including growth in population and ethnic and religious diversity that led to an increasingly multi-cultural society. Jews were the largest immigrant group from the 1880s to 1914 and then again in the 1930s. During and after the Second World War many other groups came, including non-white migrants from the New Commonwealth. Educational opportunities were also a potent force for social change and occupational mobility. The 1945 election saw the Labour Party bring with it nationalisation and welfare state legislation, which included the creation of the National Health Service. The health and life expectancy of the average person and the quality of their living conditions were transformed. Cars became the common form of transport and the layout of many towns and the pattern of shopping changed. Holidays abroad, the preserve of the upper classes at the start of the century, became increasingly common.[1] The overall increase in the average level of income greatly enhanced the ability of working-class households to purchase non-essentials. The nutritional status of the population improved at the same time as expenditure on clothing and consumer durables. Rising real incomes gave people the means to participate in new forms of leisure and recreation that was also aided by the shortening of the average working week (from 54 hours before the First World War to 40 hours by the mid-1960s). In the cultural sphere, inter-war cinemas marked a decisive democratisation of popular culture since the mainly American films were watched by an audience drawn across the social classes.[2] In 1957 the prime minister, Harold Macmillan, proclaimed that 'You will see a state of prosperity such as we have never had in my lifetime – nor indeed in the history of this country'. Whilst poverty and inequality remained, there was some substance to Macmillan's analysis.

This was an exciting, if often challenging, period in British history and theatre throughout the twentieth century reflected these changes. The *fin de siècle* saw the development of an interest in theatre that explored the moral and social issues of contemporary society. As part of this development, but at a grass roots level, left-wing political movements used theatre to agitate for social change. This book is about second generation Jewish immigrants from Eastern Europe who took part in these movements. I have chosen four key figures, all of whom originated in these movements and became famous in different aspects of the post-war British entertainment industry: Alfie Bass, David Kossoff, Warren Mitchell and Lionel Bart. This book will examine their class, politics and ethnicity and how this impacted on their remarkable contribution.

Although seminal works have been published on left-wing political theatre companies, such as the Workers' Theatre Movement and Unity Theatre, that give valuable insight into their importance of bringing political theatre to Britain during the first half of the twentieth century,[3] there is not sufficient acknowledgement given to these movements within the history of English theatre or credit for how they changed that world. A great deal of activity was centred in the East End of London and this book will explore how the seeds were sown there. The result was that working-class theatre was brought to the masses with a vital contribution from the Jewish section of the poor, but vibrant, part of the metropolis.

The contribution was made by second generation immigrants and this book will look at how they had managed to integrate into British society. Although there has been some research on Jewish participation in *traditional* theatre in this country,[4] little has been done to look at Jewish involvement in alternative and ground-breaking versions. This Introduction provides the background of the history of the Jews in the East End, Yiddish theatre, as well as Jewish interest in other East End theatres and music halls. This, together with Jewish involvement in left-wing politics, will explain the attraction for second generation immigrants to join Unity Theatre.

Unity Theatre, created in the 1930s, was a central venue for working class drama. It provided an entrance for Jewish East End actors into the entertainment industry, none more so than Alfie Bass, David Kossoff, Warren Mitchell and Lionel Bart, the figures who will form the heart of this book. They came to the forefront without having to deny their Jewishness and became famous on stage and screen for their 'Cockney' persona. They have been chosen to show their different pathways out of the East End and out of Unity. Their biographies do not stand alone but are looked at as a *collective* biography. The impact on where they lived, how they identified with the area they grew up in, their Jewish identity and how they defined themselves in order to be portrayed as Cockneys, are all explored.

The Second Generation

There have been many studies made on the lives and political involvement of first generation immigrants in the East End,[5] but there has only been a limited amount of work on their children, the second generation,[6] and no specific research that focuses on their role through the world of entertainment and especially in the theatre. This book considers the background to where the case studies' families originated from and when they arrived in Britain, to see if this had any particular impact on their Jewish identity and political involvement.

The second generation developed a world that allowed them to exist and feel attachment to both the Jewish and non-Jewish worlds. Second generation New York Jews constructed a type of ethnicity consonant with middle-class American values and succeeded in combining their experience as New Yorkers with their experience as Jews. Through the process of becoming New Yorkers, and by extension also Americans, second generation Jews redefined the meaning of Jewishness. They created a community with elements borrowed from American culture, middle-class values and urban lifestyles as well as from their immigrant Jewish heritage. They made for themselves a bilateral line of descent from their parents: selectively American on one side and selectively ethnic on the other.[7]

Likewise, the second generation's integration into British society together with anglicizing influences occurred from many directions, both informally and formally. In her study of Manchester Jews, Rosalyn Livshin showed how they were introduced informally to Englishness by mixing with non-Jewish children on the streets and through leisure and entertainment and also formally through the very institutions of the Jewish community itself.[8] The immigrants from Eastern Europe came to a Jewish community in which there already existed an established anglicized Anglo-Jewish community that had grown up during the course of the nineteenth century. With the growth of immigration from Eastern Europe the established community was faced with a new social element which threatened to distort their accepted image. The Anglo-Jewish community feared that as long as the foreign Jews remained apart they would attract hostility and abuse and would not be accepted as British citizens by the local population. In the eyes of the established community the answer to the problem lay in the transformation of Jewish foreigners into English Jews. Consequently, the great drive within the Anglo-Jewish community in the face of this problem was to anglicize the immigrant by all means within their power through Jewish schools. It was there that great emphasis was placed on speaking

English and introducing them to English life and culture and anything to do with Yiddish, the language at home, was frowned upon. This was continued in youth clubs that were modelled on non-Jewish organizations. Within one generation foreigners were turned into English Jews and the pressures towards acculturation accumulated from all directions and were too strong not to have their effect.[9]

During the inter-war period there were concerns voiced by Jewish community leaders over this 'estranged generation', as some believed they were becoming separated from Jewish life, detached from their Jewishness and Jewish peers and were being lost to secularity and mainstream culture. Yet David Dee, in his study of this generation, contends that for the most part this generation was much less distant from their Judaism than many believed.[10] There were significant shifts as many moved into jobs and careers that would have been unthinkable for their immigrant parents, that led to friendships with non-Jews and increased income that enabled them to move out to the suburbs as well as an interest in sport and leisure, activities often associated with non-Jewish society. Dee notes that such participation may have changed the second generation's perception of their Jewishness and their Jewish peers. Nevertheless, it did not mean that they abandoned their sense of being Jewish.[11] He considers that the greater exposure to non-Jewish society as well as a general desire to maintain connections with their Jewish past led to the development of a truly hybrid form of identity among the children of the immigrants. During the inter-war period a worldview developed that allowed them to exist in and feel attachment to both minority and majority society. They shaped and reconfigured their identities to facilitate their own lifestyle and life choices.[12] It enabled them to take an active part in political theatre and Unity Theatre.

Theatre in the First Half of the Twentieth Century

In order to highlight the ground-breaking work that Unity Theatre did, it is necessary to look at what was being performed in England at the time of its formation. The twentieth century heralded the beginning of the modern era in theatre with an explosion of talent led by Oscar Wilde and George Bernard Shaw together with great dramatists from abroad such as Ibsen, Strindberg and Chekhov. Theatre was at a crossroads, still controlled by a prudish and puritanical late Victorian establishment but marching towards a future which would not be to the liking of the old guard.[13] The advent of Ibsen on the English scene provided both a shock and a stimulus. *A Doll's House*, for example, performed in 1899, launched a wave of controversy that brought Ibsen to public attention for the first time.[14] The play depicts a female protagonist who dares to defy her 'duty' as a wife and mother.

In order to understand the extent of this controversy, one must consider what was performed on the stage during the preceding years. Theatre during the nineteenth century reflected what had happened as a result of the Industrial Revolution with migration from the country to towns and cities. The sheer weight of numbers introduced popular fare into the playhouses and by the 1840s melodrama and pantomime held sway. Theatres had on the whole been deserted by the middle and upper classes and the predominantly lower classes were now the new audience who enjoyed more popular fare as an escape from their dire living conditions.[15]

All works had to be submitted to the Lord Chamberlain for approval, and this affected the type of plays that people were permitted to see. Lords Chamberlains were mostly upper-middle class and reflected the views of a conservative aristocracy.[16] They felt that theatre should reflect an idealized and conventionally moral view of society and should avoid any serious questioning of orthodox values and any debating of contemporary political issues. Britain's theatre was therefore reactionary as a result.[17] Historian Andrew Davies considers that British theatre was divided into four traditions: folk theatre that usually took place in villages with content passed orally from one generation to another; popular theatre, such as music halls, that had much improvisation, spontaneity, topicality and interaction with the audiences; West End commercial theatre and alternative experimental theatre.[18]

West End Theatre

The West End was the centre of English commercial theatre, gaining its name from its geographical relationship to the City of London.[19] By the beginning of the twentieth century over 25 new theatres in the West End had been built in the Shaftesbury Avenue and Charing Cross area in an attempt to woo back the middle-class audience which had earlier in the century transferred its patronage to opera.[20]

West End theatre was founded upon two components: the star, who was often the actor-manager, and the 'long run' system whereby plays were chosen that would be popular and commercially viable. The plays appealed to a largely middle-class audience, the new West End audience, and they tended to reflect their background and values.[21] During the years before the outbreak of the First World War the West End theatres catered to audiences who were either unconcerned with or actively seeking diversion from any political or industrial struggles.[22] Drawing-room comedies, costume dramas, hilarious farces and light musicals were performed.[23] Conventional ideas prevailed and productions were detailed, elaborate and beautiful.[24]

There was a theatrical boom in the West End during the First World War caused by soldiers home on leave looking for escapist entertainment such as the farce *A Little Bit of Fluff* and *Chu Chin Chow*, a musical version based on *Ali Baba and the Forty Thieves*.[25] There was also a changing socio-economic make-up in the audience. Heavy taxes after the war had reduced the numbers of the very rich. A middle class developed due to a growth of small family businesses, the chance of home ownership and improved educational opportunities with increased numbers going to grammar schools. This was reflected in the theatre by the downgrading of settings from W. Somerset Maugham's stockbroker family houses to J. B. Priestley's middle-class villas under economic strain.[26] Most popular were the endless diet of musicals or historical period pieces such as *The Barratts of Wimpole Street*. Censorship also continued to make certain that nothing provocative or controversial would be staged.[27]

Despite such an overall conventional picture there were changes that had begun to take place that explored the moral and social issues of contemporary society. The Actresses' Franchise League was founded in 1908 to support the suffrage movement and plays were written for the cause. Away from the West End area the Royal Court put on the work of alternative theatre groups led by the Independent Theatre Society, which introduced Ibsen to Britain, and the Stage Society. These societies depended on members' subscriptions and were classed as private clubs. They did not have to submit their plays to the censor and therefore could stage George Bernard Shaw's *Mrs Warren's Profession* (about prostitution) and Harley Granville Barker's *Waste* (about an affair that leads to an abortion).[28]

It was during the inter-war period that political theatre emerged. This was a time of social discontent: depression years, unemployment and hunger marches, the rise of Fascism in Italy and then in Germany and even Mosley's Blackshirts in Britain. This period saw the rise of the Workers' Theatre Movement whose aim was to bring about social change through their work. The Unity Theatre developed from the Workers' Theatre Movement and staged plays on social and political issues to growing audiences. Its aim was to present and interpret life as experienced by the majority of the people and its work was to influence political and experimental theatre in the years to come. A new seriousness of purpose marked the content of theatre from the second half of the 1950s, such as John Osborne's *Look Back in Anger* (1956).[29] The author Julian Barnes dates modern British theatre from the date that *Look Back in Anger* was first seen at the Royal Court. Likewise, the theatre critic Michael Billington also shares this view as the play caused a stir because of its scorching attack on conventional 1950s England.[30] Others, however, argue that the revolution had come earlier. Indeed, the playwright Ted Willis considered that Unity Theatre had anticipated many of the themes aired at the Royal Court.[31]

East End Theatres and Music Halls

Theatre in the East End was in total contrast to what was shown on the West End stage due to the local population's background and history. From the late eighteenth century the East End of London developed as a major centre of trade, industry and shipping. Separated from the fashionable West End, it increasingly took on an identity fostered by its isolation. Bounded by the Thames to its south and stretching as far as Shoreditch and Hackney to the north, it seemed a world apart to those who lived elsewhere. It developed its own mythology whether through the notoriety of the Radcliffe Highway with its knife fights, prostitution and squalid saloons, or the extreme poverty of the area and the influx of immigrants. Writers sought to create and perpetuate its myths as it was a foreign and often terrifying if still enticing territory to those who lived in other districts of London. The majority of its inhabitants had either been born locally or migrated from rural areas in search of work, but there were also Jews who had settled there from their readmission to England in the 1650s onwards. This contributed to the exoticism and 'otherness' of the East End.[32]

According to the Oxford English Dictionary the term 'East End' refers to the eastern part of London and the name and the East Ender of London was referred to in *The Pall Mall Gazette* (14 August 1884).[33] The East End in the nineteenth century was a different world, an unknown space within the same city. Arthur Morrison wrote in *Tales of Mean Streets* (1896) that it was 'out beyond Leadenhall Street and Aldgate Pump' and that it was a shocking place 'where men and women live on penn'orths of gin, where collars and clean shirts are decencies unknown'. The glitter of the West End in the 1880s and 1890s was in sharp contrast to the East End and the startling existence of poverty there.[34] The contrast between the two areas was reflected in the type of theatrical entertainment that was shown and enjoyed.

The East End established itself as a generic theatrical area during the nineteenth century following the expansion of industry partially fostered by the intensive dock-building programme.[35] The East End theatres entertained huge numbers. The Pavilion in Whitechapel opened in 1828, followed in the next few years by The Garrick, The Grecian, The Effingham, The National Standard Theatre, The City of London and The Britannia. Several of these began life as 'saloons', a lower caste of venue attached to a public house. The theatres ranged in size from a capacity of 462 at The Garrick to over 3,000 at The Pavilion and Britannia.[36] Locals of all ages made up the audiences; most people walked to the theatre and ticket prices were low. The shows, which included plays, interludes or a pantomime, lasted four or five hours and were an escape from reality.[37]

Although some productions were shown both in the West End and East End, the latter had its own distinctive features. The audiences loved dramas that featured criminals and highwaymen with anti-authoritarian law-breaking heroes. Urban melodramas were popular, such as Colin Hazlewood's *The Wild Tribes of London* (City of London Theatre, 1856), which depicted aristocratic vice and working-class woe. East End theatres featured representations of London's minority communities including Jews, Indians and Africans and, unlike their representation in the West End, such characters were not always minor or comic ones.[38] Yet at times there were similar productions to those shown in the West End, where Shakespeare's plays were performed regularly alongside melodramas. Playbills for productions at The City of London Theatre in the late 1850s and early 1860s featured popular urban or crime melodramas, such as *The Robbers!* on the same bill as Shakespeare's *Macbeth* and *The Merry Wives of Windsor*.[39]

Many of the Jewish community were enthusiastic theatre-goers.[40] A reviewer at The City of London Theatre in March 1839 noted the predominance of the local Jewish population:

> It was literally a house of Israel; as if all Bishopsgate, St Mary Axe, Shoreditch and Finsbury Circus had disgorged their fusty tenantry into one huge mass of Anglo-Jewish capitalists. There were Moseses and Jacobses, and Solomons, and Isaacs, enough to have stormed and retaken old Jerusalem.[41]

By the second half of the nineteenth century theatres were catering to this audience with plays in both English and Yiddish. By the 1870s The Britannia was staging a 'Jewish Annual'. These plays included *Jewess and Christian or The Love that Kills* (1877), *Rachel's Penance or a Daughter of Israel* (1878) and the *Rabbi's Son or The Last Link in the Chain* (1879) and often featured Jewish/Gentile romances.[42] It was reported that The City of London Theatre, The Standard Theatre and the local playhouses in general were 'greatly resorted to by the Jews, and more especially by the younger members of the body, who sometimes constitute a rather obstreperous gallery'.[43]

Of great popularity in the East End in the mid-nineteenth century were the penny 'gaffs', makeshift theatres staged in a converted warehouse or similar premises, which would accommodate a couple of hundred rowdy spectators. A band would play to draw in the people and a usual programme would offer two 20-minute melodramas, with titles such as *Seven Steps to Tyburn* or the *Bloodstained Handkerchief* with a song in the interval.[44] At one time there were over 80 gaffs in the East End and they were as vital to the area as the patent theatres of the West End.[45] From the gaffs evolved the music hall. The East End accommodated 150 music halls, more than any other part of London,[46] and the bill differed little from venue to venue. Most nights the first act would be the offensively named 'nigger minstrel' followed by acts including a comic singer, a clog dancer and sword-swallower. During the course of the evening 20 to 30 patriotic and love songs would be sung.[47]

The music hall was popular amongst the Jewish population and showed their integration into local culture. It was reported that 'the variety stage can boast, and with good reason, a large number of Israelites among the members' and although it was practically impossible to name fully the most favourite Jewish entertainers of the past and present the list would be interesting alike 'to *goyim* and *yidden*'.[48] By the end of the nineteenth century the music hall had replaced theatre as a predominant mode of entertainment in the East End.[49] In 1901 only The Pavilion, The Britannia and The Standard remained, presenting similar programmes centred on popular melodramas and an annual pantomime.[50] The decline in theatre audience was partly demographic, because as the city expanded and developed, housing was replaced with industrial and commercial premises. There was also the development of the tramways from the mid-1870s and reduced fares for the working man by the Great Eastern Railways which led to a migration eastwards. The only increase in the area was in Whitechapel due to Jewish immigration and therefore The Pavilion survived with its programme of Yiddish plays.[51]

Yiddish Theatre in the East End

The Yiddish theatre in London was created by and for the Jewish immigrants from Eastern Europe who came to England in the late nineteenth century. These Jews were driven by pogroms, repressive regulations, political upheavals and, more than anything, degrading poverty. By 1911 there were 106,082 'Russians and Poles' recorded in the British census – the vast majority Jews – and most were funnelled into the East End.[52]

In all the countries where Jewish immigrants established themselves in sufficient numbers there developed a rich Yiddish cultural life. There were Yiddish books and newspapers, left-wing Yiddish and anarchist groups and an enthusiastic audience for Yiddish theatre which was the main form of entertainment for the immigrant working class. Yiddish was the mother tongue of the vast majority of Eastern European Jewry: it was the language spoken in the home and the workplace in contrast to Hebrew, the language of prayer. It is a richly expressive language based on medieval German but incorporating Hebrew, Russian and Polish words.

It was also the medium for a rich and varied folk culture, ranging from popularisation of religious texts and sentimental literature to the travelling entertainers who performed on festive occasions in the Jewish villages and towns of Eastern Europe and appeared in Purim plays. Purim commemorates the Jews being saved by Queen Esther from a massacre planned by Haman as told in the Old Testament's Book of Esther, and Yiddish theatre developed directly from the oral traditions of these entertainments.[53]

In 1883 Yiddish theatre was banned throughout the Russian empire. Many of the producers and performers forced out by pogroms or seeking employment elsewhere emigrated to western Europe and America. The impresario Jacob Adler came to London in 1883 and brought with him the first professional Yiddish actors. He presented lightweight musical comedies, melodramas and folk operas and as well as the main entertainment the actors would sing humorous or satirical rhyming couplets.[54] The early decades of the twentieth century were the heyday of Yiddish theatre in London when stars would come from Eastern Europe and America and those from Britain would perform all over the world. This fluid migration impacted on the Jewish migrants' activities and identities as ideas were shared from east to west, north to south and vice versa.[55]

Bernard Mendelovitch, a member of the Grand Palais Yiddish Company, explains that the theatre was also a meeting place for new immigrants to discuss their problems and seek help and advice and their first introduction to world literature as Shakespeare, Ibsen, Tolstoy and Strindberg were performed in Yiddish translation.[56] The theatre became a lifeline for the displaced Jewish community and kept alive their roots and values, hopes and dreams.[57] At the same time as English classics and other plays were translated, they were learning about their new environment and it served as a form of acculturation to Britain.[58]

The types of plays performed were geared to box office receipts to provide actors with good roles and audiences with laughs and thrills. The plots provided twists; the comedians turned somersaults and made vulgar puns. Melodramatic operettas added sensation and spectacle to high romance, which the audiences were already addicted to.[59] The audience was always passionately involved and many came along with their British-born children who were often fluent in both Yiddish and English.[60] As will be noted later, the Yiddish theatre was to have a great effect on Lionel Bart, composer of the musical *Oliver!*, one of the greatest musicals in British theatre history. He attended performances with his parents and acknowledged that it influenced his work.[61]

Yiddish music hall flourished briefly in the East End at the beginning of the twentieth century. Immigrant youngsters performed in local pubs and small halls and while some were professional actors, many more were ordinary workers – tailors, seamstresses, barbers, waiters – with a liking for the stage. The songs covered the whole spectrum from comic, topical to sentimental.[62] Stars such as Madame Rosa Klug sang songs such as 'A Bite to Eat Without Washing' about sex without bodily cleansing (the washing referring to Jewish purity laws). There were songs about thwarted love, the Boer War and the Titanic. It was a parallel world to English entertainment in the area and it overlapped, such as at The Wonderland Theatre where a show could include a Yiddish operatic sketch together with a viewing of a man with a ten-foot moustache.[63]

The Yiddish theatre continued to give enormous pleasure in the inter-war period but the enthusiastic faithful fell in numbers annually. This was due to demographic and social trends as immigration dropped in numbers, a decline in spoken Yiddish as children of the immigrant generation became more anglicized and the Jewish population diminished as people moved to the suburbs. The cinema was a new and powerful attraction which affected the Yiddish theatre as well as other theatres. But whereas other theatres offered a regular choice of new plays and new talents, the Yiddish theatre on the whole failed to develop a new repertoire or attract young and talented actors in sufficient numbers.[64] East Ender Louis Behr commented that young Jewish people 'wanted an outlet away from their parents. It was a bondage. They wanted to go to the West End.' By the late twentieth century London's Yiddish theatre had all but disappeared, with just occasional performances given in synagogue halls and for Jewish social functions until age and sickness took its toll and was no more.[65]

The constraints and insularity of Yiddish theatre, along with increasing pressure from outside the community for integration and anglicization, brought about its demise but not before the theatre had spawned a craving of entertainment in a new generation of aspiring performers who were ready and willing to cross into the Gentile mainstream.[66] The Yiddish theatre and music hall tended to be satirical and generally apolitical. There was, however, a different tradition of political theatre that Unity Theatre was part of.

Political Theatre

The tradition of political theatre reaches back to the origins of European drama as shown by the ancient Greek playwright Euripides who attacked the war policy of the government of his day.[67] Many playwrights held the conviction that writing plays and having them performed might help to change the way society was structured. This can be traced back to Greek drama and Aristotle's theory of *catharsis*, that by watching a tragedy we may be purged of unhealthy emotions. In later years the Christian church was willing to use drama as a means of propagating faith, giving us the word 'propaganda'.[68]

In the twentieth century theatre there grew an intention to convert to a new way of thinking, or at least to challenge old modes of thought, and it became more overtly political, questioning not so much social morality as the fundamental organization of society with the emphasis on economics rather than ethics influenced by Karl Marx's analysis of capitalism. A number of directors and playwrights, in particular Erwin Piscator and Bertolt Brecht,[69] sought to use the stage to propose socialist alternatives to the injustices of the world and helped to define what we have now come to term 'political theatre'. Piscator was the originator of the epic theatre style later developed by Brecht in plays such as *The Caucasian Chalk Circle* (1948). Epic theatre used techniques designed to distance the audience from emotional involvement in the play through reminders of the artificiality of the theatrical performance. Techniques included actors stepping out of character to lecture, explanatory captions or illustrations on a scene, flooding the stage with harsh white light regardless of where the action was taking place, or intentionally interrupting the action at key junctures with songs in order to drive home an important message. These 'alienating' and 'distancing' effects asked the audience to think objectively about the play, to reflect on its argument, and arouse a capacity for action or to take decisions.[70]

The Workers' Theatre Movement, the first organized political theatre in Britain, was founded in 1926 to conduct working-class propaganda and agitation through dramatic representation.[71] The great upheavals of the First World War and the Russian Revolution in 1917 led to a widespread questioning in British society and this applied no less to theatre. After the Russian Revolution there was a flowering of many genres: the political poster, mass dramatizations and popular street presentations.[72] There was a focus on agit-prop (agitation and propaganda), a militant form of art intended to emotionally and ideologically mobilize its audience to take particular action with regard to an urgent situation. Agit-prop was designed for the streets: portable sets, visually clear characterizations, emblematic costumes and props, choral speaking and character types familiar to a broad range of spectators.[73]

A Council for Proletarian Art was formed in Britain in 1924 and two years later changed its name to the Workers' Theatre Movement (WTM). The impetus for the WTM was built during the run-up to the General Strike of May 1926. In the years preceding the strike, the Communist Party had organized the National Minority Movement, bringing together revolutionary and non-revolutionary rank and file workers across the country. This period of activism flowed into cultural activities. These included the play *Masses Man* by Ernst Toller, performed in mining villages around Sheffield and Doncaster, revealing a transitional radical cultural movement from Germany to England. There were many local groups in the great industrial centres of the country; the idea that the working class was the 'coming class' was widespread. The WTM was formally formed in the aftermath of the General Strike. It saw itself as a theatre of action and consequently dealt with many of the issues facing the movement in the immediate fall-out of the greatest general strike Britain had seen – victimisation, police persecution and attacks on the trade unions. Short topical sketches were performed outside factory gates and were sometimes little more than choral declamation or political rewordings of popular songs.[74] Simplicity was the key factor in these street scripts since the group had to be able to 'move into position to perform it and be away before the cops got onto you'.[75]

Over 100 groups, with names such as Red Megaphones, Red Radio and the Red Front, performed in local halls, on the streets and at workers' rallies.[76] The most influential group in the early days was in Hackney – the Hackney People's Players founded by Tom Thomas. He adapted a segment of Robert Tressell's *The Ragged Trousered Philanthropist*, a novel which advocated a socialist society. The working-class audience identified with the scenario and the use of popular language and the cast of fourteen included two electricians, two clerks, a bookkeeper, a seaman, a tailor, two housewives and two cabinet makers. Thomas coined the phrase 'a propertyless theatre for the propertyless class' – there were no props or costumes.[77] The WTM produced its own publication, *The Red Stage*. The first issue with the slogan 'Art is the Weapon of the Revolution' was an indication of the growth of their movement.[78] In the next issue an article entitled 'Our Theatre Awakens the Masses' criticized mainstream theatre and cinema for not showing the realities of life and considered itself 'a new conception of the theatre, as a weapon in the workers' struggle for freedom and life'.[79]

Changes in the WTM began in the 1930s when the Communist Party changed its approach. It met the rise of Fascism with the popular front strategy in which the needs of the working class were to be secondary to building alliances with those 'progressive forces' willing to ally with the Soviet Union against Germany. The Party was no longer interested in backing workers' theatre groups and closed many of them down. Although the Party attempted to bury all memory of the WTM, its radicalism and legacy can be traced. The WTM saw itself as a modernist movement, breaking with the traditions of the theatre at that time. It attempted to get rid of conventional staging techniques, such as abolishing the curtain, and was also innovative in its repertoire. It moved beyond the written text and used an acting style to develop a new form of physical theatre and it did this with clerks, teachers and shop workers.[80]

One of these groups was the Yiddish-speaking theatre group Proltet, formed in 1909, which grew out of the Jewish Workers' Circle in Alie Street.[81] The Workers' Circle played a significant role as a social and cultural venue for the immigrant population.[82] Jewish East Ender Joe Jacobs describes the Workers' Circle as a hive of working-class activity. It was a Jewish organization set up on the basis of a friendly society with all kinds of mutual aid activities. Members included anarchists and libertarians, socialists and free-thinkers. 'Every shade of Russian and European labour thought and action were represented here.'[83] It promoted self-education, literary work and support for those who were sick or unemployed. In addition there were activities for members, many of whom were trade unionists.[84]

Between 1880 and 1914, some 2.4 million Jews left Eastern Europe. As already noted, they were driven by pogroms, repressive regulations, political upheaval and degrading poverty. London became one of the major destinations but it was an area of great overcrowding and poverty and people struggled to make a living. During this period a radical intelligentsia of socialists and anarchists created a social movement and Yiddish historian Leonard Prager referred to London as 'the Jerusalem of Jewish radicalism'.[85]

With the overthrow of the Tsar, the Soviet Union became a symbol of hope for the Jewish people and the Communist Party (CP) offered a sense of belonging to an international family.[86] Of the several distinct minority groupings traceable within the Communist Party of Great Britain (CPGB), probably the most numerous was the Jewish membership. Estimates suggest that in the Party's heyday Jewish members formed 10 per cent of the membership, a figure ten times that for the population as a whole.[87] After the Second World War there was a widespread and urgent desire for a new and different kind of Britain with many wanting a socialist society, reflected in the surprising Labour election victory of 1945. Another factor was the role played by the Soviet Red Army and Communist-led resistance movements in the defeat of Fascism. There was an upsurge of votes for Communist candidates with Phil Piratin (of Jewish origin) elected as Member of Parliament for Mile End in 1945 and several Communist councillors elected largely on the left-wing Jewish vote.[88]

In the 1930s, and throughout the Second World War, the Party established itself as the most active voice for issues of Jewish concern.[89] Often working through popular front organizations, it was at the forefront of the fight against poverty in the East End, orchestrating rent strikes against slum landlords, campaigning for proper air raid precautions and for the provision of better housing at the end of the war. Street activism appealed to the working class who were dissatisfied with the lukewarm approach of the established political parties, including the Labour Party, and the 'low profile' adopted by the Board of Deputies of British Jews.[90] 'Three-quarters of Jewish Communist activists in the 1950s joined the Party between 1933 and 1945.'[91]

On international matters, the CPGB condemned Franco in Spain and the Polish ultra-nationalists and praised Soviet Russia as the best insurance against Nazi Germany. It was able to present an image of Soviet Russia that recommended itself to the Jews in the East End. Stalinist Russia's ideological opposition to Nazism was unrivalled in Europe. It was the only state that had outlawed antisemitism and was endeavouring to improve the economic condition of the Jewish proletariat. The regime was actively promoting Yiddish culture through the World Jewish Cultural Union (1937) and the creation of the Birobidzhan Jewish Autonomous region in the Soviet Far East, an area founded in the 1930s as an alternative Jewish homeland. Pro-Soviet feeling in the East End peaked with the formation in the USSR of the Jewish Anti-Fascist Committee and the visit to Britain of two of its leading spokesmen in 1943.[92]

After the war the Party attempted to maintain its hegemony in the East End. It was active in the campaign to clear out slums and replace them with better housing. On an international level, the Party continued to promote Soviet Jewish life, especially in Birobidzhan. Yet within a decade Jewish Communism was all but extinct in the East End as well as elsewhere. This was due to changes nationally and internationally. The Communist programme for social change in East London became increasingly less relevant as the Attlee government introduced major reforms in education, medical care and unemployment benefits that ushered in the welfare state. At the same time Jews increasingly achieved their goal of upward mobility and left the East End.[93]

The problem spread further afield. After 1945, international developments put an end to many of the policy debates which had fuelled pro-Communist sentiment. At the end of the war Spain was lost, Hitler defeated, and millions had died in the Holocaust. There was less interest in class politics and more in Zionism after the formation of Israel in 1948. Jewish Communists had been overjoyed when in 1947–48 the Soviet Union pledged its support to the fledgling Jewish state. In the late 1940s, however, the rift between the two countries had already become apparent and the Soviet Union would provide almost uncritical support and arms to the Arab states. Jews were also alarmed by the reports of antisemitism within the Soviet Union that began circulating in 1948.

In February 1956, at the Twentieth Soviet Communist Party Congress, Nikita Khrushchev caused a crisis in the world's Communist movement by describing the brutal criminality of Stalin's regime. These revelations were particularly disturbing to Jews as they included a long list of antisemitic acts such as the purges of Jewish party leaders, the general shutdown of Jewish cultural institutions in the Soviet Union after 1948 and the murders in 1952 of leading Soviet Jewish writers and intellectuals. The outbreak of the Hungarian Revolution in October 1956 also shook the faith of many. In England this led to much soul-searching and there were numerous debates and heated arguments between people who had been comrades for decades. Many people left the Party.[94]

The majority of the British Jewish Communists who had joined the Party initially, before disillusionment set in, were second generation immigrants who grew up as members of both British and Jewish society. Most were found within a spectrum ranging from modern orthodox to minimal observance. 'The decline in religious belief and generational divergence both interacted with and were exacerbated by a more deep rooted and far reaching process: the integration of second generation

Anglo-Jewry into British society.'[95] Parents did not resist the process but instead encouraged it. The Anglo-Jewish elite who did not want the immigrants to stand out as an alien element set up English classes and clubs in the East End to try and make them good British citizens. New opportunities became available to Jewish youth, some of which led to joining the Party. Of the biographies of Jewish Communists on file, 90 per cent joined the Party as teenagers or soon after.[96]

Thus, given the strengths of a Jewish Communist ethnic sub-identity, it is not surprising that a Yiddish-speaking branch of the WTM was formed. Proltet modelled itself on the agit-prop style of the other WTM groups. Everyone wore the navy bib-and-brace overalls and white shirts to symbolize their sense of identity and solidarity with the working class.[97] Among the plays put on was *Strike* by Michael Gold, an American Communist of Jewish origin.[98] Ray Waterman from Proltet recalls that those in the group saw themselves as part of a movement towards socialism and that they felt responsible for what was publicly said. Fegel Firestein, also from Proltet, believed that from theatre and culture she could learn how to build a better future. Proltet functioned from 1932-34 until it became impossible to continue as some people moved away from the area and others were under pressure to use their time to fight against Fascism.[99]

Unfortunately, scant information remains about either Proltet or WTM. Howard Goorney, one of the founder members of Theatre Workshop,[100] comments that there were no written records of early agit-prop sketches as they dealt with day-to-day political issues and were by their very nature ephemeral – long forgotten notes on bits of paper if written at all.[101] He considers that it was as important a cultural and political manifestation in its own time as the alternative theatre movements that started in the 1960s. Many of these latter groups adopted agit-prop techniques, taking their theatre to non-theatrical venues and out on to the streets in the same way as WTM had done. Although the start of WTM marked the beginning of an attempt to organize left-wing theatre on a comparatively large scale, it has been almost completely ignored in the mainstream of writing about theatre history.[102] Many of its members, however, went on to work in Unity Theatre in the 1940s and 1950s and that was to have an impact on the British entertainment industry.

Unity Theatre

The transition from the WTM to Unity Theatre came mainly through the work of the Rebel Players, which as the WTM disintegrated begun to absorb members of other groups, notably Proltet and Red Radio. The core of Rebel Players was young, second-generation immigrants from the East End.[103] The first meeting of the Unity Theatre was held in January 1936 at the Workers' Circle in Alie Street. Those present were a band of amateurs formed in revolt against 'the escapism and ideology of conventional theatre'.[104] The aim was 'to foster and further the art of the drama in accordance with its principle that true art by effectively presenting and truthfully interpreting life as experienced by the majority of the people can move the people to work for the betterment of society'.[105]

In January 1936 the group acquired premises of their own, a church hall in King's Cross north of central London. King's Cross was an area with a definite working-class identity and it was important that it was outside the East End as the group wanted to broaden their appeal to a wider audience.[106] Although intended to serve as a base for the activities of mobile groups, this also represented a step towards taking the company's activities off the streets. With the voluntary help of hundreds of skilled trade unionists, the building was reconstructed.[107] Membership rose rapidly to 7,000 in May 1939 as well as the quarter of a million workers that could be reached through affiliated bodies such as the trade unions. A theatre school and workshop and film unit were also started.[108]

The group's first great success in 1938 was *Waiting for Lefty* by Clifford Odets, a landmark in the history of left-wing theatre in Britain. During the play a group of New York cabbies meet to discuss taking strike action 'to get a living wage' and while they wait for their leader Lefty Costello, they tell their stories in rapid, realistic scenes. The play ends with the news that Lefty has been shot and this provokes full support for a strike. The actors speak directly to the audience members as if they were at the meeting. Indeed, the breaking down of the barrier between actors and audience was a feature of Unity's style. Sympathetic audiences joined in with the chant of 'strike, strike'.[109] The success of the play was staggering, and it ran for 350 performances. Another great coup for Unity was when radical black American singer Paul Robeson turned down the opportunity of a well-paid contract in a West End theatre to join the unpaid amateur Unity cast for a part in Ben Bengal's *Plant in the Sun*. The play told the story of a group of teenagers in the shipping department of a New York sweet factory who hold a sit-down strike when one of them is fired for 'talking union'.[110] This was also, as in the case of the Yiddish theatre mentioned earlier, an opportunity for the flow of transitional culture from America to take place.[111]

Early programmes often included short plays about the Fascist threat. *Not For Us* imagined what might happen if the Fascists achieved power in

England and Jack Lindsey's *On Guard for Spain* dealt with the Spanish Civil War. The first significant play to come from Unity itself was *Where's That Bomb?* This was the story of a young worker poet, who was sacked from his job for writing socialist verse and who then accepts money to write for the British Patriot's Propaganda Association. He writes a 'safe' story, but the characters come to life and reject the story he has given them: the benevolent boss becomes the demon Money Power and Bolshie (who has the bomb of the title) changes from villain to hero. Unity also produced *Senora Carrar's Rifles,* the first Bertolt Brecht play in Britain (1938) and premiered Sean O'Casey's *The Star Turns Red* (1940).[112] In addition to producing plays by established playwrights, part of Unity's policy was 'the nurturing of working-class dramatists from the ranks of the people'. Among these was David Martin from a Hungarian Jewish family who wrote *The Shepherd and the Hunter* (1946) which dealt with the Arab-Jewish conflict in Palestine.[113]

In total contrast was *Winkles and Champagne,* the history of the music hall. Many Unity players had long been interested in music hall as they saw it as a popular entertainment of the working class. The show included scenes from a Regency pleasure garden, a Victorian beer hall and Edwardian music hall. Colin Chambers commented that the show's politics lay in revealing a popular tradition not in any analysis of that history and that it appealed to working class audiences.[114] The contrast between the above mentioned productions showed that Unity put on works on different levels, from the overtly political to sheer entertainment.

Unity's most interesting experiment in playwriting was its *Living Newspapers*, a method of collective authorship. The first dealt with the 1937 London's busman's strike and the technique was adopted for radio.[115] Its value was its topicality, exemplified in *Crisis*, written and rehearsed in two days on the occasion of the Munich crisis of September 1938. The script, which tried to bring out Britain's possible role as peace keeper, changed from day to day according to the situation itself.[116]

Another pre-war highlight of Unity's productions was its 'pantomime with a political point'. *Babes in the Wood* was seen by over 40,000 people and introduced a new genre. The 'babes' of the pantomime were Austria and Czechoslovakia deprived of their rights by the robbers Hit and Muss (Hitler and Mussolini), who are in league with the wicked uncle Chancellor Chamber Music (Chamberlain). The class struggle was presented through Lady Blimp who would not allow her children to mix with evacuees and who admonished them: 'So go to bed my children and mention in your prayers. To mention Mr Chamberlain with father's stocks and shares.'[117]

1. *Winkles and Champagne*, Unity Theatre 1943: The history of the music hall © as stated at the copyright holder/Victoria and Albert Museum, London © permission (Clive Gellert, Unity Theatre Trust)

Unity became a professional theatre in 1946. The performers were given two-year contracts, children's allowances and holiday with pay. Drama schools were set up to provide training not only for the amateurs affiliated with Unity but also for the professional members. For the latter their training continued alongside their professional appearances, adopting the apprentice rather than the student system. It made it possible for potential actors without financial resources to adopt the stage as a career.[118]

One such actor was Harry Landis, the son of Jewish immigrants. Born in the East End in 1931, he had an impoverished and tough upbringing living with his mother in Stepney Green. His mother originated from Poland and his father had disappeared. Landis was sent to Hebrew classes because those who attended received a pair of new boots every year. He recalls that it was a terrible time. He did not receive a proper education and left school when he was twelve years old. Two years later he started work as a welder in a factory.[119]

His love for the theatre began soon after he started work. He would go to The Hackney Empire and then go into work the following day and

2. *Buster*, Unity Theatre 1950: Harry Landis stars in *Buster*, a play about working-class East End life, Unity Theatre 1950 © as stated at the copyright holder/Victoria and Albert Museum, London, © permission (Clive Gellert, Unity Theatre Trust)

perform the show in his tea break. He recalls how the stop steward told him that he should be on the stage and suggested that he go to Unity where they performed plays about working-class people and their lives. Landis saw *All Change Here* by Ted Willis, which was about a bus strike and how it affected a family in the East End. 'I went and couldn't believe my ears. The dialogue could have been straight from my street. I was totally taken aback.' He auditioned and joined the company.[120]

Unity had a great impact on people from the East End and attracted many from the Jewish community. Margot Hilton recalls how her mother Kate played the piano for Unity and met her father there. Her mother came from a traditional Jewish family who had come from Poland in 1911.[121] Before joining Unity, Kate attended political meetings: 'Mosley was on the rise, people were stirred up...you wanted to do something, get involved'.[122] She was introduced to Unity by a friend in 1936 and attended a performance of *Waiting for Lefty* and found it inspirational to see agit-prop and the *Living Newspapers* which presented current political issues in easy to grasp documentary entertainment. She played the piano for Unity's production *On Guard for Spain*. This was a piece of journalism which originally appeared in *The Left Review* and was turned into a mass declamation which came to typify Unity's stand against Fascism.[123]

Frank Lesser, a journalist for *The Daily Worker*, joined Unity for the same reasons. His sister, Shirley Murgraff, explains that her parents came from Poland in 1912 and they were an orthodox Jewish family. Frank and his brother Sam became politicized by the threat of Fascism in the area and began to educate the family who subsequently became members of the Communist Party. She also went to shows at Unity: 'Unity was hugely important for working-class people who got encouragement and inspiration from left-wing theatre.'[124]

Similarly, Binnie Yates, born in 1931, came from a very political family that originated from Poland. Her family were close friends with the playwright Arnold Wesker's family: 'The families burst with bolshevism and so did I'. Binnie would go to Unity and was 'delighted to be part of something Communist'. She auditioned for the play *Wages of Eve* and was awarded the lead part. 'You were *kvelling* [happy and proud] that there were so many others who felt the same politically. I felt empowered.'[125]

The theatre burnt down in 1971. The land was sold and, with the proceeds, the Unity Theatre Trust was established. Harry Landis heads the Trust which awards grants to companies who work in the Unity tradition. 'It was a great education. Unity showed life as it was lived by ordinary people in order to change society.'[126] Landis has had a long career in British film and television playing Jewish cockney roles. Other well-known actors who benefited from early opportunities at Unity and became famous for their Jewish cockney roles – Alfie Bass, David Kossoff and Warren Mitchell – are discussed fully in later chapters. The background to how they were able to take on and identify with these roles now needs to be explored.

The Jewish Cockney

The concept of a Jewish Cockney and how it was constructed is core to this book. The term 'Jewish Cockney' was used to describe some of the actors from Unity Theatre who acquired fame. That was indeed how they saw themselves. When David Kossoff stated that 'although I'm Cockney, my parents come from Lithuania',[127] at first it seems incongruous. How could the second generation of East End immigrant Jews see themselves as Cockneys, growing up at a time in the East End when the Jewish and non-Jewish communities were for the most part separate and tensions between them existed?

In reality, the 'Cockney' was a construct that had evolved over time. The word was derived from the Middle English word 'cokeney', meaning cock's egg, a misshapen egg.[128] The term had originally meant a townee; banteringly it came to mean a Londoner. A 'true' Cockney was one born within the sound of Bow Bells (at St Mary le Bow) in the Cheapside district of the City of London and was first used by writers in the seventeenth century.[129]

The social historian Roy Porter characterizes the Cockney as bright, smart and street wise. He quotes writer Edwin Pugh who in 1912 commented that the Cockney is the supreme type of Englishman: 'In his sturdy optimism, in his unwavering determination, not only to make the best of things as they are, but to make them seem actually better than they are by adapting his mood to the exigencies of the occasion and in his supreme disdain of all outside influences.' By this time the working-class East Ender had become *the* Cockney, a figure quite jingoistic about London.[130]

The East End, often seen as an outcast from the rest of London, produced the Cockney mentality. 'The East End is a place and a condition of the mind. You can take a boy out of the East End but not the East End out of a boy.'[131] The Cockney character was described as someone whose 'astuteness, nonchalance, easy indifferent fellowship, tolerance, casual endurance, grumbling gusto, shallowness, unconcern for anything but the passing moment, jackdaw love of glitter, picaresque ability and jesting spirit make up a unique individual'.[132] This approach was probably of necessity in order to deal with the daily routine of life in the East End. The area to the east of Bow Bells, home to the 'Cockneys', was one of poverty and misery. The historian of London Peter Ackroyd reflected that 'it has been observed that the West End has the money and the East End has the dirt, there is leisure to the west and labour to the east'.[133]

Ackroyd points out that the chirpy and resourceful Cockney, once the native of all London, became identified more and more closely with the East End in the late nineteenth and twentieth centuries.[134] By this time the cliché Cockney was primarily associated with East End street markets and habitats. These Cockneys were the market traders, barrow boys and costermongers. Costermongering was often a hereditary occupation run by entire families, while those new to the trade were poor Irish, Jewish, unemployed tradesmen and mechanics. They lived close by and created the Cockney slang, almost incomprehensible to outsiders, which enabled them to evade police and outwit rivals.[135] The following analysis looks at the extent to which the Jewish community was influenced by its non-Jewish neighbours so that some considered themselves Cockneys and went on to achieve fame playing Cockney roles on the stage and screen.

It has been suggested that the East End is much more than a geographical label. There is an instant recognition of a way of life, an attitude of mind, far removed from that to be found in other more stable districts. It is a formidable image – sharp, dark, tough, violent, even dangerous, a battleground, a survival course. At the same time, and parallel with the dark side, is a brighter streak. A zest for life which produces its own gaiety, a certain spice, a vitality and wit which helps leaven the despair. Moreover, communal hardship produces communal loyalty and a spirit of real, practical neighbourliness.[136] It has been suggested that until the inter-war period, the term 'the East End' functioned largely as a metaphor, symbolizing problems of urban poverty and crime. It had little meaning for the residents of the area whose horizons were linked to the immediate surroundings of street and neighbourhood. These surroundings provided a localized sense of community and formed the basis of working-class networks of reciprocity.[137]

Another view is that the East End of London is not really a geographical concept; there is no such borough or postal district and it is not on an ordnance map. Yet on another level it does exist and within it, the Jewish East End.[138] Due to Jewish religious requirements whereby it was forbidden to ride on the Sabbath and Holy Days, it meant that people had to live close together and within walking distance of a synagogue. The main concentration was in Aldgate, Bishopsgate, Whitechapel and Goodmans Field, as Jewish communal institutions were in the same area.[139] During the inter-war years critical changes took place within this community. Due to a series of developments in work patterns, leisure and politics, the horizons of the Jewish residents began to expand to encompass the whole of the East End. For the first time they began to see themselves as East Enders, a local identity which included both the Jewish and non-Jewish populations of the area.[140]

Indeed, writing in 1937, an American observer William Zukerman was of the opinion that there was so much in common between the young post-war English Cockney and the young East End Jew, speaking the language and becoming English in manners and appearance. 'The truth is that what goes under the name of the East End Jew is in reality no specific type at all, it is but the general East End London labour type with which the young East End Jew has assimilated to such an extent that it is sometimes difficult to differentiate between the two.'[141]

Zukerman believed this younger Jew was more assimilated than the older English Jew who had lived in England for generations. He argues that this was due to the fact that the Jewish immigrant period in England did not last more than a quarter of a century and left no lasting mark on the younger generation, and that the number of immigrants who came during that period was too small to create a social life of its own sufficiently strong to influence the children born here. Therefore the young Jewish generation grew up in an English atmosphere, amidst English surroundings of a specific social class and assimilated within the working class. This happened at a faster rate than earlier English Jews who had assimilated chiefly with the middle or ruling classes. The latter, with their class snobbery, put certain barriers in the way of the social equality of the Jew and it took the older English Jew a few generations before breaking down those class barriers, while the young East End Jew met with practically no social barriers at all. He went to the same school as the English child, received the same education, later met socially on the same footing and shared the same social and cultural milieu. At the same time the rigid class division of English society obstructed his success into the ranks of the middle class. The result was that he grew up strongly influenced by the only section of English society where he was accepted as an equal – the working class of industrial London.[142]

Zukerman's analysis, however, is not necessarily reflected in the memoirs of Jewish and non-Jewish East Enders, where clear divisions between the two communities were reported. Elsie Shears, born at the beginning of the twentieth century, was brought up in Stepney. Her mother, a washerwoman, complained that they 'lived amongst a colony of Jews' and considered that Dempsey Street School was not good enough for her as there were too many Jews. They moved away from the area.[143]

Gilda Moss Haber, who grew up in Bethnal Green in the 1930s, recounts an incident when a boy from school stopped her in the street and asked 'where are you going Jew girl?' and ripped up the bunch of flowers she was taking to her grandmother. She felt uneasy going along Bethnal Green Road, where it was predominantly non-Jewish and breathed a sigh of relief when coming into Whitechapel.[144] Earlier, that tension was even more profound. A report in the *Eastern Post* newspaper in 1901 commented that 'when a Jewish family tried to move into a largely Irish dockland street, people poured out from every house, smashed up the van, and routed the unfortunate foreigners'.[145]

That tensions between the two communities did exist was evidenced by the findings of the Mass-Observation Project. This was a social research organization founded in 1937 which aimed to record everyday life in Britain, an 'anthropology of ourselves', through a panel of around 500 untrained volunteer observers who either maintained diaries or replied to open-ended directives. They also paid investigators to anonymously record people's conversations and behaviour at work, on the street and at various public occasions including public meetings, sporting and religious events. Its purpose was to gather facts about the thoughts, habits and activities of the ordinary 'man in the street'.[146]

As part of its work, a survey on antisemitism and the comparative sociology of Jews and Cockneys in the East End was carried out. Neville Laski, President of the Board of Deputies of British Jews, contributed £250 towards the cost.[147] The funding was for three months and in March 1939 there was a preliminary interim report of the first six weeks' work. Anthropologist Tom Harrisson, founder of the Mass-Observation Project, wrote that as the 'problem' was obscured by prejudice and difficulties of all sorts it was decided that the first month be spent studying quite objectively the differences and similarities between Jews and Cockneys in the East End and the behaviour, character and social habits of the Jews there.

Mass-Observation spent ten days wandering about the East End where they looked, listened and recorded the alleged differences that included: Jewish women walked alone more than Cockney women and were therefore more independent; 4 per cent more Jewish women went around in couples and 3 per cent of all Jewish groups were of a man with a child compared to the Cockney 0.1 per cent which showed the Jew as a family man. They noted that Cockneys spent whole evenings walking around aimlessly and going to the pub while Jews would rather spend their money in the pin ball saloons. With regard to library reading habits, Cockneys favoured more fiction and newspaper reading. Jews, who wore darker coloured clothes, were serious readers and more interested in politics and world affairs. The survey showed the 'whole subject of antisemitism appears to exist on a level not of fact but of fantasy' and that antisemitism has not emerged strongly but rather 'UNSEMITISM, i.e. Cockney and Jew living together in the same street and often in the same house, but living in different social worlds.'[148]

The Board of Deputies' reaction to the report was mixed. Although some were in favour of continuing the research, others felt it was worthless.[149] The most vehement attack came from Board member Julian Franklyn. 'The Jews have got the jitters, let's diddle them out of their dough.' He dismissed their findings and questioned their accuracy. He was more familiar with the area and culture and questioned whether the Jews they 'met' were actually Jewish as they could have been Italian or Greek. 'What pray do they regard as Cockney? Some Jews (in fact many) are Cockneys, not only because they were born within the sound of Bow Bells but because for several generations the Cockney environment has been assimilated.'[150] This was an important observation and it is borne out by the detailed case studies in this book.

The interim report was an example of the strengths and weaknesses of the field anthropology of Mass-Observation. From a positive point of view, its scope was wide and gave an insight into the everyday life, especially about leisure activities, that was missing from most contemporary sources. On the negative side, Harrisson's aim for an objective and scientific approach undermined the project. The problem was the division of the East End population into 'Jew' and 'Cockney'. It assumed that the tribes of the East End were 'Cockney' and 'Jew' and that being Jewish was incompatible with being 'Cockney'. Yet for some, such as Franklyn, many Jews saw themselves as Cockneys because the local environment had been assimilated for so long and so intensively for generations.[151]

At the time of the report, the Jews represented nearly half of Stepney's population of 200,000, many of whom were second or third generation. By this time East End culture as a whole owed much to Jewish influence. Indeed, Harrisson underestimated the complexity of what it was to be a 'Cockney'. Local identities were constantly changing. One example was food, especially types of bread, which were now part of the East Ender's diet. With such cultural intermingling, there was therefore another difficulty that Mass-Observation observers faced and that was how to identify a Jew from a non-Jew.[152] Another problem was that Harrisson's team were unfamiliar with the East End and their outsider status caused mistakes to be made as well as enabling some insights into the social dynamics of the area.[153]

Yet despite criticism levelled against Mass-Observation's quirky work and approach, the report did provide an indication of the position of the Jews in East End society in the period immediately before the war. It gave an insight into street and home life and their report has been included here to show the relationship between the two communities and where they overlapped. On the whole the report showed not the differences but the similarities between the two communities. They both enjoyed going to the cinema, music hall, boxing and billiards. Although each community had their own distinctiveness, there was much common ground. This could be seen when looking at local politics. There was a right-wing labour group dominating Stepney, made up of Irish Catholics and moderate Jews. Within the Stepney Communist Party, half or more of its 500 members were Jewish. The Communist Party did manage to unite Jews and non-Jews in political action with their involvement in the Stepney Tenants Defence League. By the summer of 1939, Jewish-Gentile cooperation was as common as the conflict represented by the clashes with the British Union of Fascists, but there were factors that complicated the overall pattern of community relations and these included individual and gender issues.[154]

Did the experience of living in the East End during the war years change people's perspectives and was there more cooperation and interchange between the two communities? Did the Blitz, especially, change the situation? Historian Tony Kushner notes that the situation was not clear cut. Although the war had united the East End in some ways through cooperation in civil defence units, there is a tendency for memories of the Blitz to become mythical and emphasize the cheerfulness and unity that evolved due to the constant aerial bombardment. The warden J. J. Mallon of East End community centre Toynbee Hall, writing in the *News Chronicle* in 1942, referred to the Blitz as a 'common sympathy, a common humanity in which differences, including the differences between Jews and Gentiles were submerged and lost', was a classic example of this tendency.[155]

In reality the situation was more complex. Quarrels broke out in shelters and there were accusations of Jews escaping the area in taxis or monopolising shelter space.[156] Yet this was offset by a great deal of cooperation whereby food, clothing and buildings were shared, and religious leaders of both communities helped to organize services. A Passover service in the Tilbury shelter in April 1941 was marked by Jews singing religious songs and Gentiles singing English folk songs. After the Blitz, Jewish-Gentile relations fell into a more settled pattern and although antisemitism did not disappear it never succeeded in being more than localized and aimed at individuals rather than the whole of Jewry.[157]

There was increased harmony within Stepney Borough Council, and this included an extraordinary meeting held in 1943 to counter antisemitic activities in the borough. There was also more cooperation within the

Borough's clubs and settlements where Jews and Gentiles mixed together, and the Jewish youth clubs practised a policy of integration. Good relations were especially evident in the Stepney Communist Party. Kushner considers it is difficult to weigh up the impact of the war on communal relations. As there were many 'East Ends' in terms of geographical location, the same was true of its institutions and perspectives would vary whether one was looking from a Gentile, Communist, religious or trade union point of view. However, his final analysis is that 'the war pushed Jews and non-Jews in the East End closer together more than it pulled them apart'.[158]

In considering what could have contributed to a more positive viewpoint, Jewish East Ender Charles Poulson points out that apart from shared wartime experiences, in reality the East End Jew and non-Jew had much in common. They had the same life experiences which included crowded accommodation, bed bugs and unemployment.[159] Interaction between the two communities occurred when they joined together to fight against injustice. Poulson was persuaded to join the Communist Party by a non-Jew, Martin Jones, whom he had met in the library. Jones convinced him 'that the only hope of the people lies in fighting the class struggle and in socialism. The alternative is unemployment, poverty and probably war again.'[160] There were situations that when threatened with opposition, the separate components of the East End united regardless of race or creed.[161] Joe Jacobs, who lived in the Commercial Road area, was surprised when he went with a huge East London contingent to the May Day parade at Hyde Park and wondered 'what had happened to the *yoks* and the Jews? We were all comrades.'[162]

The most public expression of shared positioning and support was the Battle of Cable Street, which took place on 4 October 1936 when the British Union of Fascists led by Oswald Mosley marched through the East End of London to mark the fourth anniversary of the Party's formation. It resulted in a clash between the Metropolitan Police, who were overseeing the march, and anti-Fascists including local socialist and communist groups. Bill Fishman, leading historian of the Jewish East End, recalls some 70 years later: 'We were all side by side. I was moved to tears to see bearded Jews and Irish Catholic dockers standing up to stop Mosley. I shall never forget that as long as I live, how working class people could get together to oppose the evil of racism.'[163]

Fishman's recollection was somewhat romanticized as the British Union of Fascists, led by Mosley, had opened an office in 1933 in Squirries Street (off the Bethnal Green Road), which was at the edge of the Jewish East End. They concentrated on the East End where economic hardships and poverty abutted the City. 'Mosley began to prey on the simmering resentment the impoverished white working-class East Ender felt towards others, particularly non-Christians.'[164] From their East End headquarters they produced antisemitic propaganda and their open air meetings in Victoria Park were 'driven by intimidation and aggression'.[165] In the 1937 local elections the British Union of Fascists finished second behind Labour in a three-cornered poll of three of the wards contested: Limehouse North and Mile End Old Town Centre.[166]

Nevertheless, despite the existence of Fascism in the East End, there was no doubt that the Battle of Cable Street was a significant event for the anti-Fascists. The Battle was immediately seen in terms of class. *The Daily Worker* reported the march with the headline 'Jew and Gentile Unite' and wrote that the Battle had been supported by all East End workers across ethnic lines: 'The whole of East London's working class rallied as one man (and as one woman) to bar the way to the Blackshirts. Jew and gentile, docker and garment worker, railwayman and cabinet maker, turned out in their thousands to show that they have no need for fascism.'[167] A special commemorative booklet was produced by the Communist Party which again emphasized the class-based character of the protest: *They Did Not Pass: 300,000 Workers Say No to Mosley: A Souvenir of the East London Workers' Victory over Fascism.*[168]

Success continued with the rent strikes organized by the Communist-front Stepney Tenants Defence League (STDL) which swept the East End during the 1930s. The strikes secured rent cuts or influenced legislation. The vast majority of households were tenants of private landlords which were in theory 'controlled' so that the tenants had the legal right to security of tenure. Rents could not be increased, and they were entitled to withhold 40 per cent of the rent if a sanitary inspector certified that repairs had not been done. However, houses vacated between 1923 and 1933 were 'decontrolled' which meant the landlord could put up the rent and evict a tenant at will. In practice a high proportion of tenants of 'controlled' housing were not enjoying their rights. Many landlords were overcharging and had registered their tenants as 'decontrolled' when they were not.[169]

There were sporadic rent strikes in the East End tenements between 1935 and 1937. The tenants managed to hold off the bailiff and police and the movement grew rapidly. The STDL had a grassroots structure: members would pay a penny a week and would be organized in local tenants' committees, usually representing a block of flats or a street. Women chaired most of the tenants' committees, organized opposition to eviction attempts, were in the forefront of demonstrations and even picketed shoppers in the

West End of London to draw attention to the plight of East London slum dwellers at the mercy of 'slumlords'.[170]

In 1939 rent strikes took place in street after street in rapid succession and many landlords succumbed and signed agreements with their tenants.[171] It was a time when Jewish and non-Jewish women banded together as their situation was similar: the fight against unscrupulous landlords. Father Groser, from Christ Church in Watney Street, was amazed at how families who were not directly affected by the rent increases came out to defend those who were.[172] Tubby Rosen, secretary of the STDL, commented that 'numbers of these non-Jews had gone along to almost purely Jewish areas, such as Brady Street, to help the Jews who were engaged in rent disputes'.[173]

The interaction between the two communities was also seen in regard to leisure pursuits. In addition to visits to the theatre and music hall there was boxing and gambling. Boxing had always played a major part in East London's rich cultural heritage. More world, European, British and amateur champions were born and raised between Whitechapel and West Ham than anywhere else in Britain.[174] These included world champions such as Ted 'Kid' Lewis and Jack 'Kid' Berg and national champions such as Harry Mizler, Harry Mason, Johnny Brown and Lew Lazar.[175] Sport was a unifying factor for both communities: 'In the gym all races came together.'[176]

Gambling was another great pastime in the East End and Joe Jacobs recalls that 'a large number of children and adults of all ages gambled very heavily. Mainly cards and racing.'[177] Ralph Finn remembers the bookmakers in the area and how the residents loved their little wager: 'Male and female, Jew and gentile alike, the plain and the coloured would sidle up to Abrams and push their crumpled pieces of paper at him and dream about coming up on a sixpenny each way accumulator.'[178]

Growing unemployment during the years of the Depression had not weakened the working-class taste for a 'flutter' and there was a widespread betting boom, although much of this gambling was illegal. Cash betting on horse racing, apart from at the racecourses themselves, was not allowed and resulted in fines or imprisonment on anyone deemed to be loitering to make or take bets. One could gamble on horse racing legally by having a credit account with a bookmaker, but this effectively ruled out the vast majority of working-class gamblers. Consequently, millions of working-class people had an illegal cash bet every day. This was facilitated by the bookie's runner who operated at street corners, in public houses and barber shops and at factory gates.[179]

New opportunities for gambling emerged in the 1930s with the introduction and spread of greyhound racing and football pools. Most greyhound race meetings took place in the evening which fitted in with urban patterns of work and leisure. From 1934, under the Betting and Lotteries Act, greyhound stadiums were allowed to provide legal betting facilities and 'going to the dogs' became a national and essentially working-class pastime.[180] London had seventeen tracks in the late 1940s attracting up to 600,000 attendees per week.[181]

Geoffrey Goldstein considers that most Jews in the East End gambled, and many went 'to the dogs': 'It was just like having a cup of tea'. Goldstein and his family lived in the Dun Buildings, Adelina Grove, Whitechapel. His father was a salmon filleter and curer, but the business was unsuccessful, and the family were very poor. Geoffrey explains that they could not afford to go to horse racing as it was too far away whereas dog racing was easily accessible. Three coaches, packed to capacity, would pick up people from his street at 6.30pm and take them to different tracks in time for the first race at 7.30pm. He recalls that there was good camaraderie between the Jews and non-Jews. Geoffrey lived next door to a non-Jewish family and both fathers went to the dogs together at least five times a week. A windfall from the dog tracks was his only hope of getting some extra money. Life was hard for the whole family: 'Everyone I knew was poor and gambled.'[182]

Another common activity between the Jewish and non-Jewish communities, and not far removed from the world of gambling, was crime, which was part of the cultural landscape of East London.[183] This hidden economy was oiled by informal networks of individuals seeking to increase their incomes by making deals, villains unloading their ill-gotten gains, petty traders peddling varieties of cheap merchandise and even those in regular employment making a bit on the side. 'On the fiddle', 'on the make', 'wheeling and dealing', 'ducking and diving' captured something of this opportunistic entrepreneurial culture.[184]

At the other end of the spectrum were full-time, hardcore villains, the majority of whom had served apprenticeships as petty entrepreneurs before turning professional. One such person was Arthur Harding, a king of the East End underworld. He operated in the markets of Whitechapel and Petticoat Lane and later teamed up with local Jewish boys. Harding remembers how he and the Jewish boys went on pick-pocketing expeditions. 'There were five Jewish boys in the gang – I was the only *yok*.' Harding was in charge of the operations while the others pick-pocketed.[185] He describes Whitechapel Road as being alive with thousands of people, Jews and Cockneys, all mixing together. He became acquainted with the

Jewish boys in Brick Lane. 'They took to me – they looked on me as a sort of protector.' Harding did not distinguish between Jew and non-Jew in his world. 'You didn't talk about being Jewish or English.'[186]

However, joint interaction between the two communities actually occurred at a much earlier age in the playground, as Ralph Finn recalls:

> We all played together: polacks [the children of foreign Jews)], choots [the children of English-born Jews], Gentiles, coloureds, boys and girls, the children of bookmakers, prostitutes, stall holders, auctioneers, gamblers, thieves, rabbis, shopkeepers. Boxers, barren, touts, tally men, washerwomen, chorus girls, furriers, tailors, pressers, pimps, ponies and the unemployed.[187]

What then made second generation Jewish immigrants consider themselves Cockneys? For some it was a sense of place. Cabinet maker Sam Clarke, whose father had emigrated from Russia during the pogroms, considered himself a Cockney: 'I was born in 1907 within the sound of Bow Bells so I can call myself a Cockney.'[188] Gilda Moss Haber, who grew up in the East End in the 1930s, also considered herself a Cockney because she was born within the sound of Bow Bells.[189] Her grandparents were from Eastern Europe and her parents, born in the East End, grew up in Spitalfields. She explains that there were two sections in the East End and that where she lived in Bethnal Green the majority were non-Jews. 'More Fascism, more pubs'. In contrast her grandparents lived near Whitechapel where there were kosher delicatessen and butcher shops along their street.[190] She felt an affinity for both areas: 'I loved both the *goyish* and the Jewish East End.'[191] Although describing herself as Jewish British, she also refers to herself as Cockney. She recalls going out with her non-Jewish friend Joycey, who lived on her street: 'Both Cockneys, friend Joycey Kennel and I roamed East London most Saturdays, while my operaphile mother set and permed ladies hair and my deaf, barber father shaved dockers for pub nights and Christmas.'[192] Moss Haber considers that in order to qualify as a Cockney it was not only a case of geographical location, but also a matter of being working class. Cockneys were 'saucy, full of pep, didn't grumble about poverty. Cheerful, witty and sarcastic. My father was a true Jewish Cockney.'[193]

Martin Kraft, born in 1936, also lived in Bethnal Green and considered himself a Cockney. He would help out in his family's haberdashery shop where the gangster Kray brothers were regular customers. 'As I integrated with the local children in the street and at school I adopted their thinking;

they were Cockney so I must be.'[194] Lionel Bart, whose background is explored later, also attended the same school and saw himself as Jewish and Cockney.[195]

David Cesarani considers that place and space had multiple significances with regard to the extent that the immigrant population and the subsequent second generation adopted the Cockney culture of their non-Jewish neighbours. He refers to Alexander Bloom's 1986 study *Prodigal Sons: The New York Jewish Intellectuals and their World* who emerged in the inter-war and immediate post-war years and were mostly the children of immigrants. Despite poverty and a daily struggle to exist, Jewish neighbourhoods offered young Jews a protective environment in which to learn.[196]

Bloom explains that these Jewish neighbourhoods were not only safe homes, they were also portals, a liminal space between one world and another. The parents represented another world and set of allegiances. Yet these same parents encouraged their children to embrace America, its language and culture. Bloom argues that as a result the children grew up in a schizoid environment as they matured in a half American, half Yiddish environment and they always carried with them some of that divided world.[197] It is therefore quite feasible that people growing up in the East End could be both Jewish and Cockney, taking on the mannerisms and language of those around them.

In the East End, the ease in which the second generation immigrant was able to refer to themselves as Cockneys can be attributed to interaction with their non-Jewish neighbours, whether at school, work, in politics or at leisure and the confidence that they acquired. For Harry Blacker 'the first generation stemming from the early settlers were born and nurtured in the quarter where they slowly assumed the characteristics of the native environment'.[198]

For music historian Derek Scott, the combination of being Jewish and Cockney in the East End was natural. He explains that Jewish street traders had a monopoly on the sale of oranges and lemons, the former fruit being as popular in music halls as popcorn is today in the cinema. Jews were associated with clothes and tailoring, providing the 'slap up toggery' for a Cockney night out. The father of a popular 1930s song writer, Michael Carr (born Maurice Cohen) was a boxer significantly known as Cockney Cohen. 'Whether being a Jew or being a Cockney came first was probably no more an issue than whether on Merseyside being a Catholic came before being a Scouser [Liverpudlian].'[199] It was also not an issue for both communities as together they faced the devastation that the Second World War brought to the area.

The East End after the Second World War

The Second World War fundamentally altered the East End of London. The devastation of the Blitz had fallen disproportionately on the East End. Stepney, for example, lost a third of its housing stock.[200] This affected the Jewish and non-Jewish community as hundreds of families left due to the housing shortage. Overall population totals for the boroughs of Bethnal Green, Poplar, Stepney and East and West Ham fell from nearly 1 million in 1931 to just over half a million in the 1951 census.[201]

The Jewish community's move from the East End had started before the war as second and third generation immigrants left the area when their circumstances improved. In the 1930s it was estimated that there was a Jewish population of 62,000 in Stepney, 13,000 in Bethnal Green and 4,800 in the Poplar (mainly Bow) area. As there was an estimated 234,000 Jews in greater London during this period, barely a third were living in the East End.[202] Accelerated by the heavy bombing of Whitechapel during the war, the Jewish East End population moved northwards through Hackney to Stamford Hill and westward to Golders Green, Brondesbury, Wembley, Finchley and Harrow.[203] Master tailors and furriers moved out to Hackney and Stamford Hill and eastwards into Essex. The East End furniture trade lost more than half its workshops between 1939 and 1958.[204]

John Gross, born in the East End in 1935, returned after the war to find that the area had lost a lot of its Jewish character. Nevertheless, it took a long time to die out. 'Until the 1960s, shops, businesses, markets and communal institutions gave the area a Jewish colouring which numbers alone no longer warranted.'[205] A. B. Levy, who observed the East End after the war, found that by 1948 the proportions of East End Jewry and London Jewry had been reversed. Nine-tenths of the community once lived in East London and now nine-tenths live outside it. He found that of the 25,000 people that remained, their activity in regular Jewish cultural, religious or Zionist activity was minimal. Many attended religious services for no more than an hour each year when they come to recite *Yiskor*, the memorial prayer for the dead. 'These are not Yom Kippur Jews but *Yiskor* Jews – with perhaps one ear alert for racing results. Their recreations are cinemas and solo, the wireless, the pools, the dogs.' He added that the Jewish residents continued, though slowly, to leave and couples on marrying rarely remained.[206]

In an investigation in 1949 and 1950, entitled 'Outlines of Jewish Society in London', it was reported that Whitechapel was ceasing to be the centre of the urban Jewish population. Although some communal institutions, such as the Jewish Board of Guardians and the Federation of Synagogues, remained despite the residents leaving, the children of immigrants had become secularized and were less attached to local institutions which they had not founded.[207] By the 1960s only a remnant of the once thriving Jewish population remained in the East End. Research on the history of the synagogue at 19 Princelet Street found that when various synagogue buildings came onto the market, they were not recognized as culturally or architecturally important and were allowed to become derelict and abandoned.[208]

Although Jewish activities in the area were reduced, A. B. Levy points out how well those Jews that remained had become well integrated into the local community. He cites as an example a 64-year-old Jewish dustman who was an employee of Stepney Borough Council for 25 years. He was one of 20 Jewish roads sweepers and dustmen working in the public cleaning department with 8 as lavatory attendants (total 36). Regarding the 320 on the council's staff, 64 were Jewish and there were 18 councillors (total 59). When considering the number of Jews in Stepney (25,000) and the borough as whole (100,000), the proportion of Jews in council departments did not differ greatly from their proportion among the population: 'The Jew appears to be playing an adequate part in the civic life of Stepney'.[209]

New populations were now moving in. A new wave of immigration came in the 1950s, and the biggest group were the Sylhetis from what is now Bangladesh, who lived predominantly around the Brick Lane area.[210] A. B. Levy makes reference to the 'increasing number of dark-skinned' people and that on a vacant plot, using problematic language, 'some picaninnies and Jewish tots are busy playing together'.[211] Multi-culturalism in the East End was not new. Maurice Foley, who worked at the Royal Docks for 50 years comments 'we've always been cosmopolitan. We've had Irish, Jews, we had bleeding French, Belgiques, we had a sprinkle of Chinamen. The same collective thing. Injury to one was injury to all.'[212] Actor Steven Berkoff's father catered to the non-white community. His tailor's shop in Leman Street made suits lined in satin almost exclusively for the West Indians.[213]

That such interaction had taken place in the area enabled the Jewish Cockney to be born. David Dee considers that there was a truly hybrid form of identity among the second generation – exposure to non-Jewish society and connections with their Jewish past – and that they realized that the development of a combined identity was acceptable, appropriate and often advantageous.[214] This was the case of the 'Jewish Cockneys' from Unity Theatre that contributed so much to the British entertainment industry in the second half of the twentieth century and who are at the heart of the following chapters.[215]

Performance and Masculinity

Biography

In order to examine the Jewish Cockney identity, I have looked at the lives of four well-known personalities from Unity Theatre through their biographies. The use of collective biographies can help to understand people's lives and subjective experience but in ways connecting to wider social and cultural processes.[216]

The effectiveness of the use of collective biography was shown in *Eminent Victorians* by Lytton Strachey. Published in 1918, Strachey attempted to achieve a sense of the period through the exploration of four leading figures from the Victorian era: Cardinal Manning, Florence Nightingale, Thomas Arnold and General Gordon. Each of the lives were different from one another but there were common threads. His portraits changed people's perceptions of the Victorians. With its publication, Strachey was able to breathe life into the Victorian era for future generations. Up to this point Strachey considered that Victorian biographies had been 'as familiar as the cortege of the undertaker, and wear the same air of slow, funereal barbarism'. He defied the tradition of fat volumes of 'undigested masses of material' and concentrated on four iconic figures from the period.[217] He attempted through the medium of biography to present 'some Victorian visions to the modern eye'.[218] I intend by using a collective biography in this book to give a sense of the period and the second generation East European Jews of the East End.

There have been notable changes in how biography is seen and understood historically. Prior to the twentieth century the majority of biographical subjects were significant individuals and one of the key questions which linked biography and history concerned the nature of that individual and the significance of that person's historical role. In recent times there has been a different interest concerning the way in which an individual life can reflect wider patterns within society or show the impact of social, economic and political change on ordinary people. This idea about biography has emerged from social history and from other forms of history concerned with the lives of minorities and of marginal and disempowered groups. For them the significance of a biography or a study of an individual life lies in its capacity to show in detail the experiences and the impact of historical developments on a particular individual and through this study gain a wider understanding of social and historical change.[219]

The changes in the approach to biography stems from the 1970s, with the advent of women's history, when historians saw that the capacity of individual lives could illuminate larger historical patterns and developments.[220] Biography was seen as providing a prism which enabled historians to see how particular individuals understood and constructed themselves and made senses of their lives and their society.[221]

The new approach to biography accompanied the rise of the new histories which have been so prominent since the 1970s including women's history, black history and post-colonial history. All these forms of history share a concern to explore the activities, experiences and historical agency of groups with relatively little political and economic power or social status and to locate and listen to the voices of those who had been silenced in earlier historical writing. They focus on marginal groups, including women, members of ethnic and religious minorities and indigenous peoples seeking to understand the nature of their experiences and ways in which they understood the worlds they lived in.[222] By using collective biography one is able to link life stories with wider historical processes and to illustrate particular historical developments or patterns.[223] I intend by using a collective biography in this book to give a sense of the period and the second generation East European Jews of the East End. They were ordinary working-class people who were able to enter the entertainment world due to their performance.

Performance and Masculinity

As all the case studies in this book are connected with the entertainment industry, it is important to look at how these individuals differed in performance and, when acting, whether they portrayed their Jewishness and portrayed the stereotypical Jew. The 'Faginy' Yiddish accent marks the stage Jew as different, as not really belonging to cultivated British society with its Oxbridge accent. Jews sound different because they are represented as being different. Within the European tradition of seeing the Jew as different there is a closely linked tradition of hearing the Jew's language as marked by the corruption of being a Jew.[224] The image of the 'Jew who sounds Jewish' is a stereotype within the Christian world which represents the Jew as possessing all languages or no language of his or her own; of being unable to truly command the national language of the world in which he/she lives or, indeed, even of possessing a language of true revelation such as Hebrew.[225] The extent to which the following case studies show these traits, both in terms of physicality and in speech patterns, and were internalized, will be examined as well as the different forms of masculinity that they portrayed.

The concept of masculinity has attracted much and varied scholarship in recent years. Different cultures and different periods of history construct masculinity differently. Some cultures make heroes of soldiers and regard violence as the ultimate test of masculinity and others look at soldiering with disdain and regard violence as contemptible. There are cultures that regard homosexual sex as incompatible with true masculinity whilst others think that no one can be a real man without having had a homosexual relationship. In large scale multicultural societies there are likely to be multiple definitions of masculinity and there will be differences, for example in the expression of masculinity between Latino and Anglo men in the United States and between Greek or Lebanese and Anglo men in Australia. The meaning of masculinity in working class life is different from that amongst the middle class and among the very rich and the very poor. With regard to hierarchy and hegemony, some masculinities are more honoured than others and some are actively dishonoured, such as homosexual masculinities in modern Western culture. Others are socially marginalized, as in the case of the masculinities of disempowered ethnic minorities. In total contrast are the masculinities of sporting heroes.[226]

With this background of contrasting masculinities according to different cultures and ethnic groups, how is the Jewish male represented? Jewish masculinity changed over time. After the destruction of the Temple in Jerusalem, with the emergence of rabbinic Judaism and the start of the Jewish diaspora there emerged a distinctive formation of Jewish masculine identity.[227] Jews adopted a form of manliness that was the very opposite of hegemonic Western manhood. Jews in Europe were allowed to live among Christians but always separated from them. Confined to specific areas with tight restrictions on their movements and occupations, Jews had to turn inwards. They could not participate in the Western masculine identity of citizens within the civil society. There were limitations on occupations they could participate in and they could not serve in the army. In general Jews were restricted to the lowest manual occupation such as tanning, tailoring, peddling or tradesmen, acting as middlemen between peasants and nobility. They were not allowed to own land and, as such, the traditional manly role of farmer was denied to them.

Banned from being warrior, citizen or farmer, Jewish men inhabited a manhood that defined itself by its difference from the manliness of Western tradition. Jewish masculinity reversed the traditional equation of manliness with muscularity in equating manliness with intellectuality. The ideal Jewish male, the Rabbi or Talmudic student, was indeed characterized by qualities that made him very different from, in fact almost the opposite, of 'the knight in shining armour'.[228] The highest calling for men became the study of the Talmud; the most valued of men was not the breadwinner but the scholar who did not work in a trade or a craft and whose wife maintained the household. The rite of passage for men is the *Bar Mitzvah* at 13 years of age, when a Jewish boy becomes a man by demonstrating his intellectual ability.[229]

Differences were compounded by the fact that historically the Jew was an outsider. He was outside the seat of power, excluded from privilege. The Jew is the symbolic 'other' not unlike the symbolic 'otherness' of women, gays, racial and ethnic minorities, the elderly and the physically challenged. Jewish culture is seen as an ethnic culture which allows it to be more expressive and emotionally rich than the bland norm. Jews have been characterized as emotional, nurturing and caring. Jewish men hug and kiss, cry and laugh. Historically the Jewish man was seen as less than masculine.[230]

The widely held stereotype of Jewish men were that they were non-violent and that they were 'erudite, comedic, malleable, non-threatening, part nebbish, part schlemiel, Jewish men do not fight, they talk'.[231] In contrast were the East European Jews who emigrated to America at the end of the nineteenth and early twentieth centuries from the isolated tradition bound worlds of the rural *shtetl* and the urban ghettos. Upon arrival they faced a conflict of identity. The first generation of immigrant Jewish men faced the secular commercial world with its religious and sexual freedom. Clinging to tradition prevented men from seizing new opportunities offered to them in America.[232]

Many rejected Jewish intellectuality for physicality. From the turn of the twentieth century until the Second World War, as antisemitism intensified in America and Europe and Jews established local defence organizations on a significant scale, American Jews used sports to forge a new muscular identity. Success in boxing, a sport in which Jews were heavily represented, came to symbolize working and lower middle-class Jews' determination to challenge antisemitism. Their prowess in the ring helped undermine stereotypes of Jewish males' physical incapacity, cowardice and effeminacy.[233]

By the 1950s, there were many diverse models of masculinity for all men to use as templates on which to model their behaviour and gauge their manliness. It was a decade characterized by extremes in politics and culture and these extremes found their way into the fabric of media portrayals of masculinity. The period followed wartime self-confidence based upon the sacrifice and heroism of ordinary men. A 'tough guy' masculinity permeated discussions on foreign policy and the fear of being labelled homosexual promoted a certain way of acting.[234] This book will look at men who contributed to the stage and screen from the 1950s, each with a different masculinity in terms of their own identity and how they were perceived in the public sphere.

Summary and Structure

The case studies I have chosen have been looked at individually, as well as through a collective biography, to explore their Jewish identity and

3. Lionel Bart, 1959 (Pamela Chandler), courtesy of Lionel Bart Foundation Archive

radicalism. Of the four featured, three continued in the theatre but became well-known in different spheres: Alfie Bass who starred in over sixty films and had considerable television popularity in the 1960s and 1970s with *Bootsie and Snudge*; David Kossoff, who entertained millions of viewers with his Bible stories and Warren Mitchell who became famous for his role as Alf Garnett, the London dockland bigot of the television series *Till Death Us Do Part*. The fourth is Lionel Bart, writer and composer of British pop music and musicals, including *Oliver!* Bart was a longer chapter than the others due to a richer source of archival material. These four different men were chosen deliberately as models as there were differences between them in terms of when they were born – the oldest, Bass, was born in 1916 and the youngest, Bart, in 1927 – and the different places that they grew up in the East End. Each took different career routes. Their identities will be compared, to see what they had in common and what pulled them apart. This then is a study of the interconnection between Jewishness, East End and politics of *second generation immigrants*.

Notes

1. Charles More, *Britain in the Twentieth Century:A History* (Harlow: Pearson Longman, 2007), pp. 261–2.
2. Paul Johnson (ed.), *Twentieth Century Britain: Economic, Social and Cultural Change* (London: Longman, 1994), pp. 9–11.
3. Raphael Samuel, Ewan MacColl and Stuart Cosgrove, *Theatres of the Left, 1880–1935: Workers' Theatre Movement in Britain and America* (London: Routledge & Kegan Paul, 1985); Colin Chambers, *The Story of Unity Theatre* (London: Lawrence & Wishart, 1989); Howard Goorney, *The Theatre Workshop Story* (London: Eyre Metheun, 1981).
4. Michael Freedland, *So Let's Hear the Applause: The Story of the Jewish Entertainer* (London: Vallentine Mitchell, 1984).
5. Lloyd P. Gartner, *The Jewish Immigrant in England 1870–1914* (London: Simon Publications, 1973); V. D. Lipman, *A History of the Jews in Britain Since 1858* (Leicester: Leicester University Press, 1990); David Englander, *A Documentary History of Jewish Immigrants in Britain 1840–1920* (Leicester: Leicester University Press, 1994).
6. David Dee, *The 'Estranged' Generation?: Social and Generational Change in Interwar British Jewry* (London: Palgrave Macmillan, 2017); Rosalyn Livshin, 'The Acculturation of the Children of Immigrant Jews in Manchester, 1890–1930' in David Cesarani (ed.),*The Making of Modern Anglo Jewry* (Oxford: Basil Blackwell, 1990).
7. Deborah Dash Moore, *At Home in America: Second Generation New York Jews* (New York: Columbia University Press, 1981), pp. 4, 9–11.
8. Livshin, 'Acculturation of the Children', pp. 79–80.
9. Ibid., pp. 80–5.
10. Dee, *'Estranged' Generation?*, pp. 1, 5.

11. Ibid., pp. 119, 122, 273, 315.
12. Ibid., pp. 337–8.
13. Ruth Leon and Sheridan Morley, *A Century of Theatre* (London: Oberon Books, 2001), prologue.
14. James Woodward, *English Theatre in Transition 1889–1914* (London: Croom Helm, 1984), preface.
15. Andrew Davies, *Other Theatres: The Development of Alternative and Experimental Theatre in Britain* (Basingstoke: Macmillan Education, 1987), p. xix.
16. Nicholas de Jongh, *Politics, Prudery and Perversions: The Censoring of the English Stage 1901–1968* (London: Metheun, 2000), pp. x–xi.
17. Ibid., pp. xiv–xv.
18. Davies, *Other Theatres*, pp. 4–6.
19. Martin Banham, *The Cambridge Guide to Theatre* (Cambridge: Cambridge University Press, 1995), p. 1194.
20. Davies, *Other Theatres*, p. 25.
21. Ibid., p. 47.
22. Simon Trussler, *British Theatre* (Cambridge: Cambridge University Press, 1994), p. 260.
23. Aleks Sierz and Lia Ghilardi, *The Time Traveller's Guide to British Theatre* (London: Oberon Books, 2015), p. 247.
24. A. E. Wilson, *Half a Century of Entertainment* (London: Dennis Yates, n.d.), p. 8.
25. Ibid., p. 13.
26. Ibid., pp. 24–6.
27. Allardyce Nicoll, *The English Theatre: A Short History* (London: Nelson, 1936), p. 188.
28. Sierz and Ghilardi, *The Time Traveller's Guide to British Theatre*, pp. 228–9.
29. Ibid., p. 287.
30. The play, through its portrait of working-class Jimmy Porter's marriage to the socially superior Alison, combined the sex war and the class war and expressed Osbourne's own discontent. *Guardian*, 7 February 2012.
31. Davies, *Other Theatres*, pp. 155–6.
32. Jim Davis and Victor Emeljanow, *Reflecting the Audience: London Theatregoing 1840–1880* (Hatfield: University of Hertfordshire Press, 2001), pp. 44–5.
33. J. A. Simpson and E.S.C. Weiner (eds), *The Oxford English Dictionary*, Volume 5 (Oxford: Clarendon Press, 1989), p. 36.
34. Asa Briggs, *Victorian Cities* (London: Odhams Press, 1963), pp. 326–7.
35. Davis and Emeljanow, *Reflecting the Audience*, p. 47.
36. Heidi J. Holder, 'The East End Theatre', in Kerry Powell (ed.),*The Cambridge Companion to Victorian and Edwardian Theatre* (Cambridge: Cambridge University Press, 2004), pp. 257–9.
37. Catherine Haill, 'Theatregoing in East London', East London Theatre Archive, www.elta-project.org, accessed 4 April 2017.
38. Holder, 'The East End Theatre', p. 264.
39. Ibid., pp. 269–70.
40. Davis and Emeljanow, *Reflecting the Audience*, p. 92.
41. Ibid.
42. Holder, 'The East End Theatre', pp. 266–8.
43. Henry Mayhew, *London Labour and the London Poor* (London: Charles Griffin & Company, 1865), p. 141.

44. Roy Porter, *London: A Social History* (London: Hamish Hamilton, 1994), p. 293.
45. Paul Sheridan, *Penny Theatres of Victorian London* (London: Dennis Dobson, 1981), pp. 2–3, 99.
46. Cathy Ross and John Clark, *London: The Illustrated History* (London: Penguin Books, 2008), p. 217.
47. Ed Glinert, *East End Chronicles* (London: Penguin Books, 2006), pp. 166–7.
48 . H. Chance Newton, *Idols of the 'Halls': Being My Music Hall Memories* (Wakefield: EP Publishing, 1975), pp. 218–19. Past members included Jolly Nash, Fred French, George Leybourne, Teddy Solomon, Lily Grey, Claire Romaine and Ben Nathan. The 1928 list included Ada Reeve, Lily Morris, Lowenwirth and Cohen, Hayman and Franklin, Colonel Sir Walter de Frece, Colonel Harry Day, Max Darewski, Lew Lake, Joe Peterman, Ernie Lotinga and Julian Rose.
49. Davis and Emeljanow, *Reflecting the Audience*, p. 94.
50. Jim Davis, 'The East End', in Michael R. Booth and Joel H. Kaplan (eds), *The Edwardian Theatre* (Cambridge: Cambridge University Press, 1996), pp. 211–15.
51. Ibid., pp. 202–3.
52. William J. Fishman, *East End Jewish Radicals 1875–1914* (London: George Duckworth & Co, 1975), p. 60.
53. David Mazower, *Yiddish Theatre in London* (London: The Jewish Museum, 1996), pp. 11–12. See also Vivi Lachs, *Whitechapel Noise: Jewish Immigrant Life in Yiddish Song and Verse, London 1884–1914* (Detroit, MI: Wayne State University Press, 2018).
54. Ibid., p. 14.
55. Tony Kushner, 'Jewish Migration in Fin-de-Siecle Britain', in Rachel Dickson and Sarah MacDougall (eds), *Ben Uri: 100 Years in London* (London: Ben Uri Gallery, 2015), p. 30.
56. Bernard Mendelovitch, *Memories of London Yiddish Theatre* (Oxford: Oxford Centre for Postgraduate Hebrew Studies, 1990), pp. 1–2.
57. Alan Yentob, 'Now that's what I call chutzpah: Jewish contribution to the entertainment business', *Daily Telegraph*, 22 May 2011.
58. Mazower, *Yiddish Theatre in London*, pp. 17–18.
59. Nahma Sandrow, *Vagabond Stars: A World History of Yiddish Theatre* (New York: Harper & Row, 1977), pp. 111–12.
60. Mazower, *Yiddish Theatre in London*, p. 22; Lachs, *Whitechapel Noise*.
61. David Stafford and Caroline Stafford, *Fings Ain't Wot They Used T'Be: The Lionel Bart Story* (London: Omnibus Press, 2011), p. 17.
62. David Mazower 'In Russia's Shadow: Jewish Immigrants and Radical Politics', *The Cable*, 29 (2017), p. 10.
63. David Mazower, 'Women in East End Yiddish Theatre'. Talk given at Tower Hamlets Library and Archives, London, 23 March 2017.
64. Mazower, *Yiddish Theatre in London*, p. 24.
65. Louis Behr interviewed by David Mazower, 29 October 1986. British Library Sound Archive C525/52 F11708.
66. Yentob, 'Now that's what I call chutzpah'.
67. Chambers, *Story of Unity Theatre*, p. 24.
68. Michael Patterson, *Strategies of Political Theatre* (Cambridge: Cambridge University Press, 2003), pp. 1–3.
69. Bertolt Brecht, *Brecht on Theatre: The Development of an Aesthetic* (New York: Hill & Young, 1964), p. 37.

Introduction 45

70. Michael Patterson, *Strategies of Political Theatre*, pp. 1–3.
71. Ibid., p. 72.
72. Jan Cohen-Cruz (ed.), *Radical Street Performance* (London: Routledge, 1988), p. 16.
73. Ibid., p. 13.
74. Christopher Innes, *Modern British Drama: The Twentieth Century* (Cambridge: Cambridge University Press, 2002), p. 72.
75. Samuel, MacColl and Cosgrove, *Theatres of the Left*, p. 230.
76. David Gilchrist, 'Building a Theatre of Action', *Socialist Review*, May 2015.
77. Ibid.
78. *The Red Stage*, 1 (November 1931), p. 1.
79. *The Red Stage*, 2 (January 1932), p. 8.
80. Gilchrist, 'Building a Theatre of Action'.
81. *The Cable*, 29 (2017), p. 12.
82. Samuel, MacColl and Cosgrove, *Theatres of the Left*, p. 150.
83. Joe Jacobs, *Out of the Ghetto: My Youth in the East End, Communism and Fascism, 1913–1939* (London: Janet Simon, 1978).
84. Workers' Circle Friendly Society Records 1909–1984, D/S/61, Hackney Archives Department.
85. Leonard Prager, *Yiddish Culture in Britain: A Guide* (Frankfurt: P. Lang, 1990), p. 21.
86. Chambers, *Story of Unity Theatre*, p. 38.
87. Kevin Morgan, Gidon Cohen and Andrew Flinn, *Communists and British Society* (London: Rivers Oram Press, 2007), p. 188.
88. John Green, *Britain's Communists: The Untold Story* (London: Artery Publications, 2016), p. 14.
89. Sharman Kadish, *Bolsheviks and the British Jews* (London: Frank Cass & Co., 1992), p. 246.
90. Jonathan Frankel (ed.), *The Fate of European Jews 1939–45* (New York: Oxford University Press, 1997), pp. 366–7.
91. Jason L. Heppell, 'Party Recruitment – Jews and Communism in Britain', in Jonathan Frankel (ed.), *Dark Times, Dire Decisions: Jews and Communism* (Oxford: Oxford University Press, 2005), p. 158.
92. Frankel (ed.), *The Fate of European Jews 1939–45*, p. 367.
93. Henry Felix Srebrnik, *London Jews and British Communism 1935–45* (Ilford: Vallentine Mitchell, 1995), pp. 157–8.
94. Ibid., pp. 159–64.
95. Heppell, 'Party Recruitment – Jews and Communism in Britain', p. 156.
96. Ibid., p. 140.
97. Samuel, MacColl and Cosgrove, *Theatre of the Left*, p. 151.
98. Prager, *Yiddish Culture in Britain: A Guide*, p. 536.
99. Samuel, MacColl and Cosgrove, *Theatres of the Left*, p. 153.
100. Theatre Workshop was created by a group of actors committed to a left-wing ideology. Directed by Joan Littlewood, they devised and commissioned plays by and about the working class in Britain.
101. Howard Goorney and Ewan MacColl, *Agitprop to Theatre Workshop* (Manchester: Manchester University Press, 1986), preface.
102. Ibid., pp. 199–200.
103. Chambers, *Story of Unity Theatre*, pp. 36–7.

104. N. Marshal, *The Other Theatre* (London: John Lehmann, 1947), p. 99.
105. Unity Theatre Trust Deed, V & A Theatre Archives, 01/03.
106. Chambers, *Story of Unity Theatre*, pp. 45–6.
107. Unity Theatre archive, People's Museum, Manchester, 5/1–3.
108. David Bradby and John McCormick, *People's Theatre* (London: Crook Helm, 1978), p. 99.
109. Sierz and Ghilardi, *The Time Traveller's Guide to Theatre*, p. 281.
110. Chambers, *Story of Unity Theatre*, pp. 154, 157.
111. Kushner, 'Jewish migration', p. 30.
112. Sierz and Ghilardi, *The Time Traveller's Guide to Theatre*, p. 281.
113. Marshal, *The Other Theatre*, p. 100.
114. Chambers, *Story of Unity Theatre*, pp. 243–4.
115. Ibid., p. 101.
116. Bradby and McCormick, *People's Theatre*, p. 100.
117. Malcolm Page, 'The Early Years at Unity', *Theatre Quarterly*, 1, 4 (October–December 1971), p. 65.
118. Marshal, *The Other Theatre*, pp. 102–3.
119. Harry Landis: Interview with Isabelle Seddon, 11 January 2016, London.
120. Ibid.
121. Margot Hilton: Interview with Isabelle Seddon, 29 March 2016, London.
122. Kate Hilton, *From Greenfield Street to Golders Green* (Sydney: Sydney Jewish Museum, 2011), p. 32.
123. Ibid., pp. 35-36.
124. Shirley Murgraff: Interview with Isabelle Seddon, 2 February 2016, London.
125. Binnie Yates: Interview with Isabelle Seddon, 9 February 2016, London.
126. Harry Landis: Interview with Isabelle Seddon, 11 January 2016, London.
127. *Sunday Independent* (Dublin), 22 September 1963.
128. Ben Weinreb, Christopher Hibbert, Julia Keay and John Keay, *The London Encyclopaedia* (London: Macmillan, 2008), p. 199.
129. Peter Ackroyd, *London: The Biography* (London: Chatto & Windus, 2008), p. 72.
130. Porter, *London*, pp. 302–3.
131. Piers Dudgeon, *Our East End: Memories of Life in Disappearing Britain* (London: Headline, 2008), pp. xii–xiii.
132. H. J. Massingham, *London Scene* (London: Cobden Sanderson, 1933), p. 89.
133. Ackroyd, *London*, p. 677.
134. Ibid., pp. 681–2.
135. Ross and Clark, *London*, pp. 196–7.
136. Venetia Murray, *Echoes of the East End* (London: Viking, 1989), p. 11.
137. Bernard J. Lammers, 'The Birth of the East Ender: Neighbourhood and Local Identity in Interwar East London', *Journal of Social History*, 39, 2 (2005), pp. 331–44.
138. Raymond Kalman, 'The Jewish East End – Where Was It?' in Aubrey Newman (ed.), *The Jewish East End 1840–1939* (London: Jewish Historical Society of England, 1981), pp. 3–4.
139. Kalman, 'Jewish East End', pp. 10–11.
140. Lammers, 'Birth of the East Ender', pp. 331–44.
141. William Zuckerman,'Has Anti-semitism Come to England', *Jewish Chronicle*, 12 March 1937, p. 38.

142. William Zukerman, *The Jew in Revolt* (London: Martin Secker & Warburg, 1937).
143. Elsie Shears, *The Cockney Lady* (London: New Millennium, 1995), pp. 12, 25.
144. Gilda Moss Haber, *Cockney Girl* (Derby: Derby Books Publishing Company, 2012), p. 19.
145. Chaim Bermant, *London's East End: Point of Arrival* (London: Eyre Methuen, 1975), p. 147.
146. www.massobs.org.uk, accessed 19 November 2017.
147. 'Feelings towards Jews, Jews and Cockneys in the East End', Mass-Observation Archive (MOA), TC 62-1.
148. Ibid.
149. Tony Kushner, *We Europeans? Mass-Observation, 'Race' and British Identity in the Twentieth Century* (Aldershot: Ashgate, 2004), pp. 88–9.
150. Commentary on the interim report 12 April 1939, Board of Deputies Archive C6/1/26.
151. Kushner, *We Europeans?*, p. 86.
152. Ibid., pp. 86–7.
153. Ibid., p. 90.
154. Tony Kushner, *The Persistence of Prejudice: Antisemitism in British Society During the Second World War* (Manchester: Manchester University Press, 1989), pp. 48–9.
155. Ibid., p. 54.
156. Ibid., pp. 53–5.
157. Ibid., pp. 56–8.
158. Ibid., pp. 63–5.
159. Charles Poulson, *Scenes from a Stepney Youth* (London: THAP Books, 1988), p. 87.
160. Ibid., p. 107.
161. Murray, *Echoes of the East End*, p. 12.
162. Jacobs, *Out of the Ghetto*, p. 26.
163. *Guardian*, 30 September 2006.
164. Ed Glinert, *East End Chronicles*, p. 204.
165. Ibid., p. 205.
166. Thomas P. Linehan, *East London for Mosley: The British Union of Fascists in East London and South-West Essex 1933–40* (London: Routledge, 1996), p. 64.
167. *Daily Worker*, 5 October 1936, pp. 1, 4.
168. David Renton, 'Docker and Garment Worker, Railwayman and Cabinet Maker: The Class Memory of Cable Street', in Tony Kushner and Nadia Valman (eds), *Remembering Cable Street: Fascism and Anti-fascism in British Society* (London: Vallentine Mitchell, 2000), pp. 95–6.
169. Noreen Branson, *History of the Communist Party in Great Britain, 1927–41* (London: Lawrence & Wishart, 1985), p. 197.
170. Henry Srebrnik, 'Class, Ethnicity and Gender Intertwined: Jewish Women and the East London Rent Strikes, 1935–1940', *Women's History Review*, 4, 3 (1995), p. 286.
171. Ibid., p. 288.
172. John B. Groser, *Politics and Persons* (London: SCM Press, 1949), p. 73.
173. 'The East End Rent Disputes', *Jewish Chronicle*, 2 June 1939, p. 20.
174. *Sun*, 25 February 2011.
175. Howard Fredrics, 'Jewish Boxers of the East End', *The Cable*, 1 (2006), p. 7.
176. Dudgeon, *Our East End*, p. 285.

177. Jacobs, *Out of the Ghetto*, p. 40.
178. Ralph Finn, *Grief Forgotten: The Tale of an East End Jewish Boyhood* (London: Macdonald, 1985), pp. 26–7.
179. John Davies, 'Working Class Culture in the 1930s: Going to the Dogs', *North West Labour History*, 35 (2010–2011), pp. 32–7.
180. Ibid.
181. Ferdynand Zweig, *Labour, Life and Poverty* (Wakefield: EP Publishing, 1975), pp. 31–2.
182. Geoffrey Goldstein: Interview with Isabelle Seddon, London, 19 July 2016.
183. Murray, *Echoes of the East End*, p. 292.
184. Ibid.
185. Ibid., pp. 293–4.
186. Ibid., pp. 125–8.
187. Finn, *Grief Forgotten*, p.16.
188. Murray, *Echoes of the East End*, p. 161.
189. Moss Haber, *Cockney Girl*, p. 27.
190. Gilda Moss Haber: Email correspondence with Isabelle Seddon, 10 June 2016.
191. Moss Haber, *Cockney Girl*, p. 20.
192. Gilda Moss Haber: Email correspondence with Isabelle Seddon, 9 June 2016.
193. Ibid.
194. Martin Kraft: Email correspondence with Isabelle Seddon, 15–25 July 2016.
195. *Daily Mirror*, 22 June 1965, p. 13.
196. David Cesarani, Tony Kushner and Milton Shain (eds), *Place and Displacement in Jewish History and Memory* (London: Vallentine Mitchell, 2009), p. 143.
197. Alexander Bloom, *Prodigal Sons:The New York Intellectuals and their World* (Oxford: Oxford University Press, 1986), p. 11.
198. Harry Blacker, *Just Like It Was* (London: Vallentine Mitchell, 1974), p. 109.
199. Derek B. Scott, *Sounds of the Metropolis* (Oxford: Oxford University Press, 2008), p. 181.
200. Harriet Salisbury, *The War on Our Doorstep: London's East End and How the Blitz Changed It Forever* (London: Ebury Press, 2013), p. xxvii.
201. Ibid., p. 431.
202. V. D. Lipman, 'Jewish Settlement in the East End of London', in Aubrey Newman (ed.),*The Jewish East End 1840–1939* (London: Jewish Historical Society of England, 1981), pp. 37–9.
203. Salisbury, *War on Our Doorstep*, p. 431.
204. Ibid., pp. 433, 437.
205. John Gross, *A Double Thread: A Childhood in Mile End and Beyond* (London: Chatto & Windus, 2001), p. 115.
206. A. B. Levy, *East End Story* (London: Constellation Books, 1951), pp. 98–9.
207. Ibid., p. 95.
208. Natasha Lehrer, *The Golden Chain: Fifty Years of the Jewish Quarterly* (London: Vallentine Mitchell, 2003), p. 43.
209. Levy, *East End Story*, p. 16.
210. Salisbury, *War on Our Doorstep*, p. 447.
211. Levy, *East End Story*, p. 95.
212. Salisbury, *War on Our Doorstep*, p. 454.

213. Steven Berkoff, *Free Association: An Autobiography* (London: Faber and Faber, 1996), p. 5.
214. Dee, *'Estranged' Generation?*, pp. 337–8.
215. For a study of a third-generation Jewish immigrant in the entertainment industry, see Sue Vice, *Jack Rosenthal* (Manchester: Manchester University Press, 2009).
216. Barbara Merrill and Linden West, *Using Biographical Methods in Social Research* (London: Sage, 2009), pp. 2, 95.
217. Lytton Strachey, *Eminent Victorians* (London: Penguin Books, 1986), preface.
218. Michael Holroyd, *Lytton Strachey* (London: Chatto & Windus, 1994), p. 420.
219. Barbara Caine, *Biography and History* (Basingstoke: Palgrave Macmillan, 2010), p. 22.
220. Ibid., p. 23.
221. B. Finkelstein, 'Revealing Human Agency: The Uses of Biography in the Study of Educational History', in C. Kridel (ed.), *Writing Educational Biography: Explorations in Quantitative Research* (New York: Garland Publishing, 1985), p. 45.
222. Ibid., p. 3.
223. Keith Thomas, *Changing Conceptions of National Biography: The Oxford DNB in Historical Perspective* (Cambridge: Cambridge University Press, 2005), p. 61.
224. Sander Gilman, *The Jew's Body* (London: Routledge, 1991), p. 11.
225. Ibid., pp. 12–13.
226. R. W. Connell, 'Understanding Men: Gender Sociology and the New International Research on Masculinities', *Social Thought and Research*, 24 (2002), p. 16.
227. Herbert Sussman, *Masculine Identities: The History and Meanings of Manliness* (Santa Barbara: Praeger, 2012), p. 119.
228. Daniel Boyarin, *The Rise of Heterosexuality and the Invention of the Jewish Man* (Berkeley: University of California Press, 1997), pp. 1–2.
229. Sussman, *Masculine Identities*, pp. 119–23.
230. Michael S. Kimmel, 'Judaism, Masculinity and Feminism', in Harry Brod (ed.), *A Mensch Among Men: Explorations in Jewish Masculinity* (Freedom, CA: Crossing Press, 1988), p. 154.
231. Warren Rosenberg, *Legacy of Rage: Jewish Masculinity, Violence and Culture* (Amhurst, Mass.: University of Massachusetts Press, 2001), p. 1.
232. Sussman, *Masculine Identities*, p. 125.
233. Stephen H. Norwood, 'American Jewish Muscle: Forging a New Masculinity in the Streets and in the Ring, 1890–1940', *Modern Judaism*, 2 (2009), p. 167.
234. Mark Moss, *The Media and the Models of Masculinity* (Lanham, MD: Lexington Books, 2011), p. 107.

1

Alfie Bass

Alfie Bass had the ability to combine comedy and pathos and he used his irrepressible 'Cockney' Jewish talent to establish a range of stage and television characters over the years.[1] His versatility encompassed revue, Shakespearean roles, modern drama and television, most memorably as Bootsie in *Bootsie and Snudge* and on the stage as Tevye in *Fiddler on the Roof*. Yet, despite his national fame, he stayed true to his left-wing political background and involvement with Unity Theatre where his career began. This chapter focuses on his background and the influences in his life and considers the impact they had on his famous roles. Examining his family background, his politics, his time at Unity, his career, an analysis of his performances and roles and especially his portrayal of masculinity, Bass is thus a particular model of a Jewish East Ender who retained a strong identity of both his Jewishness and radicalism after his time at Unity.

Background

Alfie Bass (his original name was Abraham Basalinsky) was born in 1916 and came from a poor immigrant Jewish East End background whose parents had fled the pogroms and whose father had come from Odessa, Russia.[2] Lloyd P. Gartner, who charts the history of immigration from Eastern Europe, argues that the turning point was 1869–1870, the year of famine in north eastern Russia when Jews were expelled from the border regions. In 1875–1876 many fled to avoid service in the armies of the Tsar during the Russo-Turkish war. In 1881–1882, the year of widespread pogroms in southern Russia, the malevolence of the Russian regime to the Jews was fully realized: 'Millions of Jews pent up in towns and villages contracted emigration fever.' Gartner points out that emigration did not just begin on account of the pogroms and gives as an example Jewish emigration from Galicia, where Jews were emancipated in 1867, yet consisted of the same proportion of Jewish emigrants as those that came from Russia and Poland.[3] As well as the main reasons cited as a trigger for departure – pogroms, religious persecution and the fear of military service – a major impulse to leave was economic. The West was perceived to be a world of unparalleled opportunity.[4]

There is no record of what Bass's father did in Odessa but living in such a cosmopolitan city might have exposed him to different experiences and viewpoints than if he had come from another area of Russia, which in turn might have influenced his children. Odessa was a city with an infamous reputation, a frontier seaport on the Black Sea whose commercial prosperity and lax legislation attracted many adventurers seeking wealth. It was a hub for contraband and vice and was multi-ethnic.

There were a number of factors that made Odessa Jewry susceptible to acculturation along distinctly European lines. These included economic incentives, the prospect of social mobility, a vibrant and westernized cultural life, a relatively tolerant political atmosphere until the pogroms and the absence of a particularly restrictive traditional Jewish communal structure. By the 1870s, many Odessa Jews had integrated and embraced elements considered suspect and innovative by Jews elsewhere in Russia. This was due to the increasingly widespread use of the Russian language by local Jews, the degree to which the more extreme orthodox elements were marginalized in communal affairs and the ritual laxity among the more traditional Jews, where Jewish economic enterprise was encouraged.[5] In Yiddish folklore, Odessa came to be associated with a life of pleasure-seeking with indifference to religion and with links to the criminal underworld. 'If Odessa could be compared at all it was only to the port cities of America and those on the frontier line like Chicago or San Francisco where a mixture of enterprise, licence and violence combined to create environments free from the restraints of the past.'[6] It differed from other 'cities of sin' such as Shanghai and New Orleans in that it was a 'judeo-kleptocracy', a city overrun and governed by Jewish gangsters and swindlers.[7]

Whatever Bass's father had experienced in Odessa, life in the Jewish East End was different and not an easy one. Bass recalls that 'there were ten of us at home in Bethnal Green so you soon got your priorities right about sharing and consideration of others'.[8] He was the youngest son and growing up with his six sisters and three brothers he quickly learnt the harsh realities of life and his circumstances contributed to his life-long belief in socialism:

> My dad was a cabinet maker and he used to flog himself silly at it. On the go – all hours he was – trying to make a proper little business if it. But the poor feller wasn't much cop as a businessman so we never had much money. My mum used to go selling carpets in the market

52   *East End Jews and Left-Wing Theatre*

> sometimes to help out. But she was paralysed when I was three and died when I was still quite young. So there was no one to look after me properly and I sort of ran wild.[9]

Bass was brought up in a non-religious household and recalls that his father was against religion. 'His view was that a good man was good whether he was religious or not.'[10] His father appeared to be more concerned with feeding and clothing his ten children. Bass said that his father cared for nothing as long as his children 'did not go naked or *borves*' (Yiddish for 'barefoot').[11]

For the majority of immigrant Jewish families, Yiddish was the language spoken at home and Bass was exposed to this culture. The first record that he chose on the BBC Radio 4 programme *Desert Island Discs* was the Yiddish lullaby *Rozhinkes Mit Mandlen*. He explained that he had selected records that were nostalgic, and this was the song that his parents sang to him.[12] This lullaby was one of the best known and loved Yiddish lullabies of all time, written by Abraham Goldfaden in 1880 as part of his opera *Shulamis*. The lyrics explain that when a baby boy is rocked to sleep, the little goat under his cradle would go to market and return with almonds and raisins.[13] By including this song in his choice of records and by mentioning a Yiddish word on a national radio programme, which he then had to translate, he did not hide his Jewish background.

Yiddish words were included in Bass's recording of two stories *Bootsie and the Beast* (based on the fairy tale *Beauty and the Beast*) and *Bootserella* (*Cinderella*). They were told in the style of the character Bootsie from the television programme *Bootsie and Snudge* and were released in 1963 during the programme's great popularity.[14] In the version of the *Beauty and the Beast* told at that time the children were girls.[15] In Bass's adaptation they were boys called Arthur, Lobbos and Bootsela. The word 'lobbos' is Yiddish for a rascal or mischievous child. In respect of the name Bootsela, by adding the 'la' on to the end of the word it is reminiscent of the Yiddish word *bubela*, Yiddish for darling, sweetheart or honey.[16] In his retelling of the story *Bootserella*, based on the story *Cinderella*, he used the name Bubela for one of the sisters.

Revealingly, Bass swore in Yiddish in a court case when he was charged under the 1843 Theatres Act for putting on the production *Here Goes* for Unity Theatre which had a very anti-American theme.[17] This outburst of Yiddish showed the possibility that Bass was bi-lingual. It has been noted that bilinguals switch from one language to another when they are tired and angry and revert to their mother tongue.[18]

In all likelihood Bass and his family would have mixed within poor Jewish immigrant circles and such contacts would have enabled Bass to get his first job. When he left school at fourteen he began work with a Russian Jewish carpenter.[19] Bass recalled how on his first day at work there was a knock on the door and the carpenter, known as old Sam, hid under the bench and told Bass to open the door. The caller turned out to be the rent collector wanting three weeks rent money owed. The next day Bass was ordered to do the same when the timber merchant came.[20]

His father wanted Bass to do clerical work rather than manual labour and Bass subsequently applied for a job with a printing firm and took his card to the labour exchange. His name was still Basalinksy as he had not yet shortened it to Bass. After looking at the Russian-sounding name on the card, the interviewer told him that he was not needed. Bass recalled how it was a terrible moment for him. 'I went out and I felt like a negro might feel or well a Jew I suppose, you know, foreigner.'[21]

Although Bass was part of a poor East End Jewish family where Yiddish was the language spoken, he grew up in a non-Jewish neighbourhood of the East End and therefore had a different exposure to those living in the heart of the Jewish East End around the Whitechapel area, where the Jewish population was 95 to 100 per cent. The impact of mass immigration on an already overcrowded East End raised some concerns among the authorities. It was amid this growing climate of concern that George Arkell was commissioned by the Toynbee Trust in 1899 to create a map illustrating the spatial distribution of the growing Jewish community in the Spitalfields and Whitechapel areas. Using the different colours ranging from deep red to deep blue, the map was created from information supplied by the London School Board who worked in the area. Jewish families were identified by their names, the schools their children attended and the observance of Jewish holidays. Those streets with the highest density of Jewish residents (95 to 100 per cent) were coloured deep blue, those with the lowest density (fewer than 5 per cent) were coloured deep red.[22] The street that Bass grew up in, Gibraltar Walk in Bethnal Green, came within the last category.

Bethnal Green was particularly hostile to Jews and it was in an area of Bethnal Green known as 'Jews Island' that verbal harassment turned into physical violence in 1903, when Jews were beaten and their properties looted. A local Jewish woman recalled that 'Bethnal Green was the worst. It was the thugs that lived in the borough. If a Jew had a beard he soon didn't have it. It was pulled off.' Apart from the new immigrants Bethnal Green had the highest proportion of locally-born residents in London. It was an inward-looking community and Jews were blamed for the decaying and squalid older housing. Overcrowding was seen as voluntary and as leading to conditions of extreme poverty rather than vice versa.[23]

Gilda Moss Haber, who lived in Bethnal Green, comments that this area had more Fascism and pubs and the smells were of salty shrimp and bacon. This was in contrast to Whitechapel, where her grandparents lived, where there were kosher delicatessens and butcher shops and the smells were chicken soup, roasting chicken, salt beef, mouth-puckering pickles and pickled herring.[24]

Bass explains how he used to mix with boys who were non-Jewish because there were only non-Jewish boys in his street: 'I knocked around with these Christian boys so to speak.' As the boys belonged to a Christian club, the Webb's Institute in Bethnal Green, he joined their club, 'rather than be separated from them I joined the club under false pretences.'[25]

But whether one was part of the Jewish or non-Jewish community in the East End, the common denominator was that life was harsh. As a result, many became involved in political activities to try and bring about change. Bass's own poverty and the difficulties experienced by those around him shaped his political beliefs.

Politics

Bass's earliest political involvement was his participation, together with his brothers, in the fight against Fascism. He took part in the Battle of Cable Street in 1936: 'If ever there was an outbreak of antisemitism, we were called on to help and we were in the forefront of the demonstrations against Mosley. I can recall helping to barricade the streets against the Blackshirts.'[26]

Like many of his generation in the East End, Bass became affiliated to the Communist Party. Aubrey Morris, who stood as a Communist Party candidate for the parliamentary constituency of Stoke Newington and Hackney North in the 1955 election, explained how Bass became involved: 'My contemporaries were people like Alfie Bass and Lionel Bart and dozens of like-minded youngsters, the sons and daughters of Jewish immigrants who settled in London's East End who came into left-wing politics as a result of their family background, the demands of the times and a yearning for justice and an end to poverty.'[27] John Green, in his study of the Communist Party of Great Britain, claims that Bass was a member of the Party.[28]

Bass became a leading figure in the Communist-inspired London Shelter Movement which emerged in the early stages of the Second World War as the Blitz ensued. From the outset of war, the tube trains kept running but the use of tube stations as shelters was forbidden. Communist groups ignored the ruling and broke into locked underground stations.[29] The Party issued 100,000 leaflets and 5,000 posters demanding the immediate construction of bomb shelters and the opening of tube stations as night shelters. The following week police raided various Party offices and bookshops and seized all the leaflets and posters they could find. These raids were also accompanied by police action to close tube station gates whenever an air raid siren sounded to prevent citizens using them as shelters. By the end of the month 79 underground stations in London were already being used as shelters for around 177,000 people. Undaunted by police raids the Party published and distributed another 20,000 leaflets demanding the construction of bomb proof shelters and the setting up of shelter committees and many Party members were involved in these committees.[30]

The Party initiative took on an organized approach. Some local shelter committees produced newsletters, such as the *Hampstead Shelterers' Bulletin*. Partly through these publications and partly through planned coordination, an all-London network grew out of this struggle. A conference was held in November 1940 with some 80 delegates from around 50 shelter committees. The conference elected the London underground station and shelterers' committee and Bass was appointed secretary.[31]

During this time Bass had become active in the Unity Theatre and they began performing shows in the shelters. They created revue material, skits, songs and jokes and the shows continued throughout the war.[32] The performers chose material that would have an immediate rapport with an audience that had not chosen to be entertained. The following, recorded by Topic Records, was sung by Bass:

> So pity the downtrodden landlord
> And his back that is burdened and bent
> Respect his grey hairs, don't ask for repairs
> And don't be behind with the rent.[33]

These words would have had significance for many in the shelters for during the 1930s rent strikes took place in the East End. Organized by the Communist Party-backed Stepney Tenants Defence League, they fought against landlords who tried to raise their rents by as much as 40 per cent or to neglect their responsibilities. It was a time when Jews and non-Jews, particularly the women, banded together to draw attention to the plight of East End slum dwellers at the mercy of 'slumlords' and organized opposition to eviction attempts.[34]

Bass often went to union meetings with an old shop steward friend, an experience which along with the struggles of his youth nurtured in him an abiding loyalty to and admiration for his own class.[35] Bass openly supported at all times, even at the height of his fame, *The Daily Worker* and later *The Morning Star*. He was publicly to the fore in campaigns against the Vietnam War in the 1960s. His profile fell somewhat during the 1970s and there is no public mention of where Bass stood on events that unfolded within the Communist movement in the last decade or so of his life.[36] There is no mention of him in the Communist Party of Great Britain archives in the People's Museum, Manchester.

If Bass stopped being active in the Communist Party in post-war years or had become disillusioned with the Party, he was not alone. After the war the Party attempted to maintain its hegemony in the East End. Yet within a decade Jewish Communism was all but extinct in the East End as well as elsewhere due to changes nationally and internationally.[37] Bass did remain politically active but it was within the auspices of the Labour Party, where he was an active campaigner on its behalf.[38] He was elected assistant honorary secretary of the Shenley Labour Party.[39] He also helped out the Labour candidate for the Hampstead constituency who hoped to topple former Tory Home Secretary Henry Brooke.[40]

Bass's commitment to left-wing politics is evident in much of the theatre work that he participated in. Apart from his work at Unity, that was backed by the Communist Party and which is discussed below, he took part in films with a political message such as *From Pillar to Post,* whose cast included postmen and other postal workers. The film showed the workers' involvement within their trade union and was hoped to have an educational value in schools.[41] Other theatre work with a political message was *No! No! McCarthy* at the Manor Hall Baths, London on 22 October 1953, billed as a concert of British talent banned on the Yankee stage.[42]

Bass considered Unity and some of the people he met there to be inspirational. One of his greatest times whilst at Unity was working with American actor Paul Robeson in *Plant in the Sun* in 1938. He considered Robeson to be 'the greatest man I ever met. He was like a beacon. He never flinched from what he felt was the truth.'[43] Some years later Bass and Robeson's paths crossed again. Bass was instrumental in arranging a Paul Robeson benefit concert at St. Pancras Town Hall on 26 May 1957. Robeson was investigated during the McCarthy era and due to his decision not to recant his public advocacy of pro-Soviet policies, he was denied a passport by the US State Department and his income plummeted. Robeson was connected by the new Atlantic telephone cable and sang over the line to a packed audience. Bass introduced Robeson to the audience and for him it was such a great occasion and emotional experience.[44] Bass's involvement in the event and his support for Robeson again showed his political beliefs.

Bass owed his acting career to Unity and the ethos behind Unity reflected his left-wing political views. Visits to Unity were popular amongst those from the East End. Ronald Davidson, whose father Andy Davidson was a great supporter, recalled going to Unity to see the annual pantomime. 'My parents had a small café just off Whitechapel which was often frequented by left-wingers and I recall Mum telling me that Dad had introduced Bass, a café customer, to Unity as he was a brilliant mimic.'[45] The café was frequented by 'many Communist Party comrades and various leading lights in the Party and the *Daily Worker* were always popping in to meet fellow members and chase up stories.'[46]

Unity Theatre

With such political leanings, it was not surprising that Bass felt an instant rapport with Unity. Actor Harry Landis explains that joining Unity was commonplace for those living in the East End of London. 'There were many from the Jewish East End. There was a lot of talent about and the political ones veered towards Unity which stood for fighting Fascism. We were doing a good job hitting at things we thought should be hit politically.'[47]

Bass's introduction to drama happened by chance when he joined a local youth club in Bethnal Green.[48] He recalls that until that time he had no theatrical ambitions. 'I wanted to be a philosopher. But I belonged to a local boxing club and the manager got up a drama group and collared me to run it. At first I treated the whole thing with derision but it appealed to me and I had no choice.' A visit to Unity reinforced Bass's growing interest in drama and he joined the group.[49] 'Everyone would muck in – mending the toilets, sweeping the stage, sewing the costumes, painting the scenery.'[50] Bass's first job at Unity when he joined as a teenager was to bring up the coal from the cellar and his teenage years were dominated by the exhilaration of learning his theatre trade there.[51]

Unity was an open university of drama which gave people self-respect and a chance to do something for a cause they believed in.[52] For many Unity became 'a second – if not – first – home, the place where people could come alive and feel useful after a deadening day either at work or on the dole.'[53] Pianist James Gibb, who started the orchestra at Unity and shared a flat with Bass for three years, explains that those involved were a close-knit group and that Unity was a very closed society. 'Life in the left and Unity was very parochial. We were in each other's company all the time. We'd go on tour together and take our van and do our play together.'[54] It would therefore appear that Bass was constantly within this left-wing political milieu.

Bass was captivated by Unity's work. He was unemployed, on the dole and started to spend all his time there: 'Everyone was devoted, especially to keeping the theatre open. We saw it as the first workers' theatre and people had sacrificed so much to get it going that the philosophy of "the show must go on" was very strong. My pride was to be appearing for the cause. I'd do any part.' He also commented that he could not imagine anything more inspiring than creating a play or revue with a real purpose. 'Everyone participated, in the décor, the music, the acting. It was a rare thing. It was special because it was collective. No one dominated except the play and its purpose.' The feeling described by Bass was a common one and it inspired intense loyalty that on occasions was akin to religious fervour.[55] Bass said that he 'believed strongly in their principle that true art, by truthfully interpreting life, can move people who work for the betterment of society'.[56]

When Unity moved to new premises in Goldington Street in Kings Cross in 1937, some 400 volunteers, many from the trade union movement, helped to convert the disused Methodist chapel into a theatre. There were craft workers of all trades including chippies, electricians, painters and specialists who came to answer the call to build a theatre for the working-class movement:

> Here, one Alfie Bass, a carpenter, went to work with a will. Soon his natural talents and clowning became the living heart of the conversation. He must have held up some work in progress with his improvisations. But after all it was theatre. The stage welcomed him as a natural. Subsequent performances on the legitimate stage and in front of the TV cameras proved his talent.[57]

Bass's acting career at Unity began with his performance in *Plant in the Sun* in 1938. The story follows a group of teenagers in the shipping department of a New York factory who hold a sit-down strike when one of them is fired for 'talking union'. The great American actor and singer Paul Robeson played Peewee, the sacked workman, and despite his star status he refused special treatment, insisting on taking turns to sweep the stage with the other actors. He had turned down several lucrative offers to play *Plant in the Sun,* which was unpaid, as all the actors were amateurs with day jobs. The play dealt with issues of solidarity across divisions of class and race. Una Brandon-Jones, an active Unity member and later professional actress, recalls the success of *Plant in the Sun*, even after Paul Robeson left the cast. The play was entered into the British Drama League Festival and won first prize with Bass given special mention: 'There was a young actor singled out by the judges – destined to become a household name – but at the time working as a cabinet maker.'[58]

Another early role at Unity was in a political pantomime, *Babes in the Wood*, Unity's biggest and most ambitious show. It opened on 15 November 1938 and ran for a record number of 160 performances until 22 May 1939, playing six nights a week to just under 48,000 people.[59] The Christmas pantomime had long been an established tradition on the English stage. Such stories as Dick Whittington and Robin Hood were constantly being revisited in new dramatizations. Unity chose a standard story for its production of a pantomime with a political point.[60] It was a political spoof based on the story of Robin Hood and included an impersonation of Prime Minister Chamberlain who was portrayed as the wicked uncle. The 'babes' represented Czechoslovakia and 'the robbers' were Hitler and Mussolini. This was before the development of political satire on television and it caused an uproar. Unity also ran into trouble with the depiction of the monarchy. Bass as King Eustace the Useless wanted to sport a beard resembling that of King George V but this was blocked as it was considered as going too far.[61]

Brandon-Jones recalls that after the first night of *Babes in the Wood*, Unity's fame spread, and articles appeared in magazines and newspapers in England and America. 'The hard-hitting topicality made it completely different from anything London had ever seen before.'[62] The final chorus reflected the mood of the theatre at the time:

> Come comrades sing with us
> Join in the workers' chorus
> Come comrades march with us
> Victory lies before us.[63]

Bass appeared in many sketches of *Sandbag Follies* that opened on 19 September 1939, the first of the wartime reviews put on at Unity the moment the ban was lifted on theatres, such as Unity, who were outside the central London radius and were permitted to give performances. A press conference was held, and Unity announced that it would be the first theatre to reopen and a show would be presented in three days' time. The show challenged official secrecy and bureaucracy and satirized life in the blackout, at work and in the army. One sketch, attacking the drive for increased

4. *Babes in the Wood*, Unity Theatre 1938 ©as stated at the copyright holder/Victoria and Albert Museum, London © permission (Clive Gellert, Unity Theatre Trust)

production through time and motion studies, had Bass as the harassed worker who, after having been told of every different way in which he could increase his production, had the tag line: 'Yes and if you give me a broom to put up my arse, I'll sweep the bloody floor for you.'[64]

The war changed Unity. The majority of those who had built, and sustained, Unity were called up for the services and could only help out when they were home on leave. Bass returned from time to time from his work as a despatch rider to help out in different capacities. In 1948 he was asked to direct the revue *What's Left*. Brandon-Jones explained that the main target in this revue were the Americans: 'Too many American troops were still in the country and the lively social aspirations of 1945 were being slowly crushed out of existence through the dictatorship of American policy.' She commented that there must have been a burst of fury at the embassy and in the CIA due to the vicious attacks that Unity were making especially as they were drawing in such packed houses. 'Two CID men came in to interview the manager as well as Bass. They were questioned at length, defending themselves mainly by silence.'[65]

Despite the start of a successful career in mainstream entertainment, Bass continued with his involvement with Unity and its provocative plays. He produced *Here Goes* at Unity in 1951 about disarmament and its subservience to American foreign policy. This coincided with the Korean War and its anti-American theme and included a song which described the Korean War as an invasion by the United States under United Nations disguise. There were reports of visits to the theatre by the CID and Special Branch officers. The resulting prosecution was seen by Unity as covert pressure from the American embassy. Bass felt that this confirmed what he had thought had happened in 1947 when the musical *Finian's Rainbow*, in which he had starred, had closed prematurely at the Embassy's request because of its political overtones. It attacked the rich and at one point the white protagonist turns black and a magic crock of gold planted in America grants the poor sharecropper's wishes.[66]

The production of *Here Goes* resulted in Bass, together with his co-director and Unity's general manager, being charged under the 1843 Theatres Act. This Act allowed the Lord Chamberlain 'to prohibit the performances of plays where he was of the opinion that it is fitting for the preservation of good manners, decorum or the public peace to do so'. At first they were issued with two summons, but the number finally rose to twelve, all related in some way to the unlicensed presentation of a new play. Bass was fined £20 but his conviction was quashed on appeal because the prosecution had not proved that he was the same Bass quoted in the programme nor that he had taken part in presenting the show on the two nights when the policemen had been at the theatre.[67]

Undeterred by the trouble caused by *Here Goes*, Bass co-wrote *Mother Goose* with Eric Paice (who later went on to write episodes of the 1960s cult

British spy-fi television series *The Avengers*). *Mother Goose*, also performed in 1951, again focused on the American threat and struggle for peace. Mother Goose was in deep trouble as she was unable to pay her grocery bills and the squire wanted to evict her because the Americans were carrying out secret research under her cottage and wanted to test a new weapon SCUM which could wipe out the earth's population.[68] *Turn It Up,* another Bass production in 1953, included skits on an ex-Nazi German industrialist singing 'I see eye to eye with ICT'; on Japanese businessmen praising democracy because it helped them to exploit their workers. The show, which also lampooned the Coronation, attracted large crowds. 'The production was lavish and full of speed under Bass's direction.'[69]

Career

Bass's career was launched at Unity in 1938. During the war years he was called up into the Middlesex Regiment as a despatch rider and he maintained his interest in acting by appearing in army film unit documentaries. On demobilisation he acted in numerous plays, films and revues, including a season at Stratford on Avon in 1948 where he played Launcelot Gobbo, servant to Shylock in *Merchant of Venice* and Grumio, a servant in *Taming of the Shrew*. 'He had the good luck to begin his professional career backed by much experience in the kind of amateur work that called for a quick wit as well as communicated enjoyment.'[70] He gave a memorable performance in Wolf Mankowitz's *The Bespoke Overcoat* at the Arts Theatre in 1953, appearing as the kindly ghost who returned to get an overcoat from the man who had 'sweated' him to death.[71]

Bass had a number of minor parts in films during the late 1940s before landing a co-starring part as one of the Lavender Hill mob in the 1951 film of the same name. He appeared in over 60 films. He was a redcoat in *Holiday Camp* (1949), a hospital orderly in *Hasty Heart* (1949) and a newspaper vendor in *The Galloping Major* (1951). The effect of these and other brief appearances was to establish him as a familiar supporting face. With the crossover of cinema audiences to television during the late 1950s, Bass switched media too.[72] By the time he was cast in a starring role in the film *Alfie* (1968), he had forged for himself a thriving television career. His television performances included *Till Death Us Do Part* and *Are You Being Served?* He became a household name in the late 1950s and 1960s when he played the character 'Excused Boots' Bisley in two popular television series, *The Army Game* and *Bootsie and Snudge*. In *The*

Army Game, which began in 1957, Bass was an army idler and the part of the bullying Sergeant Major Snudge was played by Bill Fraser. In 1960, he teamed up with Fraser to start a new series *Bootsie and Snudge* which followed the mishaps of the two characters who retire from the army at the same time and then land jobs as Boots and Major Domo at a gentleman's club in London. Snudge was the hall porter and was still telling handyman Bootsie what to do.[73] In 1968 Bass was chosen to play Tevye in the musical *Fiddler on the Roof.*

Roles

Bass's Jewish East End background stood him in good stead for *The Bespoke Overcoat*, a 37-minute film directed by Jack Clayton. It won a British Academy award in 1956 and a Hollywood Oscar in 1957 in the best two-reel short subject category and has been considered amongst the best short story films ever made.[74] *The Bespoke Overcoat* was written by Wolf Mankowitz who adapted Gogol's *The Overcoat* to Jewish characters in the East End of London after the Second World War. Bass had first performed the role at the Arts Theatre, London in 1953. The film is an ironic ghost story which touches on the themes of friendship, grief, poverty and injustice, all of which illuminate the lives of immigrant workers and which Bass knew first-hand from the struggles of his family.

Fender (Alfie Bass) works for the Ranting Company where he has clerked for 43 years. His job involves making lists of clothing while he sits in a threadbare coat with holes and freezes. His offer to buy one of their warm sheepskins with money docked from his wages is met with derision from his boss. In despair he turns to his old friend Morry (David Kossoff), a bespoke tailor with 'a needle like Paganini', and asks him the impossible task of repairing the coat. Morry compromises by offering to make him a bespoke coat at a special price. Unfortunately, Fender is callously sacked from his job and dies before he can wear it. He returns as a ghost to Morry's workshop and Morry offers him the coat. But this bespoke coat will not satisfy Fender. He wants his revenge on the man who had 'sweated' him to death. The two men enter the warehouse at night after a drunken dance outside. Fender selects his coat and having carried out a quiet revenge in the pursuit of justice fades away 'down there' where there is central heating and their old friend Lennie is doing a roaring trade in herrings.[75] Bass's gift for Jewish character comedy found its fullest expression in the roles he played in *The Bespoke Overcoat*, *The World of Sholem Aleichem* and *Fiddler on the Roof.*[76]

5. Alfie Bass (left) and David Kossoff, *The Bespoke Overcoat* © Wolfgang Suschitzky

His most famous stage performance was as Tevye in *Fiddler on the Roof*. He took over the role in 1968 from Chaim Topol, who had played the part to critical acclaim. Bass was not daunted to any comparisons that might be made as he had his own ideas about the character. He modelled Tevye on his father, who also had a hard life. 'He came from Odessa, had children and was constantly talking to God. My family was very much like Tevye's.'[77] He considered that his father was 'three hundred per cent the man in the show. He was Sholem Aleichem's Tevye the milkman.'[78] He was praised for bringing pathos to the role and for capturing 'the sense of persecution essential to the conception of the story'.[79] Bass felt that the role he played was his biggest personal success.[80] Although he was not an observant Jew (it would appear that politics was his religion) and his wife was not Jewish, he remained connected to his Jewish background and commented that 'I do feel my own Jewishness gives my work its specific flavour'.[81] He was supportive of Jewish causes and this included performing with David Kossoff in *It Should Happen to a Dog* by Wolf Mankowitz at the Royal Festival Hall in 1955, in aid of the Habonim Israel training camp scheme,[82] and opening a fete in 1967 in aid of the Israel emergency fund for the Six-Day War.[83]

The same ease with which he played Jewish roles was duplicated in his Cockney ones. Bass's immersion in the non-Jewish area of the East End where he grew up helped him in the portrayal of the Cockney. Growing up in such a tough environment as Bethnal Green, Bass recalls how as a child he used to sit on the front steps and watch the fights 'Cor, there were some fierce ones with the gangs. Knives, bottles – the lot.' He admitted that he kept a safe distance as he was small in stature, but those days helped him a great deal in his television work. 'Lots of my mannerisms and catch phrases were picked up on that doorstep.' He mentions one particular instance when he saw a little boy crying bitterly because he had dropped his bread and jam in the gutter. His mother was out working so his big sister, who was about seven years old, was in charge. She put her arms around him and tried to comfort him. 'Well, never mind, ay?' That was the first time he had heard that expression. 'But it's earned me more giggles on TV than I can remember.'[84]It was the catchphrase used by Bootsie in *Bootsie and Snudge*, the much put upon character with his appealing expression and his knack of getting into trouble that was adored by the millions who watched him on television over the years.

Whilst still at Unity Bass started to become known for his Cockney roles. He appeared in the play *Buster* by Ted Willis, performed at The Arts Theatre in July 1947. The play was about a Cockney who was awarded the George Medal and Bass had the leading role. *The Evening Standard* review pointed out that the entire cast consisted of amateurs, factory workers and several of them were Jews and that the play had unearthed Bass, a young actor of singular promise. 'He is the very essence of the cheek, the dexterity, the courage and the irreverence of the Cockney. He has feeling, humour, vitality, humanity and a natural instinct for the stage.'[85] *The Times* review commented that Buster himself, a Cockney youth with all the Cockney's natural lack of inhibitions, is a vivid figure both by virtue of the writing and the vivacity Bass brings to the part. 'Buster who was more than half way to taking the wrong turning until the war and the particular compulsion it brings to him, is in Bass's hands so living a figure.'[86]

Cockney roles became a speciality for Bass thereafter. Producer Charles Chilton asked Bass to sing a Cockney song for his BBC Home Service series *Century of Song*. Bass was such a success that Chilton suggested there should be a Cockney song programme with Bass as the star.[87] For the 1958 television programme *Alfie's Penny Gaffs,* Bass sang many of the old coster songs sung in London's forerunners of the music halls, the penny gaff. Gaff is a Cockney word for something cheap and low, especially a place of entertainment, and a penny was the usual price of admission. *Alfie's Penny Gaffs* set out to give an authentic portrayal of Cockneys and Cockney life with Bass singing many of the songs that were first bawled out a century ago by the costers and coalmen of London's penny gaffs. The BBC described him as 'a very talented graduate of London's East End whose Cockney wits were first sharpened in the knockabout neighbourhoods of Petticoat Lane'.[88] Bass also appeared in the 1950s radio programme *Journey into Space* where he played Lemmy, the timorous little Cockney. *The Evening Standard* reported that Bass was a natural for the programme as he was born within sniffing distance of Billingsgate, which made him a true Cockney.[89]

Bass became a household name as a result of *The Army Game,* a British sitcom broadcast on ITV from 1957–1961. The show was about national service conscription to the post-war British army. It dominated the network's comedy output during the 1950s and tapped into a huge vein of familiarity. The idea was simple and still fresh in the minds of most of the adult population, with the Second World War less than a decade passed, about a group of men serving their time as conscripts in the army. The show centred on a group of conscripts assigned to the Surplus Ordnance Department at Nether Hopping, Staffordshire. Billeted in Hut 29, the men were determined to work as little as possible and to have fun. The group included Bass as Private Montague 'Excused Boots' Bisley (Bootsie). His nickname 'excused boots' was due to the fact that he had bunions and had to go around in plimsolls.[90]

It was ironic that they had chosen Bass to play the part of the soldier who had foot problems, although Bootsie was a non-Jewish Cockney. The construction of the Jewish body in the nineteenth and early twentieth centuries was linked to the underlying ideology of antisemitism, to the view that the Jew was inherently different and this applied to language and movement. The foot was one example. The idea that the Jew's foot is unique has analogies with the hidden side of difference attributed to the cloven-footed devil of the Middle Ages whose shape of foot was hidden inside the shoe. By the nineteenth century the relationship between the image of the Jew and that of the hidden devil was found in a secularized scientific context. The Jew's foot was no longer the foot of the devil but of the 'bad' citizen of the new national state and is closely related to the idea of the 'foot' soldier of the popular militia. The Jew's foot marked him as congenitally unable and therefore unworthy of being completely integrated into the social fabric of the modern state. Jews could not become true citizens because they were worthless as soldiers due to their physical stature.[91]

In 1904, Joseph Rohrer[92] cited the reason that the majority of Jews called into military were released was because of their 'weak feet' and that Jewish soldiers spent more time in the military hospitals than in military service. This link of the Jews' weak feet and their inability to be full citizens was for Rohrer a further sign of the inherent intrinsic difference of the Jew. This unique gait represented the inability of the Jew to function as a citizen within a state which defined full participation as military service. Flat feet remained a significant sign of Jewish difference in German science through the Nazi period.[93]

Despite the emphasis on feet in regard to Bass's character Bootsie, there were no antisemitic connotations. Bootsie was a non-Jewish Cockney and the fact that Bass, with his Jewish background, could play him with ease showed that Bass had integrated as a second generation immigrant and had the confidence to play that role. The popularity of the show meant that the actors received celebrity status virtually immediately.[94] Bass felt that *The Army Game* was his launching pad in national terms. 'A weekly comedy series makes you recognisable all over the country. I was recognised everywhere.'[95] In 1960 Bass teamed up with Fraser to start the new series *Bootsie and Snudge*. Two years after the show commenced it nearly always appeared in the list of top ten television shows and had at times an estimated audience of 20 million.[96]

Bass had the background as well as the acting ability to play roles such as Tevye in *Fiddler on the Roof* and Bootsie in *The Army Game* with ease. In addition, he was helped by his physical attributes. 'Being small, 5ft 6 inches, with a comically large nose and sad eyes, Bass is physically ideal for roles as the pathetic, ever-suffering little underdog that made his name.'[97]

His short stature helped his career. He had a leading part in the film *The Lavender Hill Mob* (1951), a classic Ealing comedy starring Alec Guinness as a mild-mannered bank clerk whose sudden compulsion to rob the bank he works for causes havoc. He devises the robbery which will smuggle £1 million in gold bullion to France in the form of Eiffel Tower paperweights. He is helped amongst others by Bass who stars in the film as petty Cockney crook Shorty Fisher who carries not a grain of ruefulness.[98] Bass's lack of height is always emphasized in episodes of *The Army Game*. He is considerably shorter than the others and this is often used to comic effect, such as when he leaves the army and is on the train home, and he has difficulty reaching up to the luggage compartment. When he finally finds somewhere to sit and has to squeeze with great difficulty next to an obese gentleman, he announces 'ain't your body big'.[99] Although Jews were considered to be below average height, as alleged by studies carried out in

68　　　　　*East End Jews and Left-Wing Theatre*

Galicia in 1876, Bavaria in 1881 and Poland in 1906,[100] the emphasis on Bass's short stature, as with his feet, was not antisemitic and used purely for comic effect.

Performance: Mannerisms and Masculinity

The *Jewish Chronicle* described Bass as having 'an irrepressible face with the wry expression.'[101] Bass used the same facial expressions in both his Jewish and non-Jewish roles, and he adopted these far more for dramatic effect in comparison to his physical movements. When playing Fender in *The Bespoke Overcoat*, his eyes constantly open wide in surprise, his eyebrows move manically to give emphasis to what he is saying and hearing. These are considered to be Jewish characteristics.[102] His head moves from side to side when he talks to his friend Morry or his boss Renton and he uses particular expressions and mannerisms when he talks to himself. When sitting in the warehouse, hungry and cold, he describes to himself the overcoat that he would like to own. He frowns all the time and constantly raises his eyebrows.[103] These are the same mannerisms that are used in his non-Jewish role as Bootsie in *Bootsie and Snudge* when he talks to himself on the train, concerned about his future now that he has left the army: 'I wish I did have a job.'[104]

In episodes of *Till Death Us Do Part*, in which he played Alf Garnett's neighbour and drinking partner Bert, a non-Jewish Cockney, he used very similar expressions to that of the Jewish Fender. Again, there is more emphasis on facial expressions than physical movement. His eyebrows go up and down when he suggests an idea, such as Alf moving in with him and his wife so that Alf can charge his daughter and son-in-law rent on the basis of vacant possession.[105] In other episodes he nods a great deal, gives knowing looks and constantly moves his head from side to side.[106]

His Cockney performances included Jewish elements. In one episode of *The Army Game* he used a Jewish expression 'Wish you well to wear it', when he comments on the new suit that Fraser is wearing to enter civilian life again.[107] This phrase is usually said by older British Ashkenazi Jews on seeing a friend or relative wearing a new garment or accessory. It is value-neutral, not implying that the garment is nice, just that it is new.[108] The phrase could be an acknowledgement to the person with the new item that he has done well enough to afford something new, which might not have been possible for the former first generation immigrant. Bass says the phrase naturally although this is not a phrase that is used amongst non-Jews.

The ease in which this phrase was included was a sign of the times that Yiddish expressions could be casually included with the audience understanding their meaning. Elements of Jewish background crept into the work of writers and actors during this period. One example was producer Jack Rosenthal, born in Manchester in 1931, and whose parents were working class and Jewish. Aspects of his background characterized all of his work. Although he wrote *The Evacuees* (1975) and *Bar Mitzvah Boy* (1976) which specifically represented elements of Anglo-Jewish life, there are Jewish incidents and characters in many of Rosenthal's television plays and they sometimes exist at the level of small details. In *Well Thank You, Thursday* (1976) the removal man shouts 'mazeltov'[109] as he puts down Miss Shepherd's long-awaited desk.[110] Jack Rosenthal was commissioned in 1961 to write for *Coronation Street,* a soap opera set in a tightly-knit northern working-class community. 'Everything for which Rosenthal's writing became famous stems from *Coronation Street,* including his interest in the underprivileged and the underdog and their salty, everyday discourse, and in Englishness – his plays were never a resounding transatlantic success – but also in Jewishness.'[111] Although *Coronation Street* was not known for its Jewish characters, there is an episode from 1967 about Elsie Tanner's wedding where Stan Ogden asks the photographers if the photographs come out of his Japanese camera right to left only to be told 'No, pal, those are Jewish cameras'.[112]

Bass did not change his mannerisms in the roles that ranged from the tragic poor Jewish immigrant in *The Bespoke Overcoat* to the comic Cockney ones. He embraced both the Jewish and non-Jewish worlds. The ease in which he embraced both is shown in the following examples: In *The Lavender Hill Mob* (1951) he was the look-out, a timid minor villain who prefers watching the test match to a trip to Paris for a triumphant share of the proceeds; at the *Sailor Beware* (1956) nuptials he was the church organist sneaking furtive puffs on a cigarette between chords of the 'Wedding March'. In *Dance of a Vampire* (1967) Bass was a Jewish vampire with nothing to fear from a crucifix. When a tasty female victim brandishes one in front of him to save her neck, Bass gleefully brushes it aside and cackles, saying in a heavily accented Yiddish voice: 'Have *you* got the wrong vampire.'

In addition to shared mannerisms between his roles, there was a similarity in how he portrayed his masculinity. Bass is not the 'tough guy' James Bond type character that began to emerge from the 1950s onwards and which followed wartime self-confidence based upon the sacrifice and heroism of ordinary men.[113] Instead he played the part of an underdog. He is bossed around in *The Army Game* and *Bootsie and Snudge*, a hen-pecked husband in *Till Death Us Do Part* and the exploited and impoverished clerk in *The Bespoke Overcoat*. He is the weak male, and this is how the Jewish male was often represented. Historically the Jewish man was seen as less than masculine.[114] Often the Jewish male was considered effeminate due to the concept that they were considered unsuitable to serve in the army, the speed in which they spoke, their disposition to hysteria and that their nerve force was seen to be that of a woman.[115] In *The Army Game* and *Bootsie and Snudge*, Bass plays his role, Private 'Bootsie' Bisley, in a very effeminate manner: 'There are crafty nudges and hammed up performances.'[116] In the first episode of *Bootsie and Snudge,* when he leaves the army, he says in a very camp voice 'I'm free and lovely with it' as he totters in a feminine manner, exclaiming 'oh these rotten winklepickers.'[117] Private 'Bootsie' Bisley, although not Jewish, falls into the category of the weak and effeminate male, characteristics that were often attributed to Jewish men.

✳✳✳

There was a time when no British filmed seemed complete without Alfie Bass popping up in it, 'basically playing the same character, he has hopped chirpily from drama to comedy and into costume pieces and back like an energised sparrow'. His forte was playing whimsical slightly down at heel Cockney characters whose natural habitat would be the dockland café, the boxing gym or the street market to all of which he added 'an engaging warmth and sanguinity'. He was a character as 'authentically London as a pot of jellied eels'.[118]

The character remained the same, as did the political beliefs. Bass was loved for being 'one of the people' and this is what endeared him to those who watched him as Bootsie, the working-class comical character. Ted Willis, who also started his career at Unity and became famous for his television series *Dixon of Dock Green,* considered that Bass was the most unspoilt man in show business and a great socialist. He viewed the supposedly unimportant people to be the most important and that people identified with him easily. 'The man who loves the ordinary people has found a symbol for the ordinary people to love' and that Bootsie had something to say and people could identify with him.[119] He was endearing with his gentle, almost camp performance and mannerisms and the characters he played, whether Jewish or non-Jewish Cockney, were non-threatening. He was never seen as aggressive and perhaps, as he was seen in such a light, it allowed him to hold steadfastly to his more radical politics and not be judged by the general public.

Willis considered that one of Bass's greatest attributes was his ingrained habit of practising socialism. He recalled when Bass was at a film premiere, he would push aside the fur-coated stars and wealthy producers to find a working-class buddy. If that person tried to be 'posh' Bass would talk in an even louder Cockney voice. Once during their time at Unity, they were asked by the Hungarian film director Gabriel Pascal to visit him to discuss a film. They barely had enough money for the bus fare to Claridges where Pascal was staying. Upon arrival they found Pascal in his luxury suite lying on a settee in a gold-braided dressing gown. Pascal asked which of them was the poet and which the *pagliacci* (Italian for 'clown'). Bass grunted 'I don't quite get you mate but this fellow's the bleeding writer'.[120]

Bass died suddenly of a heart condition on 15 July 1987. His obituaries highlighted that he was a Jewish Cockney: 'loved and remembered as a quick, alert witty actor, frequently called upon to embody the Cockney Jewish tradition of springy resilience'[121] and for his 'irrepressible Cockney Jewish talent'[122] and that 'with his Cockney Jewish background he was eminently suitable for many of the character parts in which he appeared'.[123] He truly earned the title 'Jewish Cockney' as he epitomized a second generation Jewish East Ender who had the confidence to take on the roles of Jewish and Cockney characters and merge them into one. He remained true to his Jewish background and embraced the culture of the non-Jewish East End whilst remaining loyal to his political beliefs.

Notes

1. *The Times*, 18 July 1987.
2. 'Obituary', *Jewish Chronicle*, 24 July 1987, p. 14. Although the *Jewish Chronicle* claimed the family came to England to escape the pogroms, there is no documentation in census or nationalisation records as to the date they arrived. There is a picture of Bass in the *Jewish Chronicle*, 29 August 1969, with the caption 'setting sail to visit Odessa, birthplace of his father'. *Daily Mirror*, 23 August 1969 also featured a photograph with him and his family at Tilbury docks and stated that his father was born in the Ukraine.
3. Lloyd P. Gartner, *The Jewish Immigrant in England 1870*–1914 (London: Simon Publications, 1973), pp. 40–1.
4. Eugene Black, *The Social Politics of Anglo–Jewry* (Oxford: Basil Blackwell, 1988), pp. 243–5.
5. Steven J. Zipperstein, *The Jews of Odessa: A Cultural History 1794–1881* (Stanford: Stanford University Press, 1985), p. 151.
6. Ibid., p. 1.
7. Jarrod Tanny, *City of Rogues and Schnorrers: Russia's Jews and the Myth of Old Odessa* (Bloomington: Indiana University Press, 2011), p. 2.
8. *Evening News*, 23 October 1974.
9. *Daily Sketch*, 28 March 1961.
10. Ibid.
11. *Desert Island Discs*, PABX 4904, BBC Written Archives, Reading.

12. Ibid.
13. www.holocaustmusic.ort.org, accessed 8 April 2018.
14. *Storytime Discs*. Stars entertaining children. Catalogue CR1001, 1002, Vintage British Comedy.
15. Vera Southgate, *Beauty and the Beast* (London: Penguin, 1964).
16. www.translationdirectory.com, accessed 8 April 2018.
17. Colin Chambers, *The Story of Unity Theatre* (London: Lawrence & Wishart, 1989) p. 320.
18. Francois Grospean, 'Bilinguals', in Renzo Titone (ed.),*On the Bilingual Person* (University of Ottawa, Ottawa: Canadian Society for Italian Studies, 1989), pp. 43–4.
19. *TV Times*, 5 May 1961.
20. Ibid.
21. *Desert Island Discs*, PABX 4904, BBC Written Archives.
22. C. Russell and H. S. Lewis, *The Jew in London: A Study of Racial Character and Present Day Conditions* (London: T. Fisher Unwin, 1901).
23. Geoff Dench, Kate Gavron and Michael Young, *The New East End: Kinship, Race and Conflict* (London: Profile, 2006), pp. 16–17.
24. Gilda Moss Haber, *Cockney Girl: The Story of a Jewish Family in WWII London* (Derby: Derby Books, 2012), p. 19.
25. *Desert Island Discs*, PABC 4904, BBC Written Archives.
26. Pamela Melnikof, 'A Tevya for Two Basses', *Jewish Chronicle*, 16 February 1968, p. 33.
27. Aubrey Morris, *Unfinished Journey* (London: Artery Publications, 2000), p. 13.
28. John Green, *Britain's Communists: The Untold Story* (London: Artery Publications, 2016), p. 14.
29. www.grahamstevenson.me.uk, accessed 4 December 2017.
30. Green, *Britain's Communists: The Untold Story*, p. 202.
31. www.grahamstevenson.me.uk, accessed 4 December 2017.
32. Ron Travis, 'Unity Theatre of Great Britain 1936–1946: A Decade of Production' (unpublished MA dissertation, University of Southern Illinois, 1968), p. 108.
33. Chambers, *Story of Unity Theatre*, p. 200.
34. Srebrnik, 'Class, Ethnicity and Gender Intertwined: Jewish Women and the East London Rent Strikes, 1935–1940', *Women's History Review*, 4, 3 (1995), p. 286.
35. *The Times*, 8 July 1987.
36. www.grahamstevenson.me.uk, accessed 4 December 2017.
37. Srebrnik, 'Class, Ethnicity and Gender Intertwined: Jewish Women and the East End Rent Strikes, 1935-1940', pp. 159–64.
38. *Jewish Chronicle*, 24 July 1987.
39. *Jewish Chronicle*, 15 January 1982.
40. *Daily Mirror*, 22 March 1966.
41. *Daily Worker*, 8 September 1947.
42. *Daily Worker*, 12 October 1953.
43. Don Rowan Collection, British Library Sound Archives, C1037/54.
44. Theatre Archive Project, British Library Sound Archives, C1142/173, C1186/109.
45. Email correspondence between Isabelle Seddon and Ronald Davidson, 24 January 2016.
46. *The Cable*, 4 (2011), p. 25.
47. Harry Landis: Interview with Isabelle Seddon, 11 January 2016, London.
48. *Desert Island Discs*, PABX 4904, BBC Written Archives.

49. *Jewish Chronicle*, 16 February 1968.
50. Chambers, *Story of Unity Theatre*, p. 125.
51. www.grahamstevenson.me.uk, accessed 4 December 2017.
52. Chambers, *Story of Unity Theatre*, p. 23.
53. Ibid., p. 125.
54. *Daily Telegraph*, 3 July 2001.
55. Chambers, *Story of Unity Theatre*, p. 126.
56. *Daily Worker*, 27 January 1962.
57. Unity Theatre Archives, V & A Theatre Archives, 1/3/5.
58. Una Brandon-Jones, 'Highlights and Lowlights' (unpublished manuscript), Unity Theatre Archives (THM/9/1/3/6).
59. Chambers, *Story of Unity Theatre*, pp. 166–7.
60. Ron Travis, 'Unity Theatre', p. 83.
61. Chambers, *Story of Unity Theatre*, p. 174.
62. Brandon-Jones, 'Highlights and Lowlights'.
63. Ibid.
64. Chambers, *Story of Unity Theatre*, pp. 191–3.
65. Brandon-Jones, 'Highlights and Lowlights'.
66. Chambers, *Story of Unity Theatre*, pp. 319–20.
67. Ibid., p. 320.
68. Ibid., p. 322.
69. Ibid., pp. 330–1.
70. *The Times*, 18 July 1987.
71. *Jewish Chronicle*, 24 July 1987.
72. Terence Pettigrew, *British Film Character Actors* (Newton Abbot: David and Charles, 1982), p. 19.
73. *Daily Telegraph*, 18 July 1987.
74. Pauline Kael, *5001 Nights at the Movies* (London: Zenith, 1984), p. 50.
75. Anthony J. Dunn, *The Worlds of Wolf Mankowitz: Between Elite and Popular Cultures in Post War Britain* (London: Vallentine Mitchell, 2013), p. 57.
76. *Guardian*, 18 July 1987.
77. Pamela Melkinof, 'A Tevya for Two Basses', *Jewish Chronicle*, 16 February 1968, p. 33.
78. *Desert Island Discs*, BBC Radio 4, April 1968.
79. *Daily Telegraph*, 18 July 1987.
80. Don Rowan Collection, British Library Sound Archives, C1037/54.
81. Pamela Melkinof, 'A Tevya for Two Basses', *Jewish Chronicle*, 16 February 1968, p. 33.
82. *Jewish Chronicle*, 10 June 1955.
83. *Jewish Chronicle*, 25 August 1967.
84. *Daily Sketch*, 28 March 1961.
85. *Evening Standard*, 17 July 1947.
86. *The Times*, 14 July 1947.
87. *Daily Mirror*, 9 July 1958.
88. *Alfie's Penny Gaffs*, 9 July 1958, BBC Written Archives Centre, R86/3/1.
89. *Evening Standard*, 4 July 1958.
90. *Daily Telegraph*, 18 July 1987.
91. Sander Gilman, *The Jew's Body* (London: Routledge, 1991), pp. 38–9.
92. Joseph Rohrer was an Austrian top official and police commissioner who wrote ethnographic studies of the peoples of the Hapsburg Empire.

93. Gilman, *The Jew's Body,* pp. 40, 52.
94. www.britishcomedy.org.uk, accessed 5 December 2017.
95. Don Rowan Collection, British Library Sound Archives, C1037/54.
96. *Daily Mirror*, 28 July 1962.
97. *Daily Express*, 9 December 1978.
98. www.screenonline.org.uk, accessed 19 January 2018.
99. *Bootsie and Snudge (The Army Game),* 'Civvy Street', SO1 EO3, 23 September 1960.
100. Klaus Hoedl, 'Physical Characteristics of the Jews', Jewish Studies at the CEU, web.ceu.hu/jewishstudies.
101. *Jewish Chronicle*, 24 July 1987.
102. Raphael Patai and Jennifer Patai, *The Myth of the Jewish Race* (Detroit: Wayne University Press, 1989), pp. 219–22.
103. *The Bespoke Overcoat*, Remus Films 1955.
104. *Bootsie and Snudge* (The Army Game), 'Civvy Street'.
105. *Till Death Us Do Part*, 'Moving in with Min', S7EO1.
106. *Till Death Us Do Part*, 'The Wake', S6E05; 'A Hole in One', S7E05.
107. *Bootsie and Snudge* (The Army Game), 'Civvy Street'.
108. www.Jewish-languages.org, accessed 1 June 2018.
109. Congratulations; good luck, www.collinsdictionary.com, accessed 31 July 2018.
110. Sue Vice, *Jack Rosenthal* (Manchester: Manchester University Press, 2009), p. 165.
111. Ibid., pp. 1–2.
112. Ibid.
113. Mark Moss, *The Media and the Models of Masculinity* (Lanham, MD: Lexington Books, 2011), p. 107.
114. Michael S. Kimmel, 'Judaism, Masculinity and Feminism', in Harry Brod (ed.), *A Mensch Among Men: Explorations in Jewish Masculinity* (Freedom, CA: Crossing Press, 1988), p. 154.
115. Hoedl, 'Physical Characteristics'.
116. *Daily Mirror*, 17 October 1974.
117. *Bootsie and Snudge* (The Army Game), 'Civvy Street'. A winklepicker was a style of shoe worn from the 1950s onwards by British rock and roll fans. The feature that gave the shoe its name was the very long and sharp pointed toe.
118. Pettigrew, *British Film Character Actors,* p.19.
119. *Reynolds News*, 25 June 1961.
120. Ibid.
121. *Guardian*, 18 July 1987.
122. *The Times*, 18 July 1986.
123. *Jewish Chronicle*, 24 July 1987.

2

David Kossoff

David Kossoff was known as 'the Jewish uncle' figure of television.[1] His career comprised of three parts: an actor playing Jewish and non-Jewish roles, Bible commentator and in later years as a campaigner in his effort to rid the world of hard drugs that had killed his son. Kossoff was not a religious man in any formal definition of the term and yet in his 'three lives' he seemed to epitomize many people's ideas of an Old Testament prophet. Some of his greatest roles were playing elderly Jewish immigrant men (he specialized in aged characters even when he was still quite young) adopting the stereotypical Russian-Yiddish accents of those who lived in London's Jewish East End.[2]

By the time Kossoff was performing his Biblical and secular stories on stage and on the BBC, he had carved a role for himself that was as new to the British public as it was to the country's Jewish population. He was not appearing as a religious Jew but rather as a wise, kindly 'uncle' figure. As will emerge, Kossoff used his Jewishness to define his performing personality – the gentle Jew who portrayed a past world who was non-threatening. In his acting roles he depicted a nostalgia for the Eastern European world rather than political radicalism in any form.

Background

Kossoff was born on 24 November 1919. The youngest child of a poor Russian tailor, the poverty in which he grew up made him determined to carve out a better life for himself as well as proving invaluable background material for his career in the theatre and media.[3] His father Louis was born in Belarus in 1884 and came to England in 1910. His mother Annie, born in 1888, came from Warsaw and they met in London.[4] In the 1911 census, Louis Kossoff was living at 192 Jubilee Street, Mile End with his brother Hyman, a furrier, and Hyman's wife and two small children and working as a tailor's machinist.[5] The street that he lived in was on the fringes of the Jewish East End but the residents were 50 to 75 per cent Jewish.[6] At the time of the 1939 Register, Louis lived with his wife and three children at 28

Olinda Road, Hackney which was also not in the heart of the Jewish East End. This meant that as the area was more mixed, influences that were not solely Jewish would have had a bearing on Kossoff's life, as it had for Alfie Bass. The Register lists the family as Louis (ladies tailor machinist), Annie (not employed), Alex (warehouse stationer), Judie (ladies dress machinist) and David (precision woodwork draughtsman).[7]

Kossoff's father had a great influence on his life and work. He described his father somewhat romantically as a wonderful person; a Russian peasant with little education but with the right values. 'My father was a very wise man. A villager from Russia, an overworked tailor. He had the simple set of rules of a villager. He would tell me to always keep a dream in my pocket.'[8] Louis Kossoff would enthral his son with tales of Sholem Aleichem and his ability to tell stories evidently was passed down to his son who later found fame as a storyteller.[9]

It would appear that Kossoff did not come from a very Orthodox background or have a stringent Jewish education. This is borne out by his comment that he was quite ignorant about the Bible until he was approached by the BBC to contribute a Bible story for a programme. He chose the story of Jonah and the Whale and rewrote it.[10] 'Like most children I was subjected to the Bible too early in life. The difficult language put me off.' He added that he was not a very orthodox Jew, just someone who

6. Kossoff family, 1924 © Simon Kossoff

observed some of the festivals. Indeed, it must be emphasized that he was not a theologian but a professional entertainer and a good storyteller.[11]

Although most second generation East European Jews remained within the communal fold, they did not maintain the same emotional attachment

7. Kossoff with his brother and sister in 1940 © Simon Kossoff

to traditional religious observance that their parents had. School education exposed them to anglicising influences that weakened the hold of Old-World attachments. Fluent in English, even if Yiddish remained the language of their homes, and familiar with life outside the workshops and tenements of the immigrant quarter, and especially if they grew up on the fringes of that quarter (as Kossoff did), they became enthusiastic consumers of English popular culture. Communal and parental efforts to provide the new generation with a sound Jewish education often failed as immigrant parents struggling to survive in harsh economic climate wanted their children to acquire skills that would enable them to succeed and they assigned far more importance to their secular education than their religious one.[12]

Kossoff explains that as his father was a poor tailor, his headmaster put him in for scholarships with grants attached.[13] He won a scholarship for a design course at the London School of Architecture which indicated that there was no parental opposition to his enrolment. At 17 he decided that his family needed support, so he left college as a qualified draughtsman and started to design furniture. Meanwhile he dreamt of being in the theatre. He convinced a French café cook who had been a clown to teach him mime and he learnt from a children's elocution teacher how to use his voice.[14] Kossoff's family were not prepared for his new direction. 'I horrified my parents. I was 19 and earning three times the money my friends were getting which meant a lot to my father working day and night at his tailor's bench in the East End and still poor.'[15] Yet it was during this interwar period that second generation immigrants were branching out into other fields of work.

It was during this time that substantial numbers of men and women were entering occupations that brought them into intensive daily contact with the larger world. For a smaller number of the second generation there were two other paths out of the ghetto – the world of radical politics and the world of literature and art. Both were spheres of activity that stood outside the common run of everyday experience and above the usual divisions separating the mass of Jews from non-Jews. They were realms where both mixed more or less freely because the nature of the activity was universal, and the participants' background was irrelevant. Among second generation Jews who became alienated from Jewish observance there was a small minority who abandoned their ethnic roots as well. The commonest form of disengagement was intermarriage.[16] Three out of the four entertainers in this book – Alfie Bass, Warren Mitchell and David Kossoff – all met their non-Jewish wives whilst at Unity.

Kossoff and Unity Theatre

Kossoff joined Unity Theatre in 1942 where he encountered Alfie Bass, one of the first people to suggest that he become a full-time actor.[17] Although many joined Unity because of its left-wing political affiliations and the message that it wanted to bring to people through its work, there is no hard evidence that Kossoff had any direct Communist Party affiliation. His son Simon describes his father as a liberal and humane man, political with a small 'p' and reflects that it was highly unlikely that he was involved in the Communist Party as he worked in the United States without any problem during the Cold War period. He went to meetings of the Jewish anti-fascist movement before the War and it is probably within this mainstream East End milieu that he heard about Unity and the opportunities it might give him to advance his career.[18]

Kossoff's time at Unity was to change his life and his description of his time there as being where he 'came alive' indicates that he had found his true passion in acting.[19] Despite working alongside Alfie Bass, an active member of the Communist Party, both at Unity and at various times in his future career, Bass did not appear to have influenced him in terms of explicit left-wing ideology.

It was during his time at Unity that Kossoff wrote, directed and performed, often acting in front of scenery that he had designed, built and painted.[20] He appeared in *Spanish Village* in 1943, Unity's first classic production by Lope de Vega. The play, believed to have been written between 1612 and 1614, concerned a community who rose up against its tyrannical landlord, who had raped one of the villagers.[21] It documents the motivations behind the murder of the Chief Commander of the Calatrava, a military order founded in the twelfth century. The play was based on an historical event and Lope de Vega dramatizes the corruption of the Calatrava's leaders and the effects of the Commander's tyranny on the village of Fuenteovejuna. The Commander, while glorious in battle, lacked moral character and routinely captured and raped young women in the town. He raped the mayor's daughter Laurencia, and although the village was shocked they stood aside. But Laurencia spurred the town into action against him and he was murdered. The play was about people standing together against corruption, tyranny and abuse.[22] The choice of play showed Unity's international vision and use of history and Kossoff obviously had no objections to being involved in such a project.

Kossoff was discovered for the professional stage in 1945 whilst playing a Rabbi in *The Yellow Star*.[23] The play, written by Ted Willis, takes place in the Warsaw Ghetto under German occupation. *The Daily Worker* commented that it 'powerfully dramatizes the conflict between sadism and humanity' and pointed out that 'of special merit is the performance of David Kossoff'.[24] The theme of the play is the emergence of the new spirit of resistance amongst Polish Jews contrasted with the beginnings of the cracks and decay in the Nazi system. Among the Jewish characters there is uncertainty to begin with, together with subservience and defeatism, but gradually hope and a new will to fight emerges.[25]

The Yellow Star is set in a small town in western Poland in the late autumn of 1942 as the Nazis are moving rapidly towards Stalingrad. A Nazi commission arrives charged with organising the extermination of the Jewish population. The choice for the Jewish population is simple – resist or die. The dilemma is explored through the Rabbi, whose religious duty forbids him to kill and who takes some time to understand fully what the Nazis are planning.

At the start of the play the Rabbi approaches the Nazi commission to ask for help with the children who are dying in their hundreds from fever, hunger and cold. 'Not for ourselves sir. We understand that we are Jews, we understand that our lot is punishment and suffering. But our children, sir. They are young, they don't understand, they have done nothing.' The SS officer agrees to give rations of milk and to send medicine into the ghetto the next day and the Rabbi keeps thanking him. After he leaves the SS officer reveals that he was just lying to give false hope that night, 'the torture of hope'. Two days later, when no provisions have arrived, the Rabbi is under great emotional strain, and is unable to comfort a girl whose sister committed suicide rather than be taken by the Germans. 'I don't know my child. There is suffering for all'.[26]

The Rabbi is told by a young Jewish worker, David Levy, that all Jews are to be killed. David urges that they rise up against them. The Rabbi is against resistance: 'We will show them how to die.' David tries to convince him that 'there are over 5,000 of us...we must show them how we can live'. Yet the Rabbi adopts a fatalistic stance and begs him not to make things worse and that the situation is impossible. 'Against this what can we do? It is a punishment.'

A Russian prince, part of the Nazi commission, offers to sell the Rabbi some passes. The Rabbi considers accepting in order to let others escape. He is tempted but soon realizes that only the few that can afford to pay will be saved. 'May God forgive me for the thought! It was weak, petty, cowardly...No man's life is his own to sell. If he is free, his life belongs to his people; if he is a slave, his life belongs to a master.' He kills the Russian, egged on by his bragging about how last year he had 'roasted' a Rabbi in

Kiev: 'Don't know what I shall do when I have used all you Jews up.' The Rabbi kneels by the body: 'Curse them oh Lord, curse them. With all the curses which are written in the book of the law; cursed be they by day and cursed by night. See them apart from destruction.' He is subsequently arrested and does not flinch or struggle whilst they torture him. He learns of the threat of 200 hostages being executed in retaliation for the murder and confesses. 'He was willing to sell us our lives for money. I have never raised a finger against anyone...but I killed him and I am glad that I killed him.'[27]

Willis wanted to show both the nature of fascism and the journey of its victims from fatalism to resistance. The Rabbi appeared initially as a weak character but developed great strength. The individual courage of the Rabbi symbolized the necessity and the human cost of such resistance. Willis based his play on a newspaper story about a Rabbi in the Warsaw uprising. Kossoff's role in *The Yellow Star* portrayed radicalism and this would differ greatly from the roles that he would play in the future but, in this instance, Unity chose the play and cast. The play was a success, particularly for Kossoff.[28] It was through the strength of this performance that he was offered a repertory contract with the BBC in 1945 and his professional career began. He had shown, during his time at Unity, how he was able to take on a range of roles that were Jewish, non-Jewish, political, non-political, contemporary, historical, local and international. Yet for Kossoff it was the acting experience that was important for him rather than any personal or political beliefs. This is in contrast to Alfie Bass, who commented that he took pride in appearing in Unity for the political cause.[29]

Career

Early reports from the BBC drama department indicated that Kossoff was 'most comfortable in Jewish roles and was a natural Cockney.'[30] In this immediate post-war period it is interesting to note that being both Jewish and Cockney was acceptable and the BBC saw no differentiation, and how Kossoff's past acting experience showed that he could take on both identities. By this time the Jewish East End was starting to disintegrate due to bombings in the area during the Second World War. People were moving out and the second generation of immigrants were making their transition into everyday British life.

In an audition report dated 10 July 1945, it was written that Kossoff's 'slight Jewish accent had the most characterisation' and that although he had a lot to learn he would make a useful member of the repertory company. It was noted that he was a natural in Jewish and Cockney roles, his American accent was good, his Welsh passable but his Irish dialect poor. It was considered that he would not be of much use in straight acting work but had more than the average drive and attack and was intelligent and keen. Kossoff signed a contract on 26 September 1945 and went on to make many children's hour programmes between 1948 and 1950. Over the years he appeared in hundreds of radio plays including the sci-fi series *Journey into Space*. Kossoff's contract was terminated on 6 October 1951. A drama repertory department report commented that Kossoff was 'extremely good in certain parts but cannot be regarded as versatile'.[31]

8. David Kossoff and Robert Taylor on film location in Holland for *The House of the Seven Hawks* (1959), © Simon Kossoff

He then went freelance and in the next few years appeared in *The Love of Four Colonels* at the Wyndham's Theatre and the film *The Young Lovers* (1954), a British Cold War romance for which he won an award for promising newcomer. His many film appearances included the part of Carrington the junk dealer in the 1956 version of *1984*, the befuddled nuclear scientist in *The Mouse that Roared* (1959) and Freud's father in John Huston's *Freud* (1960). His last film was the comedy *Staggered* (1994).[32]

The BBC reconsidered their position in 1953 and reinstated Kossoff due to his ability, in their view, to portray Jewish folk humour. The BBC programmer Alan Sleath saw Kossoff perform in *The Bespoke Overcoat* at the Arts Theatre and wrote to his department on 20 April 1953 that Kossoff 'has a rich and rare fund of Jewish character studies and anecdotes which I believe would have a popular appeal to viewers'. This shows an early commitment to ethnic diversity and by selecting this genre, which was nostalgic and stereotypical of Jewish life, they chose what they felt would be comfortable for their viewers to watch. It was palatable entertainment and neither threatening nor challenging. Sleath had recognized the unique and naïve quality of Jewish humour.[33]

Jewish Folk Humour was televised on 26 September 1953. The announcement for the show was 'David Kossoff offers a programme of Jewish folk humour which he has chosen from his own collection'. Kossoff appeared as a Jewish tailor who sat by his work table sewing and humming. The tea bell rang, he put down his work, stretched and reached for his lunch. He began to talk on everyday matters to the other people in the room and then went on to tell stories from his grandfather's village. He continued until the bell rang and then he stopped and picked up his work.[34] This was quite a stereotypical way of presenting Jews to a non-Jewish audience and yet at the same time the tailor was involved in a normal work situation that viewers could relate to. During the years 1946 to 1955, the final years of BBC's monopoly of television broadcasting, the network produced a range of programmes that presented Jews, Jewishness and Judaism to a predominantly non-Jewish audience, but they were not always progressive or subtle in their representations. Indeed, some productions did elicit complaints from Jewish organizations because of their use of caricatures and stereotypes.[35]

Kossoff's childhood poverty and background enabled him to identity fully with the roles he became noted for in the next few years, especially *The Bespoke Overcoat* by Wolf Mankowitz.[36] Performed in 1953 at the Arts Theatre, Kossoff starred with his Unity contemporary Alfie Bass. The play was about poverty and exploitation and Kossoff played the part of Morry, a

9. David Kossoff in Italy whilst filming *Conspiracy of Hearts* (1960) © Simon Kossoff

poor tailor like his father. He also played Morry in the 1956 screen version of the play.

After reprising *The Bespoke Overcoat* with a Mankowitz comedy, *The Boychik,* at the Embassy Swiss Cottage in 1954, Kossoff played the narrator Mendel in *The World of Sholem Aleichem* (1955). He appeared in Wolf Mankowitz's *A Kid for Two Farthings* (1955), which was reminiscent of a *shtetl* (a small village in Eastern Europe) tale set in the world of the East End's Whitechapel Road, Petticoat Lane market and the clothing workshops. The film is sentimental, showing the East End in a nostalgic way, despite the fact that at this time rapid changes were taking place there. Kossoff is the elderly tailor Kandinsky and confidante of a young boy who buys a pet goat. We see through the young boy's eyes the little world in which he lives. He learns that a unicorn is a magic animal who can grant anybody's wish and he buys one for five shillings so that the people he loves can have what they desire to alleviate their difficulties in their impoverished lives.[37] These people include a strong man turned wrestler, a girl tired of her long engagement, a mother who longs for her husband's return and a varied assortment of people who live happily if precariously in the environs of Petticoat Lane.[38] The animal has only one discernible horn and the boy is encouraged to believe that it is a unicorn blessed with magical powers. The film won a British Oscar for the then Society of Films and Television Arts in 1956. The *Jewish Chronicle* commented that it was a beautifully acted serio-comedy of East End life in which Kossoff gives a sincere and moving performance.[39] *Today's Cinema* also gave praise: 'He combines hard work with a philosophic acceptance of life as he knows it and plays Kandinsky with genuine feeling.'[40]

Virtually every Jew has a mental image of the *shtetl*. These images are informed by a portrayal of life in a variety of media, from fiction to film. The tales of Sholem Aleichem and artist Marc Chagall's whimsical depictions of Jewish life with images of floating fiddlers contribute to the contemporary vision of the *shtetl*. Yet such a static representation of the populous and geographically dispersed Jewish communities of Eastern Europe does not reflect historical reality.[41] Thousands of *shtetls* existed in Eastern Europe at the turn of the century and while many of them shared a similar organizational structure, governed by a community council (*kahal*) that oversaw civil and religious affairs, they were not all the same as politics, dialect and religious customs varied. Yet for all the differences, the *shtetl* looms large in contemporary Jewish consciousness and that for the majority of Jews whose families originated from Eastern Europe the *shtetl* serves as a mythical point of origin, a colourful combination of religion and folk wisdom. And while *shtetl* life was inexorably changed by modernization, it was destroyed by the Holocaust. Thus, *shtetl* life is sanctified with an aura of martyrdom.[42]

Britain's television viewers had one of their first tastes of the richness, warmth and simplicity of Jewish folk humour and *shtetl* life during the peak viewing period on 26 September 1953, when Kossoff presented a one-man show. Kossoff, in the role of a typical old Jewish tailor, related a number of humorous, unsophisticated stories of the warm-hearted Jewish characters of Lublin which included Tovia the carpenter, Levy the *shochet* (ritual slaughterer) and the philosophical Herschel, still jesting though dying, with *Shema Yisrael*[43] on his lips.[44] He played many other Jewish roles throughout his career which included a Rabbi in the film *Conspiracy of Hearts* (1960), a story about Catholic nuns risking their lives to help smuggle Jewish children out of an internment camp near their convent in Italy during the Second World War so they can escape to Palestine; a member of a Yiddish Shakespearean acting troupe in Tsarist Russia in the BBC radio play *Jericho Players* by Bernard Kops (1996) and a retired American Jewish businessman starring opposite the American entertainer Eartha Kitt in *Bunny* (1972), in which 'he played the same old kindly Jewish gentleman he often plays'.[45] The portrayal of the 'old kindly Jewish gentleman' permeates throughout his roles, whether he is portraying someone from a past *shtetl* life or a modern day era; he is always sentimental and non-threatening.

In the 1960s, he starred in a Granada TV comedy *Little Big Business* as Marcus Lieberman, a wise but stubborn Jewish furniture maker and master craftsman. Having arrived in England some years before as an impoverished Latvian immigrant, Marcus was, with some justification, proud of the fact that he had built a thriving business for himself. However, when he introduced his educated but equally ambitious son Simon into the business, he was forced to modernise.[46] The show was a gentle generation gap comedy full of Jewish humour and inspired by Kossoff's own experiences of working in the furniture trade prior to becoming an actor. Once again, he was portraying essentially a non-political sentimental Jewish role, and this was repeated in *The Bespoke Overcoat*.

The Bespoke Overcoat (1955)

Kossoff appeared as the poor philosophical tailor Morry in *The Bespoke Overcoat* (1955), described in the chapter on Alfie Bass. The film opens with Fender (Bass) being taken to the cemetery on a wheelbarrow. The only mourner is Morry who returns to his workshop to light a memorial candle and to recollect his friend, who died before the coat he was making him was finished.[47] The play is a reminder of the abject poverty faced by the Jewish community in the East End and the friendships between people in this situation. It showed the humanity and poignancy of friendship and the unhappiness of unlucky men; the world of Jewish poverty and clannish bonding.[48] Love is a luxury which very poor people can afford, and *The Bespoke Overcoat* is a story of this intimate human bond. It is not a love which conquers all. Fender does not get enough food or a tailor-made overcoat in this life. He does not find satisfaction, except insofar as he is able to accept with humour and humility the deprivations forced upon him. It is because this humour and humility is shared with his friend that Fender, in spite of everything, would prefer to go on living. To prefer to go on living is to love in the context of this tale, and because this is loving at its most deprived the story is a sad one.[49]

Joseph McCulloch, rector of St Mary le Bow Church, London believes that in his role as Morry, Kossoff is the person who above all others

10. Kossoff as Morry the tailor in *The Bespoke Overcoat* (1955) © Wolfgang Suschitzky

conveyed to him a sense of the humanity of the Old Testament and that *The Bespoke Overcoat* is the greatest film ever made for its beauty and all the qualities you look for in great art. 'If Rembrandt was still alive he would have painted every shot.'[50] McCulloch admires *The Bespoke Overcoat* for its human compassion that Kossoff conveys. Kossoff explains that it is a love story, of a selfless love that only the very poor can afford, and that Mankowitz drew on memories of his own early years. 'We were contemporaries. We were both very poor from the East End and he remembered that there is a particular love that is enjoyed by people who can afford nothing else. That is what *The Bespoke Overcoat* is all about.'[51] Again Kossoff played a sentimental role in a film that was full of nostalgia for the Jewish East End that was fast fading, and a form of Old Testament Judaism that was equally non-threatening.

The dialogue between the two men is spoken in English with a Yiddish accent and again Kossoff speaks in the stereotypical manner the audience would expect a Jewish immigrant to speak. This is considered to be a linguistic bridge between languages. As Yiddish speakers traded one language for another, they invariably entered the new one with the accent of the old, wrapping their English in the warm lilting tones of Yiddish. By intertwining certain linguistic features into their speech, Yiddish speakers created their own variant of English,[52] resulting in the use of certain words and catchphrases.

The following exchange relates to Morry lighting the memorial candle for Fender and talking to himself:

Morry: Fender dead. That old man Fender dead. Funny thing. You're a good tailor, he used to say. You're a good tailor. *Nu*, your're a good tailor.[53]

In the scene when Fender comes to cancel the coat as he has lost his job and is unable to make payment:

Fender: That Ranting. He give me the sack.
Morry: After so long he give you the sack?
Fender: He give me.
Morry: Give it to you?
Fender: The sack.
Morry: *Oi*.[54]

The 'Faginy' Yiddish accent marks the stage Jew as different, as not really belonging to cultivated British society with its Oxbridge accent. In addition to portraying a 'Jewish' way of speaking, the film contained Jewish humour, despite the sad tale. Humour is the emotive language of Yiddish speaking immigrant culture. The musicality of the language and the penchant for physical and facial gesticulation all contribute to humour once

11. David Kossoff and Alfie Bass in *The Bespoke Overcoat* (1955) © Wolfgang Suschitzky

such an accent is inserted into the language of a stiffer Anglo-Saxon culture.[55]

In *The Bespoke Overcoat* there is humour and banter between the two men, such as when Morry first sees Fender in ghost form:

Morry: You not dead?

Fender: Sure I'm dead. Would I sit here in the freezing cold if I weren't dead?[56]

In the scene when Fender comes to see how Morry is progressing with the coat and Morry suggests that he tries it on, Fender is embarrassed to take off his old coat: 'What's a matter with you? You're a film starlet, you got to have a changing room else you can't take off the old coat?'[57] This is also present when Morry tries to convince Fender to buy a coat: 'I use a lovely lining; someone else would make a wedding dress from it, such a lining I use.'[58]

Jewish humour is humour created by Jews and reflects some aspects of Jewish life. It has some particularities distinguishing it from other national or ethnic styles of humour. It has deep and ancient roots found in the Bible, but it has long fulfilled an important role in Jewish life and the Jewish quest for survival during their long history as a persecuted minority. Among the many ways Jews learned to deal and cope with sad and terrible realities, humour holds a special place. It helps change, if only for a short while, the sadness of reality, twisting it into something funny and more bearable. The *shtetls* inhabited by the Eastern European Jews produced many comic figures that feature in the work of Sholem Aleichem. The *schlemiel* (the poor soul who spills his bowl of soup) and the *schlimazel* (the person he spills it on) are two such figures.[59] Poverty, fear and persecution were part of daily life and Sholem Aleichem's humour helped people to cope. By creating lovable and funny characters typical of *shtetl* life, laughing at their difficulties and knowing that they will pass and that things could be worse encouraged a certain optimism, making coping a bit easier.[60]

The humour of Sholem Aleichem has been characterized as a gracious way to overcome an unpleasant situation in which one finds oneself through no fault of one's own. It soothes the pain of a perplexing or degrading situation with inner spiritual power derived from faith in the dignity of man and in the ultimate victory of justice. Even in the most hopeless of situations such humour feigns victory in order to emphasize the meaninglessness, evil and unnaturalness of the predicament. The kind of characters that Aleichem creates such as Tevye the dairyman, Menachem Mendel and Motl and the kind of laughter he evokes, the laughter of acceptance, friendship, sympathy is essential to human dignity and sanity. Laughter is a tactic for human survival.[61]

In many ways Fender and Morry are reminiscent of characters found in Sholem Aleichem's tales. Kossoff did play these characters and appeared in *The World of Sholem Aleichem* at the Swiss Cottage Embassy Theatre in 1955. *The Stage* praised Kossoff's performance as narrator Mendel 'an itinerant bookseller of rich humour and human feeling who acts as a kind of narrator and commentator'.[62]

Throughout *The Bespoke Overcoat* there is the warmth of male friendship. Morry shows great kindness and despite his financial difficulties offers to make Fender the coat for cost:

> The trade is not good any more. Believe me, if I had a boy I wouldn't let him see a needle and thread. Things are so bad now, you know what I am doing? I'm making a ten pound coat for Fender. For ten pounds it's a wonderful coat.[63]

He badly needs some money on account and asks Fender for a few pounds. Yet he is concerned that this might be a problem: 'Can you manage a couple?'[64] After Fender loses his job, Morry assures him that he will finish the coat without payment. Morry shows understanding when Fender is embarrassed to take off his coat as his shirt is in shreds and tells Morry that he would have put on the only other shirt he owns, the one saved for best, if he had known.

> Morry: And why should you? Today is a bank holiday? Look. My own shirt. Everybody wears his own shirt for a working day.[65]

Yet Morry feels guilt over Fender's death:

> Believe me if I known you would have catched a cold and died I would have given you *mein* own coat.[66]

He also comments 'I done my best by you Fender, didn't I?' as he recites the memorial prayer.[67] Kossoff's performance throughout is given with such pathos and draws on the poor East End immigrant background that he came from.

The Larkins

Yet Kossoff did not excel in purely Jewish characterisations, which perhaps reflects his own background and life story. In contrast was his performance in *The Larkins*. *The Larkins* was a situation comedy about a lively non-Jewish Cockney family that was broadcast in six series (40 episodes) from 1958-64, three years after ITV's launch. The Larkins family consisted of hen-pecked dad Alf (David Kossoff), who worked in the canteen at a plastics factory, his battle-axe wife Ada (Peggy Mount), unemployable son Eddie and daughter Joyce with her American husband Jeff Rogers, an out of work writer of cowboy comics. They lived next door to inquisitive neighbour Hetty Pout, her husband Sam and daughter Myrtle who had a crush on Eddie. Together they find themselves in a variety of farcical situations.[68]

Although there was no Jewish content in the show, Kossoff identified himself as a Cockney. When talking about a one-man show he put on for Unity Theatre in 1963 to raise funds for the theatre, he mentioned that half the show was comprised of a series of cameos that he had written about

Eastern Europe. 'You see, although I'm a Cockney, my parents come from Lithuania.'[69] In conjunction with *The Larkins*, Kossoff recorded '*Larking About – A Cockney Sing A-long*' with the Mike Sammes Singers featuring songs such as '*Knock'd 'em in the Old Kent Road*' and '*I'm Shy Mary Ellen, I'm Shy*'.[70]

The Larkins was one of ITV's most popular early situation comedies (sitcoms). When commercial television came to Britain in September 1955 it spelt the end of the BBC's monopoly as sole supplier of home entertainment and was a trigger for radio becoming the lesser medium within a few years. The public quickly embraced the American programming style and it did not take long for American sitcoms such as *I Love Lucy*, *The Jack Benny Program* and *Sergeant Bilko* to inspire local counterparts such as *The Larkins*. A sitcom takes a routine situation and fills it with characters an audience can relate to and share many experiences with. The humour may be visual but is more likely to stem from the interaction of the characters as they cope with the situation.[71] Novelist David Lodge considers sitcoms to be light family entertainment, which aims to amuse and divert the viewers, not to disturb and distress them.[72]

The majority of sitcoms on British television (Britcoms) have been home grown and the situations firmly anchored in British society. They reflected an evolving variety of everyday concerns, characteristics and preoccupations, one of the most abiding of which was the issue of social class. When the Britcom was born, class awareness was not just alive and well but bordering on a national obsession, as Orwell had implied in 1941 when referring to England as the most class-ridden society under the sun.[73] The Britcom's subject matter was not the important thoughts, decisions and deeds of the great and the good, but rather the minor tribulations of ordinary people, like the viewers, whose trivial problems are resolved. Each episode has a happy ending or, at least finishes with the restoration of order which can then be disrupted once more in the next episode thereby starting the whole process again. The audience may realize that as the domestic problems they see on screen are similar to their own they are not alone in having to cope with such difficulties.[74]

Most series contain more or less clear markers which help viewers to readily identify the status of the characters and to judge whether they themselves are higher or lower on the social spectrum than the fictional characters. There are markers that are reasonably reliable, such as housing and language. As language can reflect a level of education its potential for social differentiation is considerable. In Britcoms, a strong local accent often suggests a lower level of education and a lack of contact with others from outside the same geographical area or social stratum, similarly ungrammatical expressions and errors of pronunciation, including the dreaded dropped or stray aitches, are typical of many working-class Britcom characters.[75]

Although the Larkins were not Jewish, Kossoff played Alf with a Cockney accent with ease and it would seem that his working-class Jewish East End background stood him in good stead. In addition, Alf's actions and the situations he got himself into were in some ways a reminder of the *schlemiel* and the *schlimazel* from Sholem Aleichem stories. Kossoff was able to incorporate and blend their actions into scenes with no Jewish story line.

Performance: Mannerisms and Masculinity

In the episode 'Wide Open House' he is asked by his wife to hang a banner to welcome home his son Eddie from the army. He is unable to do so, falls off the ladder and bursts the balloons. In 'Christmas with the Larkins' he forgets to bring home the turkey from the butcher and when he returns to the shop it has been sold. He therefore brings home a frozen turkey which he tries to defrost with disastrous results. He is not portrayed as a strong male. His campaign against having a television in the house in 'Telly Ho' and not wanting a pet cat in 'Cat Happy' are overruled by his wife and his struggle to stand up to her result in slapstick comedy.[76] Although portrayed as a rather weak and ineffectual character, he is always extremely likeable. These types of roles were similar to those played by Alfie Bass.

David Kossoff was not ashamed to let the world know his Jewish origins.[77] His Jewish persona was so entrenched in all that he did, it was comfortable and natural for him to extend it to non-Jewish roles. What the roles did have in common was that Kossoff, as did Bass, portrayed a non-threatening masculinity. The rabbis of the Talmudic era established 2,000 years ago a distinctive, non-phallic, gentle, timid and studious mode of masculinity – *Edelkayt* – which resisted norms of a martial manhood from ancient times to the twentieth century. This confirmed, in a way, the European stereotype of the feminized Jewish man.[78] This gentle masculinity can be seen in both *The Bespoke Overcoat* and *The Larkins*.

The Bespoke Overcoat was directed by a non-Jewish film maker Jack Clayton and there are some inaccuracies within the film which probably would not have been made by a Jewish film maker. Morry attends the burial of his friend Fender who was an orthodox Jew and at the cemetery he is the only mourner. As ten men are required for a *minyan* (a quorum of ten men aged over 13 for Jewish worship) this would have been highly unlikely.

Morry throws the bespoke overcoat that he made for Fender into the grave and this is also not customary but used for dramatic effect. Men are only buried with their prayer shawls which are rendered ineffective by cutting off one of the fringes.[79] The above would indicate that the film was intended for general release. Kossoff's performance is at times a caricature of an immigrant Jewish tailor speaking heavily accented and ungrammatical English with exaggerated hand movements and would suggest that he was producing an image of a Jew that a non-Jewish audience expected.

Varying arm and hand movements are constantly used. In one of the opening scenes, after he has returned home from the funeral, Morry says:

> Fender dead. That old man Fender dead. Funny thing. You're a good tailor he used to say. You're a good tailor. *Nu*, you're a good tailor. Look around. I don't care where you look, he says, you're a number one tailor.

As he speaks he points his finger in confirmation. In the scene where Fender comes to Morry to ask him to mend his overcoat, Morry responds:

> So Fender. The seams is all rotten. Look the lining is like ribbons. It can't be done. If I say it can't be done it can't be done.

His right arm goes out to make the point. He also uses a clenched fist for additional emphasis:

> Fender, listen to me Fender. A good coat like I make has got 20 years. I use good material. The best. I use a lovely lining. Someone else would make a wedding dress from it, such a lining I use.

He uses his arms in a particular way when he is confident. They are either placed on his hip – 'Fender for you I would make such a coat' – or folded. In the scene, when Morry and Fender go one night to the warehouse to steal a coat, Morry is in a buoyant mood, fuelled by alcohol. He folds his arms as he teases Fender as to whether he can walk through the wall as he is a ghost.

When showing kindness and concern to Fender, he looks him straight in the eye and leans towards him, often touching his arm, saying softly: 'Believe me you are cold.' He frequently uses Fender's name, usually towards the beginning of the sentence, when talking to him which adds an intimacy to their dialogue.

His head movements indicate contrasting moods. When sad, he hangs his head, such as during the funeral service. In contrast, when he wants to appear positive, he either puts his head to one side and smiles, such as when he tells Fender he will make him a bespoke overcoat, or looks at him directly and smiles, when he suggests what material he will use and goes through the options.

In moments of reflection, he moves his head from side to side, such as when he thinks about the hard times that he has fallen on:

> Trades no good anymore. In the old days it would be six clients a week, a coat, a suit, a spare pair of trousers, something. If I had a boy I wouldn't let him see a needle and thread.

Talking to himself, 'Fender, dead, that old man Fender', he gives a slight smile and raises his eyebrows. His eyebrows are raised when he mutters: 'I've got troubles enough.' At times where he is uncertain, he adopts various stances. He drops his head and looks to the side or puts his hand to the side of his face or his hands go to his chest: 'That lousy brandy it can kill you.' A repetition of a phrase emphasizes his uncertainty: 'I done my best by you Fender, didn't I? Didn't I?'[80] Kossoff plays the part with 'Jewish' exaggeration. At the time the film was made Jewish screen characters were divided between comic stereotypes (usually bookies and market traders; massive domineering mothers and downtrodden sons) and saintly stereotypes (noble rabbis or philosophical tailors). All of them talked with their hands, their shoulders or Cockney-Jewish accents.[81]

The following dialogues have a Jewish cadence. Fender tells Morry that if he didn't spend so much money on brandy, he would be rich. Morry considers what he would do with the money: 'I can take an off licence. I use my knowledge. A special line in brandy.' When Fender asks him how he would know it was good, he replies: 'I try every bottle, personal. I put up a smart notice. Morry's Napoleon brandy; every bottle personal tasted.' In the following, Kossoff adds extra Jewish intonation to the original text:

> Fender, You don't hold that overcoat against me, do you Fender? You ain't going to haunt me Fender? Believe me if I had known you would catched a cold and died I would have given you *mein* old coat.

In the play *The Bespoke Overcoat*, the text reads 'I would give you *my* own coat'.[82]

A particularly 'Jewish' way of talking is to end a sentence with a question, such as:

> Fender, you like the coat? What about a couple of pounds on account?
> I got expenses? Can you manage a couple?
> Listen Fender, I break my neck for the coat. You got ten pound?
> I hope you don't mind me being personal when I say what more do you want of my life?[83]

The ease with which he speaks in such a 'Jewish' way would suggest that Kossoff was drawing on memories that he had of his father and grandfather and the Jewish folk tales and humour that he heard from them.[84] Wolf Mankowitz, author of *The Bespoke Overcoat*, comments that by the time the film was made the East End Jewish community had virtually disappeared.[85] Kossoff, as with his other roles mentioned above, is steeped in nostalgia. He shows a Jewish East End of the past and does not touch on issues about the class struggle or politics that were prevalent in the area. Kossoff portrays Morry as a human being with goodness, weakness and sorrow. The conversation that passes between the two men is wholly Jewish in feeling, stress being laid on human dignity, compassion, a cheerful acceptance of adversity and a deep and abiding faith in a hereafter in which pain and sorrow vanish for ever.[86]

Kossoff brings Jewish stereotypical mannerisms into his non-Jewish roles and Jewish gestures appear in his performance in *The Larkins* in which he plays Alf, a non-Jewish Cockney. Media historian Susan Murray considers that although a performer's particular ethnic identity was rarely addressed outright in television, traces of many of the stars' Jewishness was embedded in their personas and performance styles, such as subtle inflections and gestures.[87] This was the case with Kossoff's performance in *The Larkins* and as seen in the episode 'Wide Open House' broadcast on 19 September 1958.

This episode centres around Alf's wife Ada preparing a party for her son's homecoming from the army that involves great effort and expense much to Alf's disapproval. He makes great use of hand gestures. When asking 'Where is the money coming from?' his hands go back and forth to make a point and he clenches his fist. His hand movements also reflect whether he is confident or not. When confident and wanting to stand his ground, he folds his arms, his head often goes back or he puts his hands on his hips. When making a point he moves his arms. When he is nervous his hands are close to his body.

In the scene where he is standing outside his house looking at the banner that says 'Welcome home Eddy' which he also does not approve of, he stands confidently talking to his son-in-law about all the fuss. He exclaims 'This is ridiculous' as he points to the sign. His hands then go on his hip as he says: 'I never had none of this when I came home from the army.' This hand positioning is a sign of confidence. He is also self-assured when he is talking just in the presence of other men. Taking on a role of responsibility also affects his movements. When determined to sort out a situation, such as learning that Ada has gone to great expense to hire a four-piece band and he wants to stop her, he sets off to find her, taking great strides and swinging his arms.

In Ada's presence he is less bold. When he tries to stand up to her, he pulls himself up and puffs out his chest: 'Ada will you listen to me?' He starts by being assertive with a determined voice and with his hands on his hips: 'Ada will you listen to me for one minute? A four piece band? Why do you want to go to all this rigmarole?' Yet within a short time he backs down as she takes no notice of him. He tries again: 'Will you listen to me Ada? Will you listen to me Ada?' He repeats himself twice but to no avail. His head goes to the side.

The following is a scene which again illustrates loss of confidence. Alf discovers that the army police are outside the house and he assumes that they are coming to arrest his son Eddie. He tells his son-in-law: 'We've got to keep them out at all cost. We can't have him arrested in front of all the neighbours. Think of the shame. The shock will kill his mother'. His voice speeds up, and, as he gets excited, he raises his shoulders and then brings his hands together in a very Jewish movement. When assuming charge of a situation his voice becomes louder.

His whole demeanour changes when Ada appears a few seconds later. She answers the door despite Alf imploring her not to. She lets the army men in as she thinks that they are Eddie's friends and have just come to join the party. Alf appears to shrivel in her presence and stoops forward. On many occasions when he speaks to Ada directly, he leans forward to speak. When she is around, unlike his confident stance in front of men, his arms flap. In every episode, despite trying to promote himself, he portrays a weak and rather feminine masculinity. This corresponds to the masculinity portrayed by Alfie Bass.

Although portraying a non-Jewish Cockney, Kossoff infuses Jewish intonation into his speech. In commenting on the preparations for the party, he still quips: 'What do we have here, a carnival?' When Ada makes him go up a ladder to put up the decorations, he says: 'What am I, a monument?'

When discussing his rather helpless son to whom Ada gives great credit, he remarks: 'We've got a genius in the family?' In addition, he reacts to what others say with hand gestures and answers questions with other questions. Throughout the episode he uses his hands more than anyone else and has constantly changing facial expressions in stark contrast to his son-in-law who remains deadpan throughout.[88] Jewish intonations and facial movements in a non-Jewish Cockney role were also used by Bass in *The Army Game* as discussed in the previous chapter. Although both frequently move their heads from side to side when making a point, there are subtle differences: Kossoff makes more physical movement with his arms whereas Bass concentrates more on moving his eyebrows up and down. In terms of Jewish intonation, the 'Faginy' Yiddish accent,[89] Kossoff takes on a more exaggerated tone than Bass and although in his personal life he converted to Christianity, professionally he plays the slightly more stereotypical Jew and is always non-threatening.

Storyteller

The above examples illustrate Kossoff's roles as an actor. However, he achieved even greater fame as a storyteller in the 1960s for his simple and humorous paraphrasing of the Bible into his own stories, which he read on BBC television and radio in the rich tones of an understated Jewish comedian.[90] The stories he wrote were an overwhelming success and he started to receive up to 500 fan letters a week. He admitted that he had not opened a Bible for 20 years until he was asked to do the programme and he then became obsessed with the wealth of material. He explained that he was not a very orthodox Jew, just someone who observed some of the festivals. He was not a theologian but a professional entertainer and a good storyteller.[91]

It was when he began reading the Bible seriously for source material that he discovered a great treasure. He considered what he did in translating the stories into contemporary language was 'so simple that it was idiotic'.[92] He received many accolades for his Bible story interpretations including 'he has taken on the aura of a Jewish saint with his rewriting Bible stories'[93] and emerged as a leading writer of great stories in which the heroes and villains are Old Testament characters 'all vividly brought to life by this Londoner of Russian ancestry'.[94] Kossoff acknowledged that he received a great many letters from people who said his material had uncovered 'a hunger' and emptiness in their lives.[95]

Kossoff valued simplicity in life. He commented that the original set of rules were God-given but all the subsequent 'embroideries' had been made by man and that life had become complicated by living in a competitive society. He also reflected that we complicate our lives as every time we meet someone who does not believe exactly as we believe or who does things differently, we come back with a different idea. 'We should try and simplify and get rid of the balls and the chains. It is sad to think that more people have been killed through religious arguments over the last 1,000 years than for any other reason. Humility is a wonderful thing.' Humility could only be taught by personal example and he acknowledged that was what his father had shown him.[96]

As a result of the great success of Kossoff's Old Testament stories, the BBC started to receive many letters requesting that he used the same formula for the New Testament. Kossoff admitted that he was not comfortable with this request as he was Jewish. He eventually consulted a priest who worked at the BBC about whether his use of the New Testament as source material was appropriate. The priest reminded him that Jesus was Jewish and that only a Jew could interpret the parables of Jesus. Kossoff commented that rabbinic commentaries had been compared to the parables.[97]

Kossoff then branched out further by writing *The Book of Witnesses*. The 'witnesses' of the title are several dozen fictional characters whose lives were at some point affected by the historical Jesus at different stages of his life as infant child, preacher and prophet and finally as a victim. The various accounts given by these characters in the first person, such as Jonas the drunk at a wedding, describe their contact with Jesus and the impact upon their lives. They, the narrators, as well as their accounts are the product of Kossoff's imagination although they fit within the framework of the Gospels and their style varies according to the situation of the narrator. 'It cannot be denied that the witnesses are fictional but that of which they speak is true. It is the Gospel', said Kossoff.[98]

Kossoff explained that he did not approach the Gospels as a theologian as he was an actor not a preacher. 'The whole book showed me that there are always faces in the crowd. All you had to do was find them.' He reflected that by the end he learnt a lot about Jesus and the people around him and that Jesus was the purest Jew that ever lived. 'But for the Jews the story of his life and his doings are not essential as they are a people who on the face of it are more interested in their religion than any other.' He spoke about Judaism at the time of Jesus and how it had become just a book of rules understood by the priests and was also very legalistic. 'A vast book of rules that people didn't understand. It was as if lawyers were running the world. And then along came a simple speaker who had a common touch and who got into serious trouble. Much the same thing would happen today.'[99] Kossoff's comments reflect a serious and spiritual man whose concerns are

12. David Kossoff, 1970 © Simon Kossoff

for simplicity and spirituality. He also mentioned visiting Israel where he received great spiritual refreshment as well as his love of sitting in churches to surround himself with loneliness and clarity. He subsequently converted to Christianity.[100]

Historian T. M. Endelman considers the reasons why Jews left Judaism. For some, it was the hope of improving their lives and those of their children when they realized that it would be easier to leave the liabilities of their origins behind them. It was social acceptance that the radically assimilated craved.[101] Career choice and economic status often determined who was going to convert. For Jews who entered into new occupational spheres, such as the civil service, law or science, baptism was 'either a prerequisite for admission and advancement or an emotionally and socially prudent adjustment to new circumstances'.[102] On why the insistence that Jews become Christians if they want to be accepted, Endelman is of the opinion that it is to be found in the fundamental contradiction that lay at the heart of emancipation itself: the conviction, often articulated, that Jews become worthy of incorporation only when they ceased to be Jews.[103] However, becoming Christian in the twentieth century was not a bid for status or an escape from poverty.[104] Kossoff was not changing his religion to escape the disabilities of being Jewish. It would appear that his change of religion was probably more an outcome of spiritual illumination and philosophical reflection. Perhaps his new-found faith gave some comfort when he experienced a great tragedy in 1976.

His 25 year-old son Paul, a heroin addict and the lead guitarist in the rock band Free, died of drug-induced heart failure. After his son's death Kossoff established the Paul Kossoff Foundation which aimed to present the realities of drug addiction to children. He campaigned against drugs in the late 1970s and early 1980s with his one-man show *The Late Great Paul* about the death of his son and the effect on his family. 'It was far from maudlin. He told jokes, enthralled audiences in professional theatres and small village halls with his folk tales. With a white beard and the wisdom he dispenses, he seemed more like a Rabbi than ever.'[105] In some respects he became quite evangelical in his quest to combat drugs. He had a 'cause' that was neither Jewish nor class linked but he was trying to change the world in the form of radical campaigning. The fervour in which he campaigned could have been inspired by the political radicalism he saw during his Unity days and although it lacks any specific Jewish or socialist underpinning, such as in the case of Bass, it shows that Unity's influence had not totally left him.

***

Despite playing many Jewish roles, Kossoff was never a religious Jew. He believed in God but was in no sense devout. His first marriage, which only lasted a short time, was to a Jewish girl but his second wife, Margaret Jenkins, was not Jewish. They met whilst they were both at Unity and married in 1947. She was the mother of his two sons and they lived in Golders Green. This is an area in north-west London with a large Jewish community. After the First World War Jewish families began moving from the East End into the new housing and synagogues were built to serve the community. When the boys were growing up he belonged to the local reform synagogue but did not take up any synagogue membership when he moved out of London to Hertfordshire.[106] Yet it is interesting to note that he chose to live with his family in a Jewish area. His son Simon explained that his father was not dogmatic. He did not rush down to synagogue on a Saturday morning but was proud to be on stage showing his Jewish heritage. 'He was a Jew without dogma.' His siblings, Alec and Sadie, married Jews and were more conventional.[107] Paradoxically, he did convert to Christianity which suggests that he did rely on some form of spirituality but that for him Judaism did not suffice.

Nevertheless, the Jewish world and culture of Eastern Europe permeated much of what he did. Many of the stories and short plays he used were from the Yiddish writer Sholem Aleichem, whose writings he translated. 'My father used to read his stories to us. As soon as he started he became transformed. He was no longer a simple tailor but a performer. This is the quality of Sholem Aleichem's writing. He was the number one spokesman for the immigrant and the oppressed.' [108] Despite this comment, which could have encouraged him to take an active part politically to change the impoverished lives of those living in the East End, he uses Sholem Aleichem's work to create a nostalgic vision of the East End, resembling Eastern Europe and to conjure up a lost world rather than look towards the future. In this way he was a contrast to Bass. Although they had starred together in *The Bespoke Overcoat* where they had both portrayed the pathos of the oppressed immigrant and were subsequently gentle non-threatening Jewish Cockneys in their television careers, Bass retained his political radicalism during his mainstream career whereas for Kossoff it was of no importance.

With Kossoff's dramatic roles as a Jewish tailor and Rabbi, his Jewish background was evident to all those who saw him. The *Jewish Chronicle* commented that his reputation stood high in the world of British entertainment and that he was not ashamed to let all the world know his Jewish origin.[109] In his choice of anecdotes and music for the programme

Desert Island Discs in 1964, he chose the record *Hava Nagila* sung by Harry Belafonte as his record of choice.[110] It was also on this programme that he acknowledged that Unity Theatre had given him the first wonderful opportunity to pursue his dream.[111]

David Kossoff died on 23 March 2005. The *Jewish Chronicle* noted that 'he carved out a role for himself that was new to the British public as it was to the country's Jewish community – that of the popular performer whose Jewishness was central to his act.'[112] He was the gentle Jew and in many ways the wise Rabbi. He used the same voice and mannerisms for both his telling of Bible stories and the performances about his son's life.[113] He spoke clearly and slowly, totally composed and with no exaggerated movements. In many ways he took on the role of the ideal Jewish male, the Rabbi or Talmudic student, of early modern Eastern Europe, the gentle and studious male whose origins were deeply rooted in traditional Jewish culture going back at least in part to the Babylonian Talmud.[114] He was a particular 'model' of a second generation: assimilationist, non-radical but still a Jewish Cockney and Jewish 'uncle' figure.

Notes

1. *Daily Express*, 9 October 1978.
2. Ibid.
3. *Guardian*, 24 March 2005.
4. Simon Kossoff: Interview with Isabelle Seddon, 2 December 2016, London.
5. 1911 Census, National Archives.
6. C. Russell and H. S. Lewis, *The Jew in London: A Study of Racial Character and Present Day Conditions* (London: T. Fisher Unwin, 1901).
7. 1939 Register, National Archives.
8. Bow Dialogues, Reverend Joseph McCulloch and David Kossoff, 23 August 1966, Sound Archives, British Library, C812/15.
9. Sholem Aleichem (1859–1916) was one of the founding fathers of modern Yiddish literature. A supreme Jewish humorist, he tapped into the energies of the East European spoken idiom and invented modern Jewish archetypes, myths and fables that had universal appeal.
10. *Jewish Chronicle*, 13 October 2000.
11. *Daily Express*, 16 October 1968.
12. T. M. Endelman, *Radical Assimilation in English Jewish History 1656-1945* (Bloomington: Indiana University Press, 1990), pp. 176–7.
13. *Birmingham Post*, 28 November 1972.
14. *North-Western Evening Mail*, 19 December 1959.
15. *Daily Express*, 20 June 1965.
16. Endelman, *Radical Assimilation in English Jewish History 1656-1945*, pp. 179, 181, 184.
17. *North-Western Evening Mail*, 19 December 1959.
18. Simon Kossoff: Interview with Isabelle Seddon, 2 December 2016, London.

19. Colin Chambers, *The Story of Unity Theatre* (London: Lawrence & Wishart, 1989), p. 257.
20. Ibid.
21. Ibid., p. 237.
22. www.stageagent.com, accessed 23 July 2018.
23. *TV Mirror*, 25 October 1958.
24. *Daily Worker*, 9 April 1942.
25. Ted Willis, *The Yellow Star*, V & A Theatre Archive THM/9/7169.
26. Ibid.
27. Ibid.
28. Ibid., pp. 256–7.
29. Ibid., p. 126.
30. David Kossoff file 1945-1953, BBC Written Archives Centre.
31. Ibid.
32. www.imdb.com, accessed 10 July 2018.
33. David Kossoff file 1945–1953, BBC Written Archives Centre.
34. Ibid.
35. James Jordan, 'Another Man's Faith? The Image of Judaism in the BBC Television Series Men Seeking God', in Hannah Ewence and Helen Spurling (eds),*Visualising Jews Through the Ages: Literary and Material Representations of Jewishness and Judaism* (Oxford: Routledge, 2015), p. 248.
36. Wolf Mankowitz (1924–98) was born in the Jewish East End. This background provided him with the material for three famous novels *Make Me An Offer, My Old Man's A Dustman* and *A Kid For Two Farthings,* which was adapted as a film by director Carol Reed in 1955. In 1958 he wrote the book for the hit West End musical *Expresso Bongo*. His remarkable output included novels, plays, historical studies and screenplays for many films which received awards including the Oscar, Bafta and the Cannes Grand Prix. www.bloomsbury.com, accessed 30 June 2018.
37. *Jewish Chronicle*, 13 May 1955.
38. *Today's Cinema*, 21 April 1955.
39. *Jewish Chronicle*, 13 May 1955.
40. *Today's Cinema*, 21 April 1955.
41. Joellyn Zollman, 'What Were Shtetls?' www.myjewishlearning.com, accessed 30 August 2018.
42. Ibid.
43. Shema Yisrael ('Hear O Israel') are the first two words of a morning and evening prayer ('Hear O Israel, God is our Lord, God is one') and is traditionally a Jew's last words on earth. www.chabad.org, accessed 15 June 2018.
44. *Jewish Chronicle*, 2 October 1953.
45. *Jewish Chronicle*, 22 December 1972.
46. www.nostalgiacentral.com, accessed 26 November 2018.
47. *The Bespoke Overcoat*, Remus Films 1955.
48. Anthony J. Dunn, *The Worlds of Wolf Mankowitz: Between Elite and Popular Cultures in Post War Britain* (London: Vallentine Mitchell, 2013), p. 57.
49. Wolf Mankowitz, *Five One Act Plays* (London: Evan Brothers, 1956), p. 5.

50. Dialogue with Rector Joseph McCulloch and David Kossoff, 23 August 1966. Bow Dialogues, National Sound Archive, British Library, C812/15.
51. Ibid.
52. Eddy Portnoy, 'The Disappearing Yiddish Accent', *The Forward*, 13 August 2012, www.forward.com, accessed 30 August 2018.
53. Mankowitz, *Five One Act Plays*, p. 7.
54. Ibid., p. 19.
55. Portnoy, 'Disappearing Yiddish Accent'.
56. *The Bespoke Overcoat*, 1955.
57. Mankowitz, *Five One Act Plays*, p. 16.
58. Ibid., p. 12.
59. Avner Ziv and Anat Zajdman (eds), *Semites and Stereotypes: Characteristics of Jewish Humour* (London: Greenwood Press, 1993), pp. vii–viii.
60. Ibid., p. ix.
61. Ibid., pp. 15–17.
62. Dunn, *Worlds of Wolf Mankowitz*, p. 70.
63. Mankowitz, *Five One Act Plays*, p. 14.
64. Ibid., p. 17.
65. Ibid., p. 16.
66. *The Bespoke Overcoat*, 1955.
67. Ibid.
68. Jeff Evans, *The Penguin TV Companion* (London: Penguin, 2003), p. 413.
69. *Sunday Independent* (Dublin), 22 September 1963.
70. www.allmusic.com, accessed 14 September 2018.
71. Richard Down and Christopher Petty, *The British Television Research Guide 1950-1997* (Bristol: Kaleidoscope Publishing, 1997), foreword.
72. Brett Mills, *Television Sitcoms* (London: Secker & Warburg, 1995), p. 56.
73. Orwell wrote that England was a 'land of snobbery and privilege, ruled largely by the old and silly'. George Orwell, *England, Your England and Other Essays* (London: Secker & Warburg, 1953).
74. Renee Dickason, 'Social Class and Class Distinction in Britcoms (1950s–2000s)', in Nicole Cloarec, David Haigron and Delphine Letort (eds), *Social Class on British and American Screens* (Jefferson, North Carolina: McFarland & Co, 2016), pp. 34–41.
75. Ibid.
76. *The Larkins*, 'Wide Open House', 19 September 1958; 'Cat Happy', 3 October 1958; 'Telly Ho', 17 October 1958; 'Christmas with the Larkins', 26 October 1958; ITV series.
77. *Jewish Chronicle*, 10 February 1956.
78. Thomas Kühne, 'Jewish Masculinities: German Jews, Gender and History', ed. by Benjamin Maria Baader, Sharon Gillerman and Paul Lerner (review), *German Studies Review*, 37:2 (May 2014), p. 440.
79. Lisa Alcalay Klug, 'Jewish Funeral Customs', www.Jewishfederations.org, accessed 2 September 2017.
80. *The Bespoke Overcoat*, Remus Films 1955.
81. *Jewish Chronicle*, 23 April 1976.
82. Mankowitz, *Five One Act Plays*, p. 9.
83. *The Bespoke Overcoat*, Remus Films 1955.

84. *Newcastle Journal and Daily Dispatch Manchester*, 25 September 1953.
85. *Jewish Chronicle*, 19 December 1958.
86. *Jewish Chronicle*, 2 December 1955.
87. Susan Murray, 'Lessons from Uncle Miltie: Ethnic Masculinity and Early Television's Vaudeo Star, in Janet Thumin (ed.), *Small Screens, Big Ideas: Television in the 1950s* (London: I. B. Tauris, 2002), pp. 67, 75.
88. *The Larkins*, 'Wide Open House'.
89. Sander Gilman, *The Jew's Body* (London: Routledge, 1991), p. 11.
90. *Guardian*, 24 March 2005.
91. *Daily Express*, 16 October 1968.
92. Dialogue between Joseph McCulloch and David Kossoff, 23 August 1966, Bow Dialogues, National Sound Archives, British Library C812/15.
93. *Daily Express*, 30 June 1965.
94. *Yorkshire Evening Post*, 4 November 1966.
95. Bow Dialogues, 23 August 1966.
96. Dialogue between Joseph McCulloch and David Kossoff, 14 November 1967, Bow Dialogues, National Sound Archives 1CDLR 0002983.
97. Dialogue between Joseph McCulloch and David Kossoff, 23 August 1966.
98. David Kossoff, *The Book of Witnesses* (London: Collins, 1971), book jacket description.
99. Dialogue between Rector Joseph McCulloch and David Kossoff, Bow Dialogues, 1 June 1971, National Sound Archives, British Library C812/31.
100. Bow Dialogues, 14 November 1967.
101. T. M. Endelman, *Leaving the Jewish Fold: Conversion and Radical Assimilation in Modern Jewish History* (Princeton: Princeton University Press, 2015), p. 360.
102. Ibid., p. 126.
103. Ibid., p. 362.
104. Ibid., p. 274.
105. *The Times*, 24 March 2005.
106. *Jewish Chronicle*, 16 March 1973.
107. Simon Kossoff: Interview with Isabelle Seddon, 2 December 2016, London.
108. *Jewish Chronicle*, 25 October 1953.
109. *Jewish Chronicle*, 10 February 1956.
110. Hava Nagila is a Jewish folk song traditionally sung at Jewish celebrations.
111. *Desert Island Discs*, BBC Home Service, 11 May 1964.
112. *Jewish Chronicle*, 1 April 2005.
113. *The Late Great Paul* (1992), British Film Institute.
114. Daniel Boyarin, *The Rise of Heterosexuality and the Invention of the Jewish Man* (Berkeley: University of California Press, 1997), pp. 1–2.

3

Warren Mitchell

Actor Warren Mitchell was best known for his Tory voting, racist, sexist, grumpy old man character Alf Garnett in *Till Death Us Do Part*. He played the part with his Kipling moustache and West Ham football scarf and became the vehicle for some of the hardest-hitting comedy seen on television.[1] For a decade, from 1965, he played the raging Cockney who spouted bigotry and racism with equal venom. He satirized the backlash to Britain's fast-changing cultural landscape after the war.[2] In reality, Mitchell was a lifelong, left-wing socialist.[3] This chapter will look at his family background and the influences in his life and consider that impact on the roles that he became famous for and how he became the most blatant example of a Jewish Cockney. He is a model of a second generation Jewish East Ender who stayed true to his political beliefs but had an ambiguous relationship with regard to his Jewishness/Judaism.

Background

Mitchell was born on 14 January 1926 at 22 Glaserton Road, Hackney to Annie and Montague Misell, a glass and china merchant. His family came from Russia in 1910 and were involved in the fish trade.[4] His grandmother opened a fish and chip shop on Stoke Newington High Street in the London Borough of Hackney, an area outside what was considered the heart of the 'Jewish East End' around the Whitechapel Road.[5] Until the nineteenth century, the number of Jews in Hackney was small but due to great industrialisation and a sharp increase in population and the need to build factories, offices and dwellings, the city expanded in all directions and included Hackney. Jews settled there in the years just before and after the First World War.[6]

Morris Beckman grew up in the area at the same time as Mitchell. His recollections of his childhood and life are similar to those expressed by Jews living in the midst of the Jewish East End. His father and his contemporaries kept to themselves socially and never really mastered the English language.

Everything outside of their work or businesses revolved around their synagogues and Judaic customs and tradition. Inevitably their children pulled away in all directions from the Judaic tree which gave the Jewish family unit a shock. The immigrants were Jews who lived in England. Their children were British whose faith was Jewish.

In the 1930s the Blackshirts rampaged through the East End and the dichotomy between father and son dissolved due to the fear of local fascism. There were evenings when Beckman could not walk from his home in Amhurst Road and not encounter a Blackshirt meeting.[7]

In the interwar years, whether you lived in the East End or slightly outside, there were still common characteristics. They shared the experience of migration and settlement. Their language and culture was Yiddish; Jewish knowledge and religious practice, however rudimentary or redundant, provided commonality. Although the First World War had brought increased prosperity for some involved in the trades of tailoring, leather, wood and cabinet making (through government contracts for uniforms, leather harnesses, pre-fabricated huts and furniture) which enabled them to seek accommodation outside the first areas of settlement, there was also the need to relocate due to Zeppelin and bomber raids on the East End. In 1889, 90 per cent of all Jewish families in the capital resided in the East End. Forty years later this had fallen to 60 per cent. In contrast, the foreign-born population of Stoke Newington rose from 4.6 to 6 per cent.[8]

Communities that burgeoned in suburban districts after 1918 were no more middle class than those of the interwar inner cities and suburbs. A substantial percentage worked in manual trades, as taxi drivers and traditional Jewish trades. The Jewish middle class of immigrant descent did not crystallize until the late 1950s and 1960s. These new suburban communities were distinctive not just due to those inhabiting them but due to ethnic character. The ethnic memory of those who lived in them was rooted in the inner city much as their parents had been grounded in *der Heim*.[9]

Although there were common characteristics, there were subtle differences as the Jewish population was not so intense and it did not have the same older and more established Jewish infrastructure. In an exhibition 'Sharing Our Stories: Jewish Stamford Hill 1930s–1950s' which focused on memories of the Jewish community at that time, one interviewee remarked that during that period it was still considered unusual if you heard someone speaking Yiddish in the area.[10] Indeed, living in an area that was not so intensely Jewish would have had its effect on Mitchell's attitude towards

Judaism as he would have had other 'outside' influences. This would have had a similar effect on David Kossoff, who lived in the same area.

Mitchell and his family lived above his grandmother's fish and chip shop. 'I had a lot of uncles in the business and worked in it as a kid. I often think when things are a bit slack I could always go back to frying a few flounders and a basinful of chips.'[11] He recalls his grandmother saying:

> 'Varren, venn business is good people eat fish and chips and when business is bad, people eat fish and chips. Open a fish and chip shop and you vill never go hungry'. Unfortunately for her I made the mistake of getting into a far more precarious business.[12]

It was his grandmother who thwarted his earliest acting ambitions by stopping him from appearing as Tiny Tim in a school production of *A Christmas Carol* because the Christmas pudding that he would eat at the end of the play was not kosher.[13] In contrast, his mother instilled in him a love of theatre and acting by introducing him to the world of variety shows. She would save pennies in change from the traders who came to the house and when there was enough they would go to the Holborn Empire, Finsbury Park Empire or the Palladium where they saw the variety greats, both Jewish and non-Jewish: Max Miller, Tommy Trinder and the Crazy Gang.[14] Indeed, his mother had thespian ambitions for him and he was sent to Gladys Gordon's Academy of Dramatic Arts in Walthamstow.[15]

This duality in the approach to his thespian aspirations is reflected in his family's religiosity and perhaps this accounts for Mitchell's non-observance and attitude to Judaism in later years. His family kept kosher at home but on their annual holiday to a boarding house in Clacton or Herne Bay they enjoyed having eggs and bacon for breakfast 'until it came out of their ears'.[16] His grandmother, who forbade him to take part in the Christmas play, was very orthodox and his father refused to meet Mitchell's non-Jewish wife Constance Wake until after the birth of their first child.[17] Mitchell's father became even more religious in later years and an active member of Palmers Green Synagogue.[18] In contrast his mother, when she took him out as a child to theatre outings, would visit his uncle's fish bar and order 'two haddock and chips' with an exaggerated wink. It was years later that Mitchell learnt the significance of the wink: they were eating skate, a non-kosher fish.[19]

Nevertheless, Mitchell was still expected to go to Hebrew classes three times a week and when it came to his *bar mitzvah* he did a grand solo virtuoso performance. He claimed it was the last time that he set foot in a synagogue.[20] Another rebellion against religion occurred when he was chosen to play for the school's First XI football team on *Yom Kippur* and he told his father that he was not going to fast but play the game. His father hit him and sent him to his room, but he sneaked out, played, scored a goal and at half time the team was 3-1 up. 'I looked up to the sky and said that it was all rubbish. There should have been thunderbolts.' A week after his *bar mitzvah* he decided he had no interest in the religious side of being Jewish.[21] With this anecdote it appears that he had constructed a convenient story to reject Judaism.

He was, however, unable and perhaps unwilling to deny or distance himself from his Jewish origins. He felt that, at times, being Jewish set him apart from other people. When he was studying at Oxford, for example, he felt insecure and something of an outsider. However, he had never come across antisemitism until he met the actor Richard Burton. He recalled an incident when he and Burton were having lunch with some officers after a passing out parade of the University's air squadron. An officer asked Burton, who was already an actor, about the state of the theatre. Burton told him that 'the problem is that the whole thing is controlled by Jews'. Mitchell was furious and reprimanded him. Burton, at a later stage, apologized and told him that he had never met a Jew before and, since he had made that remark he had stayed with a Jewish family and realized how wrong he had been.[22] Mitchell's fury illustrated how he defended his Jewishness from secular attack.

Unlike many of his generation in the East End, he did not have to leave school at 14, the minimum school leaving age as set out in the 1918 Education Act, in order to work to help the family finances – a reflection of the greater prosperity and aspirations of those who lived on the edges of the Jewish East End and working-class suburbia. Mitchell's family were not poor and his father made a good living.[23] He attended Southgate County grammar school and during the war studied physical chemistry at University College, Oxford on a six months' RAF officers' course. The chance meeting with Richard Burton, as mentioned above, encouraged him to become an actor as it was during this time that Mitchell realized that he *could* act. 'I found that I could masquerade as different characters. When the Americans were getting all the girls I used to pretend to be a European officer.'[24] After the war he decided not to return to Oxford and enrolled at RADA (Royal Academy of Dramatic Arts). He would perform at Unity Theatre in the evenings. Whilst at RADA his contemporaries regarded him as their pet communist.[25] 'I had two jolly years learning posh at RADA during the day and was duly de-poshed at night at Unity Theatre, where we were all socialists and communists.'[26] Mitchell had the privilege to attend RADA, one of the top drama schools in the country. The fact that he chose to take part in Unity at the same time, which was such a contrast, suggests that he was not entirely comfortable with the RADA environment.

Politics and Unity Theatre

Mitchell cut his thespian teeth at Unity in 1948. As a communist-run enterprise it was where actors got their politics and Mitchell remained a lifelong socialist.[27] Remarkably, however, he had not always had left-wing leanings and perhaps this was a reflection of his upbringing which would have been more *petit bourgeois*. His father was a shop keeper rather than a tailor or in a manual trade like many others in the East End. This was in contrast to Alfie Bass, who lived in the heart of the East End and whose father was a tailor. He was a decade older than Mitchell and like many of his generation had taken part in the Battle of Cable Street and as a result of his family background it was natural for him to embrace left-wing politics. Mitchell's early beginnings and where he lived were very different. He admitted that up until he left the army he was 'an awful little Tory'. It was when he travelled back home on the boat from Canada that he came under the influence of a fellow passenger who 'converted him', gave him literature to read and convinced him that communism was the only ethical way to run the country. Prior to that, he had remarked that 'if that bounder Attlee gets in, I don't want to go home'. Upon his return to England he was introduced to the Squatters Union in St John's Wood who were helping to get flats for people who had lost their homes in the war as well as to Unity Theatre.[28]

Fellow Unity actor Harry Landis also remarked that Mitchell's time at Unity was the beginning of his political education which continued throughout his life.[29] There were times he sold socialist newspapers on the street.[30] He never joined the Communist Party and it does not appear that he took an active part in any political party. However, he was always ready to align himself with left-wing politics and appeared to be to the left of the Labour Party. Just before the 2010 election, he said that he would rather there was a hung Parliament than a Tory win.[31]

His first appearance at Unity was in *Six Men of Dorset* (1948), the story of the Tolpuddle Martyrs, the farm workers put on trial for trying to form a union.[32] Mitchell recalled that when the verdict of guilty was brought in, the audience wanted to lynch the judge.[33] He also appeared in *Cousin Elwyn*

(1949) where he played Elwyn, a successful American businessman who visits his English cousin who runs a 200 year-old shoe shop. Elwyn transforms the middle-class English home with a range of gadgets and is finally sent back home to America having disrupted the household but also having taught the shoemaker how to introduce a few useful improvements. He considered his role in *The Ragged Trouser Philanthropist* (1949), a socialist classic about conditions of the building trade at the turn of the century and how workers created the wealth but did not receive any, as one of the highlights of his time there. He commented that it said so much about socialism in wonderful and humane terms and showed how as the workers made the house richer their lives disintegrated under the force of capitalism.[34] All of these roles were non-Jewish in their focus.

When Mitchell arrived at Unity he had ideas about how he wanted to act that had been influenced by his RADA training. He recalled how he was soon put in his place by the director Bill Rowbotham.[35] Mitchell was a devotee of the Russian actor and stage director Stanislavski and 'the method'.[36] 'Rowbotham would take the mickey, "What does Mr. Stanislavski

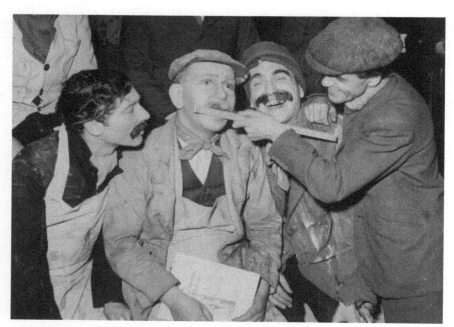

13. *The Ragged Trousered Philanthropist,* Unity Theatre 1949 © as stated at the copyright holder/Victoria and Albert Museum, London © permission (Clive Gellert, Unity Theatre Trust)

say…Warren move over to the other stage…Oh what does Mr. Stanislavski say?" I learnt that if a director asks you to do something, you do it. I took away from Unity a very pragmatic down to earth approach'. He also considered Rowbotham to be his shining light at Unity.[37] Mitchell called Unity his 'alma mater'.[38] He adored his time there: 'I just succumbed to the place. To be in something revolutionary that got up people's noses as well as Unity did.'[39]

The seeds of Mitchell's left-wing political identity were sown at Unity and in later years he commented that he mostly identified with the working class but not 'when they are being obtuse about some union matter and behaving like a lot of sheep'.[40] In 1995, he said that he wanted to see the Labour Party win the next election but was worried at the sight of so many Labour policies being chucked out of the window in the pursuit of power. 'I'd like to have seen a radical alternative to the present system and something done to reverse the philosophy of greed.'[41]

Early Career

The understanding of life and its difficulties were soon experienced by Mitchell when he left RADA and began his professional career. He became an old campaigner at the employment exchange, squarely on the left of the Labour Party.[42] He struggled to find stage work and earned a living as a porter at Euston Station and in an ice cream factory.[43] His early stage work was varied. He was one of a singing trio with the Ambrose Band Show and stooged for Abbot and Costello.[44] Mitchell changed his name in 1951 when he stood in for DJ Pete Murray as a presenter on Radio Luxembourg. They said that no one was ever going to write in their request to a Warren Misell, a foreign and alien sounding name, and they obviously wanted Mitchell not to appear different from his listeners and suggested a surname that they could easily relate to.[45] Listeners would not be aware of his Jewish origins as he had a polished actor-trained voice.[46] This would not be the case, however, for the roles that he was offered during the 1950s.

By this time he had become a competent character actor in straight and comedy roles, while premature baldness gave him the ability to play a wide age range. After appearing in the popular radio show *Educating Archie,* he got his television break in 1955 in a number of episodes of *Hancock's Half Hour.* It was the first of many screen appearances. Although he yearned to play classic parts, all his early roles were Jewish or foreign character parts. 'I suppose I was offered them because of looking dark and Jewish and being able to speak several foreign languages.'[47]

He played non-Jewish roles at Unity but those who came to watch the productions were not the mainstream Jewish public. They were interested in left-wing causes and had a more open mind to who and what was being portrayed. At the start of his career, before he became famous as Alf Garnett in the 1960s, his looks and background were ideal to embody the role of the foreigner. With his baldness and command of Eastern European accents he was often cast as an alien villain.[48] He was thus a 'natural' as a comic or sinister foreigner hailing from a wide range of destinations typically from somewhere along an arc curving through Eastern Europe and the Mediterranean.[49] In most films he played small character parts, such as a tailor in *Two Way Stretch* (1960), a comedy about a group of prisoners who break out of jail, commit a robbery and then break back into jail again, thus giving them the perfect alibi; Spencius in *Carry on Cleo* (1964);[50] Abdul in the Beatles' *Help* (1965), Mr Zanfrello in *The Spy who Came in from the Cold* (1965), a British Cold War spy film and Popov in *Diamonds for Breakfast* (1968), a comedy about four thieves who try to steal the Imperial Jewels of Russia. 'I played a succession of sinister foreigners, pathetic foreigners, funny foreigners, in film and on television but no natives until 1964 when I was offered Alf Garnett. I revelled in portraying his awfulness for 24 years.'[51]

Till Death Us Do Part

Mitchell shot to fame as the Cockney Alf Garnett in *Till Death Us Do Part*. His East End character was famed for his racist, sexist, homophobic and antisemitic views.[52] To achieve such fame, as someone with a Jewish background playing such a character, would appear somewhat incongruous but he had grown up with exposure to both the Jewish and non-Jewish world and therefore he was able to take on such a role with ease.

It changed Mitchell from being a small part, character actor, a natural choice for the Italian taxi driver or male foreigner, to someone who was highly sought after.[53] British television had never seen a character like Alf Garnett when he first appeared in Johnny Speight's controversial British sitcom (1966–75) which spanned more than 50 episodes, briefly moving to ITV for a 1981 *Till Death Us Do Part* series, and then back to the BBC for *In Sickness and in Health* (1985–92). It was one of the most popular and controversial programmes of its generation. Some 16 million people a week would watch the hectoring foul-mouthed pro-monarchist 'Cockney' who loudly condemned anything and anyone who did not conform to his ideas of what made Britain great. There was an uncomfortably familiar ring of truth about this scowling know-it-all; the first character to regularly use the word 'bloody' on mainstream television.[54] It was the first great working-class comedy. Television producer Tony Moss commented that it showed domestic life with larger-than-life monsters at the heart and that 'the characters reminded us of our parents.'[55]

The show highlighted the pressures felt by the white working class at a time of great social change in Britain. It broke a number of taboos with a high level of swearing and insulting references to racial minorities and was condemned by television campaigner Mary Whitehouse as a sign of the BBC's declining moral standards. It was ironic that Mitchell, a left-wing Jewish Spurs supporter, played a Conservative Party-voting antisemitic West Ham fan.[56]

Mark Ward, who wrote a companion guide to *Till Death Us Do Part*, points out that the programme broke down the boundaries of comedy for ever.[57] It offended many people yet, for millions, it was the most exciting show on television. Alf Garnett became a British institution, his profane language a national treasure. The characters were grotesque but still loved by many. The series centred on the working-class Garnett family (Alf and his wife Else, daughter Rita and her husband Mike), trapped together by circumstances in a seemingly endless series of arguments. The show was path breaking. Critics loved its realism, the constant flow of ideas and challenges to authority. Audiences loved the electric atmosphere of the show as it trod the edge of what was permissible on television.[58]

Few television shows have created such an impact and controversy and few characters have bitten so deeply into the public's consciousness as Garnett. No previous television character had provoked such extreme reactions, from the protests of clergymen, a Conservative MP and Mary Whitehouse[59] at Alf's language to those who were enthusiastic with every word he said. He shocked and delighted people with his outspoken bigotry. It was a send up, although Alf voiced views that many held privately (and were indeed given credulity by Alf). Any attempt to historicize the racial sitcom may well begin with the arrival of *Till Death Us Do Part*. It was not a programme primarily focused on race, yet it is remembered very much in racial terms.[60] Alf Garnett was 'the ambivalently monstrous Enoch Powell of the sitcom'.[61] But despite its racial legacy, the programme was conceived as an iconic working-class comedy, intended to give comic voice to the daily lives of ordinary poor Londoners. Speight's intention was a desire to create characters 'warts and all' and not to sugar coat or romanticize the attitudes and experiences of daily life.

To provoke his political views Alf was challenged by his son-in-law Mike, who was a socialist and anti-monarchist. Mike's views and indeed the world in general reduced Alf to rage on a weekly basis. Time and time again the subject leading to argument was race or immigration, an issue which divided Mike and Alf on predictable lines of racism and anti-racism. Race relations dominated the political background of British society during the programme's production. It was set against the background of Powellism,[62] of African-Asian expulsions and the Race Relations Act of 1965 and 1968 and the Immigration Act 1971. Speight argued that the heated race rows in the programme brought murky hidden views about these issues to the surface and performed a valuable social function in the process. His idea was why not bring racial prejudice into the open, show people how ignorant they are about it and make them laugh at themselves? This strategy sat at the heart of Speight's work and became the central defence of the racial sitcom as a genre. In the character of Alf Garnett he created an ideal and iconic vehicle to bring it to life. Mitchell seized the opportunity to plunge into the aggression and frustration of his character. Mitchell's self-identification as a committed character actor set the tone of the programme,[63] and his time and training at Unity was invaluable.

The premise was deceptively simple: its biting parody relied on the exact inverse of what Alf was saying in order to aim its barbs at attitudes toward royalty, religion, sex and sexuality, race and politics. The more Alf blindly defended his beloved ultra-conservative 'standards' the more the audience realized that those standards were intended to be lampooned. It was a dangerous game and Speight was well aware that Alf's tirades could be taken at face value. They were careful to show that Alf was always the loser yet even this was to backfire on them as the success of the series enabled Alf to dominate it.[64] It was rather ironic that Mitchell, whose views were the opposite of Alf in real life, would be the one for the role. Yet Mitchell loved playing Alf as he reflected 'how daft racism was' and he felt that through the brilliance of Johnny Speight's writing he gave a true portrayal of a bigot.[65] However, although some of the audience would have realized the parody, others would not.

Speight was a committed socialist from a working-class background, the son of a docker. He claimed that he utilized the character of Alf Garnett to explode popular prejudices and attack the British class system. *Till Death Us Do Part* offered critical insight into the political and social dynamics of the British working classes and ultimately enhanced historical understanding of British race relations in this period. The show was designed as a mechanism for Speight as a working-class writer to offer original and sharp social commentary, highlighting the class and generational tensions of British society through the vehicle of the Garnett family.[66] Although this was his intention, there was always the danger that it would not work. Unfortunately, the world was full of Alf Garnetts who shared his views. The British public probably warmed to Garnett because he could be identified with the kind of reactionary and prejudiced figure that existed in the country at the time and who shared their views on race. How wonderful it was for them to seemingly laugh at his outrageous comments and secretly agree with him.

Race was a major and recurring theme in the programme. Both Speight and the BBC were adamant that voicing racial prejudice through the character of Alf Garnett would serve as an educative function, forcing ordinary people to laugh at the character's stupidity and bigotry. The racial attention of the programme was almost entirely focused on Britain's rising black and Asian community. Alf constructed these immigrants as essentially different to indigenous Britons and sometimes alleged that these differences were biological and at other times cultural.

Alf's belief in racial difference is epitomized in the episode entitled 'The Blood Donor' (19 January 1968) in which he volunteered to donate blood. When he saw a black man was donating, he said that the blood should be segregated. In another part of the episode Alf voiced ideas of racial difference with reference to the failure of the first surgical attempt at a heart transplant which had taken place in South Africa. The patient, a Jewish man called Louis Washkansky, survived the operation but died eighteen days later from pneumonia. Alf explained the death in respect of racial difference. It was because his own body rejected the foreign heart that the doctors put in: 'Your Washkansky was a Jew. An if your doctors had a Jewish heart put in him...he'd have been alright...cos his body would accept that you see'.[67]

Alf's antisemitic thoughts on Jews appear in *The Thoughts of Chairman Alf*. When contemplating why England had deteriorated, he considers that 'the real rot started with Jack the Ripper, otherwise known as Gladstone the Jew. Queen Victoria knew this was so and that was why she would not leave Windsor Castle whilst Gladstone the Jew was roaming around with his little black bag.'[68] He blamed Hitler's madness on his having to have a blood transfusion after he was bitten by a bat and Goebbels was the only doctor nearby. As he was a vet and got his bloods mixed up, he gave Hitler the Jewish blood that he kept for his pet vampires.[69] He considered that Israeli Prime Minister Golda Meir, whom he called Goldwyn Meyer, only became Prime Minister because her husband being Jewish put the country in his wife's name 'an old Jewish dodge that is, to avoid tax and bankruptcy'.[70]

Despite these antisemitic outbursts there was a recurring joke in which Alf's family alleged that he was Jewish (something he hotly denied).[71] It was his Jewish looks that led to a famous episode in which he was accused of being 'a yid'. Mitchell said repercussions were few and both the *Jewish Chronicle* and the Campaign Against Racial Discrimination were of the view that the programme had helped to combat prejudice.[72] The programme did produce fits of moral apoplexy from viewers who took the show's irony for the bald truth. The *Jewish Chronicle* commented that the difficulty was that in order to expose an idiocy you have to demonstrate it and Johnny Speight's writing was especially liable to misinterpretation because of the savage relish with which he depicts the ignorance of his characters. Yet it considered that the programme was no more a contribution to antisemitism than Jonathan Swift's advice on how to cook children was an incitement to cannibalism.[73] *Till Death Us Do Part* worked best as a satire against bigotry rather than a mouthpiece for it.[74]

Yet was Warren Mitchell's Alf Garnett Jewish? Was he the ultimate Jewish Cockney? In a discussion about Jesus in the episode 'God was Church of England. Jesus was after the Oil', Alf asked his daughter Rita where Jesus came from and she replied that he was from England. Alf told her she was correct and added that the first two English names in the Bible were Mary and Joseph. Rita told him that Joseph was a Jewish name.

> Alf: Ok, he might have been a bit Jewish on his father's side.
> His wife Else retorted, with a knowing look: 'like you'.[75]

In another episode entitled 'Holiday in Bournemouth', Alf and Else take a taxi from the station to the hotel and start to moan that they should not have come to Bournemouth as they have the sea back home in Wapping. The taxi driver then announced:

> Taxi driver: That's the trouble with Bournemouth. Too many Jews… We've got more Jews down here than they got in Israel. And they're more trouble.
> He points out: Another Jewish hotel there. They got their own private Jewish beach. They paddle there with the *yarmulkes* on.
> Alf: The what?
> Taxi driver: You know, the skull caps. Them little round hats.
> Else (gives Alf the same knowing look): 'you know'.

When they get out of the taxi, the driver takes a good look at Alf, puts his hands on Alf's chest and says with a large shrug of his shoulders in a very Jewish accent:

Taxi driver: Sorry, I didn't realise you was a yiddisher boy.
Alf: I ain't no bloody yiddisher boy. (He shakes his fists in the air.)
Taxi driver: Not a yiddisher boy. Whose he kidding?[76]

The driver had probably initially assumed that Alf was not Jewish as he had talked during the journey about living in Wapping and working on the docks (not a Jewish occupation or a Jewish area of the East End). Yet when he saw him get out of the car and took a good look at him, something about his looks and demeanour must have convinced him that Alf was Jewish.

References to Alf's Jewishness and his denial are shown again in the episode 'Intolerance'. Alf was vitriolic that he was not seen by his usual doctor at the surgery but by the replacement Dr Agawalla whom he referred to as a 'sambo' and a 'coon'. This resulted in an argument with his daughter Rita, and son-in-law Mike, who criticized Alf for this blatant racism and asked him how he would like it if he called him 'a yid'.

Alf: Eh? What are you talking about – yid. I'm not a yid.
Mike: You're Jewish.
Alf: I'm not Jewish.

Mike tells him that everyone in the area knows that he is Jewish and that his grandfather had a fish stall in Petticoat Lane and was known as Solly Diamond the fish king. Alf tells him that it is all lies. Mike tries to appease him by saying that there is nothing to be ashamed of by being Jewish.

Alf: I'm not Jewish I tell you.
Mike: Gerroff – look at your hooter. Blimey that's a right kosher honk you got there.

Alf gets more and more irate and starts insulting Mike's Irish heritage by calling him 'a mick', but Mike tells him that he is proud to be Irish and that Alf should be proud to be Jewish.

Alf asked his daughter to tell her husband to stop telling lies about him.
Rita: What are you ashamed of? What's it matter if you are Jewish?

Alf still argued and said that there was nothing Jewish about him, his nose was 'roman' and that his grandfather changed his name from Garnett to Solly Diamond for business reasons.

Alf: You wanna get on up in that Whitechapel you're better off, changing your name to Jewish and making out you're one of 'em.

But Mike, looking at Alf's plate, still insisted and said that old Solly Diamond would turn in his grave if he saw Alf eating egg and bacon. Alf then threw the plate at Mike.[77]

Television producer Tony Moss comments that Alf was a brilliant characterization of human frailty and stupidity. 'He rails about not being Jewish when he clearly is. The more irate he gets, the more Jewish he becomes. It was a wonderful insight into the myopic nature of most of us.' He added that bigots missed the point and took Alf as their champion.[78] Alf presents himself as a non-Jew, denying but ultimately knowing that he is Jewish and he constantly tries to prove the point and is the only one that will not acknowledge his origins. He is both Jewish and Cockney and this is something that a second generation immigrant was able to be.

Although he played a Cockney character, Mitchell integrated Jewish physical movements into his performance. When he gets excited or irate and wishes to make a point, he gesticulates wildly with one arm and makes a jabbing gesture. This is similar to the movements made by Kossoff in *The Larkins,* described in the previous chapter, despite the fact that Mitchell is playing an aggressive male and Kossoff a hen-pecked husband. This is in line with the findings of David Efron who studied the spatio-temporal aspects of the gestural behaviour of Jews from Eastern Europe and southern Italians in New York City, living under similar as well as different environmental conditions. Efron found that Jews used a limited range of motions, mostly from the elbow. Their movements were jabbing, and they tended to use one hand and used pointing motions frequently. They tended to gesticulate with up and down motions, and it was rare for them to use both arms for the same movement. Individuals had a tendency to gesture in zig-zag like and erratic motions with punctuation represented by 'jabs'. Their movements also seemed to be very deliberate and 'choppy'. This was in contrast to Italians who used more curved lateral gestures which pivoted from the shoulder. They tended to use both arms and one gesture usually flowed into the next one, making it a smooth and regular motion.[79] The use of such body language by Mitchell and Kossoff, despite being in such different roles, draws on their background.

One could say that, in Garnett, Mitchell merged aspects of his Jewish origins together with his exposure to the non-Jewish world. His experiences in life and where he grew up certainly enabled him to understand and portray Alf. His time at Unity stood him in good stead as he acknowledged that Alf's loud and rough Cockney accent was a direct copy of how Unity's George Tovey spoke.[80] He had come across such characters, the know-all and the barrack room lawyer, when he worked at Euston station as a porter and at Walls' ice cream factory on the night shift.[81] The derogatory way in which Alf spoke was not unlike the way his father spoke when talking about non-Jews. His father used to say at Christmas 'Look at 'em. Look at 'em drinking. They don't eat all year, then they eat and drink like lunatics.'[82]

Mitchell's father clearly pointed out that Jews were different, and this is something Mitchell felt. He considered the fact that he never was given the opportunity to play major heroic Shakespearean characters due to his physical appearance.[83] Although he regarded himself as versatile, he was bound by the limitations of his body. 'I don't think I even look particularly English. I've always found it extremely strange that I was asked to play this quintessential, representative Englishman, Alf Garnett. I look like what I am – the descendant of a Russian Jew.' He also said that 'when I started in rep I could never play all those characters who do everything in dinner jackets. I have to laugh, shout, roar, let go completely on stage.'[84] This comment illustrates his personification of what it is to be English and that he saw himself as 'the outsider'.

Mitchell considered that he had a 'Jewish' temperament as he was extrovert and demonstrative. 'My emotions are fairly near the surface. I don't sit on them. I explode when I need to and break down when I need to. I can easily come close to weeping. Maybe that's a Jewish thing.'[85] This acknowledgement is reflected in his theatre work where his Jewish background comes to the fore, whether playing Jewish or non-Jewish roles and his 'Jewish' interpretation is in evidence, partly due to his family background and Jewish mentors at an early stage in his career.

Theatre Roles

One of his first professional appearances was in *The Golden Door*, a comedy drama about Jewish immigrants' life on the Lower East Side, New York, at the Embassy Theatre in Swiss Cottage in 1950, where he understudied both Alfie Bass and the Yiddish actor Meir Tzelniker.[86] 'I learnt a great deal from both of them. I could imitate Tzelniker's mannerisms so well that no one would believe I wasn't him.'[87] Meir's daughter Anna Tzelniker, also a Yiddish actor, recalled that Mitchell often said he learnt how to act by watching her father from the wings.[88] She also described how many of these Yiddish productions were melodramatic as the poor immigrants saw such plays as escape from their drab surroundings.[89] Bass and Kossoff also appeared at

122   *East End Jews and Left-Wing Theatre*

the Embassy Theatre in other Jewish roles at the start of their professional careers after Unity.

This immersion in a style influenced by Yiddish theatre can be seen in his role of Solomon in *The Price* by Arthur Miller, for which he won an Olivier award in 2004. Mitchell excelled himself as Solomon, an ancient Jewish furniture dealer, bidding for the piled-up furniture belonging to a long-dead millionaire ruined in the 1920s Wall Street crash. He is called in by two brothers to divide the contents of their late father's house. 'The icing on the cake is Mitchell's comic turn as the ancient and very Jewish dealer with the knack of survival.'[90]

Mitchell admitted that Meir Tzelniker had greatly influenced his performance.[91] The Yiddish humour is evident in a scene where he has just climbed the stairs to the garret in which the play is set. He coughs, splutters and holds up his hands to the two other characters Esther and Victor as if to say 'wait a minute, I'll speak soon'. Esther offers him some water and in a Russian Yiddish accent Solomon says: 'Water I don't need. A little blood I could use.'[92] The *Guardian* considered that Mitchell was in his element as Solomon:

> …bent-backed, hamming furiously, his caterpillar eyebrows doing a whole separate show of their own and this woeful, Topol-like accent wrapping itself round nuggets of wisdom such as, the average family, they love each other like crazy, until the parents die, and then…shrug, shrug, the eyes roll, the hands go up.[93]

It was also felt that 'the real joy of the play lies in the character of the wily, life loving 89-year-old Solomon who contradicts the image of Miller as a writer of graveyard solemnity. Far from overacting, Mitchell plays him to perfection.'[94]The *Evening Standard* wrote that Mitchell gave the loveliest performance of a lifetime as a second-hand dealer looking for a last good deal and imparts delectable comedy and pathos. 'He wheedles in a Russian-Yiddish accent to the manner reborn. Mitchell's manipulative Solomon, with a woozy eye on the main chance, is an exquisite comic creation.'[95]

A few years afterwards, and again in his later career, Mitchell plays Mr Green, an 86 year-old orthodox Jewish New York dry cleaner in *Visiting Mr Green* by Jeff Baron, performed at the Trafalgar Studios in London in 2008. Green is living alone in a down at heel apartment on the upper west side of Manhattan. His beloved wife of 59 years has recently died, he is not eating properly, is at a dangerously low ebb and has narrowly escaped being killed by a speeding car. His visitor is 29 year-old Ross Gardner, an almost waspish but Jewish gay New Yorker, the driver of the car. The judge has ordered Gardner to make weekly visits to Green as part of his community service.

The two hander begins predictably with the stubborn Mr Green, whom the *Jewish Chronicle* referred to as a Yiddish Alf Garnett, not liking Ross until he knows that he is Jewish (Ross persuades him to eat kosher food). Then he doesn't like him again when he finds out he is gay.[96] Mr. Green turns icily homophobic and Jewish fundamentalist.[97] We discover that Green, with his late wife, sat *shiva* (Jewish week of mourning) for their only daughter after she married a non-Jew. Over a period of time mutual suspicion between the two men, both Jewish, lonely and burdened, turns into a tender relationship.

Mitchell received acclaim for his acting but at the same time, as already highlighted with regard to his role as Mr Green, there were references made to the Cockney Alf Garnett. The *Telegraph* said that Mitchell had not lost his touch for testy irritation that was such a performance in *Till Death Us Do Part*. 'His comic timing is spot on and he has an astonishing touching old man's gait, half weary shuffle, half hopeful skip. Best of all are the actor's moments of sudden tenderness, when Mitchell seems to be living the role rather than acting it.'[98]

The Times pointed out that Mitchell proved as credible a cantankerous maverick as when he brought Alf Garnett to television. 'To see Mitchell shuffling across the stage or cannily observing his visitor while firing off one-liners one is reminded of what was clear from performances as different as his malicious tramp in Pinter's *The Caretaker* and his feisty title character in Miller's *Death of a Salesman* that Mitchell is one of our major actors.'[99] Mitchell appeared in *Death of a Salesman* at the National Theatre in 1979 for which he won an Olivier award.

If Mitchell was unable to escape comparisons to Garnett with whatever he did, he also could not escape the influences of his Jewish background or the area in which he grew up. Such an influence could have contributed to his Jewish interpretation of roles that were not necessarily Jewish, such as Harold Pinter's *The Homecoming* (1990). Speculation that *The Homecoming* concerned a Jewish family began immediately after its original premiere although this was denied by Pinter. Significantly, Mitchell chose to interpret the role in a Jewish way despite Pinter not being in agreement.

In *The Homecoming* (1990) Mitchell played Max, the bullying head of an all-male family whose hierarchy is disrupted by the return of his elder son and wife. Mitchell argued with Pinter as he felt that it was a Jewish family and showed Max's reaction to his son marrying a non-Jew despite Pinter saying that 'he didn't write it specifically Jewish'. In Michael

Billington's biography of Pinter, it was revealed that the play was seeded by a reaction of Pinter's family to his non-Jewish wife. Mitchell went ahead with his own interpretation: 'I did play it with a strong Cockney Jewish accent. It seemed to fit.'[100] Here Mitchell identifies with being both Jewish *and* Cockney. He also would have identified with the situation as his wife was not Jewish and, as noted, his father would not meet with her until after the birth of their first child.[101]

The play is about close but abrasive families, rejection, suppressed violation and sex. Mitchell's portrayal of Max was 'as a sort of demonic Alf'. He sees the play, set in the East End he knew so well, as a portrait of a Jewish family closing ranks against a non-Jewish girlfriend being brought into the household by the returning successful academic son from America. Their arrival leads to disturbing realignments within the family.[102]

Critics commented on the similarities to Alf Garnett, commenting that he 'repeats all the shrugging East End mannerisms and truculent bombast that made his reputation as Alf Garnett'.[103] The two roles have a lot in common and Mitchell accentuates the similarities. 'Both characters are illiberal, xenophobic and generally contemptuous of women.'[104] Mitchell said that he invented a biography for Max – what happened to him and why he was the way he became. He used the time of the 1950s and gangsters in the area as this would have been the sort of atmosphere where Max flourished.[105] As Mitchell did not grow up in the heart of the Jewish East End, he would have come into contact with a greater range of characters in the East End itself. Kossoff, who grew up in a similar area as Mitchell, chose to play the stereotypical immigrant Jew and those from a bygone age.

In his roles Mitchell exercised a particular masculinity that was not typical of the traditionally-held view of the Jewish man. The widely held stereotype of Jewish men were that they were non-violent and that they were 'erudite, comedic, malleable, non-threatening, part nebbish, part schlemiel, Jewish men do not fight, they talk'.[106] Bass and Kossoff fitted this mould. In contrast, Mitchell embodied a 'tough guy' masculinity which, as pointed out in the Introduction, was a stance adopted by some immigrant Jewish men as they adapted to their new surroundings, and this was portrayed in *The Homecoming*.

Yet, at the same time, reviews commented on the 'Jewish stance'. *The Times* wrote that Mitchell gave a towering performance and that he modulated his Alf Garnett voice from West Ham to Stamford Hill. He played Max 'very Jewish', transforming the play into a study of what happens to a male Jewish family in the absence of a strong mother figure.[107]

The *Guardian* felt that by casting Mitchell as Max, the patriarchal ex-butcher, director Peter Hall brought out the play's Cockney-Jewish humour and Pinter's sharp awareness of the way sentimentality frequently dissolves into aggression.[108] The *Daily Telegraph* said that the speech tended to become more overtly Jewish in inflection as the play proceeded.[109] The *Observer* pointed out that Mitchell played the role in a natural Jewish Cockney idiom that had not been present when Paul Rogers played the role in the original production in 1995.[110] Theatre director Peter Hall remarked that Mitchell was great, 'full of Cockney Jewish speech rhythms, paternal vituperative one moment, maternally sentimental the next, and in the end strangely moving as, in craven capitulation, he begged Ruth for a kiss'. Pinter also thought he was very good but, ever anxious for *The Homecoming* not to be defined as a Jewish play, questioned the accent. 'It doesn't make sense for Max to be Jewish if the rest of the family isn't.'[111] (Pinter does not give a surname to the family.) Mitchell thought otherwise and went ahead regardless.

Mitchell drew on past experiences from both the Jewish and non-Jewish worlds. When he played the role of the tramp Davies in Harold Pinter's play *The Caretaker*, he used memories of the tramps he met while signing on at various labour exchanges during his unemployed days. At that time he had known poverty. He remembered being desperately poor and on the verge of giving up acting and selling hats on a stall in the market.[112] When he married in 1952, he was unable to afford a wedding ring.[113]

In *The Caretaker*, two brothers use an old tramp Davies (Mitchell) to unite them when their relationship was in danger of disintegrating. Aston has been through some electro-convulsive therapy and in the process has become a laconic passive creature and his brother Mick finds it difficult to communicate with him. When Aston brings back Davies, an aggressive down and out, to his junk-littered room, Mick's jealousy causes him to plot the undermining of his brother's relationship by offering the tramp a job as caretaker and provoking him to revile his brother. *The Times* felt that 'Mitchell brings the outlandish assertiveness of Alf Garnett to the role of the tramp and in the role of the tramp and in their bigotry proves that both Garnett and Pinter's caretaker are brothers under the skin'.[114] The *Sunday Telegraph* commented that Mitchell gave a bravura performance made up of innumerable tics and gestures that seem to have accumulated not from one lifetime but many.[115]

This is even reflected in the way that he plays 'the supposedly' non-Jewish Alf Garnett. He uses the hand gestures that were mentioned previously as a Jewish trait as did Kossoff in *The Larkins*, but in his case he does so in an aggressive and confrontational manner that is in contrast to Kossoff's helplessness. He continually shouts, swears, yells and when he wishes to make a point to someone he leans forward and puts his face directly in front of his opponent at a distance that is inappropriately close. This confrontational behaviour, bordering on the menacing, occurs in every episode and is illustrated in all the clips entitled 'Five Best Moments' that cover all sorts of situations including his anger at the BBC and their licence fee, pushing his wife in a wheelchair in the middle of the road and his abuse at the driver who wants to move him, arguing with his wife who will not make his dinner, getting ready to go out for a party and a political debate with his son-in-law.[116] In one episode when he lights up a cigarette in a hospital waiting room and the nurse tells him to stop smoking, he gives a Nazi salute.[117]

His aggressive demeanour is in total contrast to that of his friend Bert (Alfie Bass) who is a gentle Cockney. In the episode 'Christmas Club Books', the two are in Alf's home. Bert watches as Alf works on the paying-in books for the Christmas Club that is managed by Alf. The neighbours have been contributing to the club for the past year and are expecting to be paid out from their savings as it is four weeks before Christmas. It is obvious from the start that the books will not tally, money is missing, and Alf is trying to cover this up, pretending that he must have written down something incorrectly. Bert, in all innocence, sits quietly by Alf's side and tries to point out what might have gone wrong. He acts nervously, his eyebrows go up and down and he looks puzzled as Alf is either erasing information or tearing pages out from the book. At every comment Bert makes, Alf either stares at him with venom or erupts into anger. He bangs his fists on the table, waves his arms in the air, swears or leans forward to talk to Bert to a point when he is practically touching him. Bert is nervous in his presence, twitches and mutters to himself 'I won't say nothing, won't interfere' but turns away from Alf as he does so. He then decides to go to the pub but before leaving he stands behind Alf's chair and when he sees that he is engrossed in working out a balance sheet, Bert quietly mentions, with somewhat trepidation, that people in the pub were hoping that they would be paid that evening. He leaves when he realizes that this will not happen. He is totally non-confrontational and the opposite to Alf.[118]

Not surprisingly, Mitchell adopts the same voice and mannerisms as the Cockney Garnett when he appears as a Jewish character, such as his role as Ivan Fox in the six-part television series *So You Think You Have Troubles* (1991). Ivan Fox was reluctantly relocated from London to Belfast to manage a small tobacco factory. Eagerly welcomed by the tiny Jewish community in Northern Ireland, his troubles deepen at work when he has to decide whether or not to hire Catholics in an all-Protestant company. He uses the same voice and mannerisms as he did as Alf Garnett: the shoulder shrug, his head movement and raising his eyebrows when he is talking. He also walks with the same determined stride.[119] Mitchell remained the Jewish Cockney despite the fact that he was not in the East End. The place made no difference upon his being. He remains aggressive even in the explosive sectarianism of Belfast.

Mitchell's threatening behaviour extended to those who worked with him. Dandy Nichols, who played Alf Garnett's long-suffering wife Else in *Till Death Us Do Part*, decided after ten years in the role that she could no longer work with Mitchell and had to leave. In the series it was explained that she had left for Australia to visit her sister.[120] Fenella Fielding, who co-starred with Mitchell on stage in *The Miser* by Moliere in 1985, said 'he was horrible to everyone, including me'.[121] The persona remained the same when one met him in real life. Indeed, the author sat next to Mitchell at a dinner that followed a talk he gave about his career at Burgh House in London. He ranged from being taciturn to extremely rude to all those around him. He also gave 'the stare' that he gave on *Till Death Us Do Part* when someone tried to engage with him and it was extremely uncomfortable to be in his presence.[122] It was as if it was Alf Garnett at the table.

∗∗∗

Warren Mitchell was unable to shed the Alf Garnett persona. He not only maintained the Cockney element to his career but became THE Cockney on television. He admitted that there was something of himself in the character. 'He could be waspish and combative.'[123] It was commented that 'it was a fine irony that Alf Garnett, the ignorant, pig-headed brutish, racist, anti-Semite, now as recognisable an Englishman as any character from Dickens should be played by a Jewish actor of radical leanings'.[124] Yet it would appear that in real life he was Alf Garnett and had an aggressive masculinity. His family referred to him as 'bully bottom' and he admitted that 'I do bully. I do shout a bit. I am opinionated'. He also commented that he was always successful in a role when he had known the man immediately.[125]

His obituary in The *Telegraph* commented that 'he could be forceful, even aggressive company, always seeing himself as something of an outsider'.[126] That feeling of being an 'outsider', the Jew, appeared always to remain with him and he constantly referred to his Jewish background. He recalled that he was often asked to play Jewish roles and if he thought they gave a bad impression he turned them down. 'I once released a part which I regarded as unintentional antisemitism. The only Jewish character in the play was a fence. There are a great many people who have never met a Jew and gain all their impressions from the television. So we have to be careful.'[127] However, he claimed that he had no interest in the religious aspect of Judaism and that his Jewishness was a fondness for Jewish jokes and food and nothing more.[128]

His identification with his Jewish background, however, was more than just jokes and food. Mitchell had considered living in Israel as he felt it was a socialist country and England lacked idealism. He and his wife spent six months studying Hebrew in London but after his wife visited Israel to consider their prospects it was decided that there would not be sufficient acting work available and they stayed in England.[129] Even though he felt Israel to be a socialist country and a preferable place to live, there were other socialist countries in the world that he could have relocated to but never considered. He was a regular visitor to Australia, frequently appearing on the Sydney stage. In 1989 he took dual British-Australian citizenship saying that he preferred its egalitarian culture to the hidebound structure of British society.[130]

He admitted that when he became famous, he did not – even when asked – automatically attend every Zionist function if he was critical of the country's policies at the time. There were occasions when he found himself in conflict with the majority of the Jewish community who he accused of supporting Israel in the way they support Arsenal. He was not prepared to believe Israel was always right just because he was Jewish, but he refused to surrender his Jewishness. 'I don't believe in my country right or wrong as far as England is concerned and I don't believe that Israel is right because I'm Jewish. I'm interested only in justice for all people concerned and I'm deeply suspicious of nationalism.'[131] He did give his support to numerous local Jewish fundraising events, as did Kossoff. These included raising funds for the Jewish care home in Cardiff, a retail therapy walk through the West End of London for Chai Cancer Care, a British Ort annual dinner and support for Young Jewish Care's talent show and Manchester Jewish Students' charity committee.[132]

He was proud of his heritage and always declared it. When he drew the winning ticket in the lottery at the first division game between Tottenham Hotspur and Southampton at White Hart Lane one Boxing Day, he announced to the crowd at half time: 'On behalf of all the Jewish supporters of Spurs, may I wish all the *goyim* (non-Jews) a good Yom Tov and well over the fast!'[133] Mitchell thus played with the porous boundaries of Jew/non-Jew through local identity. This was clearly a message for the Spurs fans as those from Southampton might have been somewhat perplexed as their local Jewish community at the time was miniscule and they would probably not have been familiar with what Mitchell was referring to.[134] The quip reflected who he was: buoyant in a very masculine environment, speaking to the Spurs fans as a 'local boy', saying a statement that shows he is Jewish but at the same time was totally ridiculous as 'well over the fast' refers to the Day of Atonement that was in October that year.

Mitchell's choice of records and events he spoke about in *Desert Island Discs* gives an indication of what was important to him. He was more than happy to acknowledge his time at Unity Theatre. It had played an important part in his life as it did for Alfie Bass, who also spoke on *Desert Island Discs* about how performing at Unity gave him a great sense of purpose.[135] Throughout the programme he mentioned his Jewish heritage. He explained that he had a strange dichotomy within him with regard to his Russian background and that although he was the grandson of a Russian lady from the Caucasus, he loved England. He was keen to go to war to fight for his country after going to Liverpool Station in 1938 to collect a girl, Ilse Moses, who was on the Kindertransport,[136] and came to live with his family and that he was shocked to hear about her experiences in Frankfurt. This anecdote illustrates his family's involvement in helping a Jewish child and Mitchell's thankfulness and love for a country that had given him safety. Included in the programme was a Jewish joke about being stranded on a desert island and one of his records was the music to the dance of the Kazatsky,[137] as it reminded him of his grandmother dancing at a Jewish wedding.[138]

If at times there was a dichotomy within him as illustrated by the phrase 'I'm an atheist, thank God',[139] there was no ambiguity with regards his political beliefs. He was in reality the antithesis of Alf politically, an active and enthusiastic socialist all his life, as was Bass, giving his support to many left-wing campaigns.[140] This was in contrast to Kossoff who had no interest in radical politics. It was his time at Unity that really cemented his newly-found socialist beliefs and he considered his time there as 'marvellous' and gave specific mention to Unity, which showed its importance in his life, whilst talking on *Desert Island Discs*.[141] Actor Harry Landis, another Unity graduate, described him as 'a good socialist fella'.[142] Warren Mitchell was 'Jewish, atheist and socialist down to the marrow of his Stoke Newington bones.'[143]

Notes

1. *Morning Star*, 16 November 2015.
2. *The Times*, 16 November 2015.
3. *Morning Star*, 16 November 2015.
4. *Daily Telegraph*, 14 November 2015.
5. The first Jewish settler in the area was Isaac Alvarez in 1688. At that time Hackney was just far enough away from the city to avoid the soot that prevailing winds blew to blight the nearby Bethnal Green. During the first half of the nineteenth century there was an influx of some wealthy Jewish families. In 1842 William Robinson noted that there were very few of that persuasion in the parish. Morris Beckman, *The Hackney Crucible* (London: Vallentine Mitchell, 1966), pp. vii, xiv–xviii.
6. Ibid.
7. Ibid., pp. xxi–xxii.
8. David Cesarani, 'A Funny Thing Happened on the Way to the Suburbs: Social Change in Anglo Jewry Between the Wars 1914-1945', *Jewish Culture and History*, 1 (1998), pp. 6, 8.
9. Ibid., p. 21.
10. *Hackney Citizen*, 9 September 2016.
11. *Sunday Express*, 1 December 1968.
12. *Sunday Express*, 27 November 2005.
13. *The Times*, 16 November 2015.
14. *Observer Review*, 24 September 1995.
15. *Jewish Chronicle*, 18 November 1966.
16. Warren Mitchell interviewed by Sue Lawley, *Desert Island Discs*, BBC Radio 4, 3 December 1999.
17. *Jewish Chronicle*, 11 December 2015.
18. *Jewish Chronicle*, 18 November 1966.
19. *The Times*, 31 December 1990.
20. *Evening Standard*, 8 October 1976.
21. *Jewish Chronicle*, 25 October 2002.
22. *Daily Mail*, 27 April 1996.
23. *Desert Island Discs*, 3 December 1999, BBC Radio 4.
24. *Sunday Express*, 1 December 1968.
25. *Evening Standard*, 30 October 2000.
26. *Independent*, 10 February 2000.
27. *Guardian*, 16 November 2015.
28. *Desert Island Discs*, 3 December 1999, BBC Radio 4.
29. Harry Landis: Interview with Isabelle Seddon, 11 January 2016, London.
30. *Daily Mail*, 14 November 2015.
31. *Ham & High*, 25 March 2010.
32. The Tolpuddle Martyrs were a group of nineteenth-century Dorset agricultural labourers who were arrested for and convicted of swearing a secret and illegal oath as members of the Friendly Society of Agricultural Labourers, a forerunner to a trade union. The men sought only to resist a reduction in wages, but the government feared rural unrest and they were sentenced to seven years penal transportation to Australia.
33. *The Story of Unity Theatre*, Unity Theatre Trust recording 2009, British Library Sound Archives 1DVDR0001737.

34. Ibid.
35. Bill Rowbotham (Owens) was an actor and songwriter who became famous for his role in the British sitcom *Last of the Summer Wine*.
36. Constantin Stanislavski (1863–1938) developed a naturalistic performance method technique known as 'method acting' that allowed actors to use their personal histories to express authentic emotion and to create rich characters. www.biography.com, accessed 15 August 2018.
37. *The Story of Unity Theatre*, Unity Theatre Trust recording, 2009.
38. Chambers, *The Story of Unity Theatre*, p. 307.
39. *The Story of Unity Theatre*, Unity Theatre Trust recording, 2009.
40. *Observer*, 19 September 1976.
41. *Observer*, 24 September 1995.
42. *Daily Mirror*, 23 March 1967.
43. *Morning Star*, 16 November 2015.
44. *The Times*, 16 November 2015.
45. Mitchell is an English and Scottish surname derived from the name Michael.www.ancestry.co.uk, accessed 15 August 2018. The name was also adopted by Yvonne Mitchell (1915–79), an English Jewish stage, television and film actress who changed her name by deed poll from Yvonne Frances Joseph in 1946. Yvonne Mitchell, *Actress* (London: Routledge & Paul, 1957).
46. *Daily Mail*, 14 November 2015.
47. *Jewish Chronicle*, 18 November 1966.
48. Ibid.
49. www.screenonline.org.uk, accessed 19 January 2018.
50. The *Carry On* films were British comedies whose humour was in the British comic tradition of the music hall and bawdy seaside postcards.
51. *King Lear Programme*, West Yorkshire Playhouse, 22 September–28 October 1995.
52. *Daily Star*, 15 November 2015.
53. *Daily Mail*, 20 March 1969.
54. *Jewish Chronicle*, 11 December 2015.
55. www.independent.co.uk, 31 July 1998, accessed 20 March 2018.
56. 'Warren Mitchell', BBC News, Entertainment & Arts, 14 November 2015.
57. Mark Ward, *A Family at War: The Unofficial and Unauthorised Guide to Till Death Us Do Part* (Tolworth: Telos Publishing, 2008).
58. Johnny Speight, *Alf Garnett: The Thoughts of Chairman Alf: Alf Garnett's Little Blue Book Or Where England Went Wrong* (London: Robson Books, 1973), pp. 6–10.
59. Mary Whitehouse was the founder of the National Viewers and Listeners Association and the Clean Up National TV Campaign.
60. Gavin Schaffer, *The Vision of a Nation. Making Multiculturalism on British Television 1960-80* (Basingstoke: Palgrave Macmillan, 2014), p. 190.
61. A. Medhurst, *A National Joke: Popular Comedy and English Cultural Identities* (London: Routledge, 2007), p. 38.
62. Enoch Powell was a right-wing Conservative politician famous for the 'Rivers of Blood' speech in Birmingham 1968 in which he criticized the Commonwealth immigration policy and the proposed anti-discrimination legislation.
63. Schaffer, *The Vision of a Nation*, pp. 188–9.
64. Speight, *Alf Garnett: The Thoughts of Chairman Alf*, pp. 6–10.
65. *Desert Island Discs*, 3 December 1999.

66. Gavin Schaffer, 'Till Death Us Do Part and the BBC: Racial Politics and the British Working Classes 1965–75', *Journal of Contemporary History*, 45: 2 (April 2010), pp. 454, 459.
67. Ibid., p. 464.
68. Speight, *The Thoughts of Chairman Alf*, pp. 21–2.
69. Ibid., p. 39.
70. Ibid., p. 83.
71. Ibid., pp. 461, 463.
72. *Jewish Chronicle*, 18 November 1966.
73. *Jewish Chronicle*, 11 January 1974.
74. *Jewish Chronicle*, 20 November 2015.
75. Alf Garnett, 'God was Church of England. Jesus Was after the Oil', www.youtube.com.
76. 'Holiday in Bournemouth', *Till Death Us Do Part*, BBC 1, SO4EO3, 27 September 1972.
77. 'Intolerance', *Till Death Us Do Part*, BBC 1, SE1E04, 27 June 1966.
78. Tony Moss was executive producer of the BBC2 programme *A Tribute to Johnny Speight*, 1 August 1998, www.independent.co.uk, accessed 20 March 2018.
79. David Efron, *Gesture, Race and Culture* (The Hague: Mouton, 1972), p. 81.
80. *Morning Star*, 16 November 2015. George Tovey (1914–82) went on to appear in films *Frenzy* (1972), *Doctor Who* (1963) and *Steptoe and Son Ride Again* (1973).
81. *The Times*, 31 December 1990.
82. *Independent*, 7 December 2000.
83. The same applied to Bass who only appeared in minor roles as a servant at the 1948 Shakespeare season, Stratford on Avon.
84. *King Lear Programme*, West Yorkshire Playhouse, 22 September–28 October 1995.
85. Ibid.
86. Meir Tzelniker (1894–1982) appeared mainly in Yiddish theatre but was a character actor in English language plays and films such as *It Always Rains on Sundays* (1947) and *Expresso Bongo* (1959).
87. *Jewish Chronicle*, 18 November 1966.
88. *Daily Express*, 13 December 2003.
89. Steven Berkoff, 'Exploring the Vanishing Jewish East End', www.towerhamlets.co.uk, accessed 1 September 2018.
90. *Daily Express*, 19 September 2003.
91. *Jewish Chronicle*, 21 December 2007.
92. Ibid.
93. *Guardian*, 10 September 2003.
94. *Guardian*, 12 September 2003.
95. *Evening Standard*, 12 September 2003.
96. *Jewish Chronicle*, 3 March 2000.
97. *Evening Standard*, 9 April 2008.
98. *Daily Telegraph*, 9 April 2008.
99. *The Times*, 9 April 2008.
100. *Jewish Chronicle*, 18 January 1991.
101. *Jewish Chronicle* 11 December 2015.
102. *The Times*, 31 December 1990.
103. *Evening Standard*, 11 January 1991.
104. *Financial Times*, 11 January 1991.
105. *Independent*, 9 January 1991.

106. Warren Rosenberg, *Legacy of Rage: Jewish Masculinity, Violence and Culture* (Amhurst, MA: University of Massachusetts Press, 2001), p. 1.
107. *The Times*, 24 January 1991.
108. *Guardian*, 12 January 1991.
109. *Daily Telegraph*, 11 January 1991.
110. *Observer,* 13 January 1991.
111. Michael Billington, *Harold Pinter* (London: Faber and Faber, 2007), p. 325.
112. *Evening Standard*, 14 November 1980.
113. *The Times*, 16 November 2015.
114. *Evening Standard*, 12 November 1980.
115. *Sunday Telegraph*, 16 November 1980.
116. 'Five Best Moments', *Till Death Us Do Part*, www.youtube.com.
117. 'Wheelchair in the Road', *Till Death Us Do Part*, www.youtube.com.
118. 'Christmas Club Books', *Till Death Us Do Part*, www.youtube.com.
119. www.troublesarchive.com; britishclassiccomedy.co.uk, accessed 5 December 2017.
120. Dandy Nichols, www.museum.tv, accessed 1 September 2018.
121. Fenella Fielding and Simon McKay, *Do You Mind If I Smoke?* (London: Peter Owen, 2017); *Guardian*, 13 September 2018.
122. 'Lifelines: Evening with Warren Mitchell', 6 October 2005, Burgh House, Hampstead, London.
123. *The Times*, 16 November 2015.
124. *Evening Standard*, 8 October 1976.
125. *Desert Island Discs*, 3 December 1999.
126. *Daily Telegraph,* 14 November 2015.
127. *Jewish Chronicle*, 18 November 1966.
128. *Jewish Chronicle*, 10 September 1971.
129. *Jewish Chronicle*, 18 November 1966.
130. www.telegraph.co.uk, 14 November 2015, accessed 11 May 2018.
131. *Jewish Chronicle*, 10 September 1971.
132. *Jewish Chronicle*, 30 November 1990; 15 August 2003; 30 September 2006; 6 November 1998; 18 October 1990.
133. *Jewish Chronicle*, 2 January 1981.
134. The Jewish population in Southampton, according to the Jewish Year Books of 1966 and 1991 were 150 (1965) and 105 (1990), www.jewishgen.org.
135. *Desert Island Discs*, PABX 4904, BBC Written Archives.
136. The Kindertransport was an organized rescue that took place during the nine months prior to the outbreak of the Second World War. The United Kingdom took in nearly 10,000, predominantly Jewish children, from Germany, Austria, Czechoslovakia and Poland. The children were placed in British foster homes, hostels, schools and farms and often they were the only members of their families that survived the Holocaust.
137. A Russian squatting dance.
138. *Desert Island Discs*, 3 December 1999.
139. *Jewish Chronicle*, 7 September 2007.
140. *Morning Star*, 16 November 2015.
141. *Desert Island Discs*, 3 December 1999.
142. Harry Landis: Interview with Isabelle Seddon, 11 January 2016, London.
143. *Jewish Chronicle*, 21 November 2015.

4

Lionel Bart

Lionel Bart epitomized the start of the 1960s in Britain, which he uniquely captured in song and spirit. He was one of the few composers to deal non-condescendingly with the working classes, transposing their life styles and vernacular to the musical stage. 'Nobody tries to be la-de-la uppity, there's a cuppa tea for all', sings the Artful Dodger to Oliver in the musical *Oliver!*[1] The success of *Oliver!* and other musicals including *Blitz!* and '*Fings Ain't Wot They Used T'Be* owed much to his East End Jewish background. Bart is an example of one who followed the most commercial path, and to what extent his time at Unity Theatre, and whether his left-wing political views were superficial, will be explored. His exposure to the non-Jewish East End Cockney world that influenced his work and enabled him to be both a 'Jewish Cockney' and so commercially successful, will also be interrogated.

Background

Lionel Bart was born Lionel Begleiter at Mother Levy's at 24 Underwood Road, East London on 1 August 1930. This was a Jewish maternity home and many of East European migrant origin chose to be here rather than the local large London Hospital, as it was more intimate and they felt at ease surrounded by a nursing staff sympathetic to Jewish ritual and culture.[2] Bart's parents, Morris Begleiter and Yetta Darumstundler, were originally from Sambor, Galicia (then part of the Austro-Hapsburg Empire). They married in 1910 and arrived in Britain in 1912. Davina Gold, Bart's niece and the daughter of his sister Renee, recalls different stories circulating among the family as to why they came to Britain in 1912. Some said that it was due to the pogroms, but Gold felt that in all likelihood it was because Bart's aunt was already here, and they were looking for a better life.[3]

David Cesarani considered why many immigrants constructed tales about escaping pogroms, which were not always necessarily true, and passed them on to their children in such a way that it formed the back of their identity as Jews in Britain. One explanation was the public debate over mass immigration. From the time of the great protest against pogroms in

February 1882, the Anglo-Jewish leadership explained that the Tsarist government was driving Jews out by a combination of religious intolerance, political repression and economic victimization. The immigrants were characterized as refugees and were seeking asylum in Britain. This formula was designed to appeal to liberal opinion and to mask the underlying economic opportunism behind the steady stream of emigration that had been underway since the 1860s. The use of the asylum formula was hardened by the political struggle over legislation to restrict alien immigration which began in the mid-1880s and culminated in the Aliens Act of 1905. Genuine refugees, those defined as seeking to enter the country to avoid persecution or punishment on religious and political grounds, were exempted. After the 1906 fall of the Conservative government that had passed the Aliens Act, the new Liberal Home Secretary Herbert Gladstone issued instructions to immigration officers and boards that benefit of doubt should be given to those from areas of Eastern Europe where pogroms had occurred and who claimed refugee status. It was therefore in the interests of Anglo-Jewish representatives and the immigrants themselves to characterize the flow of migration as a flight from persecution. For the immigrants at the point of arrival, the stated reasons for their migration could make the difference between admission to Britain and instant deportation.[4]

The debate over immigration and the implementation of the Aliens Act were responsible for homogenising accounts of migration and settlement and helped to generate a myth of origin. In respect of Bart's family, there were no pogroms in Galicia. Other functions of the myth of origin were to manifest as patriotism and love of the new country. Tales of murder and pogroms made immigrants glad to be British and loyal subjects of the King. The alibi of forced conscription into the Russian army was tuned to a liberal English audience who loathed standing armies and conscription. These myths could serve as an alibi for opportunist migration and a way of creating and transmitting group memories, establishing and preserving a sense of community.[5]

It seems very likely that Bart's family left Galicia not because of pogroms but due to poverty and lack of opportunities to better themselves. Yet life in England presented its difficulties. Morris Begleiter was interned on the Isle of Man for two months from 15 November 1915 as Galicia was considered enemy territory as it was in the Austro-Hungarian Empire.[6] On 5 August 1914 Home Secretary Reginald McKenna rushed through Parliament an Aliens Restriction Act. The speed with which it was enacted resulted from years of prior planning inspired by war scares and spy mania.

Under the Act there was control over the landing of aliens and areas were set up where they were not allowed to reside. From August 1914 to May 1915 the government implemented a policy of selective arrest and internment of Germans and Austrians of military age. The number in captivity reached 10,000 by late 1914. After the sinking of the ocean liner *Lusitania* by a German submarine on 7 May 1915, a wave of popular anti-alienism prompted the government to order the internment of all enemy alien males. The number of those interned rose to 32,000 over the next two years.[7]

Anti-alienism persisted after the First World War ended. It was fuelled by wartime animosities, the repercussions of the Russian revolution, economic dislocation and a prolonged socio-political crisis. Anti-alien rhetoric figured prominently in the General Elections of 1918 and 1924. Between 1919 and 1929 aliens were subject to a set of draconian practices extending from registration to expulsion. The 1919 Aliens Restriction Act added new restrictions to the civil and employment rights of aliens already resident in Britain. This partly reflected concern about rising unemployment. Dozens of Jews were expelled for allegedly engaging in subversive Bolshevik activities. It was a criminal offence for any alien to promote industrial unrest. Those residents in the country since 1914 were prohibited from changing their name and were excluded from employment in the civil service and could not serve on a jury. The 1919 Act elevated anti-alienism to a new level of viciousness which was then sustained throughout the 1920s by constant public debate and a series of measures against aliens in general and specific groups: Jews, Chinese and Blacks.[8]

Non-naturalized East European Jews who had arrived before 1914 formed the largest body of aliens in Britain. They found themselves labouring under a body of regulations whereby they could be deported for trivial offences. Non-British born Jews, even if they were naturalized, and their children were denied employment in the civil service and local government. They were also barred from council housing and council scholarships in London. Alien Jews were held in second-class status by the long delay and high costs of naturalization. Home Office officials covertly operated a racial hierarchy by which Slavs, Jews and other races from central and Eastern Europe were obliged to wait far longer than the statutory period before naturalisation was given. Anti-alienism continued during the 1920s and as unemployment rose after 1929 the government had little option but to keep immigration down to a trickle.[9]

Morris Begleiter applied for naturalization on 15 May 1939. In it he wrote: 'In 1926 or 1927 I was sued at Whitechapel County Court for £6 in respect of goods bought on credit'. He noted that the sum had been paid back in full. Other instances were in 1929 when 'I was sued for about £8, this sum being the balance of a loan granted by the plaintiff' and in 1930 when he was sued for £3 for balance of rent due for his workshop. In both instances he stated that judgement was made in favour of the plaintiff. The references that accompanied the application were from people who lived and worked in the East End and knew him professionally and socially, tailors D. Nzdus, Myer Scheincle and Alf Mansfeld, who carried out insurance transactions for him.[10] The choice of referees showed that his life did not extend out of the East End area as if it did he would probably have chosen referees from a more established English background. Revealingly, his application was rejected. Government policy also made it very difficult for aliens in the country who had not been naturalized in terms of access to public housing and education. In addition, there was the threat of deportation, especially for those who had broken the law which was relevant in the case of Bart's father.

His next application was signed on 24 September 1948 and witnessed by officials from the Metropolitan Police (Special Branch).[11] A police report that accompanied the application dated 30 June 1947 stated that he had been operating his business under the name Morris Berg without having received exemption under the Aliens Restriction Amendment Act 1919 and had not registered under the Registration of Business Names Act 1916. Begleiter expressed ignorance of the regulations.[12] The report also highlighted that Begleiter's earlier application was not entirely accurate. He was sent to Brixton Prison for non-payment of debts from 1 March 1927 for fourteen days. Begleiter claimed that he was in prison for only two days and payment was made in full. It was also mentioned that Begleiter had been summoned to Whitechapel County Court in 1930 and 1931 for debts of £10.3.6d and £11.9.8d but they had not been paid to date. Nevertheless, the report stated that his English was adequate, and he and his wife were of good character. In the slightly more tolerant climate of the post-war era, naturalization was now granted.

It would appear from the above that Begleiter lived on the edge of respectability and his dealings were probably not always strictly within the law. William Goldman who worked for Morris Begleiter described him as a lazy, self-important bully whose recreations were betting, drinking brandy and taking vapour baths and who confided that he had practised seventeen variations of the sexual act.[13] Money would have been a constant concern as Bart's niece Andrea Mattock recalls that her grandfather was a great gambler, as was her grandmother who loved going to the dog races. Unable to read or write English she would just point out the numbers that she wanted to bet on. Yet at the same time she brought up her family in a 'traditional' Jewish way, observing Jewish beliefs and practices.[14]

Bart was very aware of his Jewish heritage. His life was coloured by his family life and growing up in the heart of the Jewish East End.[15] His mother had eleven children but only seven survived. His siblings were Stan, Fay, Harry, Sam, Debbie and Renee. He considered himself an afterthought – 'the last shake in the bag' as his father called him.[16] There was an interval of six years between him and his sister Renee. 'Mum was 46 and Dad in his 50s when I was born. I was always known as Baby and fussed over a lot. Sometimes I was neglected being the youngest. Other times loved to distraction.' Bart believed himself to be the runt of the litter. He acknowledged that his constant craving for admiration and affection throughout his life had their origins in those days of self doubt. In compensation he persuaded himself he was special and that one day the world would share his belief that fame was due.[17]

Bart's description of his family contrasts with the usual image of the loving Jewish traditional family. There is myth-making about the Jewish family in modern times. Jews and Gentiles alike have constructed and perpetuated a romantically idealized image of the Jewish family as warm, supportive and ever-nurturing. This image was derived in part from the nostalgia of the Jews who had moved from the relatively insular communities of traditional Jewry into the anonymity and tension of modern Western society. Looking back these Jews saw the family of their childhood as their refuge in a new and sometimes hostile environment.[18]

Yet Bart admitted in an interview on the *South Bank Show* in 1964 that his father was a slave driver and his parents had a love-hate relationship.[19] Bart's creativity was not always appreciated. Broadcaster Ned Sherrin recalls that when Bart came home from the Royal Air Force (RAF), he found that his paintings had been thrown out. He realized that he needed to leave home and prove himself.[20] Andrea Mattock, whose mother was Bart's oldest sister and who spent a lot of time in Bart's household, has a different perspective. She remembers the family as being very close knit and that Bart was adored by his mother.[21]

The loving traditional family life was not always experienced by the others featured in this book. Alfie Bass's mother died when he was young, and his father struggled to care for his family. 'There was no one to look after me properly and I sort of ran wild.'[22] Warren Mitchell experienced tensions within his household as his grandmother was very orthodox and forbade him to appear in a school Christmas play because the Christmas pudding he would eat at the end of the play was not kosher,[23] whereas his mother would feed him non-kosher food when they were out.[24] His father appeared to have a temper and hit him when Mitchell refused to fast on *Yom Kippur*.[25] This lack of direction and tension could have contributed to their not following a conventional Jewish path. In contrast David Kossoff, who was more traditional, appeared to have had a more secure childhood and adored his father.[26]

Bart's beginnings were humble. He lived at 43 Ellen Street, Whitechapel, before moving to 1 Princelet Street in 1936 and 39 Stepney Way, Stepney in 1941.[27] Ellen Street and Princelet Street were in the heart of the Jewish East End as shown in the 1899 map produced by Charles Russell and H. S. Lewis of Jewish London mentioned in the Introduction. Bart's first home in Ellen Street was marked by a medium blue colour which indicated that there were between 75 and 95 per cent Jews on that street and when he moved to Princelet Street, the area was dark blue which showed that the population was 95 to 100 per cent Jewish.[28] David Roper, Bart's biographer, observes: 'To be brought up in such a Jewish milieu was bound to have had an influence on Bart. Shoreditch, Whitechapel, Bethnal Green and Mile End were the boundaries of Bart's world'.[29] By the 1930s, there were 333,000 Jews in England, 183,000 in London. Some 60 per cent of London's Jews lived in the East End, over half of them in Stepney, an area with the largest Jewish population in the country. By 1931, a quarter of Stepney's population had been born abroad, more than any other borough in the country. Most were Jewish immigrants.[30] Bart is the only one of those studied in this book who lived in such a predominantly Jewish part of the East End. Bass lived in Bethnal Green which had a higher percentage of non-Jews and Kossoff and Mitchell lived on the edge of the East End that had even fewer Jews.

Bart's father was a tailor (as were the fathers of Bass and Kossoff), and this profession was adopted by nearly everyone in the family, with a workshop at the bottom of the garden next to the outdoor toilet. 'On a good week he'd turn out 50 ladies' coats. In the early days there were not many good weeks.'[31] He was a high-spirited child and niece Davina Gold recalled a family story about his cutting off the fingers of his aunt's gloves when she came to visit.[32] Despite his naughtiness, there were inklings of his creativity at an early age. When he was six his father bought him a violin from Petticoat Lane market after his headmistress said he was an artistic genius. He had lessons and also learnt to play the piano with one finger, then four. At the age of thirteen he was one of nine students to win a junior scholarship to St Martin's School of Art in Charing Cross Road on the edge of the Soho

140   *East End Jews and Left-Wing Theatre*

district.[33] It was this opportunity that allowed him to venture out of the East End.

At this point Soho was a cosmopolitan district that attracted immigrants of many origins, bohemians, drinkers, teenagers and sexual adventurers. It encompassed European and African street life, restaurants, after-hours drinking clubs and jazz. It was also the capital's 'sexual gymnasium' for people of every persuasion.[34] Soho was irresistible to the young as it offered freedom. In the early 1950s London was suffering from post-war depression and it was a revelation to discover people who behaved outrageously without a twinge of guilt and drank so recklessly that when they met the next morning they had to ask if they needed to apologize for the day before.[35]

Bart was quick to adapt and lived a double life. At St. Martin's he encountered a whole new world of ideas and people. One of the first models he had to draw was the writer and raconteur Quentin Crisp.[36] The recreational geographical divide ran along the axis from the West End to the East End. The West End was the antithesis of the East End. It was the location of mainstream popular culture with its galleries and bookshops unlike the Yiddish theatre of the East End. The Lyons Corner House that served traditional British light refreshments was an alternative to Jewish cooking. 'All offered a glimpse of sex and the promise of forbidden liaisons conducted beyond the gaze of watchful elders.'[37]

Exposure to another world away from the confines of the Jewish East End probably stood Bart in good stead for his time in the RAF. In 1948 he was called up for National Service and it was there that he became friends with John Gorman. They met on the train to basic training at RAF Padgate and had an instant rapport. Gorman was not Jewish but they both came from modest East End backgrounds and were of similar leftish political persuasions.[38] Gorman, who was from Stratford in the East End, was the son of a carpenter and domestic worker and a member of the Communist Party. Gorman considered their meeting a moment of fate and that they were destined to be business partners as well as lifelong friends. They were posted to various stations together, shared billets and worked in the same sections throughout their time in the RAF.[39] Their fellow servicemen were a cross-section of society, from all over Britain and from widely different cultural backgrounds. Gorman recalled that they all lived as an intimate and artificial family sharing a common ambition – to be demobbed.[40]

After finishing National Service, Bart and Gorman started a silk screen printing business at 53 Underwood Road, Hackney, named G & B Arts after the two initials of their surname.[41] They went through hard times financially, living from week to week on a cash basis.[42] It would appear that his close relationship with Gorman probably had an influence on his political outlook. Gorman joined the Communist Party in 1949 whilst serving in the RAF. David Roper, Bart's biographer, felt that 'Bart's relationship with Gorman took them both into the Communist Party'.[43]

Politics and Unity Theatre

Bart joined the Stamford Hill branch of the Communist Party in 1951. As discussed in the Introduction, it was not unusual for someone of Bart's background to join the Party although he did so at quite a late date. 'It was the thing for him to do', comments Andrea Mattock.[44] Gorman points out that Bart was sympathetic to left-wing causes. His brother Sam was a docker who had fought with the International Brigade in Spain while he himself had witnessed the antisemitism of Mosley's fascists in the East End. Davina Gold said her mother would recall how Sam would teach her and Bart to sing the left-wing anthem 'The Internationale' in the kitchen and that her grandmother would tell them to be quiet.[45] Bart listened to the street corner Communists in Stepney, especially the charismatic orator Solly Kaye.[46] Bart accepted the Communists as stalwart anti-fascists and champions of the poor.[47]

Yet how deeply political was Bart? David and Caroline Stafford's only mention of Bart's politics in the biography *Fings Ain't Wot They Used T'Be* is that two years of exposure to Gorman's dogged rhetoric finally coaxed him into becoming a card-carrying Communist.[48] Gorman, who was very active in the Party until he left in 1956, does not mention Bart in the chapters 'Comrades and Friends' or 'All in the Cause' in his autobiography *Knocking Down Ginger* when he describes his political involvement and activities in great detail.[49]

At the same time that Bart joined the Party, he became active in the International Youth Centre, a club for left-wing young people.[50] Another attendee, John Gold, recalled how they put on regular cabarets and in 1952 wrote the club's annual revue.[51] They were so encouraged by its success they went to the Unity Theatre in 1952 to audition for a part in Leonard Irwin's *The Wages of Eve*, a Romeo and Juliet story which took place across the picket line of an industrial dispute. Bart began to embrace the world and ideology of Unity. The Communist Party backed Unity and Bart readily joined his new friends, Communist writers and actors that included Alfie Bass, who worked late in the night with Bart on new ideas for shows.[52]

It would appear that Bart joined in with what was expected of him amongst the people he mixed with. Unity member John Gold did not feel that Bart was overtly political.[53] Actor Harry Landis who worked with Bart on several projects in Unity shared the same view. 'He put his mind to it and wrote some left-wing songs. He was an East End boy from an area where people struggled. He was partly involved but not all that committed.'[54] Their views are probably accurate as there appears that Bart had no active involvement with the Communist Party once he achieved fame and fortune. Indeed, there is no mention of him in the documents held at the Communist Party of Great Britain Archive.[55] This was unlike Bass and Mitchell who always maintained their connection with left-wing politics even when they achieved fame.

To be part of Unity, and to work with those involved, was a great opportunity for Bart. At Unity he got the feel for the world of entertainment. 'Everything was beginning to change in the early 1950s and I was lucky to be in at the beginning.'[56] Muriel Walker, the daughter of Jewish immigrants from Lithuania and a production manager at Unity, has tellingly argued that Bart was not political but simply ambitious.[57] It was during his time at Unity that Bart gained confidence and began to develop his skills. Una Brandon-Jones remembered Bart's early days in Unity when he came with John Gold to audition for *The Wages of Eve*. She described Bart as 'a lean fresh looking Jewish lad'. Gold was given the lead part and Bart the understudy.[58]

Binnie Yates, who played the part of Eve in *Wages for Eve*, remembered Bart fondly. 'All the time he was there he was at the piano trying out tunes. He was self-effacing and sweet. He was not a good actor but he looked after me and was reassuring.' Yates came from a family of Russian-Polish Jewish origin who were members of the Communist Party.[59] She felt that Bart's time as an understudy was fruitful. 'For it was hanging around the theatre at rehearsals that he got to know Jack (Grossman) and the rest of us and that the idea matured for the two of them to collaborate in writing a revue.'[60]

Bart recalled that there was a board at the theatre and a notice went up to ask if anyone interested in writing some songs. 'So I did a couple for a laugh. I sang the songs to someone who could write notations, pinned them on the notice board. Alfie Bass collared me and said he thought they weren't half bad.'[61] The song-words were for a tune called *Turn It Up* and they appeared in the political revue of the same name which was directed by Bass. This was the start of Bart's career in the theatre.[62] *The Stage* review commented that Bart had a definite gift for both lyrics and witty music.[63]

Documentary film maker Jack Grossman described Bart's involvement in *Turn It Up*. A theme would be decided, and Bart would come back the next day with lyrics. He also did not think that Bart was at all political but had a great talent for picking a headline in the newspaper, extracting its essence and making a song of it. He pointed out that a lot of people used Unity as a stepping stone and Bart was no exception. 'I always knew he would fit into whatever surroundings he chose. He was a bit of a chameleon and he's always been a good bluffer. He loved rubbing shoulders with famous people.' He also considered Bart to be very much in the spirit of the times. 'Here was a working class boy taking advantage of the fact that there were no longer any social rules. Nobody said you can't do that or you can't go there...come the hour, cometh the man.'[64]

Bart began to map out his destiny and this included changing his name. He was not the only one at Unity to have done so. Alfie Bass, the director of *Turn It Up,* had been born Abraham Basalinsky. Warren Mitchell's surname had been Misell. It was all part of launching their careers and to be more acceptable to the non-Jewish world. Bart's new name was plain, simple and memorable. Lionel Begleiter was not. A story about how Bart's change of name came about was that he was on a bus passing St Bartholomew's Hospital and decided upon the name Bart – although there are no official records of his having made an application to change his name by deed poll.[65]

The new name was not the only change for Bart at this time. His involvement with Unity was about to alter his life dramatically. His lyrics were regularly commissioned and were included in an agit-prop version of *Cinderella* and the revue *Peacemeal.* He became one of Unity's main writers and the driving force behind several shows. His first musical was *Wally Pone,* an updating of Ben Jonson's *Volpone,* a Jacobean comedy of manners about a successful conman who is finally unmasked by those he duped.[66] It was set in the contemporary world of the Soho vice barons and satirized the fashionable coffee bar culture that preceded the swinging 1960s. It ran for eight weeks from 18 July 1958. *The Stage* review pointed out that the play spanned the centuries with ease but that in using classics as a peg for social comment, the satire needed to be brilliant. It was not enough to aim at the target; the lyricist must score bull's eye. Bart does this with 'Money Maketh Man' and 'The Parasite'.[67] The choice of lyrics shows Bart's empathy with the underdog against the oppressor so maybe he was not totally apolitical although he could have been opportunist in producing works along the lines of what Unity would want.

The road to success beckoned. Bart acknowledged that Unity had a profound and lasting influence on his work and credited his time there with teaching him everything he knew. He learnt the power of simplicity in composition and theatrical effect, stagecraft, how a show was put together from the ground up and what it was that actors and singers did and what he needed to do to improve. 'He witnessed at first hand the atavistic spell that those old belting oom-pah music hall styles could weave over an audience. Most of all he learned that he was good at it.'[68]

Marc Napolitano, author of *Oliver! A Dickensian Musical* felt Bart gained much from his time with Unity including experience with a collaborative and somewhat frenetic production methodology that would come to define many of his later theatrical projects. Looking back on his career, Bart said that he hated working alone and had to work to a deadline with a team. Unity encouraged its members to immerse themselves in all elements of staging a show and Bart was given an unparalleled hands-on education in the theatrical production process. He began his career under the tutelage of a group of artists who were committed to preserving the entertainment traditions of the working classes. Just as music hall would prove essential to Bart's shows, it was likewise an integral part of the Unity repertoire.[69]

Unity felt that Bart was indebted to them. Bart's agent Jock Jacobsen had written to Unity director Heinz Bernard on 23 May 1958 with a contract in respect of royalties to be paid if Bart's work transferred elsewhere or appeared on television and radio. 'All amounts of percentages that the Unity Theatre Society are to receive shall be limited and not exceed £300.' Bernard responded in a letter dated 30 May 1958 that more leeway should be allowed as Unity was always in financial difficulty and always took risks putting on new plays. If a play transferred and was successful, Unity should get a proper financial reward which would enable them to put on other plays. 'As you are probably aware Lionel Bart was himself a very active member of Unity Theatre for a number of years. His present, well deserved success must in no small measure be due to the opportunity this theatre gave him to develop his talent.' In response Bart agreed to a royalty of 1.5 per cent on box office receipts on all professional productions in the UK for two years following the last production at Unity. The contract was signed on 23 June 1958.[70] In 1963, when he had become famous, he did remember to still give support and his name was included among a list of sponsors of the Unity Theatre Trust who were raising the £50,000 needed for the purchase and reconstruction of a new theatre building. The names included playwright John Osbourne, actors Sybil Thorndike, Alec Guinness and theatre director Joan Littlewood.[71] Littlewood, who ran the Theatre Workshop in Stratford East, was often called 'the mother of modern theatre'.[72] It was whilst Bart was at Unity that his talent was spotted by Littlewood and his career started to develop.

Career

To be chosen by Littlewood was fortuitous for Bart. His first real success came in 1959 writing songs for a play called *Fings Ain't Wot They Used T'Be*, a Cockney comedy, and by the end of 1959 both this musical and *Lock Up Your Daughters*, based upon an eighteenth-century comedy by Henry Fielding, were running successfully in London's West End. It was also in the

14. Lionel Bart, 1959, taken for the launch of the LP record *Bart for Bart's Sake* (Pamela Chandler), courtesy of Lionel Bart Foundation Archive

late 1950s that he wrote songs for the early British rock and roll stars Tommy Steele ('Rock with the Caveman' and 'Little White Bull') and Cliff Richard ('Living Doll') that topped the musical charts. Despite his chart success, he yearned to have his songs performed in the theatre. In June 1960 he opened the show *Oliver!* to immediate success. In 1968 Colombia Pictures released the film version of *Oliver!* which received 11 Academy Award nominations. There were other fairly successful shows such as *Blitz!* and *Maggie May* but they never achieved the same success and acclaim as *Oliver!* In 1965, in order to finance his next musical show *Twang!,* he signed away all the rights to *Oliver!* The show received disastrous reviews and Bart was declared bankrupt in 1972. His fall from grace was as dramatic as his ascent and he ended up an impoverished alcoholic living in shabby obscurity.[73]

As mentioned above his ascent began at Stratford East. One of the plays that Littlewood read was a script *Fings Ain't Wot They Used T'Be* by Frank Norman, a young writer who had been brought up in care and had spent time in prison for petty crimes. Littlewood told Norman that what he had written was marvellous but it should not be put on as a straight play 'like all that rubbish that the West End management put on', but it should be a musical and she had met 'a marvellous nutcase called Lionel Bart who had agreed to write some songs'.[74] In addition to being familiar with Bart's work at Unity, Littlewood had met him through British theatre and film director Oscar Lewenstein, who was general manager and artistic director of the Royal Court Theatre and a former manager at Unity.[75] Post-war theatrical discourse was dominated by talk of the Royal Court Theatre and Theatre Workshop. Unity was the elder statesman of these leftist troupes.[76]

Littlewood understood the power of music hall as a working-class institution. The interactive nature of music hall entertainment was conducive to creating the type of theatrical environment Littlewood hoped would draw working-class patrons to Stratford East. Bart was intrigued by her use of music hall to foster camaraderie between the audience and cast. He felt an affinity with this approach from his childhood when he went to the Yiddish theatre.[77]

The show *Fings Ain't Wot They Used T'Be* had its roots in Unity as some of the ideas from *Wally Pone* were incorporated, notably the opening song 'G'night Dearie'. Yet Bart has been accused of losing sight of his Unity roots and that the Unity chapter of his career never received the full attention that it deserved regarding his development as a theatrical composer. Unity veteran Harry Landis considered that Bart thought it sounded better to have said that he started his career with Joan Littlewood's theatre as it was well known. Despite these accusations, Bart attributed his success to both. He said in an interview with the *Belfast News Letter* that Unity was a turning point in his life but also acknowledged the importance of Joan Littlewood as writing for the stage had been a closed shop and she opened doors of opportunity for him.[78]

Fings Ain't Wot They Used T'Be opened at the Theatre Royal Stratford on 17 February 1959 and the lyrics and music by Bart contributed a great deal to the success of the show. It was a rousing knockabout East End 'knees up' style of theatre that owed a great debt to popular variety entertainment.[79] Its playwright Frank Norman commented that the theatre was packed out night after night with Cockneys, most of whom had never been to a theatre in their lives. Littlewood said that previously the voice of the Cockney was one long whine of servitude.[80] The cast revelled in the Cockney slang and competed to see who could be the boldest, funniest and most obscure and not play out the usual comic charladies and 'gor blimey' dustmen.[81] The local audience appreciated not only its colour but its language that came from their streets and was perceived as authentic.[82]

In this play, Fred Cochrane, the hero, is a down at heel gangster about to make a comeback. Lil Smith is his loyal moll, a tart with a heart of gold, who longs for respectability and keeps a marriage licence ready for her lucky day. Fred's gambling den provides a refuge for the failures of the underworld: Paddy the gambler, Tosher with his girls Betty and Rosey, and Redhot, a sad little burglar who never manages to get warm. They all look to Fred for a living and when he wins on the horses it seems that the gang may be back in business. Fred redecorates the place and at the opening the horrible Percy Fortesque comes to gamble and a rival leader Meatface is beaten in a razor fight. The play ends with a wedding. Fred and Lil are giving up crime and handing over their business to Sergeant Collins who has long wanted to go crooked.[83] The audience resonated with the story and the musical transferred to the Garrick Theatre in the West End in February 1960 where it ran for just over two years with the Jewish actress Miriam Karlin in the lead role of Lil Smith. It was Bart's first West End show and it was acknowledged that it was due to his input that it won the 1960 *Evening Standard* Award for Best Musical.[84]

Other opportunities presented themselves to Bart. Gorman recalled that Bart started to find it hard to get to work on time as he was spending half the night in bars playing in skiffle groups. This brought him into contact in 1956 with a young merchant seaman called Tommy Hicks, playing under the name Tommy Steele. Before long Bart was writing songs for Steele, who said that Bart had the wonderful gift of being able to portray the thoughts and conversation of the ordinary Cockney. Singer and actor Anthony

Newley said Bart was the first person to use catchphrases for titles of songs, such as 'Do you mind?'[85] When Steele appeared on a new teenage television programme performing Bart's song 'Rock with the Caveman', Bart appeared on the show for an interview. To be seen on television at that time carried enormous prestige and brought instant recognition.[86] He was about to embark on the next period of his life and he stopped working with Gorman. 'He no longer had the commitment, his heart was somewhere else. It was as though he was seeking to fulfil the needs of an inner compulsion.'[87]

Other successful shows followed – *Lock Up Your Daughters*, *Oliver!*, *Blitz!* and *Maggie May*. The magic touch seemed infallible. Broadcaster David Jacobs remarked that 'never since the days of Ivor Novello has one man had such success in the musical theatre. A one man band of show business. A phenomenon who can't write or read music.' Jacobs considered Bart a showbiz phenomenon who in just a few years had become an institution in British theatre.[88] The Variety Club of Great Britain named Bart as Show Business Personality of the year in 1960. A review in *The Stage* commented that Bart had a very special distinction. He was the first British musical composer to strike the public imagination since the days when Ivor Novello and Noel Coward were the glamorous leading lights in this sphere of theatre. In those days, before their musicals opened, there was excitement as they cast a magic spell and Bart created the same effect. 'Mr Bart is a real man of the theatre with an uncanny knack of composing hummable tunes and writing words that stick in the mind with their direct application to contemporary feeling and outlook.'[89]

Oliver!

Bart's greatest success was *Oliver!*, based on the Charles Dickens novel *Oliver Twist*. John Gorman remembered the day that he and Bart had time off from their RAF duties and went to see the film *Oliver Twist* starring Alec Guinness as Fagin. On the way back Bart told Gorman that one day he was going to write a musical based on the story and it would be better than any musical to date. These were prophetic words for in producing *Oliver!* Bart created a new genre for stage musicals for many decades to come.

> The clipped received English accents of earlier British musicals were replaced with raucous Cockney and English as spoken with mid-European Jewish pronunciation. Gone were Busby Berkeley high kicking chorus lines, replaced with dance routines that had more in common with a good old East End knees up. It was a musical that

drew inspiration from the bubbling street markets of the East End studded with working class wit and characters from London street life.[90]

Marc Napolitano argues that *Oliver!* proved that a Cockney-Jewish East Ender could change the course of the history of the English musical forever.[91] It reflected many of the concerns that dominated the post-war English stage, including the struggle to define a new Englishness in the face of a globalized culture. If the central contrasts between the pre-war and post-war British theatre are best exemplified by the decline of Terence Rattigan and the rise of John Osborne – the rejection of the drawing room and the acceptance of the kitchen sink drama – Bart's musicals conveyed a similar shift away from the glitzy and glamorous world of the pre-war operetta towards a gritty, working-class musical genre. Theatre producer Sir Cameron Mackintosh considers *Oliver!* to be the musical equivalent of John Osborne's *Look Back in Anger*. This play premiered at the Royal Court Theatre on 8 May 1956, a date often taken to signify the start of the post-war British theatre revival.[92] *The Stage* considered that Bart wrote what was arguably the greatest British musical of all time.[93]

Bart's Jewish heritage was indispensable to his conception of *Oliver!* and remains perhaps the most ironic paradox: remarkably a Jewish East Ender conceived of a stage musical in which the hero is based on a Victorian literary character who embodied abhorrent antisemitic stereotypes. Bart's reinterpretation of Fagin was a bold attempt to present him in a unique and sympathetic light.

The Jew in English literature had rarely been presented positively. They had played a notable role in English writing from the time of Chaucer and their earliest characterization was largely contingent on popular superstition, political convenience and folk mythology. The Jew of medieval and renaissance literature was, for the most part, a composite of negative characteristics. Even after the readmission of the Jews to England in 1656, the way they were represented in literature did not substantially change. They remained on the outskirts of English society and were depicted as essentially separate from the mainstream. The image of the Jew in English literature had as its base the figure of the Christ killer. The Christ murderer, sometimes presented as the devil or the devil in disguise, hovered in the background. This association is seen through Chaucer, Shakespeare and Dickens. In Chaucer's *The Prioresses Tale* one finds the medieval view of the 'cursed Jewes' as kidnappers, mutilators and murderers of innocent Christian children.[94] Shylock in Shakespeare's *Merchant of Venice* is the best-known Jew in English literature. His name entered the language as a term of abuse and the Jewish presence in English literature took its form from Shylock. He endures as a man and a monster. Fagin, a character created by Dickens more than two centuries after Shylock, stands in a direct line of descent from Shakespeare's villain and echoes the medieval view.[95]

It is thought that Dickens based Shylock on Ikey Solomon (Isaac Solomon) who was tried at the Old Bailey in 1830 for charges of theft and receiving stolen goods. It was likely that Dickens, who started off as a court reporter, would have attended at least one of Solomon's trials and used him as a basis for Fagin (although unlike Fagin, Solomon was not hanged but transported to Tasmania).[96]

Solomon, who was one of London's leading fences, was born in 1765 and grew up in the streets between Aldgate and Petticoat Lane. His father Henry had come from Bavaria around 1758.[97] It is believed that Henry Solomon traded in stolen goods. It appears that most Jewish receivers in London started off humbly and innocently enough as itinerant rag and bone men or buyers of old clothes and second-hand goods. They soon became aware that it was not often in their best interest to ask too many questions or perhaps it was because their English was imperfect. Therefore, often without realising it at first, these small-time Jewish merchants discovered that they had crossed over the fine line that divided dealer from receiver.[98]

Ikey Solomon started hawking goods on the streets around Petticoat Lane at an early age and was soon involved in gangs of pickpockets. He became a receiver on a large scale and there were accounts of him buying up whole warehouses of stolen property and purchasing stolen watches in bulk.[99] A colourful personality, his trial was given great coverage in the newspapers and would have provided ripe material for Dickens to incorporate into a story.

Throughout history certain fictional characters in literature have achieved an illusion of reality due to their popularity. In the main they became enduring stereotypes and influenced social judgment. As well as Shylock, Fagin ultimately became one such 'profile' of a Jew that embedded itself in popular culture and prejudice and the stereotype was perpetuated.[100] Jeet Heer writes in an Afterword to Will Eisner's book *Fagin the Jew* that in *Oliver Twist*, when Oliver is snared by a gang of thieves led by Fagin, Dickens' first description of Fagin is of a 'very old shrivelled Jew, whose villainous and repulsive face was obscured by a quantity of matted red hair'. This description is intended to match his character. He is a corrupter of the young and lives off their labour, teaching street urchins how to pick pockets and deliver the stolen goods into his greedy hands. Fagin has no loyalty to anyone and informs on some of his criminal partners after he no longer needs their services. He is utterly bereft of decency, seems hardly human and is frequently linked to either animals or the devil. When describing Fagin making the rounds at night, Dickens sets the scene by describing how the mud was thick on the ground, there was a black mist and everything felt cold and clammy to the touch.

> It seemed just the night when it befitted such a being as the Jew to be abroad. As he glided stealthily along, creeping between the shelter of the walls and doorways, the hideous old man seemed like some loathsome reptile, engendered in the slime and darkness through which he moved: crawling forth, by night, in search of some rich offal for a meal.

Heer points out that in the above passage and elsewhere in the novel, Fagin is not referred to by name but as 'the Jew' as if Jews were a species and he represents them. When not compared to creatures such as reptiles, Dickens describes Fagin as wearing 'an expression of villainy perfectly demonically'. Nancy, a member of Fagin's gang, describes him as 'the devil...and worse than devil'. Villain Bill Sikes says Fagin looks 'like the devil when he has his great coat on'. These characterizations of Fagin are fully vindicated when Fagin convinces Sikes that Nancy has informed on him which leads to Sikes murdering Nancy.[101]

Through Dickens' description of Fagin as a Jew, the Jew is portrayed as filthy, a criminal, corrupter of children, who values money above all, a Judas-like betrayer, an animal, a murderer, a devil. A large part of what makes Fagin's character so oppressively unforgettable is that he combines in one package centuries of loathsome antisemitic stereotypes.[102] Dickens created Fagin out of material provided by centuries of Christian myth-making while reflecting ideas that still permeated British society at that time. Jews were still second-class citizens when Dickens started his career as a writer. They were unable to open a shop within the city of London, be called to the Bar or to sit in Parliament. The intensity of Dickens' writing ensured that Fagin continued to live on in the popular imagination and became a household word.[103] In David Lean's 1948 film *Oliver Twist* Alec Guinness impersonated Fagin with brilliant and frightening effect, putting heavy stress on the idea of the archetypal Jewish villain.[104] Lean presented Fagin faithfully as the duplicitous criminal of evil conscience and the film gives full weight to a portrait of rare nastiness. Beneath a surface warmth is utter viciousness.[105]

Bart's interpretation is in total contrast. He converted one of literature's most hated villains into a lovable rogue. He gave him a heart that was absent in both the novel and the film. Bart's Fagin is an entertaining showman and Jewish den mother, as opposed to the conniving devil, antisemitic stereotype. The maternal element in Fagin was essential to Bart's conception of the character.[106]

In the notes he made entitled 'Thoughts on Fagin', Bart suggested that Fagin's physical image and demeanour should be that of:

> Some kind of zany chicken, with red hair and beard sticking out spikily awry, out from his bright eyed face. This chicken-like figure of a man – a mother hen protecting the little villains and pick-pockets who are his chicklets; sometimes with mock violence; sometimes with a matriarchal quality, at which moments he becomes a brooding hen.

He also stated that he did not want Fagin to be portrayed with anything approaching Dickens's ghetto-like image of the Jew and that as he had lived in London all his life, his dialect, accent and argot should be that of a *Cockney*. 'The melodies of his songs are quite sufficient to tell us the background of his heritage without the use of any accompanying Jewish gesture, attitude or verbal inflection.'[107]

These melodies and the music he heard growing up would prove essential to the writing of the score. Bart's childhood was characterized by a wide diversity of musical idioms, from the Cockney ballads of the music hall to the Jewish songs of the Yiddish theatre to the vibrant street cries of the East End buskers. Bart in later years recalled an elderly Jewish busker Solomon Levy who had a grotesque clown effect. The image of the frightening yet clownish East End Jew who had the power to entertain and to terrify simultaneously is evocative of Bart's Fagin. The conventions of the music hall singer, the synagogue cantor and the East End busker would all find their way into *Oliver!*[108]

Ron Moody, the legendary Fagin of the stage and screen version of *Oliver!*, recalled the first night with the curtain calls going on forever. He attributed Bart's success to going back to his roots: 'Back to his East End, Cockney, *heimishe* Jewish roots where cockles and mussels formed an alliance with salt beef on rye *mit* a pickle. He was of the people, for the people.'[109] Although *Oliver!* was based on a Victorian text that endorsed middle-class morality, the true centre of Bart's musical adaptation is the working-class East End community of the mid-twentieth century. The fragility of that community is shown in the break-up of Fagin's gang. The ending is melancholy optimism based heavily on the Jewishness of his main character.[110]

Moody felt that Bart 'filleted Fagin of all the characteristics that make Jews shudder and antisemites applaud, turning him into a public benefactor who gave orphans a better fed life than they would have got from the authorities, even if it meant picking a pocket or two'.[111] Moody agreed with Bart's interpretation. 'Bart is as Jewish as I am and we both felt an obligation to get Fagin away from a vicious racial stereotype and instead make him what he really is – a crazy Father Christmas gone wrong'.[112] Muriel Walker said that Bart would have loved to have played Fagin as he was close to the character but he could not act or sing a note.[113]

Bart acknowledged how he was influenced by Yiddish theatre and Jewish music. His parents took him to the Yiddish theatre, and he remembered watching plays by Sholem Aleichem. 'I used to make a beeline for the pit and lean over and watch the fiddlers and the drummers and be really close up to the actors so you could see the greasepaint. I had the buzz even then.'[114] He constantly heard music, both at home and on the street. 'And there was Jewish music everywhere.' Although his family were not religious, his father went to the synagogue once a year on *Yom Kippur*. He recalled going there with him and how he loved the music and the sound of the ram's horn when it was blown. 'It said something to me.'[115] Jewish music was present in *Oliver!* The show introduced Fagin with violins in a Chassidic nigun of Bart's inspiration.[116] A nigun is a tune or melody, often without words, sung by Chassidic Jews. The tunes range from devotional melodies, melodies of yearning and melodies of joy. In the wordless tunes, meaningless syllables such as ay-ay-ay, ya-ba-bam, ta-ta-da-ri-da are interjected.[117] Bart also used tunes from the Passover Haggadah, particularly 'Chad Gadya' that was the basis of 'Reviewing the Situation'.[118]

Marco Napolitano analyses 'You've Got to Pick a Pocket or Two' and 'Reviewing the Situation' and considers that they are defined largely by their Jewish rhythms and can be traced back to the music hall in terms of their comic patter.[119] The tenets and practices of Yiddish theatre were quite similar to those of the early English music halls. Yiddish actor Meier Tzelniker claimed that whereas general theatre separated plays into genres such as comedy, drama and musicals, Yiddish theatre incorporated them into one, a song, a laugh and a tear.[120] Although Bart was not a religious man, Jewish secular and religious traditions were important to his sense of identity. Bart's main interest in Jewish matters were cultural, incorporating music and theatre, and it was natural that Bart would be drawn to the conventions of Yiddish for this was the language of the people and the language around him in the East End.[121] In short, the Jewish East End that he grew up in coloured a great deal of his work.[122]

East End Identification

Similarly drawing on his Jewish East End background was *Blitz!*, a wartime nostalgia musical that opened at the Adelphi Theatre on 8 May 1962, the anniversary of VE Day. It was about the East End of London during the heavy bombing of the Second World War. Bart admitted that the show was 'in a way about me' as well as being about intolerance and the effect of the bombings on East End Jews and Cockneys.[123] 'I remember the Blitz vividly. The energy you get as a kid is very strong.'[124] Bart was evacuated on a number of occasions but disliked the countryside and would return to London. 'Every time I came back to London the Blitz got worse. They called me the jinx.'[125] *Blitz!* tells the sentimental story of a Jewish mother trying to keep her family together but eventually bestowing her blessing on her daughter's marriage to a non-Jewish boy, the '*goy* next door'. Mrs Blitztein is the matriarchal pickle seller with hand gestures and Cockney Yiddish.[126] Brenda Evans, Bart's personal assistant for nearly 20 years and who runs the Lionel Bart Foundation Archive, said that he based the Blitztein characters on his own family.[127] Bart's handwritten notes about *Blitz!* state that the story is a child's eye view and the characters include a Yiddishe mama who has raised a large family, the child who is also the storyteller, the child's elder brother and the girl he loves, 'the *shixsa* next door'.[128] Bart's brother Harry married a non-Jewish girl, Rosie, and Bart was fascinated by her and her family and would spend as much time with them as possible when he visited the East End.[129]

The character of Mrs. Blitztein embodied much of the spirit and courage of his own mother. The musical is set in Petticoat Lane in 1940 and much like the stories of *Romeo and Juliet* and *West Side Story* revolve around two feuding families, the Blitzteins run by Mrs Blitztein, and the Lockes, run by a non-Jew Alfie Locke who sold fruit and vegetables. Carol Blitztein and George Locke fall in love. People die. Children are evacuated and Carol goes blind. There is a desertion, a marriage and in the end when Mrs Blitztein is buried in the rubble, it is her arch enemy Alfie Locke who dug her out.[130]

As mentioned earlier, there was greater cooperation and interchange between the Jewish and non-Jewish communities during the Blitz period. An article in the *News Chronicle* in 1942 commented that the Blitz was 'a common sympathy, a common humanity in which differences, including the differences between Jews and Gentiles, were submerged and lost.' Tony Kushner considers that the situation is not clear cut and cautions that the memories of the Blitz can become mythical and emphasize the cheerfulness and unity that evolved during the constant aerial bombardment and that in reality the situation was more complex, and quarrels did break out in shelters. Yet the common suffering of both communities did have an impact on their relationship. Within the shelters although there were tensions it also proved that despite their differences the two communities had much in common and that adversity could create harmony.[131] Bart reflected this in *Blitz!*

Bart's formative years in the East End, and wartime Blitz nights in the underground shelters near Petticoat Lane, left a deep mark. 'I think it affected my work a great deal. When you were underground it didn't matter if you were Jewish, coloured, Irish or Cockney. There was a marvellous atmosphere.'[132] Bart was a combination of Jewish and Cockney and this early experience could have been a contributing factor. He learnt from an early age to defend himself. He survived on the streets because he was able to think up rude words to popular songs and he survived as a Jew in the Air Force due to his ability to make fun of himself. 'I figured that Fagin could do that too. London humour and Jewish humour come together in the way the Cockney and Jew can laugh at themselves.'[133]

He was determined to survive and succeed. His humble beginnings in the East End contributed to the driving force where he was burning the candle at both ends. He noted that 'maybe at the back of my mind I'm remembering the broken down gaff we all lived in Whitechapel and when we were pretty poor and my Dad often had no wages at the end of the week'. He loved the East End and the way that people helped each other as well as 'the barrer boys, the hopscotch on the chalked out cobblers'.[134] He was referred to as 'the Cockney Cole Porter'.[135]

Even so, a certain tension was present within Bart. On some occasions he prided himself on being an East End boy and yet at other times aimed to become someone else. He began to reinvent himself by changing his name from Lionel Begleiter, his voice and his facial appearance. The changes were a desire to integrate into English society. This was an opportunity to give himself some class and to secure, even illicitly, admission to the circle which had at its centre his hero Noel Coward.[136] This was in contrast to the other case studies who never camouflaged their background at any time in order to enter a social circle and even if they wanted to it was not an easy path. The systematic discrimination against British-born subjects of non-British born parentage, the obstacles placed in the way of the naturalization of

156 *East End Jews and Left-Wing Theatre*

aliens and their consequent vulnerability was underpinned by the common racist assumptions that these groups did not or could not fully belong to the nation. 'British nationality was conceptualized and constructed in legal terms so as to exclude a racialized Other, be it Russian Jews, Chinese or black seamen.'[137]

Bart's looks gave him self-doubt and anguish. Following plastic surgery on his nose, he began to work on the inner man, 'cultivating the mannerisms (including an intermittent Churchillian lisp,) polishing the affectations, refining the Cockney twang into a hep-cat dialect rather than a gor-blimey embarrassment'.[138] Such changes are a desire for invisibility, the desire to become 'white' which lies at the centre of the Jew's flight from his or her body, a desire to transform the difference heard in the sound of his or her voice into a positive sign.[139]

It appears he invented his own language early on in his career. In 1958 singer Tommy Steele described him as speaking in a hybrid of East End, Hollywood and Noel Coward. His voice was a whisper, a hiss. It could be gossipy-confidential or deadpan funny or conspiratorial like a spiv's tale or scary in the manner of Marlon Brando as the godfather Don Vito Corleone. His audience were forced to lean forward and listen to no one else but him.[140] He talked with a slow drawl that became a trademark.[141] Unity actor Harry Landis reckoned the voice and the language were developed, deliberately or otherwise, as a form of class eradicator, an alternative to the telephone or interview voice people adopt. Landis said that it enabled him to rub shoulders with cab drivers and princesses without feeling out of place. Landis said that the quiet voice disguised his true persona, which was a Cockney loudmouth.[142]

Roper considers that these changes reflected Bart's need to be rich and to escape his East End Jewishness.[143] Those who worked closely with Bart take a different view. Brenda Evans reflected that it was fame that he craved and he never lost being an East End boy.[144] Muriel Walker felt he never changed. 'He just had posher friends.'[145] His niece Davina Gold said he never rejected his Jewishness.[146] Certainly without his Jewish background it would be inconceivable that he could produce musicals such as *Oliver!* and *Blitz!* Marc Napolitano points out that his Jewishness and East End upbringing are arguably the defining traits of his life story, his personality and his career; they are also in many respects the defining traits of his dramatic/musical canon and their relevance to the conception and execution of *Oliver!* cannot be overestimated.[147]

Despite the affectations mentioned above, Bart was at heart an East End Jewish boy made good who loved to flaunt his success but did not forget his origins. This is shown in a scene from the BBC's documentary series *One Pair of Eyes*, entitled '*Who Are the Cockneys Now?*' In the summer of 1968 in the immediate wake of Enoch Powell's 'Rivers of Blood Speech', in which he warned of the consequences he foresaw if immigration to the Commonwealth remained unchecked, actress and singer Georgia Brown returned to the East End of her youth to record an episode and to see how an area that was once largely populated by Jews had become home to the Bengali community. In the opening scene Brown is accompanied by Bart, her childhood friend, as they drive in his open-air Bentley convertible. They both visited their old school in Deal Street, which in their day had a 70 per cent Jewish population, and now catered to the new wave of immigrants. Bart told a little boy that the area had good memories for him. He mentioned how he and Georgia Brown grew up together and that both their families were gamblers. 'When my father got cleaned out, I used to eat round her place.'[148] This incident shows the dichotomy within Bart. He had left the East End and become successful but the area was still important to him.

Yet he was still riddled with self-doubt and insecurity and had the notion that other successful people around him were 'proper', whereas one day he would be found out.[149] Bart's overnight success coupled with the insecurities from his childhood began to be reflected in his behaviour. He would either present himself as an East End boy from an impoverished Jewish background or flaunt himself in a most ostentatious manner, according to who he was with. Those brought up in strained circumstances adopt a range of attitudes about childhood, either playing on the poverty or full nostalgia for the family and neighbourhood or bitter and angry. Bart tried all approaches depending on who he was talking to. With reference to his childhood he would either blame his mother as being too old when he was born and without the strength to give him love and affection he needed (at the time of his bankruptcy hearing in 1972) or 'he could turn up the schmaltz' about his wartime childhood when promoting his show *Blitz!*[150] Bart's friends referred to his constantly altering the facts of his childhood and taking liberties with the truth. When he was looking for a writer to help ghost his memoirs, several noted authors turned him down as they were concerned that he would not tell the truth.[151] He was known to stretch the truth to its breaking point.[152]

In all probability, Bart's difficulties arose from his childhood and would lead to his ambiguity about his East End origins. He would show great nostalgia, saying that 'he missed the smell of dried up horse manure on the streets'.[153] However, he would also admit that he was driven to the limits of his excess by the same impulses that drove him to the limits of success – the impulse to be rich and escape his East End Jewish roots. Alcohol and drugs were the quickest route to oblivion which he hoped would enable him to drown his increasing self-loathing and would mask the lack of a stabilising emotional anchor.[154]

Lifestyle

In the 1960s Bart was the Andrew Lloyd Webber of the West End. As well as finding fame with his musicals and his songs for Tommy Steele, he wrote hit songs for Cliff Richard, such as 'Living Doll' and the theme song for the James Bond movie *From Russia with Love*. Unable to write or read music, he would sing into a portable tape recorder, often while driving. The media adored the trimmings – four cars with their own telephone. This was 'as rare as hen's teeth' at the time.[155] He made a quantum leap from Stepney to a millionaire's lifestyle in Chelsea. His prodigious output made him millions.[156] He suddenly found he was everybody's friend. He loved his new celebrity status and was flattered that the famous were happy to sit at the table of the son of a Jewish East End tailor. There were wild parties at his home for the Beatles and Rolling Stones. Royalty and nobility turned up along with his close friends Judy Garland, singer Alma Cogan and Beatles' manager Brian Epstein.

His friend John Gorman saw the change in him after he started to become well known. 'Fame can be a drug and Bart, who had an obsession to become famous, was hooked.' Gorman was not surprised by his success as he felt Bart possessed a mix of inspirational genius and ambition and would work with enormous enthusiasm and creative ability towards any goal he set himself. He had no limits. 'He had a childlike charm that drew people to him yet the same qualities could produce dramatic tantrums if he was thwarted.'[157]

Despite (or because of) his impoverished childhood, he had a strange disregard for money. Gorman recalled how, when they were working together in the design studio in 1951, they were reduced to drawing just 15 shillings a week for their subsistence. It was at that time that Bart began to demonstrate his strange attitude to money when he would give away half of their money for the week to an old woman who was taking a street collection for flowers or ordering dinners that he could not afford. Bart with his extravagant lifestyle claimed that he was dyslexic with figures, especially money. He had been known to receive a cheque for £10,000 but claimed it was for £100,000. Bart assumed that he should not have to worry about money as it was just there to be spent.[158]

15. Lionel Bart (Vivienne), courtesy of Lionel Bart Foundation Archive

When the money began to flow from the first Tommy Steele hits, Bart began to indulge in stylish clothes and spent hours at the hairdressers. In 1964 the *Daily Mirror* reported that his wardrobe included 40 suits, 25 pairs of shoes, 40 shirts and that he would only wear white gold cufflinks.[159] He loved to lie back in his bath and hear himself earn £3 in four minutes on *Housewives Choice* (that was his share of royalties for a record that played for that time).[160]

He spent money as soon as he received it. 'At the time I hated money. As a kid I was brought up with the knowledge that my dad was a gambler. Gamblers and bank managers were not my kind of people.' He used to keep a bowl containing £1,000 and this would be prominently displayed in his house. 'It was my way of saying, it's only money, take it.' At the height of his fame he had five homes – a Kensington mews house next to the artist Francis Bacon, a mansion in Fulham with 27 rooms, a castle in Tangier, a New York apartment and a house on Malibu beach.[161] He was considered 'an astonishing golden boy of show business, a fabulous one man musical enigma'.[162]

It was suggested that Bart made a vast fortune, but the millions disappeared. Muriel Walker, who had been friends with Bart from his Unity days and was his personal assistant from 1964–66, recalled her office with its green silk walls, the chandelier in Bart's living room that was from the set of the 1964 film *Becket* and the toilet that was in the form of a throne. One of her jobs whilst working for Bart was to spend a whole day at Harrods just before Christmas to buy all his presents for family and friends. The chauffeur-driven Rolls Royce would collect her in the morning and take her back in the evening. His accountant and solicitor advised him to curb his spending, but he could not stop.[163]

Despite all the fame and attention, Bart remained insecure and had a desire to be loved and admired constantly. He knew from childhood that he would never be his father's *mensch* (Yiddish for honourable) as his father had said that was all he wanted him to be and that he would never be able to introduce his mother to the right girl.[164] *The Belfast News Letter* wrote: 'His bank balance makes him an eligible bachelor but he has no wish for what some might call a normal private life.'[165] As Brenda Evans poignantly said, 'Everybody loved Lionel but no one loved him the best.'[166] He never found someone to share his life with and this lack of emotional security resulted in the desire to be loved not consistently but constantly.[167]

Masculinity

Bart's inability to be in a public relationship was due to his homosexuality – a form of masculinity in contrast to the previous case studies. The change in the law came too late for Bart and others of his generation – not morally or physically too late but mentally they were unable to change. They had learned and subconsciously accepted a way of living in two worlds – visible in one, invisible in the other. When the law was passed in 1967, legalizing the sexual act between two consenting males over 21 in private, they were unable to shed the cloak of self-deception.[168] His bachelorhood was a subject for speculators who liked to see every show business name linked to another.[169] This must have added to his internal pressure and a pressure in respect of his family. Andrea Mattock said the family always hoped he would find a nice Jewish girl and they chose to be in denial.[170] Was his self-loathing born as a result of his father's comment that he only ever wanted him to be a *mensch*? What humiliation he must have felt when his father took him to the public baths and ridiculed him over the size of his penis and whether he had been born a girl.[171]

Although known in the profession to be gay, it was not until the 1990s that Bart described himself as 'out at last'.[172] He was in the same position as his friend Brian Epstein, the Beatles manager who changed the face of pop music and whose name, like Bart, became synonymous with the Swinging Sixties. Epstein's success concealed a tragic lonely figure. Beneath the façade of a flamboyant tycoon was an isolated man, a Jewish homosexual.[173] Bart was in a similar situation.

Bart first met Epstein in Liverpool in 1964 when he went to absorb the atmosphere of the city for his musical *Maggie May*. They became close friends when Epstein moved to London and their friendship centred on a group of entertainment figures who met regularly at the home of singer Alma Cogan who lived in Kensington. Cogan was also Jewish and they both loved her. If Lionel was ever to have married, Alma seemed the perfect partner. Her extrovert bubbling personality and keen interest in clothes struck a chord with him. Epstein was just as infatuated, and he took her to Liverpool to introduce her to his parents. Their affection for each other was never to be clouded with talk of his homosexuality.[174] As this was a time when homosexuality was a criminal offence, Cogan was the perfect partner to accompany Bart in public. He referred to her as his girlfriend and said that Epstein was also very taken with her.[175] Davina Gold recalled that when Cogan died of cancer aged 34 in 1966, Bart was so devastated that he ran away to the States. His inability to cope with the death of those he loved was also reflected when he would not visit his mother when she was dying in 1970. She also considered that Bart did not want his mother to see the state he was in.[176] Bart was already drinking heavily and taking drugs, as was Epstein. Bart commented that it was necessary for them to be part of what was going on in the pop music world. 'He and I were experimenting, trying to find something good in life but using oneself as a test tube.'[177]

Gillian Jesson met Bart in 1977 when she and her husband Tim, who was bi-sexual, would party at Bart's home. Jesson recalls how Bart drank large quantities of Remy Martin, would be the life and soul of the party, then become depressed and sob on the telephone to Keith Moon of the rock band *The Who*. Jesson realized that Tim was having an affair with Bart as Bart paid their telephone bill, taxi fares and other expenses. Jesson remembers Bart fondly for his kindness and great generosity to all around him. She saw him once more by chance in a coffee shop in 1988. By this time he had lost all his money but his generosity still remained. 'He still left the biggest tip.'[178] Jesson's recollection shows the vulnerable Bart – his battle with alcoholism, his instability and need for constant attention and his extravagant spending that would contribute to his downfall.

Downfall

Bart's real downfall began in 1965 when *Twang!*, a burlesque version of the Robin Hood story, was savaged by the critics. *The Stage* called it a spectacular failure.[179] Bart was so desperate to keep the show in production

16. Lionel Bart, courtesy of Lionel Bart Foundation Archive

that he ignored the advice once given to him by Noel Coward to never invest one's money in one's own shows. *Twang!* closed after just eight weeks.[180] Did Robin Hood, as champion of the poor, strike a chord with the political leanings from this youth? He considered essential the extreme authenticity of the period and that it should be filmed in Sherwood Forest for realism. Bart intended that the language was to be understandable to modern viewers while retaining an authentic feel for the period. The story was to deal primarily with the conflict between Robin Hood and the barons whereby Robin Hood becomes the champion of the poor serfs. The serfs' plight should be realistic 'and absolutely no punches pulled in the presentation of this'. Bart wrote that he did not want Robin Hood to be shown just as an Errol Flynn figure that leaps about from tree to tree but to be portrayed as 'a quick witted con man who has risen from a lowly background and has developed a supreme confidence to match his wit and connivance with that of the gentry. It must be shown that it is more important to him to con the money than to keep it. In fact he gives it away unprohibitively.'[181] This reflected Bart's attitude to money which he spent and gave to others extravagantly. When asked if the fortune he made, coming from East End poverty to earning over £1 million a year, had affected him as a person, Bart said that talking about money brought him down and it was finding people and talent that was his real inspiration.[182]

The show opened at the Palace Theatre, Manchester on 3 November 1965. Muriel Walker, who worked on the production, said that it was obvious from the beginning that it was going to be a disaster, but Bart went on regardless. 'He did not know when to stop. He was his own worst enemy. Generous and foolhardy.' In terms of its storyline, Bart had moved away from his usual East End territory and Walker was of the opinion that it failed because Bart was not familiar with the Robin Hood story. She also blamed Joan Littlewood, the first director, who was very subversive.[183]

From the outset Littlewood was a strange choice for director. She had put herself forward as, although she had never been connected with West End commercial theatre before, she wanted to direct *Twang!* in order to raise money for her Fun Palace in Hammamet, Tunisia. The possibility of working with a director who had directed his first hit *Fings Ain't Wot They Used T'Be* appealed to Bart. Many had their reservations since the production represented in effect a direct confrontation of two extreme camps in contemporary theatre, the traditional designer Messell and Littlewood, a neo-Brechtian of the improvised, informal theatre. Bart was probably in awe of her as he went ahead despite his remarks that Littlewood did not think much of the work that he had done that she had not staged and that 'she walked out at the intervals of *Blitz!* and *Oliver!* and thought *Maggie May* 'was a right load of rubbish.'[184] The failure of *Twang!* left Bart with debts estimated at £80,000. He had also mortgaged past and future royalties and some copyrights to finance the production, a move which put his future in jeopardy. He filed for bankruptcy in 1970.[185] Much of his fortune had been dissipated by his generosity to hangers on and by the ease with which casual sex partners could rob him.[186]

Walker points out that for someone who used to stuff cardboard into his shoes, he had no idea what to do with money and fame. 'He got too much too soon.'[187] Bart, who had once lived in a bizarre home in the style of Metro Goldwyn Tudor ended up in a two bedroom flat in Acton, west London.[188] He signed away everything that he would earn for the next four years and in return was given £300 a month to live on. This was the man whose royalties from *Oliver!* at one time made him £1 a minute.[189] He had thought that he was immune from disaster. 'I used to think I was safe in traffic – I was an East End street boy – it would bounce off me.' It was also at this time that he remembered his origins and came to terms with his fall from grace and living in Acton. He admired the sense of community there. 'It reminds me of my childhood with its strong Jewish community.'[190]

Bart never gave up writing despite battling alcoholism.[191] Down on his luck, he remained optimistic that he would succeed again and questioned why he always had to prove that he was not just 'a flash in the pan'. He admitted that he was not an intellectual like John Osborne and described himself as 'an ordinary Cockney bloke'.[192] Bart, as a second-generation immigrant, had strongly identified with being both Jewish and Cockney. His heart and soul had always been in the East End and his nephew reflects that one of the reasons he went off the rails was that he moved from the East End into a totally new world.[193] Although he had mixed with stars and royalty and despite affectations he may have made, the East End boy was always there even at the height of his fame. Bart recalled how one day, when he was walking near his house in Malibu, California he heard a voice call out 'Mile End Road'. It was the film director Mel Brooks who had spent time in the East End as a child. When Bart asked him how he knew where he came from, Brooks told him it was by the way he walked.[194] Andrea Mattock recalls that Bart loved everything about the East End. 'It was his roots and his life. His real pleasure was to be there.'[195] Social historian Piers Dudgeon comments that the East End is a place and condition of the mind. 'You can take a boy out of the East End but not the East End out of a boy.'[196]

Elliot Davis collaborated with Bart during the last few years of his life. He first met him in 1994 when they worked together on a Warner Bros animation film and Davis transcribed his musical ideas. Davis considered him to be brilliant. 'He had that ability to combine the Jewish East End experience with that of the Cockney. He just knew them both. Davis acknowledges that he was a tortured soul. His homosexuality had been a problem. He had wanted to marry Alma Cogan but she saw through the

17. Lionel Bart, 1994 (Michael Le Poer Trench), courtesy of Lionel Bart Foundation Archive

situation.' Davis adds that other partners were badly chosen, people took advantage of him and he would not listen to advice. He saw himself as an outsider.[197] He was at times an opportunist, taking the best from Unity and identifying with the socialist world but not allowing himself to be radicalized. Above all he was a brilliant mimic and creator but was never happy in his own skin.

Bart never recouped his fortune or achieved his former success. He died of cancer on 3 April 1999. The service was conducted at Golders Green crematorium by Northwood Liberal Synagogue's Rabbi Andrew Goldstein. Brenda Evans said that he had not belonged to a synagogue but had requested that he did not want to be buried but wanted 'Kaddish', the memorial prayer, to be recited as 'I came in as a Jew and need to leave as a Jew'.[198] He always maintained his Jewish identity.

✳✳✳

During the 1960s Lionel Bart was in the centre of all that was happening in the popular musical world in Britain. Long before the days of Andrew Lloyd Webber, he was the first composer to have three shows running simultaneously in the West End and his songs featured predominantly in the music charts. His photograph was on the covers of magazines and he mixed with royalty and celebrities. He straddled both pop music and theatre and *Oliver!* revolutionized musical theatre. Yet at the same time he battled with internal demons. He was a complex personality who became famous overnight but who was unable to nurture his phenomenal talent.

Bart's spectacular rise and fall can be attributed to his Jewish East End background. It was a double-edged sword. It was the backbone to his most successful works when he drew on his experiences and which influenced his witty lyrics and understanding of melody and yet the insecurities that plagued him in respect of his immigrant background, together with his sexuality, were to contribute to his excessive and reckless behaviour and his ultimate downfall. Bart's homosexuality and masculinity were in contrast to Mitchell's aggressive masculinity and to Kossoff and Bass who were more like the image of the stereotypical and traditional non-threatening Jewish male.

With his new-found fame, his earlier left-wing political leanings were no longer obviously in evidence. He shied away from the left-wing musical that he was expected to produce as a result of his Unity days. 'I feel I am not the kind of man to hammer home politics from a soap box.'[199] Although, after Unity, he had worked with Joan Littlewood's Theatre Workshop, which would have indicated a continuation of his left-wing politics, his socialism appears to have been superficial. He had joined the Communist Party when it was not that unusual for his contemporaries in the East End to do so and his time at Unity was a stepping stone for his career. Most critically, and in partial contrast to the other cases studies in this book, he was keen to become mainstream and famous. He could have invested his new-found wealth in political theatre and left-wing causes but instead he chose to have homes decorated with great opulence, and spent excessively on cars, clothes and material possessions. Even so, there was a residue of its influence, sentimentally expressed, whether in *Oliver!* or *Twang!* of empathy with the poor and oppressed and a carefree attitude to money that was against its accumulation.

The East End had a great influence on his work and he was most successful when he drew on these memories, such as *Oliver!, Blitz!* and *Fings Ain't Wot They Used T'Be.* Lyricist Don Black commented that his work had an East End quality that could capture the mood of the people. 'He grew up in the East End where these characters lived and the modern counterparts have not changed. They will cut your neck and at the same time help your granny across the road. With Lionel they do it to music.'[200] He captured the East End Cockney spirit and it was only when he ventured into unfamiliar territory such as *Twang!* that he failed.

Indeed, his Jewish background had an over-riding influence on *Oliver!,* his greatest work. Actress Barbara Windsor considers that Bart's East End Jewishness and love of London was a perfect match. Similarly, theatrical producer Cameron Mackintosh claims that it was Bart's inherent Jewishness that made the story work so well. He used his cultural heritage to great effect.[201] Bart might have tried to change who he was through his voice and plastic surgery, but he was unable to shed his origins. The Jew remains a Jew even when disguised. It is in their 'painted and over-barbered essence. There is no hiding from the fact of constructed difference.'[202] The East End boy always shone through. Don Black said that Bart would walk around town very flamboyantly. 'He was like royalty but there was something very East End about him.'[203] He remained the Jewish East End boy whose background was paramount to his success and left songs that brought joy to millions of people and are still performed all over the world. Bart had the confidence as a second generation immigrant, and the ability to fuse the rich Jewish heritage of his immigrant parents with the vibrant world of the Cockney East End, as did the previous case studies, although they took on different roles and personae. Mitchell became the ultimate aggressive Cockney in *Till Death Us Do Part*, whereas Kossoff and Bass were able to portray the gentle and humorous Cockney in *The Larkins* and *The Army Game*. In Bart's case, the genius of this 'Jewish Cockney' left a lasting mark.

Notes

1. *Independent,* 4 April 1999.
2. Lara V. Marks, *Model Mothers: Jewish Mothers and Maternity Provision in East London, 1870–1939* (Oxford: Clarendon Press, 1994), p. 125.
3. Davina Gold: Interview with Isabelle Seddon, 26 November 2016, London.
4. David Cesarani, 'The Myth of Origins: Ethnic Memory and the Experience of Migration', in A. Newman and S. W. Massil (eds), *Patterns of Migration* (London: Jewish Historical Society of England/Institute of Jewish Affairs, 1996), pp. 248–9.
5. Ibid., pp. 250–2.
6. National Archive, HO 21699 350/48/6087.
7. David Cesarani, 'An Alien Concept? The Continuity of Anti-Alienism in British Society Before 1940', in David Cesarani and Tony Kushner (eds),*The Internment of Aliens in Twentieth Century Britain* (London: Frank Cass, 1993), pp. 34–5.
8. Ibid., pp. 37–9.
9. Ibid., pp. 40–1.
10. National Archive, HO B.21699.
11. National Archives, HO 350/48/6087.
12. National Archives, HO 39/6/18.
13. Willy Goldman, *East End My Cradle* (London: Faber & Faber, 1940), pp. 110–11.
14. Andrea Mattock: Interview with Isabelle Seddon, 17 January 2017, London.
15. Davina Gold: Interview with Isabelle Seddon, 26 November 2016, London.
16. David Stafford and Caroline Stafford, *Fings Ain't Wot They Used T'Be: The Lionel Bart Story* (London: Omnibus Press, 2011), p. 11.
17. David Roper, *Bart!* (London: Pavilion Books, 1994), pp. 6–7.
18. Steven M. Cohen and Paula E. Hyman (eds.), *The Jewish Family: Myths and Reality* (New York: Holmes & Meier, 1986), pp. 3–4.
19. Stafford and Stafford, *Fings,* p. 14.
20. *A Handful of Songs: Tribute to Lionel Bart,* BBC Radio 2, 12 August 2015.
21. Andrea Mattock: Interview with Isabelle Seddon, 17 January 2017, London.
22. *Daily Sketch,* 28 March 1961.
23. *The Times,* 16 November 2015.
24. *The Times,* 31 December 1990.
25. *Jewish Chronicle,* 25 October 2002.
26. Dialogue between Reverend Joseph McCulloch and David Kossoff, 23 August 1966, Bow Dialogues, National Sound Archives, British Library, C812/15.
27. National Archives, HO B.21699; HO 350/48/6087.
28. C. Russell and H. S. Lewis, *The Jew in London: A Study of Racial Character and Present Day Conditions* (London: T. Fisher Unwin, 1901).
29. David Roper, *Bart!,* p. 15.
30. Cable Street Group (eds), *The Battle of Cable Street 1936* (London: Cable Street Group, 1995), section 3.
31. Stafford and Stafford, *Fings,* p. 11.

32. Davina Gold: Interview with Isabelle Seddon, 26 November 2016, London.
33. David Roper, *Bart!*, p. 7.
34. Cathy Ross and John Clark, *London: The Illustrated History* (London: Penguin Books, 2008), p. 284.
35. Daniel Farson, *Soho in the Fifties* (London: Michael Joseph, 1988), p. 7.
36. Stafford and Stafford, *Fings*, pp. 22–3.
37. David Cesarani, 'Putting London Jewish Intellectuals in their Place', in David Cesarani, Tony Kushner and Milton Shain (eds), *Place and Displacement in Jewish History and Memory: Zakor V'Makor* (London: Vallentine Mitchell, 2009), p. 147.
38. Aubrey Morris, *Unfinished Journey* (London: Artery Publications, 2000), p. 180.
39. John Gorman, *Knocking Down Ginger* (London: Caliban Books, 1995), p. 126.
40. Ibid., p. 131.
41. Ibid., pp. 151–2.
42. Ibid., p. 169.
43. David Roper, *Bart!*, p. 12.
44. Andrea Mattock: Interview with Isabelle Seddon, 17 January 2017, London.
45. Davina Gold: Interview with Isabelle Seddon, 26 November 2016, London.
46. Solly Kaye was the son of Jewish Lithuanian immigrants who joined the Communist Party in 1934. He was active in the Battle of Cable Street, campaigned against slum landlords and was elected as one of the three Communist councillors to Stepney Council in 1960. *Guardian*, 4 May 2005.
47. Gorman, *Knocking Down Ginger*, p. 134.
48. Stafford and Stafford, *Fings*, p. 32.
49. Gorman, *Knocking Down Ginger*, pp. 197–219; 221–41.
50. Ibid., p. 172.
51. David Roper, *Bart!*, pp. 12–13.
52. John Gorman, *Knocking Down Ginger*, p. 175.
53. David Roper, *Bart!*, p. 15.
54. Marc Napolitano, *Oliver! A Dickensian Musical* (Oxford, Oxford University Press, 2014), p. 34.
55. Labour History Archive, People's History Museum, Manchester.
56. David Roper, *Bart!*, p. 7.
57. Muriel Walker: Interview with Isabelle Seddon, 23 November 2016, London.
58. Una Brandon-Jones, High Lights and Low Lights (unpublished manuscript), Unity Theatre Archives (THM/9/1/3/6).
59. Binnie Yates: Interview with Isabelle Seddon, 9 February 2016, London.
60. Ibid.
61. David Roper, *Bart!*, p. 13.
62. Colin Chambers, *The Story of Unity Theatre* (London: Lawrence & Wishart, 1989), p. 331.
63. *The Stage*, 19 March 1953.
64. David Roper, *Bart!*, pp. 14–15.
65. Ibid., p. 15.
66. Ibid.
67. *Stage*, 24 July 1958.
68. Stafford and Stafford, *Fings*, pp. 37–8.
69. Napolitano, *Oliver!*, pp. 33–4.

70. Unity Theatre Archives, THM 9/2/1/15.
71. *Stage*, 24 December 1963.
72. Littlewood started as a commercial actress but together with a group of actors committed to a left-wing ideology devised and commissioned plays by and about the working class in Britain. The company experimented with physical approaches to characterisation. She broadened the classic repertoire and discovered new writers. She combined slapstick humour with serious satire to set a new style in improvised theatre. BBC News, 'Obituary: Theatre's Defiant Genius', 21 September 2002, accessed 3 December 2016.
73. *Daily Mail*, 11 January 2012.
74. Howard Goorney, *The Theatre Workshop Story* (London: Eyre Metheun, 1981), p. 112.
75. Chambers, *Story of Unity Theatre*, p. 265.
76. Napolitano, *Oliver!*, p. 33.
77. Ibid., p. 39.
78. *Belfast News Letter*, 17 April 1964.
79. Nadine Holdworth, *Joan Littlewood* (London: Routledge, 2006), p. 31.
80. Goorney, *Theatre Workshop Story*, p. 114.
81. Stafford and Stafford, *Fings*, p. 69.
82. David Roper, *Bart!*, p. 29.
83. Frank Norman, *Fings Ain't Wot They Used T'Be* (London: Samuel French, 1960), Introduction.
84. Roper, *Bart!*, p. 30.
85. 'Blitz on Bart', British Library sound recording CB43/58.
86. John Gorman, *Knocking Down Ginger*, p. 192.
87. Ibid., p. 175.
88. 'Blitz on Bart', British Library sound recording CB43/58.
89. *Stage*, 12 April 1962.
90. Gorman, *Knocking Down Ginger*, p. 138.
91. Napolitano, *Oliver!*, p. 30.
92. Martin Banham: *The Cambridge Guide to Theatre* (Cambridge: Cambridge University Press, 1995), p. 828.
93. *Stage*, 8 April 1999.
94. Derek Cohen and Deborah Heller (eds), *Jewish Presences in English Literature* (Montreal: McGill-Queen's University Press, 1990), pp. 3–6.
95. Ibid., p. 25.
96. Judith Sackville-O'Donnell, *The First Fagin: The True Story of Ikey Solomon* (Melbourne: Acland Press, 2002), p. ix.
97. J. J. Tobias, *Prince of Fences: The Life and Crimes of Ikey Solomon* (London: Vallentine Mitchell, 1974), pp. 1–3.
98. Ibid., p. vi.
99. Sackville-O'Donnell, *The First Fagin*, p. xvi.
100. Will Eisner, *Fagin the Jew* (Oregon: Dark Horse Books, 2013), p. 123.
101. Ibid., p. 130.
102. Ibid.
103. Ibid., pp. 131–2.
104. Irving Howe, *Selected Writings: 1950–1990* (New York: Harcourt Brace Jovanovich, 1990), p. 371.

105. *Jewish Chronicle*, 3 May 2013.
106. Napolitano, *Oliver!*, p. 153.
107. Lionel Bart, 'Thoughts on Fagin', 23 January 1967, Lionel Bart Foundation Archive.
108. Napolitano, *Oliver!*, pp. 31–2.
109. *Jewish Chronicle*, 9 April 1999.
110. Napolitano, *Oliver!*, p. 21.
111. *Jewish Chronicle*, 9 April 1999.
112. *Jewish Chronicle*, 3 July 2015.
113. Muriel Walker: Interview with Isabelle Seddon, 23 November 2016, London.
114. Stafford and Stafford, *Fings*, p. 17.
115. Ibid., pp. 14, 18.
116. *Jewish Chronicle*, 8 July 1980.
117. Macy Nulman, *Concise Encyclopedia of Jewish Music* (New York: McGraw Hill, 1976), p. 97.
118. *Jewish Chronicle*, 2 December 1994.
119. Napolitano, *Oliver!*, p. 115.
120. Anna Tzelniker, *Three for the Price of One* (London: Spiro Institute, 1991), p. 9.
121. Napolitano, *Oliver!*, pp. 116–17.
122. *Stage*, 8 April 1999.
123. Roper, *Bart!*, p. 59.
124. Stephen Williams in Conversation with Lionel Bart, British Library Sound Archives, C704/31.
125. Stafford and Stafford, *Fings*, p. 20.
126. *Jewish Chronicle*, 14 September 1990.
127. Brenda Evans: Interview with Isabelle Seddon, 15 November 2016, London.
128. Notes on *Blitz!*, February 1961, Lionel Bart Foundation Archive.
129. Andrea Mattock: Interview with Isabelle Seddon, 17 January 2017, London.
130. Stafford and Stafford, *Fings*, p. 123.
131. Tony Kushner, *The Persistence of Prejudice. Antisemitism in British Society During the Second World War* (Manchester: Manchester University Press, 1989), pp. 53–5.
132. *Jewish Chronicle*, 27 May 1960.
133. *Jewish Chronicle*, 2 December 1994.
134. *Daily Mirror*, 13 September 1962.
135. *Daily Mirror*, 22 June 1965.
136. Roper, *Bart!*, p. 15.
137. David Cesarani and Mary Fulbrook (eds), *Citizenship, Nationality and Migration in Europe* (London: Routledge, 1996), pp. 62–3.
138. Roper, *Bart!*, pp. 53–4.
139. Sander Gilman, *The Jew's Body* (London: Routledge, 1991). pp. 235–6.
140. Stafford and Stafford, *Fings*, p. 135.
141. *Belfast News Letter*, 17 April 1964.
142. Stafford and Stafford, *Fings*, pp. 135–6.
143. Ibid., p. 14.
144. Brenda Evans: Interview with Isabelle Seddon, 15 November 2016, London.
145. Muriel Walker: Interview with Isabelle Seddon, 23 November 2016, London.
146. Davina Gold: Interview with Isabelle Seddon, 25 November 2016, London.
147. Napolitano, *Oliver!*, p. 30.

148. *One Pair of Eyes: Who Are The Cockneys Now?* 17 August 1968, BBC Four London Collection.
149. Stafford and Stafford, *Fings*, p. 117.
150. Ibid., pp. 14–15.
151. *Independent*, 4 April 1999.
152. Napolitano, *Oliver!*, p. 30.
153. Stafford and Stafford, *Fings*, p.15.
154. Ibid., pp. 149–50.
155. David Roper, *Bart!*, p. 1.
156. *Jewish Chronicle*, 28 August 1992.
157. Gorman, *Knocking Down Ginger*, p. 193.
158. Ibid., p. 163.
159. Stafford and Stafford, *Fings*, pp. 136–7.
160. Roper, *Bart!*, p. 38.
161. *Daily Express*, 11 November 1994.
162. *Daily Mirror*, 13 September 1962.
163. Muriel Walker: Interview with Isabelle Seddon, 15 November 2016, London.
164. Roper, *Bart!*, p. 9.
165. *Belfast News Letter*, 17 April 1964.
166. Brenda Evans: Interview with Isabelle Seddon, 15 November 2016, London.
167. Roper, *Bart!*, p. 9.
168. Ibid., p. 11.
169. Ibid., p. 65.
170. Andrea Mattock: Interview with Isabelle Seddon, 17 January 2017, London.
171. Roper, *Bart!*, p. 8.
172. *Independent*, 4 April 1999.
173. Ray Coleman, *Brian Epstein: The Man Who Made the Beatles* (London: Penguin Books, 1990), p. 348.
174. Ibid., pp. 373–4.
175. Deborah Geller, *The Brian Epstein Story* (London: Faber, 2000), p. 60.
176. Davina Gold: Interview with Isabelle Seddon, 25 November 2016, London.
177. Geller, *Brian Epstein*, p. 374.
178. Gillian Jesson: Interview with Isabelle Seddon, 22 November 2016, London.
179. *Stage*, 3 February 1966.
180. *Jewish Chronicle*, 28 August 1992.
181. Lionel Bart's initial thoughts on *Twang!*, 19 June 1964, Lionel Bart Archive, London.
182. Stephen Williams in Conversation with Lionel Bart, British Library Sound Collection, C704/31.
183. Muriel Walker: Interview with Isabelle Seddon, 23 November 2016, London.
184. 'Twang! The Final Word', Personal papers of Muriel Walker, London.
185. *Jewish Chronicle*, 28 August 1992.
186. *Independent*, 4 April 1999.
187. Muriel Walker: Interview with Isabelle Seddon, 23 November 2016, London.
188. *Daily Mirror,* 6 February 1965.
189. *Daily Mirror*, 13 April, 1971.
190. Roper, *Bart!*, p. 8.
191. *Stage*, 8 April 1999.

192. *Daily Mirror*, 6 February 1965.
193. *Jewish Chronicle*, 13 February 1995.
194. Will and Tricia Adams, *A Nostalgic Look at the Capital since 1945* (Peterborough: Past and Present Publishing, 1997), p. 7.
195. Andrea Mattock: Interview with Isabelle Seddon, 17 January 2017, London.
196. Piers Dudgeon, *Our East End: Memories of Life in Disappearing Britain* (London: Headline, 2008), p. xii.
197. Elliot Davis: Telephone interview with Isabelle Seddon, 23 January 2017.
198. Brenda Evans: Interview with Isabelle Seddon, 15 November 2016, London.
199. Roper, *Bart!*, p. 68.
200. *A Handful of Songs: The Lionel Bart Story*, 28 February 2007, BBC Radio 2.
201. Ibid.
202. Gilman, *Jew's Body*, p. 193.
203. *A Handful of Songs: The Lionel Bart Story*, BBC Radio 2.

Conclusion

This book has focused on four second generation Jewish males born in the East End of London who later became famous in the entertainment industry in the second half of the twentieth century. On the surface, in spite of their common background and formative years in Unity Theatre, they had little in common. Their political affiliations ranged from Bass's lifelong adherence to radical politics, Mitchell's attraction to socialism during his twenties and then a continued involvement, Bart's partial commitment, to Kossoff's non-involvement in any political party. Bart, as a composer, was the most successful; Kossoff had a great following as a storyteller; Bass excelled in comic roles and Mitchell's Alf Garnett was probably the most famous Cockney character ever on television. There were also differences in their masculinity – Bass was gentle, bordering on camp; Kossoff was the prophet figure; Mitchell was macho and aggressive and Bart, although not a performer *per se* but very much in the public eye, had to disguise his sexuality. However, despite their major differences and the fact that they all left the East End, they became known as 'Jewish Cockneys'.

The differences in their personalities, politics and interests is reflected in comments made when all four took part in the BBC 4 radio programme *Desert Island Discs* in the 1960s.[1] *Desert Island Discs* was first broadcast in 1942. Each week a guest – a 'castaway' – is asked to choose eight recordings and a luxury item that they would like to take if they were to be cast away on a desert island, whilst discussing their lives and the reasons for their choices. To be chosen for this programme indicated that they were indeed household names. Bass, through the television sitcom *The Army Game* and *Bootsie and Snudge*, was recognized in the street; Kossoff had popularized how religion was broadcast; Mitchell's Alf Garnett was television's most controversial character and Bart, who had written one of the greatest British musicals, partied with stars and royalty.

The interviews showed to what extent they were indebted to Unity, how politics and their Jewishness impacted on their lives and reflected their similarities and differences. When asked to choose a luxury item, Bass demonstrated his modesty through his reluctance to choose one at all whilst

Bart went to the other extreme and with his confidence and sense of entitlement asked for Nelson's Column. All, apart from Bart, who just talked about coming from the East End, acknowledged their Jewish background (although elsewhere Bart never denied it). Bass explained that he chose records that were nostalgic, in particular the Jewish lullaby Rozhinkes Mit Mandlen that his parents sang to him. David Kossoff chose 'Hava Nagila', an Israeli song usually sung at Jewish celebrations, as his record of choice and mentioned his initial reluctance to read New Testament Bible stories on the BBC as he was Jewish. Mitchell mentioned that he was born in Stoke Newington and that his parents had to give him a name that began with a 'W', in memory of a relative, as it was a Jewish custom to be named after someone in the family who had died.

Their choice of recordings shows that they had been exposed to a range of music with an emphasis on classical. Kossoff's selection included Puccini and Beethoven as well as a lesser known violin concerto by Soviet composer Khachaturian. Mitchell chose modern jazz together with Mozart, Bach, Wagner and Sibelius. Bart chose predominantly Broadway musicals and the 'Symphonic Poem – Don Juan' by Richard Strauss. For Bass, the preference was for Handel, Mozart and Beethoven but perhaps an unexpected choice was 'Land of Our Fathers', the Welsh national anthem which is such a patriotic and emotive song and showed that he could be moved by this in the same way as his choice of Yiddish lullaby.

In respect of Unity Theatre, it was only Bart that omitted to mention his time there. Mitchell considered it was 'marvellous' and Kossoff felt it to be the best theatre in the world. Bass spoke the most about the importance of its message and purpose and indeed he was always the most vocal about his socialism. After they achieved fame, they all apart from Bart (again reflecting his apolitical later career), publicly acknowledged their time and gratitude to Unity as it was a launching pad for their careers. Kossoff produced a one-man show in 1963 to raise money for Unity when they had financial trouble. Nonetheless, their political affiliations in later years varied from Kossoff's indifference to Bass's life-long commitment to socialism. Mitchell remained sympathetic to left-wing causes and Bart indulged in a lifestyle of extravagance. Despite the differences they were still unified by identifying themselves and being identified as Jewish Cockneys. This was how they saw themselves and others saw them, both Jews and non-Jews, and no one queried this coupling.

Second-generation Jews living in the interwar period were developing and adopting new approaches to being Jewish and being a Jew in England. It appeared that few sought complete estrangement from their family and community. Even if they had wanted to escape their identity there were reminders such as antisemitism when Jews sought out employment and housing opportunities outside of the Jewish areas and pre-existing immigrant trades. It provided the impetus for young Jews to feel and protect their Jewishness and Jewish community. An example of this was the reaction to fascism and political antisemitism in the 1930s, when many Jews were on the front line of the Spanish Civil War and the Battle of Cable Street to protect Jews and Jewish freedom. Greater exposure to non-Jewish society, including the hostile elements within it, and a general desire to maintain connections to the Jewish history, culture and community led to a hybrid form of identity among the second generation. They were thus reconfiguring their identities to suit their environment and their life choices. This ability to exist in and understand both cultures was often beneficial, whether it be in business or political organisations. They were redefining their Jewishness and creating something that was both separate from, yet influenced by, the background that they came from. What appeared to develop was a worldview that allowed them to exist in and feel attachment to both minority and majority society.[2]

What occurred during this period was an evolution of Jewish identity in a British context. The way that their Jewishness was conceived and expressed was influenced both by their background and external forces. They found a new way of being and feeling both Jewish and British in the interwar Jewish, British and British-Jewish environments in which they lived.[3] This was applicable beyond the East End. Second generation David Daiches, son of an orthodox Rabbi and who grew up in Edinburgh, commented that he was equally at home in both worlds.[4] Jack Caplan, who grew up in the Gorbals, a working-class area in Glasgow with a large immigrant Jewish community, reflected 'I love the Scots. After all, I am Scottish too. My loyalty and devotion is divided equally between Scotland and Israel.'[5]

This compatibility is evident in early reports from the BBC drama department indicated that Kossoff was 'most comfortable in Jewish roles and was a natural Cockney'.[6] This statement showed that the BBC, an establishment organization, acknowledged Kossoff's ease with his Jewishness but, at the same time, acknowledged that he was also a Cockney and that he could have *both* identities. It was significant that they were chosen to play Cockneys in the first place. Kossoff had a leading role as a hen-pecked Cockney factory worker in *The Larkins*. This was an early ITV sitcom at a time when the network was trying to establish itself after years of BBC's monopoly as the sole supplier of home entertainment. It is clear that they were confident that Kossoff could embody this role – likewise with

Conclusion

Bass, who was chosen to play Cockney Bootsie in the *Army Game* and *Bootsie and Snudge*. Mitchell's Alf Garnett in *Till Death Us Do Part* was the most famous Cockney character on television.

At the same time, they endorsed their Jewish identity. Bass swore in Yiddish in a court case when he was charged under the 1843 Theatres Act for putting on a production for Unity with an anti-American theme.[7] Bart was always proud of his East End origins and this was reflected in the programme *One Pair of Eyes* when he went back to the East End to show where he had grown up.[8] Mitchell always defended himself against any antisemitic attack, such as the time when actor Richard Burton made negative remarks.[9] Mitchell clearly stated his Jewishness at a Tottenham Hotspur football match on Boxing Day where he said 'On behalf of all the Jewish supporters of Spurs may I wish all the *goyim* (non-Jews) a good *yom tov* (good day) and well over the fast.'[10] This was a totally inappropriate remark for that time of the year but he wanted to put his message across. Although all four were non-practising Jews and married non-Jews (apart from Bart who was homosexual and did not marry) they always acknowledged their background.

Bass's obituaries highlighted that he was a Jewish Cockney: 'frequently called upon to embody the Cockney Jewish tradition of springy resilience'[11] and for his 'irrepressible Cockney Jewish talent'.[12] The *Jewish Chronicle* commented that 'with his Cockney Jewish background he was eminently suitable for many of the character parts in which he appeared'.[13] Bart was referred to as a 'Cockney Cole Porter'.[14] When Mitchell appeared in Pinter's *The Homecoming*, it was said that he played the role in a natural Jewish Cockney idiom.[15] And crucially, to repeat, they saw themselves as Jewish Cockneys. Kossoff commented that although he was a Cockney, his parents came from Lithuania.[16] When Bart appeared on BBC's *Woman's Hour* he stated that he was 'obviously very pro-Cockney at heart'.[17] These comments show the confidence they had as second generation immigrants to be able to identify as Jewish Cockneys in the post-war era, and for them to be accepted freely as such in non-Jewish society. It was a remarkable form of cultural adjustment, performance and successful integration.

Notes

1. *Desert Island Discs* BBC Radio 4, Lionel Bart 26 September 1960; David Kossoff 11 May 1964; Warren Mitchell 13 November 1967; Alfie Bass 1 April 1968; BBC Written Archives, Reading.
2. David Dee, *The 'Estranged' Generation? Social and Generational Change in Interwar British Jewry* (Leicester: Palgrave Macmillan, 2017), pp. 337–8.

3. Ibid., p. 342.
4. David Daiches, *Two Worlds* (Edinburgh: Canongate, 1997), p. 3.
5. Jack Caplan, *Memories of the Gorbals* (Durham: Pentland Press, 1991), pp. 95–6.
6. David Kossoff file 1945–1953, BBC Written Archives, Reading.
7. Colin Chambers, *The Story of Unity Theatre*, p. 320.
8. *One Pair of Eyes*, BBC Four London Collection, 17 August 1968.
9. *Daily Mail*, 27 April 1996, p. 31.
10. *Jewish Chronicle*, 2 January 1981, p. 15.
11. *Guardian*, 18 July 1987.
12. *The Times*, 18 July 1986.
13. *Jewish Chronicle*, 24 July 1987.
14. *Daily Mirror*, 22 June 1965.
15. *Observer*, 13 January 1991.
16. *Sunday Independent* (Dublin), 22 September 1963.
17. Lionel Bart file, 1958–62, BBC Written Archives Centre.

Bibliography and Sources

ARCHIVAL MATERIAL
Lionel Bart Foundation Archive, London
'Notes on *Blitz!*', February 1961.
'Lionel Bart's initial thoughts on *Twang!*, 19 June 1964.
'Thoughts on Fagin', 23 January 1967.

BBC Written Archives Centre, Reading
Alfie's Penny Gaffs, 9 July 1958, R86/3/1.
David Kossoff file, 1945–1953.
Lionel Bart file, 1958–62.
Desert Island Discs, PABX 4904.

British Library, London
'Blitz on Bart', Sound Archives, CB43/58.
Louis Behr interviewed by David Mazower, 29 October 1986, Sound Archives, C525/52 F11708.
Bow Dialogues, Reverend Joseph McCulloch and David Kossoff, 23 August 1966; 14 November 1967; 1 June 1971; Sound Archives, C812/15; ICDLR 0002983; C812/31.
Alfie Bass interview, Don Rowan Collection, Sound Archives, C1037/54.
Stephen Williams in conversation with Lionel Bart, Sound Archives, C704/31.
'The Story of Unity Theatre', Unity Theatre Trust Recording 2009, Sound Archives, 1DVDR0001737.
'The Story of the Yiddish Theatre in the East End of London', BBC Radio 4, 16 October 1987, Sound Archives, B3410/2.
Theatre Archive Project, Sound Archives, C1142/173, C1186/109.

Hackney Archives, London
Workers' Circle Friendly Society Records, 1909–1984, D/S/61.

London Metropolitan Archives, London
The Board of Deputies Archives

Marx Memorial Library Archive, London
The Archive of the *Daily Worker* Newspaper

Mass-Observation Archives, The Keep, Sussex
Report on Antisemitism 1939-51 TC 62.
Notes on Antisemitic Feeling 1939–45, 62-1-B.

East End Study 1939, 62-1-A.
Feelings towards Jews and Cockneys in the East End, 62-1.

Muriel Walker Personal Archive, London
Muriel Walker was a member of Unity Theatre and personal assistant to Lionel Bart.

The National Archives, London
1911 Census.
1939 Register.
HO B.21699.
HO 350/48/6087.
HO 39/6/18.

People's History Museum, Manchester
Labour History Archive, People's History Museum, Manchester.
The Papers of the Communist Party of Great Britain 1920–1994.
Unity Theatre Archive, 5/1–3.

Working Class Movement Library Archive, Manchester
Workers Theatre Movement collection.
Unity Theatre Archive.

V & A Theatre and Performance Collection, London
Unity Theatre Archives 1932–2001.
Una Brandon-Jones, Highlights and Lowlights, THM/9/1/3/6.
Ted Willis, *The Yellow Star*, THM/9/7169.

INTERVIEWS WITH THE AUTHOR
Davis, Elliot, 23 January 2017 (telephone).
Evans, Brenda, 15 November 2018, London.
Gold, Davina, 26 November 2016, London.
Goldstein, Geoffrey, 19 July 2016, London.
Hilton, Margot, 29 March 2016, London.
Jesson, Gillian, 22 November 2016, London.
Kossoff, Simon, 2 December 2016, London.
Landis, Harry, 11 January 2016, London.
Mattock, Andrea, 17 January 2017, London.
Murgraff, Shirley, 2 February 2016, London.
Walker, Muriel, 23 November 2016, London.
Yates, Binnie, 9 February 2016, London.

NEWSPAPER AND PERIODICALS
Belfast News Letter
Birmingham Post
Cable
Daily Express
Daily Mail
Daily Mirror

Daily Sketch
Daily Star
Daily Telegraph
Daily Worker
Evening News
Evening Standard
Financial Times
Guardian
Hackney Citizen
Ham and High
Independent
Jewish Chronicle
Morning Star
Newcastle Journal and Daily Dispatch Manchester
North-Western Evening Mail
Observer
Observer Review
Red Stage
Reynolds News
Socialist Review
Stage
Sun
Sunday Express
Sunday Independent (Dublin)
Sunday Telegraph
The Times
Today's Cinema
TV Mirror
TV Times
Yorkshire Evening Post

AUTOBIOGRAPHIES

Beckman, Maurice, *The Hackney Crucible* (London: Vallentine Mitchell, 1966).

Berkoff, Steven, *Free Association: An Autobiography* (London: Faber and Faber, 1996).

Blacker, Harry, *Just Like It Was: Memoirs of the Mittel East* (London: Vallentine Mitchell, 1974).

Fielding, Fenella and Simon McKay, *Do You Mind If I Smoke?* (London: Peter Owen, 2017).

Finn, Ralph, *Grief Forgotten: The Tale of an East End Jewish Boyhood* (London: Macdonald, 1985).

Goldman, Willy, *East End My Cradle* (London: Faber & Faber, 1940).

Gorman, John, *Knocking Down Ginger* (London: Caliban Books, 1995).

Gross, John, *A Double Thread: A Childhood in Mile End and Beyond* (London: Chatto & Windus, 2001).

Hilton, Kate, *From Greenfield Street to Golders Green: 90 Years of 20th Century London Memories* (Sydney: Sydney Jewish Museum, 2011).

Jacobs, Joe, *Out of the Ghetto: My Youth in the East End, Communism and Fascism 1913-1939* (London: Janet Simon, 1978).

Kops, Bernard, *The World is a Wedding: From East End to Soho* (Nottingham: Five Leaves Publications, 2008).

Mendelovitch, Bernard, *Memories of London Yiddish Theatre* (Oxford: Oxford Centre for Postgraduate Hebrew Studies, 1990).

Mitchell, Yvonne, *Actress* (London: Routledge & Kegan Paul, 1957).

Morris, Aubrey, *Unfinished Journey* (London: Artery Publications, 2000).

Moss Haber, Gilda, *Cockney Girl: The Story of a Jewish Family in WWII London* (Derby: Derby Books, 2012).

Poulson, Charles, *Scenes from a Stepney Youth* (London: THAP Books, 1988).

Shears, Elsie, *The Cockney Lady* (London: New Millenium, 1995).

Tzelniker, Anna, *Three for the Price of One* (London: Spiro Institute, 1991).

OTHER PRINTED PRIMARY SOURCES
Evans-Gordon, W., *The Alien Immigrant* (London: William Heinemann, 1903).

Kossoff, David, *The Book of Witnesses* (London: Collins, 1971).

Levy, A. B., *East End Story* (London: Constellation Books, 1951).

Massingham, H. J., *London Scene* (London: Cobden Sanderson, 1933).

Mayhew, Henry, *London Labour and the London Poor* (London: Charles Griffin & Company, 1865).

Russell, C. and H. S. Lewis, *The Jew in London: A Study of Racial Character and Present Day Conditions* (London: T. Fisher Unwin, 1901).

TALKS
Mazower, David, 'Women in East End Yiddish Theatre', 23 March 2017, Tower Hamlets Library and Archives, London.

Mitchell, Warren, 'Lifelines – Evening with Warren Mitchell', 6 October 2005, Burgh House, Hampstead, London.

THEATRE PROGRAMME
King Lear, West Yorkshire Playhouse, 22 September – 28 October 1995.

INTERNET
Alcalay Klug, Lisa, 'Jewish Funeral Customs', www.jewishfederations.org, accessed 2 September 2017.

BBC News, 'Joan Littlewood Obituary: Theatre's Defiant Genius', 21 September 2002, accessed 3 December 2016.

BBC News, 'Warren Mitchell', 14 November 2015, accessed 31 August 2018.

Berkoff, Steven, 'Exploring the Vanishing East End', www.towerhamlets.co.uk, accessed 1 September 2018.

Haill, Catherine, 'Theatregoing in East London', East London Theatre Archive, www.elta-project.org, accessed 4 April 2017.

Hoedl, Klaus, 'Physical Characteristics of the Jews', Jewish Studies at the CEU, web.ceu.hu/jewishstudies, accessed 12 August 2017.

Portnoy, Eddy, 'The Disappearing Yiddish Accent', *The Forward*, 13 August 2012, www.forward.com, accessed 30 August 2018.

'Wonderland/Rivoli Cinema – 236–7 Whitechapel Road', www.arthurlloyd.co.uk, accessed 4 April 2017.

Zollman, Joellyn. 'What Were Shtetls?' www.myjewishlearning.com, accessed 30 August 2018.

WEBSITES
www.allmusic.com, accessed 14 September 2018.
www.biography.com, accessed 15 August 2018.
www.bloomsbury.com, accessed 15 August 2018.
www.britishcomedy.org.uk, accessed 5 December 2017.
www.chabad.org, accessed 15 June 2018.
www.collinsdictionary.com, accessed 31 July 2018.
www.grahamstevenson.me.uk, accessed 4 December 2017.
www.holocaustmusic.ort.org, accessed 8 April 2018.
www.imdb.com, accessed 10 July 2018.
www.independent.co.uk, accessed 20 March 2018.
www.jewishgen.org, accessed 14 May 2018.
www.jewish-languages.org, accessed 1 June 2018.
www.massobs.org.uk, accessed 19 November 2017.
www.museum.tv, accessed 1 September 2018.
www.nostalgiacentral.com, accessed 26 November 2018.
www.screenonline.org.uk, accessed 19 January 2018.
www.stageagent.com, 23 July 2018.
www.telegraph.co.uk, accessed 11 May 2018.
www.translationdictionary.com, accessed 8 April 2018.
www.troublesarchive.com, accessed 11 May 2018.

VIDEO
Bootsie and the Beast, Bootserella, Storytime Discs. Stars Entertaining Children, Vintage British Comedy.
Bootsie and Snudge (The Army Game), 'Civvy Street', SO1 E03, 23 September 1960.
One Pair of Eyes. Who are the Cockneys Now?, 17 August 1968, BBC Four London Collection.
The Bespoke Overcoat (1955) Remus Films.
The Larkins, 'Wide Open House', 19 September 1958; 'Cat Happy', 3 October 1958; 'Telly Ho', 17 October 1958; 'Christmas with the Larkins', 26 October 1958; ITV series.
The Late Great Paul (1992), British Film Institute.
Till Death Us Do Part, 'Intolerance', SE1E04; 'Holiday in Bournemouth', SO4EO3; 'The Wake', S6EO5; 'Moving in with Min', S7EO1; 'A Hole in One', S7EO5; 'Christmas Club Books', SO6EO7; 'Five Best Moments'; 'God Was Church of England. Jesus Was After the Oil'; 'Wheelchair in the Road', www.youtube.com.

RADIO
Desert Island Discs, 26 September 1960; 11 May 1964; 13 November 1967; 1 April 1968, 3 December 1999, BBC Radio 4.
A Handful of Songs. The Lionel Bart Story, 28 February 2007, BBC Radio 2.

UNPUBLISHED DISSERTATION
Travis, Ron 'The Story of Unity Theatre 1936-1946 – A Decade of Production' (MA dissertation, University of Southern Illinois, 1968).

184   East End Jews and Left-Wing Theatre

SECONDARY SOURCES

Ackroyd, Peter, *London: The Biography* (London: Chatto & Windus, 2008).

Arkell, George E., *Jewish East London, 1899 map* (Botley, Oxford: Old House, 2012).

Banham, Martin, *The Cambridge Guide to Theatre* (Cambridge: Cambridge University Press, 1995).

Barker, Clive and Maggie B. Gale, *British Theatre between the Wars, 1918–1939* (Cambridge: Cambridge University Press, 2001).

Barltrop, Robert, 'Prize Fighting in East London', *Cockney Ancestor*, 12 (Autumn 1981), p. 3.

Behr, Louis, 'Boxing Memories', *East London Record*, 5 (1982), pp. 34–6.

Bermant, Chaim, *London's East End: Point of Arrival* (London: Eyre Metheun, 1975).

Bertolt Brecht, *Brecht on Theatre: The Development of an Aesthetic* (New York: Hill & Young, 1964).

Billington, Michael, *Harold Pinter* (London: Faber and Faber, 2007).

Black, Eugene, *The Social Politics of Anglo-Jewry, 1880–1920* (Oxford: Basil Blackwell, 1988).

Bloom, Alexander, *Prodigal Sons: The New York Intellectuals and their World* (New York: Oxford University Press, 1986).

Booth, Michael R. and Joel H. Kaplan, *The Edwardian Theatre* (Cambridge: Cambridge University Press, 1996).

Boyarin, Daniel, *The Rise of Heterosexuality and the Invention of the Jewish Man* (Berkeley: University of California Press, 1997).

Bradby, David and John McCormick, *People's Theatre* (London: Crook Helm, 1978).

Bradshaw, Ross, 'Children of the Revolution', *Jewish Renaissance* (January 2017), pp. 28–9.

Branson, Noreen, *History of the Communist Party in Great Britain, 1927–41* (London: Lawrence & Wishart, 1985).

Briggs, Asa, *Victorian Cities* (London: Odhams Press, 1963).

Brook, Stephen, *The Club: The Jews of Modern Britain* (London: Pan Books, 1987).

Burke, Thomas, *The Real East End* (London: Constable & Co, 1932).

Cable Street Group (eds), *The Battle of Cable Street 1936* (London: Cable Street Group, 1995).

Caine, Barbara, *Biography and History* (Basingstoke: Palgrave Macmillan, 2010).

Caplan, Jack, *Memories of the Gorbals* (Durham: Portland Press, 1991).

Cesarani, David and Mary Fulbrook (eds), *Citizenship, Nationality and Migration in Europe* (London: Routledge, 1996).

Cesarani, David and Tony Kushner (eds), *The Internment of Aliens in Twentieth Century Britain* (London: Frank Cass, 1993).

Cesarani, David, 'A Funny Thing Happened on the Way to the Suburbs: Social Change in Anglo Jewry between the Wars 1914–1945', *Jewish Culture and History*, 1 (1998), pp. 5–26.

Cesarani, David, 'An Alien Concept? The Continuity of Anti-Alienism in British Society Before 1940', in David Cesarani and Tony Kushner (eds), *The Internment of Aliens in Twentieth Century Britain* (London: Frank Cass, 1993), pp. 25–52.

Cesarani, David, 'Putting London Intellectuals in their Place', in David Cesarani, Tony Kushner and Milton Shain (eds), *Place and Displacement in Jewish History and Memory: Zakor V'Makor* (London: Vallentine Mitchell, 2009), pp. 141–53.

Cesarani, David, 'The Myth of Origins: Ethnic Memory and the Experience of Migration', A. Newman and S. W. Massil (eds), *Patterns of Migration* (London: Jewish Historical Society of England/Institute of Jewish Affairs, 1996), pp. 247–54.

Bibliography and Sources

Cesarani, David, Tony Kushner and Milton Shain (eds), *Place and Displacement in Jewish History and Memory* (London: Vallentine Mitchell, 2009).

Chambers, Colin, *The Story of Unity Theatre* (London: Lawrence & Wishart, 1989).

Cheyette, Bryan, 'East Ender: Bernard Kops', *Jewish Quarterly*, 33, 1 (1986) pp. 32–4.

Cohen-Cruz, Jan (ed.), *Radical Street Performance* (London: Routledge, 1988).

Cohen, Derek and Deborah Heller (eds), *Jewish Presences in English Literature* (Montreal: McGill-Queen's University Press, 1990).

Cohen, Steven M. and Paula E. Hyman (eds), *The Jewish Family: Myths and Reality* (New York: Holmes & Meier, 1986).

Coleman, Ray, *Brian Epstein: The Man Who Made the Beatles* (London: Penguin Books, 1990).

Comas, J., *Racial Myths in Race and Science* (New York: Columbia University Press, 1961).

Connell, R. W., 'Understanding Men: Gender Sociology and the New International Research on Masculinities', *Social Thought and Research*, 24 (2002), pp. 13–31.

Craig, Sandy (ed.), *Dreams and Deconstructions: Alternative Theatre in Britain* (Ambergate: Amber Lane Press, 1980).

Daiches, David, *Two Worlds: An Edinburgh Jewish Childhood* (Edinburgh: Canongate, 1997).

Dash Moore, Deborah, *At Home in America: Second Generation New York Jews* (New York: Columbia University Press, 1981).

Davies, Andrew, *Other Theatres: The Development of Alternative and Experimental Theatre in Britain* (Basingstoke: Macmillan Education, 1987).

Davies, John, 'Working Class Culture in the 1930s: Going to the Dogs', *North West Labour History*, 35 (2010–2011), pp. 32–7.

Davis, Jim and Victor Emeljanow, *Reflecting the Audience: London Theatregoing 1840-1880* (Hatfield: University of Hertfordshire Press, 2001).

Davis, Jim, 'The East End', in Michael R. Booth and Joel H. Caplan (eds), *The Edwardian Theatre* (Cambridge: Cambridge University Press, 1996), pp. 221–8.

de Jongh, Nicholas, *Politics, Prudery and Perversions: The Censoring of the English Stage 1901-1968* (London: Metheun, 2000).

Dee, David, *The 'Estranged' Generation?: Social and Generational Change in Interwar British Jewry* (London: Palgrave Macmillan, 2017).

Dench, Geoff, Kate Gavron and Michael Young, *The New East End: Kinship, Race and Conflict* (London: Profile, 2006).

Dickason, Renee, 'Social Class and Class Distinction in Britcoms (1950s–2000s)', in Nicole Cloarec, David Haigron and Delphine Letort (eds), *Social Class on British and American Screens* (Jefferson, North Carolina: McFarland & Co, 2016), pp. 34–57.

Down, Richard and Christopher Petty, *The British Television Research Guide 1950-1997* (Bristol: Kaleidoscope Publishing, 1997).

Dudgeon, Piers, *Our East End: Memories of Life in Disappearing Britain* (London: Headline, 2008).

Dunn, Anthony J., *The Worlds of Wolf Mankowitz. Between Elite and Popular Cultures in Post War Britain* (London: Vallentine Mitchell, 2013).

Efron, David, *Gesture, Race and Culture* (The Hague: Mouton, 1972).

Eisner, Will, *Fagin the Jew* (Oregon: Dark Horse Books, 2013).

Endelman, T. M., *Leaving the Jewish Fold: Conversion and Radical Assimilation in Modern Jewish History* (Princeton: Princeton University Press, 2015).

Endelman, T. M., *Radical Assimilation in English Jewish History 1656–1945* (Bloomington: Indiana University Press, 1990).

Englander, David, *A Documentary History of Jewish Immigrants in Britain 1840–1920* (Leicester: Leicester University Press, 1994).

Evans, Jeff, *The Penguin TV Companion* (London: Penguin, 2003).

Farson, Daniel, *Soho in the Fifties* (London: Michael Joseph, 1988).

Finkelstein, B., 'Revealing Human Agency: The Use of Biography in the Study of Educational History', in C. Kridel (ed.), *Writing Educational Biography: Explorations in Quantitative Research* (New York: Garland Publishing, 1985), pp. 45–59.

Fishman, William J., *East End Jewish Radicals 1875–1914* (London: George Duckworth & Co, 1975).

Frankel, Jonathan (ed.), *Studies in Contemporary Jewry: The Fate of the European Jews, 1939–1945: Continuity or Contingency?* (New York: Oxford University Press, 1997).

Fredrics, Howard, 'Jewish Boxers of the East End', *The Cable*, 1 (2006), p. 7.

Freedland, Michael, *So Let's Hear the Applause: The Story of the Jewish Entertainer* (London: Vallentine Mitchell, 1984).

Freedman, Maurice (ed.), *A Minority in Britain* (London: Vallentine Mitchell, 1955).

Gartner, Lloyd P., *The Jewish Immigrant in England 1870–1914* (London: Simon Publications, 1973).

Geller, Deborah, *The Brian Epstein Story* (London: Faber, 2000).

Gilman, Sander, *The Jew's Body* (London: Routledge, 1991).

Glinert, Ed, *East End Chronicles* (London: Penguin Books, 2006).

Goorney, Howard and Ewan MacColl, *Agitprop to Theatre Workshop* (Manchester: Manchester University Press, 1986).

Goorney, Howard, *The Theatre Workshop Story* (London: Eyre Methuen, 1981).

Green, John, *British Communists: The Untold Story* (London: Artery Publications, 2016).

Groser, John B., *Politics and Persons* (London: SCM Press, 1949).

Grospean, Francois, 'Bilinguals', in Renzo Titone (ed.), *On the Bilingual Person* (University of Ottawa, Ottawa: Canadian Society for Italian Studies, 1989), pp. 35–54.

Heppell, Jason L., 'A Rebel Not a Rabbi: Jewish Membership of the Communist Party of Great Britain', *Twentieth Century British History*, 15, 1 (2004), pp. 28–50.

Heppell, Jason L., 'Party Recruitment: Jews and Communism in Britain', in Jonathan Frankel (ed.), *Dark Times, Dire Decisions: Jews and Communism* (Oxford: Oxford University Press, 2005), pp. 148–167.

Holder, Heidi J., 'The East End Theatre', in Kerry Powell (ed.), *The Cambridge Companion to Victorian and Edwardian Theatre* (Cambridge: Cambridge University Press, 2004), pp. 257–76.

Holdworth, Nadine, *Joan Littlewood* (London: Routledge, 2006).

Holroyd, Michael, *Lytton Strachey* (London: Chatto & Windus, 1994).

Howe, Irving, *Selected Writings 1950–1990* (New York: Harcourt Brace Jovanovich, 1990).

Innes, Christopher, *Modern British Drama: The Twentieth Century* (Cambridge: Cambridge University Press, 2002).

Johnson, Paul (ed.), *Twentieth Century Britain: Economic, Social and Cultural Change* (London: Longman, 1994), pp. 9–11.

Jordan, James, 'Another Man's Faith? The Image of Judaism in the BBC Television Series Men Seeking God', in Hannah Ewence and Helen Spurling (eds), *Visualising Jews*

Through the Ages: Literary and Material Representations of Jewishness and Judaism (New York and Oxford: Routledge, 2015), pp. 247–64.

Jordanova, Ludmilla, *History in Practice* (London: Hodder Arnold, 2006).

Kael, Pauline, *5001 Nights at the Movies* (London: Zenith, 1984).

Kalman, Raymond, 'The Jewish East End – Where Was It?', in Aubrey Newman (ed.), *The Jewish East End 1840–1939* (London: Jewish Historical Society of England, 1981), pp. 3–15.

Kavaloski, Laini, 'Bernard Kops: Fantasist, London Jew, Apocalyptic Humorist', *Comparative Drama* 48, 3 (Fall 2014), pp. 315–18.

Kimmel, Michael S., 'Judaism, Masculinity and Feminism', in Harry Brod (ed.), *A Mensch Among Men. Explorations in Jewish Masculinity* (Freedom, CA: Crossing Press, 1988), pp. 153–6.

Kühne, Thomas, 'Jewish Masculinities: German Jews, Gender and History', ed. by Benjamin Maria Baader, Sharon Gillerman and Paul Lerner (review), *German Studies Review*, 37, 2 (May 2014), p. 440.

Kushner, Tony, 'Jewish Migration in Fin-de-siecle Britain', in Rachel Dickson and Sarah MacDougall (eds), *Ben Uri: 100 Years in London* (London: Ben Uri Gallery, 2015), pp. 24–34.

Kushner, Tony, *The Persistence of Prejudice: Antisemitism in British Society During the Second World War* (Manchester: Manchester University Press, 1989).

Kushner, Tony, *We Europeans? Mass-Observation, 'Race' and British Identity in the Twentieth Century* (Aldershot: Ashgate, 2004).

Lachs, Vivi, *Whitechapel Noise: Jewish Immigrant Life in Yiddish Song and Verse, London 1884–1914* (Detroit: Michigan Wayne State University Press, 2018).

Lammers, Benjamin J., 'The Birth of the East Ender: Neighbourhood and Local Identity in Interwar East London', *Journal of Social History*, 39, 2 (2005), pp. 331–44.

Laybourn, Keith, 'King Solomon's Mines Can Not Compare with the Money That Has Been Raked in by Greyhound Racing: Greyhound Racing, its Critics and the Working Class 1926-51', *Labour History* 55, 5 (2014), pp. 607–21.

Lehrer, Natasha, *The Golden Chain: Fifty Years of the Jewish Quarterly* (London: Vallentine Mitchell, 2003).

Leon, Ruth and Sheridan Morley, *A Century of Theatre* (London: Oberon Books, 2001).

Linehan, Thomas P., *East London for Mosley: The British Union of Fascists in East London and South-West Essex 1933–40* (London: Routledge, 1996).

Lipman, V. D., *A History of the Jews in Britain Since 1858* (Leicester: Leicester University Press, 1990).

Lipman, V.D., 'Jewish Settlement in the East End of London', in Aubrey Newman (ed.), *The Jewish East End 1840–1939* (London: Jewish Historical Society of England, 1981), pp. 17–40.

Livshin, Rosalyn, 'The Acculturation of the Children of Immigrant Jews in Manchester, 1890–1930', in David Cesarani (ed.), *The Making of Modern Anglo Jewry* (Oxford: Basil Blackwell, 1990), pp. 79–96.

Mankowitz, Wolf, *Five One Act Plays* (London: Evan Brothers, 1956).

Marks, Lara V., *Model Mothers: Jewish Mothers and Maternity Provision in East London,1870–1939* (Oxford: Clarendon Press, 1994).

Marshal, N., *The Other Theatre* (London: John Lehmann, 1947).

Mazower, David, *Yiddish Theatre in London* (London: The Jewish Museum, 1996).

Medhurst, A., *A National Joke: Popular Comedy and English Cultural Identities* (London: Routledge, 2007).

Merrill, Barbara and Linden West, *Using Biographical Methods in Social Research* (London: Sage, 2009).

Mills, Brett, *Television Sitcoms* (London: Secker & Warburg, 1995).

More, Charles, *Britain in the Twentieth Century: A History* (Harlow: Pearson Longman, 2007).

Morgan, Kevin, Gidon Cohen and Andrew Flinn, *Communists and British Society, 1920–1991: People of a Special Mould* (London: Rivers Oram Press, 2007).

Moss, Mark, *The Media and the Models of Masculinity* (Lanham, MD: Lexington Books, 2011).

Murray, Susan, 'Lessons from Uncle Miltie: Ethnic Masculinity and Early Television's Vaudeo Star', in Janet Thumin (ed.), *Small Screens, Big Ideas: Television in the 1950s* (London: I. B. Taurus, 2002), pp. 66–87.

Murray, Venetia, *Echoes of the East End* (London: Viking, 1989).

Napolitano, Marc, *Oliver!: A Dickensian Musical* (Oxford: Oxford University Press, 2014).

Newton, H. Chance, *Idols of the 'Halls'* (Wakefield: EP Publishing, 1975).

Nicholson, Steve, *British Theatre and the Red Peril* (Exeter: University of Exeter Press, 1999).

Nicoll, Allardyce, *The English Theatre: A Short History* (London: Nelson, 1936).

Norman, Frank, *Fings Ain't Wot They Used T'Be* (London: Samuel French, 1960).

Norwood, Stephen H., 'American Jewish Muscle: Forging a New Masculinity in the Streets and in the Ring, 1890–1940', *Modern Judaism*, 2 (2009), pp. 167–93.

Nulman, Macy, *Concise Encyclopedia of Jewish Music* (New York: McGraw Hill, 1976).

Orwell, George, *England, Your England and Other Essays* (London: Secker & Warburg, 1953).

Page, Malcolm, 'The Early Years at Unity', *Theatre Quarterly*, 1, 4 (October-December 1971), pp. 60-66.

Patai, Raphael and Jennifer Patai, *The Myth of the Jewish Race* (Detroit: Wayne University Press, 1989).

Patterson, Michael, *Strategies of Political Theatre* (Cambridge: Cambridge University Press, 2003).

Pettigrew, Terence, *British Film Character Actors: Great Names and Memorable Moments* (Newton Abbot: David and Charles, 1982).

Porter, Roy, *London: A Social History* (London: Hamish Hamilton, 1994).

Powell, Kerry (ed.), *Victorian and Edwardian Theatre* (Cambridge: Cambridge University Press, 2003).

Prager, Leonard, *Yiddish Culture in Britain: A Guide* (Frankfurt: P. Lang, 1990).

Renton, David, 'Docker and Garment Worker, Railwayman and Cabinet Maker: The Class Memory of Cable Street', in Tony Kushner and Nadia Valman (eds), *Remembering Cable Street: Fascism and Anti-Facism in British Society* (London: Vallentine Mitchell, 2000), pp. 95–108.

Roper, David, *Bart!* (London: Pavilion Books, 1994).

Rose, Millicent, *The East End of London* (Bath: Cedric Chivers, 1973).

Rosenberg, Warren, *Legacy of Rage: Jewish Masculinity, Violence and Culture* (Amhurst, Mass: University of Massachusetts Press, 2001).

Rosenfeld, Lulla, *Bright Star of Exile* (London: Barrie & Jenkins, 1978).

Ross, Cathy and John Clark, *London: The Illustrated History* (London: Penguin Books, 2008).

Bibliography and Sources 189

Sackville-O'Donnell, Judith, *The First Fagin: The True Story of Ikey Solomon* (Melbourne: Acland Press, 2002).

Salisbury, Harriet, *The War On Our Doorstep* (London: Ebury Press, 2013).

Samuel, R., 'The Lost World of British Communism', *New Left Review*, 154 (1985), pp. 3–53.

Samuel, Raphael, *East End Underworld: Chapters in the Life of Arthur Harding* (London: Routledge & Kegan Paul, 1981).

Samuel, Raphael, Ewan MacColl and Stuart Cosgrove, *Theatres of the Left 1880–1935* (London: Routledge & Kegan Paul, 1985).

Sanderson, Michael, *From Irving to Olivier: A Social History of the Acting Profession in England 1880-1983* (London: Athlone Press, 1984).

Sandrow, Nahama, *Vagabond Stars: A World History of Yiddish Theatre* (New York: Harper & Row, 1977).

Schaffer, Gavin, '*Till Death Us Do Part* and the BBC: Racial Politics and the British Working Classes 1965–75', *Journal of Contemporary History*, 45, 2 (2010), pp. 454–77.

Schaffer, Gavin, *The Vision of a Nation: Making Multiculturalism on British Television 1960–80* (Basingstoke: Palgrave Macmillan, 2014).

Scott, Derek B., *Sounds of the Metropolis* (Oxford: Oxford University Press, 2008).

Sharman, Kadish, *Bolsheviks and the British Jews* (London: Frank Cass, 1992).

Sheridan, Paul, *Penny Theatres of Victorian London* (London: Dennis Dobson, 1981).

Sierz, Aleks and Lia Ghilardi, *The Time Traveller's Guide to British Theatre* (London: Oberon Books, 2015).

Simpson, J. A. and E. S. C. Weiner (eds), *The Oxford English Dictionary*, Volume 5 (Oxford: Clarendon Press, 1989).

Southgate, Vera, *Beauty and the Beast* (London: Penguin, 1964).

Speight, Johnny, *Alf Garnett: The Thoughts of Chairman Alf: Alf Garnett's Little Blue Book Or Where England Went Wrong* (London: Robson Books, 1973).

Srebrnik, Henry Felix, *London Jews and British Communism 1935–45* (Ilford: Vallentine Mitchell, 1995).

Srebrnik, Henry, 'Class, Ethnicity and Gender Intertwined: Jewish Women and the East London Rent Strikes, 1933-1940', *Women's History Review*, 4, 3 (1995), pp. 283–99.

Stafford, David and Caroline Stafford, *Fings Ain't Wot They Used T'Be: The Lionel Bart Story* (London: Omnibus Press, 2011).

Steinweis, Alan E., *Studying the Jew: Scholarly Antisemitism in Nazi Germany* (Cambridge, Mass: Harvard University Press, 2006).

Strachey, Lytton, *Eminent Victorians: Top Biography Collections* (London: Penguin Books, 1986).

Sussman, Herbert, *Masculine Identities: The History and Meanings of Manliness* (Santa Barbara: Praeger, 2012).

Tanny, Jarold, *City of Rogues and Schnorrers: Russia's Jews and the Myth of Old Odessa* (Bloomington: Indiana University Press, 2011).

Thomas, Keith, *Changing Conceptions of National Biography: The Oxford DNB in Historical Perspective* (Cambridge: Cambridge University Press, 2005).

Tobias, J. J., *Prince of Fences: The Life and Crimes of Ikey Solomon* (London: Vallentine Mitchell, 1974).

Trussler, Simon, *British Theatre* (Cambridge: Cambridge University Press, 1994).

Vice, Sue, *Jack Rosenthal* (Manchester: Manchester University Press, 2009).

Ward, Mark, *A Family at War: The Unofficial and Unauthorised Guide to Till Death Us Do Part* (Tolworth: Telos Publishing, 2008).

Weinreb, Ben, Christopher Hibbert, Julia Keay and John Keay, *The London Encyclopedia* (London: Pan Macmillan, 2008).

Will and Tricia Adams, *A Nostalgic Look at the Capital Since 1945* (Peterborough: Past and Present Publishing, 1997).

Williams, Caroline, 'Personal Papers: Perceptions and Practices', in Louise Craven (ed.), *What Are Archives? Cultural and Theoretical Perspectives* (Aldershot: Ashgate, 2008), pp. 53–67.

Wilson, A. E., *Half a Century of Entertainment* (London: Dennis Yates, n.d.).

Woodward, James, *English Theatre in Transition 1889–1914* (London: Croom Helm, 1984).

Zipperstein, Steven J., *The Jews of Odessa: A Cultural History 1794–1881* (Stanford: Stanford University Press, 1985).

Ziv, Avner and Anat Zajdman (eds), *Semites and Stereotypes. Characteristics of Jewish Humour* (London: Greenwood Press, 1993).

Zukerman, William, *The Jew in Revolt* (London: Martin Secker & Warburg, 1937).

Zweig, Ferdynand, *Labour, Life and Poverty* (Wakefield: EP Publishing, 1975).

Index

Note: Bold Page Numbers denote photographs and page numbers followed by 'n' denotes notes.

Ackroyd, Peter 23, 24
Actresses' Franchise League 6
Adelphi Theatre 154
Adler, Jacob 10
agit-prop style 13, 17
Aleichem, Sholem 90, 102, 103n9
Alfie (1968) 62
Ali Baba and the Forty Thieves 6
Aliens Act of 1905 135
Aliens Restriction Act 135
Aliens Restriction Amendment Act 1919 137
American sitcoms 92
   I Love Lucy 92
   The Jack Benny Program 92
   Sergeant Bilko 92
Anglo-Jewish community 3
Anglo-Jewish elite 17
Anglo-Jewish leadership 135
anti-alienism 136
antisemitism 40, 54, 66
Arab-Jewish conflict 19
Aristotle 12
Arkell, George 53
Arnold, Thomas 37
Arts Theatre 63, 65, 83, 85
asylum, Britain 135
Attlee government 16

Babylonian Talmud 103
Barker, Harley Granville, *Waste* 6
Bar Mitzvah Boy (1976) 69
Barnes, Julian 6
Baron, Jeff 122

The Barratts of Wimpole Street 6
Bart, Lionel 2, 11, **41,** 42, 134–68, **145, 159, 162, 165**
   background 134–41
   career 145–54
   downfall 162–8
   East End identification 154–8
   lifestyle 158–60
   masculinity 160–2
   Oliver! 148–54
   politics and Unity theatre 141–4
   Wally Pone, 143, 146
Bart for Bart's Sake **145**
Basalinsky, Abraham 143 *see* Bass, Alfie
Bass, Alfie 2, 22, 42, 50–74, **64,** 76, 78, 79, 85, **89,** 97, 121, 143
   background 50–4
   career 62–3
   mannerisms and masculinity 68–71
   performance 68–71
   political involvement 54–7
   roles 63–8
   Alfie's Penny Gaffs 65, 66
   Are You Being Served? 62
   The Army Game 62–3, 66, 67, 69, 70, 98, 168, 174
   Bootserella 52
   Bootsie and Snudge 42, 50, 52, 62, 63, 65, 67, 69, 70, 174
   Bootsie and the Beast 52
   Unity Theatre and 57–62
Battle of Cable Street 54, 176
Becket (1964)160
Ben Bengal 18

Berkoff, Steven 36
Bernard, Heinz 144
The Bespoke Overcoat (1955) 62, 63, **64,** 68,
   69, 83, 85, 86, **87,** 87–93, **89,** 102
Bethnal Green 53
Billington, Michael 7, 123–4
biography 37-8
Black, Don 167
Blacker, Harry 34
Blitz! 134, 146, 148, 154, 157, 164
Bloom, Alexander 34
Book of Esther 10
The Boychik (1954) 85
Brandon-Jones, Una 61
Brecht, Bertolt 12, 19
The Britannia Theatre 8, 9
Britcoms 92, 93
British Ashkenazi Jews 68
British Drama League Festival 59
British Patriot's Propaganda Association 19
Bunny (1972) 86

Carr, Michael 34
catharsis 12
The Caucasian Chalk Circle (1948) 12
censorship 6
Century of Song, BBC Home Service 65
Cesarani, David 34, 134
Chagall, Marc 85
Chamberlain, Lord 5, 61
Chambers, Colin 19
Chaucer, *The Prioresses Tale* 149
Chilton, Charles 65
Christianity 102
Chu Chin Chow 6
Cinderella 143
The City of London Theatre 8
Clayton, Jack 63, 93
Cockney 65, 82
Cockney ballads 152
   'I'm Shy Mary Ellen, I'm Shy' 92
   'Knock'd 'em in the Old Kent Road' 92
'Cockney Cole Porter' 177
'Cockney' persona 2
Cockney roles 65, 97, 98
Cogan, Alma 161

Cohen, Cockney 34
collective authorship 19
collective biography 37
Communist Party (CP) 13–15, 22, 30, 54,
   79, 140–2, 167
Communist Party of Great Britain (CPGB)
   15, 54, 56, 142
Conspiracy of Hearts (1960) **84,** 86
Coronation Street 69
Council for Proletarian Art *see* Workers'
   Theatre Movement

Daiches, David 176
Dance of a Vampire (1967) 69
Davies, Andrew 5
Davis, Elliot 164
Dee, David 4, 36
Desert Island Discs 52, 103, 129, 174
Dickens, Charles 148
Dixon of Dock Green 70

East End furniture trade 35
East End immigrant Jews 23
East End of London 2, 7, 11, 22, 24, 25, 34,
   57, 63, 102, 124, 140
   after Second World War 35–7
   bomb shelters 55
   boxing 31
   cash betting 31
   communal hardship 24
   costermongering 24
   dock-building programme 7
   economic hardships 29
   exoticism 7
   gambling 31, 32
   multi-culturalism 36
   otherness 7
   rent strikes 31
   Yiddish theatre in 9–12
East End theatres 2, 7–9
Eastern Europe 2, 9, 50, 102, 103
Edwardian music hall 19, 80
The Effingham Theatre 8
Eisner, Will 150
Eminent Victorians 37
Endelman, T. M. 101

Index

English Jews 4
epic theatre style 12
Esther, Queen 10
Euripides 12
The Evacuees (1975) 69
Brenda Evans 160

Fagin the Jew 150
'Faginy' Yiddish accent 38
fascism 14, 30, 54, 81
Fiddler on the Roof 50, 63, 64, 67
Fielding, Fenella 127
Fielding, Henry 145
Fings Ain't Wot They Used T'Be (1959)134, 141, 145–7, 163
Finn, Ralph 31, 33
Firestein, Fegel 17
First World War 6, 13, 102, 136
Franklyn, Julian 27
Fraser, Bill 63
Freud (1960) 83

The Galloping Major (1951) 62
Garnett, Alf 42
The Garrick Theatre 8
Gartner, Lloyd 50
General Strike of May 1926 13
Gibb, James 57
Gladstone, Herbert 135
Gogol, *The Overcoat* 63
Gold, John 141, 142
Gold, Michael 17
The Golden Door (1950)121
Goldfaden, Abraham 52
Gordon, General 37
Gorman, John 140–1, 148
Grand Palais Yiddish Company 10
Green, John 54
Groser, Father 31
Grossman, Jack 142
Guinness, Alec 148, 151

Haber, Gilda Moss 25, 33, 54
Habonim Israel training camp scheme 64
Hackney People's Players 13
Hall, Peter 125

Hampstead Shelterers' Bulletin 55
Harding, Arthur 32
Harrisson, Tom 26, 27
Hasty Heart (1949) 62
'Hava Nagila' 103, 106n111, 175
Hazlewood, Colin 8
Heer, Jeet 150
Hilton, Margot 22
Holiday Camp (1949) 62
The House of the Seven Hawks (1959) **82**
Housewives Choice 159
Huston, John 83

Ibsen 4, 10
    A Doll's House 4
immigrants 134, 135
Independent Theatre Society 6
Industrial Revolution 5
inter-war cinemas 1
inter-war period 4
Irwin, Leonard 141
Isle of Man 135
Israel emergency fund 65
It Should Happen to a Dog (1955) 64

Jacobs, David 148
Jacobsen, Jock 144
Jenkins, Margaret 102
Jericho Players 86
Jerusalem of Jewish radicalism 15
Jewess and Christian or The Love that Kills (1877) 8
Jew in literature 149, 150
Jewish Annual 8
Jewish Anti-Fascist Committee 15
Jewish anti-fascist movement 79
Jewish Cockneys 22, 23–34, 37, 102, 134, 174, 177
Jewish Communism 56
Jewish Communist ethnic sub-identity 17
Jewish Folk Humour (1953) 83
Jewish-Gentile cooperation 28
Jewish-Gentile relations 28
Jewish immigrants 2, 10
Jewish masculinity 40
Jewish uncle *see* Kossoff, David

Jewish Workers' Circle 14
Jews Island 53
Jonson, Ben 143
Journey into Space, radio programme 66, 82
judeo-kleptocracy 51

Kaye, Solly 169n46
Khrushchev, Nikita 16
A Kid for Two Farthings (1955) 85
Kindertransport 133n136
Kitt, Eartha 86
Klug, Madame Rosa 11
Kops, Bernard 86
Kossoff, David 2, 22, 23, 42, 64, **64,** 75–106, **82, 84, 87, 89, 100,** 139
  background 75–8
  The Bespoke Overcoat (1955) 87–93
  The Book of Witnesses 99
  career 81–7
  The Late Great Paul 101
  mannerisms and masculinity 93–8
  Old Testament prophet 75
  performance 93–8
  political radicalism 101
  storyteller 98–103
  and Unity Theatre 79–81
Kushner, Tony 28, 29

Landis, Harry 20, **20,** 21, 22, 57, 129, 142, 146, 156
The Larkins 91–3, 125, 168
  'Cat Happy' 93
  'Welcome home Eddy' 97
  'Wide Open House' 93, 96
The Lavender Hill Mob (1951) 67, 69
Lean, David 151
left-wing ideology 170n72
left-wing political theatre companies 2
Lesser, Frank 22
Levy, A. B. 35, 36
Lewenstein, Oscar 146
Lewis, H. S. 139
Lindsey, Jack 19
Little Big Business – ITV sitcom (1963-65) 86

A Little Bit of Fluff 6
Littlewood, Joan 163, 170n72
Living Newspapers 19, 22
Livshin, Rosalyn 3
Lock Up Your Daughters (1959) 145, 148
Lodge, David 92
London Shelter Movement 54
Look Back in Anger (1956) 6, 7, 149
The Love of Four Colonels (1951), 83

Macbeth, 8
Mackintosh, Sir Cameron 149, 167
Macmillan, Harold 1
Maggie May (1964), 146, 148, 161, 164
Manchester Jews 3
Mankowitz, Wolf 62–4, 85, 96, 104n37
Manning, Cardinal 37
Martin, David 19
Marx, Karl 12
Masculinity 38-41
  Jewish masculinity 40
  'tough guy' masculinity 41
Masses Man 13
Mass-Observation project 26
  anthropology of 27
Maugham, W. Somerset 6
McCulloch, Joseph 88
McKenna, Reginald 135
melodramas 9
  Bloodstained Handkerchief 9
  Seven Steps to Tyburn 9
melodramatic operettas 11
Mendelovitch, Bernard 10
Merchant of Venice 62, 149
The Merry Wives of Windsor 8
middle-class American values 3
Middlesex Regiment 62
Mike Sammes Singers 92
Miller, Arthur 122
  The Caretaker 123, 125
  Death of a Salesman 123
  The Price 122
Moliere, 127
  The Miser 127

Index

Mitchell, Warren 2, 22, 42, 78, 107–33, 138, 143
  background 107–11
  early career 113–21
  politics and Unity Theatre 111–13
  Theatre roles 121–9
  Till Death Us Do Part 114–21
Morris, Aubrey 54
Morrison, Arthur 7
Mosley, Oswald 29
The Mouse that Roared (1959) 83
Munich crisis 19
Murray, Susan 96
Music Halls 7–9
  'nigger minstrel' 9

Napolitano, M. 144, 149, 153, 156
National Health Service 1
National Minority Movement 13
The National Standard Theatre 8
National Theatre 123
New York Jews 3
Nightingale, Florence 37
non-naturalized East European Jews 136
No! No! McCarthy (1953) 56
Norman, Frank 146, 147

O'Casey, Sean 19
Odessa 51
Odets, Clifford 18
Oliver! 11, 42, 134, 146, 148–54, 164, 166
Oliver Twist 148, 150, 151
One Pair of Eyes (1968) 157, 177
Osborne, John 6, 149, 164
'Outlines of Jewish Society in London' 35

Paice, Eric 61
Pascal, Gabriel 71
Paul Kossoff Foundation 101
The Pavilion Theatre 9
People's Museum, Manchester 56
Penny gaffs 9
Pinter, Harold 123, 125
  The Caretaker 123, 125
  The Homecoming (1990) 123, 177
  The Price 122

Piratin, Phil 15
Piscator, Erwin 12
pogroms 9, 14, 33, 50, 134
political theatre 4, 12–17
politics
  Bart, Lionel and 141–4
  Bass and 54–7
  Mitchell, Warren and 111–13
Porter, Roy 23
Poulson, Charles 29
Powell, Enoch 131n62, 157
Prager, Leonard 15
Priestley, J. B. 6
Proltet 14, 17, 18
Pugh, Edwin 23
Purim plays 10

rabbinic Judaism 39
Rabbi's Son or The Last Link in the Chain (1879) 8
Rachel's Penance or Daughter of Israel (1878) 8
Rebel Players 18
Red Front 13
Red Megaphones 13
Red Radio 13, 18
Registration of Business Names Act 1916 137
Richard, Cliff 146
Robeson, Paul 18, 56–8
Rogers, Paul 125
Rohrer, Joseph 67
Roper, David 139, 141
Rosen, Tubby 31
Rosenthal, Jack 69
Royal Court Theatre 146
Royal Festival Hall 64
Russell, Charles 139
Russian Revolution 13
Russo-Turkish war 50

Sailor Beware (1956) 69
Scott, Derek 34
second generation immigrants 2, 3-4, 42, 78
  estranged generation 4

Second World War 1, 15, 34, 40, 54, 63, 66, 82, 86, 154
   East End of London after 35–7
Shakespeare 8, 10
Shaw, George Bernard 4, 6
   Mrs Warren's Profession 6
Shema Yisrael 104n44
Shenley Labour Party 56
The Shepherd and the Hunter (1946) 19
Sherrin, Ned 138
shtetls 85, 86
Sikes, Bill 151
Simon, Kossoff 102
Six-Day War 65
Sleath, Alan 83
South Bank Show 138
Soviet Communist Party Congress 16
Soviet Red Army 15
Soviet Union 14–16
So You Think You Have Troubles (1991) 126
Spanish Civil War 176
Stafford, Caroline 141
Stafford, David 141
Stage Society 6
Staggered (1994) 83
The Standard Theatre 9
The Star Turns Red (1940) 19
Steele, Tommy 146, 156, 158
Stepney Borough Council 28
Stepney Communist Party 28, 29
Stepney Tenants Defence League (STDL) 28, 30, 55
Strachey, Lytton 37
Strauss, Richard 175
street activism 15
Strindberg 10

Tales of Mean Streets (1896) 7
Taming of the Shrew 62
Taylor, Robert **82**
The Grecian Theatre 8
Theatre, Twentieth Century 4
Theatre Royal Stratford 147
Theatres Act, 1843 61
Theatre Workshop 17, 166
Thomas, Tom 13, 14

Till Death Us Do Part 42, 62, 68, 69, 107, 114–21, 127, 167
   'Christmas Club Books' 126
   'Five Best Moments' 126
Toller, Ernst 13
Tolpuddle Martyrs 130n32
Toynbee Trust 53
trade union movement 58
Tressell, Robert *The Ragged Trousered Philanthropist* 13
Twang! (1965) 146, 162, 163
Tzelniker, Meir 121, 122, 132n86

Unity theatre 2, 4, 6, 7, 12, 17–23, 36, 37, 50, 52, 55, 57, 65, 103, 175
   Bart, Lionel and 141–4
   Bass, Alfie and 57–62
   Kossoff, David and 79–81
   Mitchell, Warren and 111–13
Unity theatre policy 19
Unity theatre productions
   All Change Here 21
   Babes in the Wood 19, 59, **60**
   Buster **21,** 65
   Finian's Rainbow 61
   Here Goes 61
   Mother Goose 61, 62
   On Guard for Spain (1937) 19, 22
   Peacemeal 143
   Plant in the Sun 18, 56, 58, 59
   Sandbag Follies 59
   Senora Carrar's Rifles 19
   Spanish Village 79
   Turn It Up 62, 142, 143
   The Wages of Eve 22, 141, 142
   Waiting for Lefty 18, 22
   Where's That Bomb? 19
   Winkles and Champagne 19, **20**
   The Yellow Star 79–81
Unity Theatre Trust 22
urban melodramas 8
   The Robbers! 8
   The Wild Tribes of London (1856) 8
Visiting Mr Green (2008) 122
Volpone 143

Walker, Muriel 153, 160, 163

Index

Wally Pone (1958) 143, 146
Warsaw Ghetto 79
Warsaw uprising 81
Waterman, Ray 17
Webber, Andrew Lloyd 158, 166
Well, Thank You, Thursday (1976) 69
Wesker, Arnold 22
West End of London 31, 140
West End theatre 5–7, 18
 '*Who Are the Cockneys Now?*' (1968)
  157
Wilde, Oscar 4
Willis, Ted 7, 21, 65, 79, 81
Windsor, Barbara 167
Woman's Hour 177
The Wonderland Theatre 11
Workers' Theatre Movement (WTM) 2, 6,
 12–14, 17
 'Art is the Weapon of the Revolution'
  14
 'Our Theatre Awakens the Masses' 14

World Jewish Cultural Union 15
The World of Sholem Aleichem (1955) 63,
 85, 90

Yates, Binnie 22
Yiddish cultural life 10
Yiddish folklore 51
Yiddish language 52
Yiddish lullabies 52
 Rozhinkes Mit Mandlen 52, 175
Yiddish music hall 11
 'A Bite to Eat Without Washing' 11
Yiddish theatre 2, 11, 12, 122, 140, 152, 153
 in East End of London 9–12
 heyday of 10
Yom Kippur 139, 153
Yom Kippur Jews 35
The Young Lovers (1954) 83

Zionism 16
Zukerman, William 25